The Bride Can't Cook

&

Susan Gee Heino

"If you can't cook, you'd better be darn good at other things!"
—*Granny Snowden*

The Bride Can't Cook

Garden Falls, Book 1

Susan Gee Heino

Dedication

To Melody.
Thanks for the idea for this story,
and for the recipes I mangled while writing it.
Your kitchen is a happy place.

Other Romance
by Susan Gee Heino

Three Tempting Tales of Lord Larry
The Earl's Passionate Plot
The Earl's Intimate Error
The Earl's Christmas Delivery
Miss Farrow's Feathers
Miss Wheaton's Whiskers
Yuletide Lies
Passion and Pretense
Temptress in Training
Damsel in Disguise
Mistress by Mistake

Chapter 1

The old cowbell on the front door at *Granny's Kitchen* clattered. Again. Marti's left eye twitched. She supposed she ought to be grateful for the business, but today she just wasn't up to it. The smoky drama of the weekend had left her slump-shouldered and defeated. Not to mention, her hair still smelled funny. Waiting tables with a fake smile plastered on was even harder than usual today.

Unfortunately, this morning's *Gazette* made Saturday's calamity seem like the most exciting thing to hit Garden Falls in a long time. Where'd they get off using words like "inferno" and "conflagration", anyway? Who in this little town even knew what a conflagration was?

She and Granny spent Saturday night and all day Sunday scrubbing and scouring—hence the funky hair smell—and they got up every grimy trace of soot and smoke. Last night Granny announced the place fit for business today and she didn't even mentioned the whole disaster was Marti's fault in the first place. All she did was declare that today's special would be bologna and kraut. She said cooking that ought to cover any lingering, er, aroma.

Their customers didn't seem to want to talk about anything else, though. Nope. Half the town had drifted through the doors today to check out the damage. They were probably taking bets on what Marti's next big catastrophe was going to be. Clearly they found this way more exciting than anything else *The Gazette* had written up.

But why didn't anyone notice any of the other newsworthy stuff in the paper? What about the article explaining how developers were planning to drain the pristine wetlands out off Beaverbend Road? And what about the little blurb way back on page six about the local recycling plant shutting down? Or heck, what about the front page interview of the only famous person ever to come out of this Podunk town?

John Easton Smith. Until Marti's indoor bonfire, little Johnny Smith from next door was big news. Heck, it wasn't every day a hometown boy got fired from a national TV show and a divorce from America's queen of the cutlery all in one fell swoop. Surely someone around here wanted to waste time gossiping about *that* rather than gawking at Marti's infamous ineptitude. For sure, Johnny's life was way more exciting than hers. She wouldn't have minded listening in on some of that gossip, in fact.

But apparently she was the only one thinking about him today. Or yesterday, or pretty much every day for the past ten years. Better get her mind back on business before something else caught fire. She stared at the gurgling coffee maker.

The pot she'd stuck in there was full. Okay, it was a little more than full. Coffee was pouring over the sides of it, actually, and making a big steaming puddle on Granny's clean floor. Oops.

Marti managed to get the over-boiling stopped and only burned herself a couple times in the process. At least Granny was in the back for this debacle and didn't see the mess. Marti toweled it up quickly.

No more daydreaming. So what if she'd come crawling back here with her career in tatters and her tail between her legs? She was here to help Granny get through a rough time and—by golly—that's what she was going to do.

Oops. Her order pad fell into the ice chest. Well, no harm. The ink didn't smear too badly. She stared at it and frowned. Did Lloyd Schneider order fried eggs, or "dried figs"? Had to be the eggs. She'd better get that turned in.

She dropped off her orders and gathered up drinks for table six—Phil and Joetta Townsend. The pot of decaf for Phil and a pitcher of Diet Coke for Joetta. And extra creamer for Phil, of course. Jeez, did the guy bother to put it into his coffee or just drink it straight out of the little ceramic cow? She took a deep breath and headed toward them.

"Looks like you've just about outgrown that outfit there, Marti," Phil said, his bug-eyes coming to rest on the bric-a-brac neckline of the peach colored uniform she'd worn since she first started working here in high school.

She smiled politely and shoved a menu up in front of those eyes. "How about some scalding hot coffee while you look at the menu?" she suggested cheerfully.

"I just can't decide," Joetta said, fidgeting with her menu in the tight booth. She finally sighed and propped her expensive new breasts on the table, the menu resting on them. "What would you recommend?"

"Bologna and kraut is always a favorite," Marti said, doing her very best to ignore the gratuitous boob propping.

"It's so nice that Granny was able to open the place today," Joetta went on, lovingly running a finger over the deserts page on her menu. "After what happened this weekend, and all."

Sigh. Marti recited the same thing she'd been saying all day. "It was just a small electrical fire. Wiring in the kitchen. Nothing bad."

No, not bad at all. Just a huge, inferno-ish conflagration that melted a wall and fried their big refrigerator unit. Heck, with all Granny's medical bills and other problems, this disaster was hardly noticeable.

"Well, I'm just glad no one was hurt," Joetta said, looking around as if she were appraising the place. "And the building is intact."

Which is, of course, what the Townsends really cared about. This building butted up next to their real estate office and Joetta had been itching to expand for some time now. Well, it would be a cold day in Borneo before Granny let them get their mitts on this place. The Townsends were bad news.

They were paying customers, though, so Marti kept on smiling and topped off their drinks. She waited patiently while they pretended they were going to order salads from Granny's "lite-side" menu but in the end, of course, they went with the Special. Never had a Townsend refused Granny's special fried bologna and sauerkraut.

Marti turned in their orders, made the rounds with the coffee pot, and delivered Lloyd Schneider's noodle soup and fried eggs. He asked about his dried figs. Really? Another oops.

Granny stuck her salt-and-peppered head out of the kitchen and wiggled her eyebrows in Marti's direction.

"Marti, I just got off the phone and I think I ought to warn you—" she began when Marti got over to her.

"I know what you're going to say," Marti interrupted, taking up the two plates of today's special.

Granny lived in near-terror that Marti would actually tell the Townsends what she thought of them. Well, she wouldn't. Not today, anyway. For Granny's sake.

"It's okay. I won't let my personal feelings get in the way of my job. Even though Phil and Joetta are the driving force behind that mindless ecological destruction out off

Beaverbend Road, I'll keep it nice and friendly here."

"Glad to hear it, but I was going to warn you that—"

"I know, I know." Marti sighed. "They want you out of here so they can take over the building. Vultures. I promise, I won't let them know how bad the fire really was. Now I'd better go check on some figs."

She didn't give Granny time to offer any more cautions. It was hard enough pretending for the Townsends that she didn't hate what they were trying to do to those perfectly good wetlands. She didn't have the stomach to pretend for Granny, too. Best just to keep moving.

"Smells as good as it looks, darlin'," Phil said when she made it back to deliver their bologna.

Marti couldn't figure how Phil's words were high praise.

"I'm sure you'll enjoy it, Mr. Townsend," she said, phony smile still firmly in place.

She refilled their drinks and was actually very neat about it. No splashing or ice cubes landing where they shouldn't or anything like that. Granny would be proud. Marti made remarkably amicable small talk about the weather, but Phil's next question caught her off guard.

"So, you've been keeping up with the gossip on your old next-door-neighbor?"

Her eye twitched again, but she managed a casual shrug.

"Johnny and I sort of lost touch when I went off to college," she said.

Joetta patted her arm in an unnecessary show of compassion. "That's understandable, dear. You never did catch Johnny's eye in *that* sort of way, did you?"

She pretended she had no clue what Joetta meant. God, but this stupid smile was starting to hurt.

"Johnny and I did what kids do; we grew up. I went on to college and, well, he didn't."

"No," Phil said. "Guess he sure didn't need to waste his time in college. Managed to do all right for himself without all that stuck-up education."

Joetta apparently wasn't about to let her husband sound like the only ignoramus in the family. "But you must have really liked college, Marti. What was it, eight years before you graduated?"

Clench teeth. Be polite.

"Not quite. I got my bachelor's degree a year early, then spent two years in the Galapagos Islands working on my master's and finally finished up my doctorate with a government grant to monitor invasive algae in industrial runoff. A little short of eight years."

Phil was too clueless to be impressed. "Hmm, yeah. Granny always talks about that environmental stuff you do. Probably not as much fun as working in Hollywood like Johnny, huh?"

Keep smiling. Keep smiling. Don't throw anything.

"Maybe if you'd have kept up with him he could have found you something a little better than industrial algae," Joetta suggested.

"Yeah, wouldn't that be great?" Marti said, although now her teeth just wouldn't quit clenching. "I could've been on TV with Johnny doing a mindless cooking show. Golly. Kind of a shame his career is down the toilet now, huh?"

Joetta's smile was just as fake as Marti's. "Yeah, just like it's a shame about your career, too. Such a pity. Too bad things didn't work out for you with that doctor Granny kept bragging to us about. Must have sure broke your heart when he left you."

All the clenching was giving her a headache. Dear God, why couldn't these cretins just choke on their bologna and die already?

"Actually, Dr. Hedgeman is still back working at our project in the Everglades," Marti explained sweetly, fantasizing about dumping the pitcher of Diet Coke into Joetta's polyester-clad lap. "I'm the one who left."

Yeah, she came back here because Granny needed her. And because she really had nowhere else to go. Not after Dr. Hedgeman made her the fall guy when she found out about his unethical—and environmentally immoral—business dealings. No, she wasn't bitter about that, or anything.

The cowbell clanged again against the diner door and Marti winced. Would the lunch rush never end today? She glanced over to see who the newcomer was, finding it hard to imagine a body in town who hadn't already come in to gawk at some point today.

It took a couple seconds for the face on the body in the doorway to register.

Good grief. It was HIM, flesh and blood and all grown up. And two thousand miles away from Hollywood. John Easton Smith: her old best friend and the only guy who ever actually did break her heart.

The Diet Coke slipped for real out of her hand.

———

John Easton Smith pulled off his sunglasses and sauntered into *Granny's Kitchen*. Ah, the familiar sound of clattering dishes and that wonderful cowbell. Sounds he hadn't heard for far too long. This was one place in Garden Falls he was actually glad to see again.

And smell again. Mmm. Nobody could feed a growing boy like Granny could. And he sure hadn't found anyone to cook like her out in California. What was it today? Bologna and kraut—and something else. Burnt plastic? That was weird.

He let his eyes adjust to the indoor lighting. The place hadn't changed much. Same patchwork curtains, same brown plastic booths, same—

Marti Snowden. There she was, apologizing over the Townsend's, who also looked pretty much the same except that they were wet. Was that an entire pitcher of Coke? More important, was that the same little peach-colored uniform Marti used to wear? It fit a lot better now.

She bent over to start wiping up the floor. Oh yeah, the uniform fit a *whole* lot better these days. Hell, he'd thought he was prepared for seeing her again. He'd thought wrong.

Phil Townsend quit leering at Marti long enough to glance up and notice him.

"Well, look what the cat dragged in!"

His wife craned her neck and squealed. "Ooo! It's Johnny Smith!"

Everyone froze. Every eye in the place shifted to stare at him. He didn't really care. He was used to that. Besides, he was busy staring at Marti.

Scuttling out from under the table, she conked her head. When she tried to stand up, she conked it again. This knocked her down onto her bouncy little backside and she was left sitting in a puddle of Coke, blinking up at him in shock.

Wow, he'd missed her.

"Hi, Marti," he said.

"And what in God's name are *you* doing here?" she asked.

Ouch. He'd kind of been hoping for a nice warm smile and maybe some friendly banter. She must be having a bad day. Kind of looked like one although, to be honest, this wasn't too far from normal for Marti.

"Can I help you up?" He reached out a hand toward her.

"I'm fine, thanks," she said.

She scrambled to her feet. The foaming floor didn't make it easy and nothing about her movement was graceful, but she got up all right. Without any help. Typical Marti.

"I heard you were back," he said, surprised by their difference in height. He'd grown a couple inches since that summer after graduation. She had too, but not in height. He tried not to think about where she *had* gained a couple inches.

"Yeah. I'm back. For a while."

Okay, so she wasn't in a conversational mood. She was probably upset over the Coke and Joetta's dampened polyester.

"I heard about Granny's surgery," he said, determined to give it another shot. "I hope she's doing all right."

"She's at the serving window. You can go ask her. I need to get back to work."

With that she grabbed up the empty pitcher where it lay on its side and flounced back through the swinging doors into the kitchen. So much for the sappy reunion he'd sort of dreamed about. Oh well. He knew he shouldn't have expected much. He hadn't exactly left things on a high note ten years ago.

"You're better off without her," Joetta was saying, dabbing at her clothes. "That girl has a nervous disorder, or something. Probably brought it back from those Galloping Islands."

Okay, that didn't make much sense. But neither Townsend bothered to explain. Instead, they invited him to join them.

"So, Johnny, take a load off and tell us what you've been up to."

Joetta giggled and batted her big moony eyes. "Oh, but

we can't call you Johnny anymore, can we? You're J. Easton Smith now."

"I figured I'd stand a better chance of getting noticed if I went as something other than John Smith," he said, wishing right now that he hadn't been noticed. Not by Phil and Joetta, at least.

"Then if everyone else in the world calls you East," Joetta said. "We will, too."

Actually, not everyone called him East. His ex-wife called him Holy-Crap-Are-You-Home-Already. But that was only once, when he showed up unexpectedly to find her with his personal trainer. And they hadn't exactly been doing yoga. He didn't really feel much like sharing this with the Townsend's, however.

"East. I like that," Phil said philosophically. "It's geographical, like land. And funny you should mention it, because Joetta and I are in the land business..."

Oh, hell. Now he was stuck listening to some pitch about a big real estate project they were involved in. Apparently they thought he managed to walk out of his so-called marriage with cash burning a hole in his pocket. Well, he hadn't.

The only hole in his life right now was the one Marti left ten years ago. That's what he came back for, not some glossy development brochure Joetta dug out of her purse. Marti might have made it very clear she couldn't care less about him, but he wasn't ready to give up just yet. All he needed was an ally.

A sweet little gray haired ally who was waving at him from the pick-up window.

Chapter 2

Marti could see him, even when she tried not to notice. What on earth was he doing back in town? More importantly, what were he and Granny so deep in conversation about?

Somehow he'd extricated himself from the clutches of the Townsend's and their inevitable sales pitch and now he was fawning over Granny like she was his favorite person. Maybe she was. Marti was pretty sure he was Granny's favorite. Years ago she'd rescued him from his Dad's insurance office and put him to work in her kitchen, teaching him how to make her custard pie just the way she'd perfected it and glowing with pride when he mastered her two-spatula burger technique. Marti still wasn't even allowed near the grill.

Yeah, Johnny had been a kitchen prodigy and Granny loved him. It was probably a good thing she never knew what really went on between the two of them that last summer before... well, before Marti went one way and Johnny went another. Marti supposed she should be glad to see someone making Granny smile this way. The poor gal hadn't smiled enough lately.

She just wished she'd been able to provide some of those smiles. So far all she'd provided was another insurance claim. Sometimes she had to wonder if it had been such a good idea to come back, after all.

———

Granny had given East the biggest hug he'd had in years when he made his way over to talk to her. Pretty powerful hug for a little old lady who just had hip surgery a few weeks ago. He liked it.

He liked the lunch she shoved at him, too, when she dragged him over to a booth and plunked him down for a thorough conversation.

"Eat," she ordered. "I can't be sure anyone's been feeding you out there in that land of camera-happy skinny people."

"I've been feeding myself, thank you very much. Did you forget all those summers I worked here? No one works for Granny Snowden and doesn't learn to cook."

He noticed Granny's quick glance out over the lunch counter. Marti was there, struggling with her order pad and delivering the wrong meals to the wrong tables.

"Well, almost nobody," he corrected himself with a chuckle.

"She tries so hard." Granny sighed, shaking her head.

"It's great she could come back to help you."

"Yeah, it is. And I'll bet your mom's just beside herself having you back here for a while, too" Granny said, those gray eyes glittering.

"And Dad's ready to sign me up as one of his agents already."

"What? C.J.'s still after you to sell insurance? Bah. You never were cut out for that. You'd be terrible at it."

"That's what I keep telling him."

Granny had been about the only one in town who ever thought East might do something else with his life but follow in his father's footsteps. Well, her and Marti. But he guessed it didn't matter much now what Marti used to think of him, did it?

Granny must have caught him following her with his eyes as she headed back into the kitchen, returning a plate of something suspicious to the kitchen.

Granny sighed. "She didn't exactly do cartwheels when you came in here."

He tried to act like Marti's cool reception hadn't bothered him. "I have a feeling it would take a little bit more than my two-year stint on The Culinary Network to impress Dr. Marti Snowden. You must be really proud of her. She's got your hard-working attitude as well as your smarts."

Granny waved away his flattery, but she beamed. "Oh, she's way smarter than me. Who'd have thought there'd ever be a PhD in my ignorant family?"

"Anyone who ever met you or Marti, that's who. It's all Marti ever talked about; going off to school and getting those letters after her name. And you know she never lets anything get in the way of her goals."

Granny frowned. "Well, she never used to, anyway. Maybe you don't know about it, but... well," she gave a big, tired sigh before she went on. "Marti's had kind of a rough time lately. I think she was glad for the excuse to come back here and help me."

East nodded. Yeah, he knew a little about that. His mom had filled him in. "You mean that guy. Doctor some-body-or-other."

"Hedgeman. Doctor Leland Damn Hedgeman. Marti was just crazy nuts for him; followed him all over the country from project to project, doing his work for him and earning him grants and all. I thought for sure she'd found her match."

"Yeah. That's what mom said." He'd heard all about Dr. Damn Hedgeman and how Marti was so happy with him. Hell, that was probably what sent him over the edge and convinced him to go ahead and marry Treeva Kincaide, one of his more lamentable impulses.

"Things seemed to be going so well for her," Granny said. "Then a few months ago something happened. I don't know what. All I can gather is that fool Hedgeman started making it look like Marti wasn't doing her job, or something. He even got her kicked off the project, he did. Off the project and out of his life, just like that."

"Shit."

He'd heard Marti was single again, but he didn't realize it had been quite that traumatic. Or recent. She must feel like crap. And he felt like an asshole because all he could think of was how he might be able to use this to his advantage. She'd need someone with a shoulder to cry on, right? Hell, Marti on the rebound would be way better than no Marti at all.

"Well, working here helps keep her mind off her worries," Granny went on. "And I sure am glad to have her back at the house. Plus, I gotta say, with Marti here to make the place so lively, business has really picked up."

"I don't know if she'd be so glad to hear you say that," he said with a chuckle. No, Marti would probably *not* like to know her fabled mishaps were drawing a crowd.

"It's just nice to think folks have an excuse for coming here again."

"Hey, no one needs an excuse to eat here," he assured her. "What did you do to this custard pie? It was always my favorite, but now it's even better."

Well, that had been the right thing to say. The worry lines went away and a smile spread wide on her face. "Oh, a little tweaking here, a little something extra there. I've been perfecting it over the years in hopes of… well, I'm glad you like it."

The smile faded slightly. It was still there, but not the same. It kind of made the room feel like the lights just dimmed.

"What? Perfecting it for what?"

"Nothing. I'll get you the recipe so you can bake 'til your heart's content. Glad to know it'll be put to some good use after all."

"Hey, don't be too quick to pass out your recipes, Granny. Wouldn't want them falling into the wrong hands."

"I'll just be glad knowing once this place is shut down somebody's still eating my recipes somewhere."

Now *that* was like someone just turned the lights off all together.

"Once the place is shut down? You're not considering that, are you?"

She tried to shrug it off, but the truth was obvious. She'd been considering it, all right. Wow.

"I can't even imagine Garden Falls without *Granny's Kitchen*," he admitted.

And would Garden Falls without *Granny's Kitchen* mean there'd be no Marti, as well? That was like someone just extinguished the sun. He had to remind himself to breathe.

Granny, however, didn't seem to think it was such a big deal.

"Hey, you certainly don't expect me to spend all my golden years stuck behind a lunch counter, do you? Nah, it's high time I think about retiring. I'd have done it already if I hadn't been so sure…" Her voice trailed off.

"So sure about what?"

She sagged. "That silly contest. I thought for sure I'd get in it this year."

Oh. Man, he'd forgotten that was usually around this time of year. So she missed out on her chance for that Patchwork Platter again? That really sucked.

"You didn't make it? Jeez, I'm sorry to hear that."

"Yeah, I made it to the final round, but still came up short. I'm just first alternate."

"First alternate? You mean, like if someone's restaurant burns down between now and the competition you get to take their place?"

She snorted. "As if that's going to happen. But it's not all bad news. Your friend Arv got in."

"Arv Koch?"

"Yeah, he and his wife, Charleen, moved up to Finster last year and opened their own place. They got one of the spots from our district."

"I thought he was an engineer?"

"What, don't you keep up with him, either? Well, when the Pedersund plant here shut down he took his severance and opened up a restaurant. Folks say it's pretty good."

Huh. This was something he hadn't heard. He'd sort of lost track of Arv back when, well, when Arv went off to college with Marti and East didn't. He'd heard the two of them started dating. Arv always had a crush on her so it made sense they'd get together. But that was ten years ago. East shouldn't still want to strangle his old pal after all this time, should he?

"I hope they win it. Arv's a good kid," Granny was saying. "But Marti was pretty upset. Disappointed for me, and all. I think she knows this was our last shot at it."

That sounded way too ominous. "Come on, there's always next year."

"No, there isn't. The diner ain't going to make it into next year. I'm tired and it's flat worn out. I'd have sold out already except that, well, the only folks who seem to want it are them Townsend's."

"The Townsend's want to go into the diner business?"

"No, they want the building. You heard about that big

development they've got planned?"

"Yeah, I heard about it."

"It figures they'd try to hit you up. They've got half the town lined up to invest in it so they think they're big stuff and need more office space. They're in the building next door, and now Joetta's got plans for knocking out this wall and expanding."

"And of course Marti won't have anything to do with selling out to them."

"Not on your life, she won't! Says their plan is an assault on the planet. She's used to being out there fighting against people like them. Now here she is having to smile and serve them their lunch." Granny sighed. "I sure love the girl, but it just ain't fair for me to keep her here."

He understood that sigh. It was the sigh of someone stuck in between what they had and what they really wanted. He knew it well.

Granny shook her head and slumped. "I need to unload this place and let Marti get back to her bugs and her swamp things. I was just hoping I'd get lucky and some poor schmuck might come along wanting to go into the restaurant business and give me a fair price. Oh well. I can hang onto it a couple months longer, but then I'll need to let it—and Marti—go."

Apparently Granny was done with lunch. She pushed her half-eaten pie back and swiveled in her seat to get up. Propping her hand on the table, she winced as she got ready for what must be the painful effort of standing up. East put his hand over hers to stop her.

"Let me help you," he said.

"Naw, I can get up. It just takes me a minute."

"No, I mean with the diner. Let me help you."

Granny gave him a confused glare. "What, you going to

go wash dishes for me?"

"No. I'm probably the biggest schmuck likely to walk in here today, so I guess I'd better make an offer. I want to buy your diner."

———

It was dinnertime, but Marti wasn't hungry. Seeing Johnny—East—today had kept her off balance all afternoon. It's a wonder the place was still standing after the last couple hours of Marti the Menace at her very best.

Damn him! Why'd he have to show up here *now*? Why not six months ago when everything in Marti's life was still peachy and she was five states away?

No, luck and timing had never been on their side, had they? Why should today be any different?

Because they were frigging grown-ups now, that's why! After ten years he shouldn't still have the power to make her knees go weak just by smiling at her. And memories of him shouldn't be so damn pleasant. He'd left, after all. Taken off with nary a farewell. And she was fine with that.

Yeah, right. So why'd she drop a pitcher of Diet Coke, knock over the ficus, pour salt in a sugar dispenser, and put Honey Dijon instead of caramel sauce on Emily Timmer's bread pudding? All Easton Smith's fault.

Granny'd sat and chatted with him forever, keeping him lingering around long after they were done with their lunch. Marti had no idea what on earth they'd been going over, but at one point East had even gotten out a notebook and started writing stuff down. Trading recipes, maybe? Whatever.

At last he'd gone finally, but Marti was still a wreck. Granny watched her break dishes and screw up orders until nearly four o'clock. It was awful. Finally Granny came up with some excuse about needing to go home and rest. The dinner staff came in and Granny claimed Marti needed to take her home and Marti was only too glad to play along. *Granny's Kitchen* couldn't take much more.

So, home they went and Marti fussed over Granny and Granny let her as long as she could stand it. Then she put herself to bed for a nap and told Marti to walk the dog. Marti was almost afraid to attempt that given how her day had been, but somehow she'd managed to get Granny's sausage-shaped little dog around the block and back home safely. Thank God.

Granny was still napping when Marti came tiptoeing into the house carrying a panting Trixie. Okay, so the dog really only walked halfway around the block and made Marti carry her the rest of the way, but it was the thought that counted, right? Besides, the necessary business had been attended to so Marti wouldn't end up having to mop the floor. Unless she dumped dinner all over it, or something.

Aw, shoot—dinner! Marti had told Granny she'd take care of that tonight. Rats. She'd meant to just bring something home from the diner but with all the excitement from her many disasters she'd forgotten. Well, maybe she could whip something up herself and sort of make up for the rotten day she'd given them all.

Actually, that wasn't a bad idea. Nothing would make Granny happier than to see that all the years of trying to pass down her secrets hadn't been entirely wasted. The house was always full of food, so putting together a simple dinner ought to be easy. Hell, she was Milly Snowden's granddaughter. She could do dinner. Right?

Except that a quick scan of the fridge proved there were no simple entrees at hand. Just the raw ingredients—items foreign to Marti like something wrapped in butcher's paper labeled "stewing beef" and sour cream that didn't already have onions or Ranch seasoning in it. Huh. What did people do with that?

Feeling brave, she peaked into the cupboard under the toaster. There, way in the back was an old canister that said "flour". She pulled it out and peered inside. Ah ha, it was still there: Granny's ratty old file box with her precious recipes in it. Many a Garden Falls biddy would have given her eye-teeth for half an hour alone with this and a copy machine.

Flipping through the battered note cards and magazine cut outs, all of which were practically illegible from all the changes and additions Granny had scribbled on them, Marti found the heading "Meat Dishes". Well, that sounded good. She skipped the ones marked "chicken" or "pork" or—God forbid—"organs" and found "beef".

A few minutes more and she smiled. Ah, this was just the thing. Granny made it all the time and always went on and on about how easy it was. Marti laid the chosen card out on the counter and carefully put the cherished box back in its hiding place.

She washed her hands and opened the fridge.

"Okay, stewing beef, you are about to become dinner," she said and gave an evil laugh.

See? Cooking could be fun after all. Trixie made a nervous whining sound and waddled back toward the bedrooms. Well, what did she know? Marti had never seen dogs be especially particular about what went into their mouths.

She brought out the meat and set to collecting the rest of her ingredients. Yep, seemed like Granny had everything she'd need. And other than the deplorable handwriting and grease stains, the recipe looked easy enough to follow. Granny was going to be so proud.

Marti measured the spices carefully and didn't even sneeze in the pepper. Going good. She was feeling better already. Maybe cooking was therapeutic like some people said. Usually she felt more likely to need therapy after cooking, but that was just her.

In no time the beef was sizzling in Granny's skillet and Marti was patting herself on the back for being not quite so hopeless in the kitchen as was commonly believed. So what was the big deal? Anyone could read a recipe and throw stuff in a pan. And she did, exactly as it said on the note card.

But after a minute or two it started to smell— well, not so good. What had gone wrong? She'd done everything so far according to the recipe; right down to the last letter, which wasn't easy considering Granny's extra-curly handwriting.

Granny's bedroom door banged open.

"What in God's name are you doing?" she hollered as she came loping into the kitchen as fast as her gimpy leg would let her. Trixie stayed in the hall and just peeked around the corner to watch.

"I'm fixing dinner for us."

"Put down the spatula and step away from the skillet," Granny ordered, surveying Marti's project and grabbing up the note card.

"It's okay, Granny. Nothing's on fire. I don't even have the oven heating up yet. And I was real careful with your recipe box."

"But I smell cloves!"

Of course she did. And so she should. Marti had just put a bunch of them in the stewing beef.

"There's no cloves in my Special Stew!" Granny railed, waving the recipe in Marti's face.

Now Marti was getting ticked. "Yes, there are. It's right there in the recipe."

She shoved the scribbly card back under Granny's nose. Granny pushed it out to arm's length and squinted at it.

"Right there," Marti pointed for her. "It says: one 'LG' clove. I figured 'LG' meant 'large' and that would be a tablespoon since that's larger than a teaspoon."

And Marti had been pretty darn impressed with herself for figuring that out, especially the way Granny had run this ingredient's listing right on top of the next one: garlic, minced.

But Granny just started cackling like this was the funniest thing she'd ever heard. "I swear, Martha Snowden, you had better marry you a man that can cook or you'll end up starved to death."

Well, she hadn't starved so far, had she? And she sure as heck hadn't had some man cooking for her. Or doing anything else for her in a long, long time, for that matter. But hey, as long as God made frozen dinners and instant oil change places, who needed a man anyway?

Granny kept chortling away. "You might be able to save the rainforest, honey, but you sure as shooting can't read a recipe."

"Oh? Then what does it really say?"

"It says 'one large clove garlic, minced'," Granny explained between belly laughs. "There's no cloves in my stew!"

"Well what the heck is a 'clove garlic'?"

Granny just guffawed her way over to a basket on the counter. She pulled out some little onion looking thingy and held it up in front of Marti's nose. "This is garlic."

Yes, it was. Marti pushed it away.

"The little knob here is called a 'clove', but it don't have anything to do with the spice called cloves that you pulled out of the cupboard!" And the old woman laughed and laughed. Then she ordered Marti to wash off the stewing beef and start over. With no cloves.

And so Marti started over; this time with Granny hovering behind her. Well, it was an honest mistake. Anyone could have done it. Probably some really great chefs started out this way.

Probably not two days after they burned down the kitchen, though.

Chapter 3

Aw, hell. Another plate on the floor and they were still serving breakfast. Well, at least this one didn't have someone's nice hot pancakes on it. Damn. She never really was good for anything on a Friday.

"I'll get it," Granny's long-time assistant cook, Peg said, leaving the counter she'd been scrubbing down and coming to push Marti out of the way of the broom. She probably would have rather pushed her right back out the door into the alley. Peg was being a good sport about things, but Marti's recent bout of especially bad luck was starting to take its toll on the older women. Peg was a bit twitchy these days.

Marti wisely got out of her way and stood by, mute, simply handing over the dust pan when Peg had the shattered pieces all swept into a pile. She glanced at Marti with a wary look that said she'd have rather been wearing a haz-mat suit for coming in that close contact with her. The way things were going, maybe Granny ought to start issuing them.

"Thought I heard you come in here."

Marti glanced up to find Granny standing in the doorway, coming in from the dining area. The look on her face said she'd already been pricing the haz-mat suits.

"Yeah, that was me," Marti acknowledged. "Only broke one plate, though."

"And a coffee cup," Peg added.

"Oh." Marti sighed. "I guess I didn't see that."

"No matter," Granny said, stooping to help Peg with the rest of the clean up.

"No, I can get that," Marti said quickly, rushing in to finish the job before poor old Granny ended up hurting herself.

"No!" both gray-haired ladies practically shouted.

Marti jumped back. Great. Now not only was she going to have to remember to deduct the cost of an additional plate *and* coffee cup from the miniscule paycheck she'd be writing out for herself today, she'd be feeling guilty for standing around watching senior citizens clean up after her. What else did she need to make her day any worse?

"Is that Hurricane Marti back here?"

Oh, God. That's what she needed to make her day worse.

Here came East, sauntering in all broad-shouldered and perfect-teethed. Jeez, he was gorgeous. Yep, this was pretty much just exactly what she needed to make her day worse. Charming, beautiful East making fun of her and her legs going weak just to look at him.

She ignored him as hard as she could.

"It was my fault," Peg and Granny both said at the same time.

Oh brother.

"No, it was my fault," Marti corrected. "I knocked some dishes off the counter."

"Huh. Something different for a change," East said, blinding her with a grin.

Why oh why did he still have to be so damn good-looking? She turned her back to him, but she knew he was watching her. He was still grinning, too; she could feel it. It made the air in the kitchen sizzle.

"Did you get your pictures from the drug store this morning?" Granny asked as she brushed up the last of the fragments. Peg helped tug her back up to standing and Granny returned the favor. Muscles creaked and joints popped in both of them.

"Yeah, they were ready," Marti said, pointing to the photo envelope lying on Granny's desk.

"Did they turn out all right? Is your friend in the government going to be able to use them, do you think?" Peg asked.

Granny harrumphed. "I don't know why anyone in the government would want pictures of lizards, though."

"You took pictures of lizards for the government?" East asked, stepping into the room and dangerously closer to Marti.

"No, I didn't," she said, happy to disagree with him.

"Yeah, you did. Come on and show us," Granny prodded.

"I'm pretty sure you don't want to see them," Marti said.

"Well, I'll bet Johnny does," Granny said.

East nodded and took another couple steps closer to her. Marti gulped and stepped back, which put her right next to Granny's clunky old desk that had never really fit properly in the kitchen. The backs of her legs banged into the chair, and Marti plopped down into it. Hard. East just smiled.

"Yeah, I'd love to see Marti's lizard." His deep, warm voice didn't exactly sound like he was talking about reptiles.

"I don't have a lizard," she assured him.

He just shrugged, his August-sky eyes agreeing that he was not, indeed, discussing cold-blooded creatures. "How about you just show me what you do have?"

God, wasn't he ashamed of himself for talking that way in front of two old ladies?

"Go ahead, Marti," Granny suggested. "Show him your pictures. He'd probably get a kick out of it."

"I didn't get prints," she said. "Just a disk."

"Fine," East said, unphased. He picked up the envelope, then handed it slowly to her and nodded toward the computer on Granny's desk. "Get the machine running and let's slide it inside."

Holy hormones, the way he said that was positively indecent! What on earth was wrong with her? She was around the guy five minutes and her brain slipped right into the gutter.

Then his arm brushed her shoulder as he reached past her to open up the disk drive. Oh, *that* was why. Even after ten years his touch still melted her into a pile of helpless jelly. God, how on earth was she going to survive him being back in Garden Falls?

Mostly just to distract herself from him, she turned to pop the disk into the computer. Oddly enough, her audience suddenly dispersed. Peg ambled across the kitchen to empty her dustpan full of shards and Granny went to talk to the waitress who came in asking if she could substitute fried bologna for a side salad. Must be the Townsend's stopping in for a snack.

But this left Marti alone at the computer with East leaning over her. *Looming* over her was more like it. His hot breath touched her all over, making the hair on the back of her neck stand up and other parts of her body joined in. Mortifying.

Why did he still do this to her? It's not like he was anyone to her. Not anymore. And it wasn't like she'd ever in a million, jillion years want to get involved with him again. Hell no! He'd been a scrawny, unmotivated kid ten years ago and getting involved with him nearly destroyed her. What on earth would it do to her if she let herself slip up with the big time TV-star and certifiable heartthrob he'd become?

"Open it up," he said in her ear. "Let's see what you've

got."

"Take it easy," she said, hoping he could hear how much he annoyed her. "This old machine is slow."

She felt him let out a low breath. Was he complaining, or laughing at her? She didn't dare turn her face up to look at him. He was waaaaay too close for that.

"Take your time," he said as she tapped her finger nervously on the desk. "I'm sure it'll be well worth the wait."

Her pulse rate increased and she cursed it. This was only East, for heaven's sake. He was the goofy kid next door, the one who could have been the class jock but decided to do show choir and drama club instead. He was the kid who was better at making everyone laugh than at remembering his homework; the guy who seemed to think there wasn't any such thing as tomorrow and that nothing else mattered except having fun.

Well, he'd been wrong. Time and life had proven that. There really was tomorrow, and there really were important things that did matter. She was working on one of those things right now. She needed to concentrate on *that*.

"Got those pictures up?" Granny asked. Apparently she'd sorted out the bologna/salad dilemma and was coming back over to the computer. Thank God.

East acknowledged Granny's presence by putting some air between him and Marti. She drew a deep breath and thankfully could smell more pulled pork than she could East. Breathing in too much of him was making her hungry. The wrong kind of hungry.

"Well, look at that," Granny said with sincere amazement when the photos finally popped up and Marti selected one to enlarge it. "Peg, come and see this awful thing."

"No, I've got dinner rolls that need made," Peg called back from the sink where she was scrubbing down like a surgeon. "You look at your lizards, but leave me out of it."

"It's not a lizard," Marti repeated.

"What did you say it was?" Granny asked, peering closer at the murky picture on the screen. "A hellsmacker, or something?"

"It's a hellbender," East said. He even made that word sound sexy.

"Not exactly pretty is it?" Granny muttered, tipping her head sideways as if that would make the photo look better.

"They're really hard to photograph in the wild," Marti explained.

"Nice of the little fellow to come up and pose for you like that," East added.

"Maybe he knows his future depends on letting me get his picture," Marti said, trying desperately to keep her mind on the important stuff.

East didn't seem to believe in important stuff. "What, you're going to get him a job selling car insurance?"

"Funny. I don't suppose you have any clue what this picture really means," she said, scooting the chair over enough so that she could turn and look up at him. "Do you?"

"Uh, oh," Granny sighed. "I smell a lecture coming on."

But East didn't look like he'd mind a lecture just now. He leaned against the desk, crossed his perfectly tanned arms over his sculpted pecs, and nodded.

"Yeah. A hellbender isn't really a lizard, it's an amphibian; the largest salamander in North America. My guess is you're all fired up because, as far as I know, nobody's seen any around here in a long, long time."

Huh. He spouted that off as if he memorized it somewhere. It didn't seem likely those were lines he'd ever used on his cooking show, but anything was possible. The important fact was that he'd been right.

"Well, now somebody's seen one," she said proudly. "Me. Right here in Tyler's Branch."

He looked surprised. "Really? Here, behind the diner?"

"No, not here in town. Out a ways. Out off… well, out off Beaverbend Road."

Oh no, just mentioning the place made her face get all warm. Surely she wasn't blushing, was she? Yeah, she was. Finding a rare salamander wasn't the only memorable experience she'd had out there off Beaverbend Road. She'd spent the last ten years trying really, really hard not to think about the other ones.

But East didn't seem to have the same hang-up. He made a kind of "hmm" sound and leaned closer to the monitor for a better look. It was almost like he didn't remember Beaverbend Road was where they… well, they drove out there a few times.

"So just how big is that ugly thing?" Granny asked.

"This one was only about thirteen or fourteen inches, I think," she replied. "But they can get even bigger."

Granny let out a low whistle. "They get bigger than *that*? Shoot, that's one hell of a hellbender. Peg, did you get a look at this thing?"

Shaking her head, Granny left the computer area and headed over to harass Peg with tales of gargantuan salamanders overtaking the earth. This left Marti alone with her hellbender. And East. She wasn't sure which one was slipperier.

"So, are you especially fond of the bigger hellbenders, or doesn't size matter?" he asked softly.

Oh no, she wasn't going there. She kept her reply strictly business.

"Any hellbender in this county is an important find."

"Yeah, but you act like a fourteen inch hellbender is no

big deal. Personally, I think that's something to brag about."

"Not really. They get bigger."

He leaned closer to her and his eyes were almost violet. "You mean, with special handling he could grow?"

"They don't usually like to be handled."

"Maybe you haven't been doing it right."

Good grief, was the guy stuck in middle school? Well, if he was, then so was she because darned if she didn't feel her face go redder and a giggle try to escape. Oh, East had no right to affect her this way! She'd be better off with the salamander.

"Tell me," he was saying. "Exactly how big can these hellbenders get?"

"Some have been found up to twenty inches."

Now he looked downright impressed. "Did you actually see these twenty-inch wonders, or did they just *tell* you they were that size?"

"I've seen a few."

"I bet you have."

"Shut up, East."

"Come on. You're smiling," he said.

"I am not."

"Yes, you are. Good thing, too. I was starting to think maybe you hated me."

"That would imply I have time to waste any emotion at all on you," she said. "I don't. Now get out of the way so I can e-mail this. Someone at the statehouse is bound to be interested in a protected species living right where the Townsend's are planning to build condos."

"Oh, so that's the deal. Your little buddy here is going to stop the destruction."

"Exactly."

"So, then I guess in this case, size really doesn't matter."

"No, just the fact that he's here at all."

"So a twenty-inch hellbender somewhere else would not be nearly as good for you as an eight inch hellbender right here in Garden Falls?"

"Yeah, pretty much."

"Good to know."

The smile he gave her had no doubt melted many a female. Well, not this female. Not anymore.

"An eight inch hellbender is obviously underdeveloped and immature," she said evenly. "It might be hard to find support for adequate protection."

"I've always supported adequate protection."

He was not giving up, was he? Then neither was she. She met his eyes. "You know, it's kind of hard to work here with you sitting on my computer."

"So don't work," he said. "Talk to me instead. Tell me all about what you've been doing the last ten years. My mom says you've traveled. Is that right?"

Oh, he was good. She almost believed he was interested in her life. Almost.

"I've been busy. I'm busy now, as a matter of fact," she said and tugged at the mouse cord. It was wedged securely under his taut butt and seemed perfectly happy to stay there. She really couldn't blame it.

"Is that my invitation to leave?"

"No, that would be rude," she said and kept up the sweet smile for him. "Besides, you seem pretty good at leaving all on your own without an invitation."

"Ouch. Is that your non-rude way of reminding me what a jerk I was?"

"Was?"

"I like to think I've grown up a bit since high school."

"And I like to think I'm a willowy blonde, but it doesn't

make it automatically true."

He caught her off guard then by reaching toward her. She sucked in a shocked breath as his finger touched her cheek then slid over her temple to push back a strand of mussed pony tail.

"You're sort of blonde," he said.

Grr. Nobody wanted to be "sort of" blonde. Even while being touched by J. Easton Smith.

"So I guess maybe you're just sort of a jerk?"

"I've missed you, Marti," he said.

Oh, God. She was melting again. Of course, deep down she knew if he really *had* missed her he could have got her phone number and called, or friended her online, or tracked down her address and shown up on her doorstep in something approximately like what he was wearing now minus the shirt and jeans. Yeah, he could have done that. But he didn't. He left and never looked back.

She pushed his hand away and was disappointed that he let her.

"Please say we're still friends," he said.

No, of course they couldn't still be friends. They quit being friends ten years ago on a hot August night after a movie and a box of carry-out chicken. They couldn't be friends because ever since then she couldn't even eat chicken without remembering, without wondering where he was, what he was doing, who he was with.

No, when a guy ruins your dinner for ten years straight, you pretty much can't still be friends.

"Yeah, we're still friends," she said. Pathetic.

"Good."

"But get off my mouse cord. I need to get these pictures sent. Groundbreaking is set for next month."

"Well don't let me stand in the way of you standing in the

way of progress," he said and scooted over so she could finally free her mouse.

"And I don't like working with someone looming over me," she hinted.

"I like looming over you."

She just glared.

"All right," he said, finally stepping away. "I'll see you around."

"Yeah." *Not if she could help it.*

He didn't seem to notice her insincerity and called over to Granny. "Well, Granny, you ready?"

Granny smiled and came to collect her purse out of the desk drawer. What was this? East was taking off with Granny? They hadn't mentioned this to her. What was going on? She frowned at both of them.

"Don't worry. I'll have her back in an hour or so," East said with a wink.

"Maybe," Granny added, giggling and heading for the back door.

They were just going to take off, without explanation. That was weird. Granny always told her where she was going, what she was doing. Marti didn't think she liked this one bit. But what could she do? It wasn't like she was jealous of her own grandmother, or anything. No, that would be ridiculous.

"East?" Marti called after him just as he disappeared through the back door.

He poked his head back inside. "Yeah?"

She kept her eyes firmly on the computer and forced a disinterested scowl. East waited patiently for her to continue. She finally slid her eyes up to meet his.

"Eight inches? I don't think so. Nothing changes that much, even after ten years."

She turned quickly back to the monitor, but his warm laughter washed over her and trailed away as he followed Granny out into the alley. Wow. How had she existed all these years without East's laughter? Maybe she really hadn't.

Chapter 4

Charleen Koch checked her watch. They might just make it on time. Maybe.

"Got your seatbelt on, Josh?" she called back to her son.

"Yeah," he grumbled.

She glanced over her shoulder to make sure. Okay, next question: "Got your backpack?"

She knew he did; she handed it to him with his jacket as they dashed out the back door of their restaurant.

"Yeah, I've got it," he said. "I hate this old car. Why can't we drive the van?"

Charleen sighed. She hated the clunky old Chevy, too, but Arv needed something a little more presentable for his meeting with the bank people over in Garden Falls today and it was unlikely this pitiful excuse for transportation would actually make that forty-minute trip. So she'd parted with the custom painted *"The Dutch Pantry"* van for a day.

The car stalled at a stop sign. A huge pick-up truck behind them honked and Charleen swallowed a few select words she would have rather screamed out loud. Until this year she never even thought curse words. Now her kids were scolding her for them practically every day. Rough year.

Who'd have thought building a dream would be so frustrating? And after all the hard work, what did they have to show for it? Two mortgages, eighty-hour workweeks, and Arv had to drive around in this danger-mobile every day.

How did he do it without complaining?

Sometimes she resented his faultlessly positive outlook. He even believed they'd win that silly cook-off thing he'd gotten them invited to. Sure, she believed their food was good enough, but how was winning a cook-off supposed to help them? It just seemed like a lot of extra work. She'd only agreed to do it because it got them a free weekend in a fancy hotel in Cleveland. Her parents lived up there, and it would be great for the kids to see them again. It would almost be like a vacation.

After a couple grinding tries she got the engine running again. That meeting at the bank was pretty important. It was a darn good thing she hadn't let her husband head off in this heap. A lot was riding on that famous Arv Koch charm and personality. She checked the time again. Well, for right now she'd just be glad to get Josh across town for kindergarten.

She watched him in her rear-view mirror. He was scowling. She knew why.

"Don't worry, honey. After this weekend Daddy will have some time for you."

"How many days is that?"

She knew it would feel like a hundred, for all of them. The weekends always did. "Today's Friday. Then comes Saturday…"

"When we go stay with Mamaw Koch, right?" Josh asked. He used to get excited about weekends with Arv's parents. Neither of the kids did anymore. They missed their own house.

"That's right. You and Annie will get to stay with Mamaw and Papaw, and they'll bring you back on Sunday night. And then comes Monday."

"And no restaurant."

"No restaurant and no catering on Monday." Their one,

blessed day off.

"Do we hafta go to school?"

"Yes, but then we'll have all afternoon together. Just us at home."

Josh couldn't help but smile. "Good. I like that."

"Me, too, sweetheart."

"I hate the restaurant."

Charleen was glad to pull up in front of Lincoln Elementary School. She hated this conversation every time. "I know you do, honey. But the restaurant is Mommy and Daddy's job. We have to work. Everybody's Mommy and Daddy works at something, don't they?"

"Dillon's Mommy just takes care of him, and after school he gets to go home instead of sitting in a hot smelly kitchen. And at night his Daddy comes home from his job and eats dinner with them. And Ashley's Daddy has his job in their house! She says he works on his computer in his underwear all day long and he can give her peanut butter sandwiches anytime she wants one."

Charleen rolled her eyes. Oh sure, the Beaver Cleavers of kindergarten were corrupting her child. "Well, that's how their life is and this is how our life is."

"Well our life sucks."

"Josh! We don't talk like that."

"You do."

He had a point. "Okay, here we are. Get your things together."

She slowed the car and stopped at the curb in the long line of moms dropping off afternoon kindergarteners. Dillon's Mom was right in front of them with her big shiny SUV and tight little butt that came from having plenty of time to work out. Charleen smiled sweetly and returned her wave as she got out to open Josh's door for him. It creaked loudly and

Josh dragged himself slowly out onto the sidewalk.

"Hurry up, honey. You don't want to be late," she said.

He grumbled something that sounded vaguely like he did want to be late and included another word she was sure she should have scolded him for. She pretended she didn't hear it.

"You got all your things?"

"Yes, Mom."

"Where's your jacket?"

"I don't need it."

"Yes, you do!"

"But it's summer now," he whined.

"No, it's spring, and it's still chilly. Is your jacket in your backpack?"

"No, I left it at the restaurant. We can go back and get it!"

She sighed and made herself count to five. "No, we cannot go back and get it. You'll just have to be cold at recess today."

"I won't be cold. I'm fine."

"Good. Now get in there!"

She gave him a little nudge to set him walking toward the building. Remembering that Dillon's perfect mom was nearby, she called after her grumbling little boy. "Have a great day, sweetie! I love you! Oh, and don't forget, you and Annie will take the bus home today."

He turned back to her with the hint of a smile. "Home?"

"Well," she amended. "To the restaurant."

He didn't even respond but turned and hoisted his backpack more securely onto his sagging shoulder. Dillon gave his mommy a final kiss then ran to catch up with Josh. Yuppie-boy was talking a mile a minute, but Josh hardly seemed to notice. They disappeared into the building to meet up with their teacher and the rest of their class.

Charleen scanned the giggling, squealing children out on

the playground, but it didn't look like Annie's second grade class was outside right now. She'd hardly said two words to her daughter this morning in the rush to get everything ready for the day. And she'd be too caught up with dinner preparations when the bus dropped the kids off at the corner near the restaurant after school. Well, she'd get them home before seven and maybe there'd be time for a little maternal bonding during bath and bedtime.

They'd hardly seen their father since Monday, so at least she was ahead of Arv in this parenting game. Not that she was really keeping score. It just gave her something to compare to. Something other than Dillon's tight-butt-perfect mommy.

Why did it all have to be so hard? She reminded herself that for generations families worked long hours in less than perfect conditions to support themselves. This was actually a fairly normal lifestyle by worldwide standards.

She liked to tell herself that her children were lucky to be able to spend time with them at the restaurant instead of being stuck in an impersonal day-care somewhere, or spending the entire day at school in the latchkey program. They were meeting people and learning valuable skills. Someday they'd be glad for everything this restaurant meant to their family.

She noticed the time as she climbed back into the rumbling car and tugged at her stubborn seatbelt. Their new manager at The Dutch Pantry, Andrea, was turning out to be a great asset, but Charleen hated to leave her alone for too long right in the middle of the lunch hour. She gunned it past Dillon's mom and cut off a lady in a station wagon. With Arv out of town, she needed to get back there and look after things.

She heard the sirens about half a mile away from the

school. They sounded close and she had a moment of terror when she was afraid maybe something had happened to one of her kids, but ahead at the next intersection she could see the flashing lights of fire trucks turning the other way. Her heart pounded in relief.

That's right, the fire station was just around the corner. That's one of the first things she looked for when they moved to Finster last year. If the restaurant was close to a fire station, they could get a deduction in their insurance. She made sure they bought a building within the required radius. Their house, too. Every little bit they could save meant that much more they could put into the business.

She followed the sirens for a while, and when she turned onto Park Street she could smell smoke. Her heart started pounding again. The fire trucks were blocking the road and she couldn't even get to her parking lot from here. Was the convenience store across the street on fire? Oh, hopefully not the furniture store next door! That would be a disaster.

No, she couldn't see for sure from this distance, but the firemen were running toward… Oh, no! They were dragging those big hoses right in through the front doors of The Dutch Pantry!

She pulled off into a no parking zone and jumped out. At first she took comfort in knowing her kids were safe, and Arv was in Garden Falls. Okay, at least that was good. But what about the employees? And all their lunchtime customers?

This couldn't be anything bad, it just couldn't be. It had to be a drill, or maybe an alarm got set off accidentally.

Oh, God! There was smoke pouring out from the back of the building!

———

The Bride Can't Cook

Well, they'd done it. East was now part owner of Granny's Kitchen. They'd met up with the attorney at the bank and done the deed. All that was left now was to buy a new fridge, line up some electricians to up-grade the place, and start actively looking for a buyer who wasn't Phil or Joetta Townsend.

Oh, and they needed to tell Marti.

They came out of the bank and headed for his car. The May weather was great this year and he half wished he hadn't been Granny's chauffeur today. He could have really used the walk. Between all the home cooking he was getting from Granny as well as his mother, he was really going to have to start watching things if he didn't want to go hopelessly to flab. He missed his personal trainer. Not only was Paulo the best at keeping his abs photo-ready, but East still owed the guy a big thank-you for taking Treeva off his hands.

He was just helping Granny into his car when a van in the bank parking lot caught his attention. *The Dutch Pantry* was emblazoned on it in big, old-fashioned lettering. That sounded vaguely familiar. Why? The address and phone number painted were in Finster. Hmm, did that ring a bell? Who did he know up in Finster?

"Oh look," Granny said, pointing. "There's Arv!"

He followed her gesture and saw a man leaving the bank and heading toward the van. It only took a minute to recognize him. Yep, Arv.

"Hey, Arvie Koch!" Granny called, clambering back out of the car.

The man stopped, then broke into a huge grin. He loped over their way. "Well, I don't believe it. Granny, is that the long-lost Johnny Smith with you?"

East took his hand when Arv offered it. He shook it with gusto, too. Well, hell. He was damn glad to see the guy, even if he had been the one Marti chose over him. For a while, anyway.

"He's a big star now, Arv. Everyone says we've got to start calling him Easton," Granny said.

"That's right," Arv laughed. "You're somebody now."

"Yeah, who'd have ever thought, huh?" East laughed with him.

Had it really been ten years? Sure didn't feel like it now, standing here on Piccolo Street with Granny and Arv. All that was missing was Marti.

"We figured you'd do okay," Arv said. "You always did."

That just showed how much his old buddy didn't know. But Arv seemed to have done all right for himself.

"Granny says you're all married and settled down now. Up in Finster, huh?" East asked.

"Yep. Two kids, big mortgage, in-laws, the whole nine yards."

"And a restaurant?"

Arv stood up taller and beamed. "That's right, sold the house here and started up our own place in Finster."

"Yeah, I heard about Pedersund closing up."

"That was pretty tough on a lot of people here," Arv said. "It worked out okay for me, though. Guess engineering wasn't really what I wanted to do."

"But restauranting is?"

Arv shrugged. "Maybe all those summers peeling potatoes and pouring iced-tea at Granny's weren't wasted, huh?"

"Apparently not," East said.

He hoped none of what he was thinking showed up on his face or in his voice. He'd never thought Arv's summer after summer working for Granny had anything to do with dedication to a job. It was a handy access to Marti. Sort of like East's reason for working there.

"But what about you? You back in Garden Falls for long?" Arv asked.

East decided not to mention that he'd sort of gone into the restaurant business himself—with Marti, even though she still didn't know about it—and that his stay here might be a little longer than expected.

"Naw, just a visit."

They caught up a little on the past ten years. East didn't even mind answering his old friend's questions about Hollywood and all the famous people he'd managed to meet there—or rather, the super-famous people he hadn't met.

Arv didn't seem overly impressed by East's career. It was just a good, old-fashioned friendly conversation. That was nice.

Arv talked about his wife, Charleen. They met in college, he explained. East didn't ask, but he guessed they must have met right after the thing with Marti, judging by their kids' ages. That was kind of a surprise. East would have expected Arv to have been too upset after his breakup with Marti to run out and get married right away. Oh well. Everyone had their own ways of dealing with things. Sounded like Arv's way worked out pretty good for him.

They talked about the past, their summers at Granny's Kitchen, and some of the stupid things they'd all done in high school. Arv even made a few jokes about Principal Monroe. Funny, but those years usually seemed like a lifetime ago. Talking to Arv now, it all came back like last week.

Memory Lane was interrupted, however, by Arv's cell phone. It played *"The Sun'll Come Out Tomorrow"*. East cringed.

"My wife programs my phone when I'm not looking," Arv said sheepishly. "She knows I hate show tunes."

East tried to imagine his ex-wife ever doing something like that. Heck, Treeva didn't even bother to program her own phone. That, among other menial tasks, was the reason other people existed, of course. Treeva the Diva didn't get her nickname by being the salt of the earth.

She did, however, like show tunes.

"Hey, it's my wife," Arv said, covering the tiny mouthpiece. "She sounds upset, so I'd better find out what she needs."

"Sure. Great seeing you again, Arv."

"Don't be a stranger!" Granny called. "And kiss those babies for me before they get too grown up."

Arv nodded. "And you guys come on up to Finster and get a decent meal for a change."

Arv turned his attention back to his phone and headed for his van. East caught a quick glimpse of Lorelei Jennings and her giggly daughter, Marie, heading their way to suck him into another excruciating conversation about how it would be really great if he would help out at the community theatre while he was in town. Purely for self-preservation, he ignored Granny's claims of independence and hoisted her into his car. He made it into the driver's seat just in time. Lorelei and Marie had to make do with quietly waving long-distance at him.

——

The lunch crowd was just about done when East's tall, magazine-cover body breezed in through the door. Marti tried not to notice him. She glanced at the Dr. Pepper clock on the wall over the hall to the restrooms. He and Granny had been gone over an hour. Wonder what they'd been up to? Not that she'd ever come out and ask either of them. As far as they were concerned, she couldn't care less about East's comings and going.

Except that right now he was coming toward her. Oh, rats! Now she was smiling at him over the tray stacked high with today's pulled pork with sweet coleslaw sandwiches and Granny's famous black bean soup. He was bound to think she was glad to see him, or something.

She tried to get involved in casual small talk with the customers around her, but it was awfully hard to breathe with East in the building. It didn't matter anyway. No one in the diner really cared about small talk with her right now. They all wanted to watch what was going on between the town hunk and Swamp Girl.

She finished doling out the plates on her tray and retreated to an empty table nearby to pull out her order pad and double check a few things. She wasn't sure what, exactly, needed double-checking, but at least it got her a couple feet away from the curious customers. And East. He followed, though.

"Serving up anything I might like?" he asked when it was obvious she wasn't going to speak first.

He was using that same voice from earlier, the one that said one thing and meant another.

"The soup's really good," she said, not looking up at him.

"Then I guess it's not your day to cook, huh?"

"Very funny," she said and remembered she needed to get Mavis McAulley an extra spoon. Chuckie McAulley was notorious for throwing things.

"Yeah, the town's in luck," she said under her breath as she hustled off to find a spoon. "Granny and Peg are responsible for today's food. Society as we know it is safe."

Lloyd Schneider laughed at them. Oh yeah, his soup was waiting on the counter. She went and got it for him and even remembered the figs this time, too. East still followed. Lloyd snickered some more. Marti let his soup slop onto the table as she served it to him.

East grabbed a wad of napkins out of a canister on the next table and wiped up her mess. Lloyd just grinned at them.

"This smells like good soup, Miss Marti," Lloyd drawled and turned his beady eyes on East. "You come here for some soup, son?"

"If that's what she's serving up, Mr. Schneider," East answered easily.

Honest to God, he winked at the old man. Lloyd laughed until he coughed. Marti refilled his water glass for him and marched herself away before she started dropping things again.

Lloyd might have been saying something about needing a spoon, but she wasn't about to go back and find out. Maybe Lloyd would get lucky and Chuckie would pitch one his way.

"If it's lunch you're looking for," she snapped at East, dropping off the coveted utensil at the McAulley table. "Maybe you ought to go find someplace to sit."

"Yeah, but I hate eating alone."

"Hmm. Lloyd's got an empty chair."

"How about that empty table in the back with a couple empty chairs?" East suggested, trailing her into the kitchen. "A chair for me and a chair for you."

She turned on him, a little more confident without the whole town out there staring. "East, I'm trying to work here. Quit messing around."

He shrugged. "Who's messing around? I'm asking you to have lunch with me."

Well, there went that blood pressure again. "No, I can't. And where the heck is Granny? Didn't you bring her back?"

"Doctor's appointment."

Oh, that's right. Marti was supposed to drive her over to Dr. Traynor's this afternoon. Guess she had East take her, instead. What was going on between those two, anyway?

"You should have just waited there at the doctor's office rather than coming back here." Yeah, that would have kept him busy all afternoon. Granny's appointments with Doc Traynor lasted ages, for some reason.

"But I'm hungry," East reminded her. "Want to hear my order?"

"No, not really. What were you and Granny doing all day, anyway?"

"Oh, we talked a bit."

"What about?"

"Well, not you, so don't be all flattered."

"I'm not. Trust me."

"Well, let's see then. She mentioned how you nearly burned the diner down last Saturday, how you pulled the doorknob off—from the inside—on the closet with the cleaning supplies, how you put regular dish soap in the dishwasher and flooded the place with suds, how you..." He paused for a moment then grinned. "Okay, so I guess we were talking about you. Go ahead and be flattered."

Marti groaned. He ignored it and offered a chair.

"How about soup for two?"

"After all Granny's been telling you, don't you think it's a bit dangerous to ask me to sit so close?"

"Yeah, you're dangerous, all right," he said. His voice was low and his eyes had their own kind of danger in them.

Yeah, dangerous was the word for letting herself get this close to East. Dangerous and stupid. And he was close. Too close. Her face felt warm.

"Come on Marti, take a break," he coaxed. "Let's have lunch."

She refused to be flattered. She couldn't let herself wonder what it meant that he was so gung-ho about eating with her. Probably he really just didn't want to eat alone. Probably he knew he could go home and eat with his mother or sit here alone and take his chances that Phil and Joetta would come along and join him. It really wasn't saying much that he'd prefer her company to theirs.

Then again, wasn't it in everyone's best interest if she kept Phil and Joetta away from East? He probably had money to burn after all those years living it up in Hollywood. He'd be easy prey for them.

Maybe she should agree to sit down with him for a few minutes, just to be sure they weren't going to show up and start prying money out of him. How did she know East could be trusted not to get sucked in by their smarmy smiles and promises of instant profit?

Besides, her feet were kind of hurting. Okay, for the sake of ecological responsibility and her sore feet, she'd give East fifteen minutes. They had almost a full staff today and the lunch rush was thinning out. Just fifteen minutes would be okay. It wasn't like she was going to get all weak-kneed and goo-goo eyed over him in that time. Was it?

"All right," she agreed. "Have a seat and I'll bring lunch. You want the special?"

"Is that easy for you?"

"You mean, can I handle it? Yeah, I think so."

"I mean I don't want to make extra work for you," he said. "I know you can handle it."

The way he was looking at her said he might still have a few memories of certain things she'd been known to handle. Or she could just be imagining that. Yeah, probably just imagining. She hoped.

"I'll get you some food," she said and turned away before

those blue eyes made her start imagining a few more things.

"Hurry back," he said just loud enough for her to catch it. "I have a deep, dark confession to make."

Chapter 5

She escaped into the kitchen to turn in East's lunch order and get a bowl of soup for herself. Peg must have been watching them because she ordered Marti to take a break and assigned Trisha, who was just coming in to start her shift, to look after her tables for her. When Peg mentioned something about East liking his soup nice and hot, Trisha glanced over at Marti and giggled.

Apparently nobody in town had anything better to do than speculate on Marti's personal life. And apparently they thought that personal life seemed to include East. Boy, were they wrong. Wouldn't everyone be disappointed when he headed back for California in a few days, or hours or whenever it would be.

Marti put two glasses of tea on her tray. She stuck three lemon slices on the side of one glass. East liked extra lemon in his tea. Peg winked at her from her spot by the grill.

"Tell him I've saved out one strawberry shortcake just for him," she said quietly.

Marti was floored. "What? I've been telling people for half an hour that we're out!"

"We are out, except for his. I just figured he'd probably show up again today and he might want some."

"You know, it's no wonder the man thinks the earth revolves around him," Marti sighed.

And here she was, bringing him his extra lemon, just the

way he liked it. Pitiful.

Her weakness of character was rewarded by a dazzling smile when she emerged from the kitchen. East was inordinately happy to get his triple-lemon tea. She tried not to swoon. He was just a customer, and she was just doing her job, after all. It wasn't like she wanted him to appreciate her extra effort, or anything.

"Your food will be ready in a couple minutes," she said. "Anything else I can do for you?"

His mouth slid into a grin. Oops. She hadn't meant to use those words exactly. The last thing Mr. One-track needed was encouragement.

"I'd like you to sit down and have lunch with me," he said after a slight pause.

Huh. So maybe there really wasn't anything else he wanted her to do for him. All his double entendres and dark, steamy looks were probably all just teasing. Well, good. That's as it should be. She'd agreed to be friends, and that's what friends did. They never, ever took steamy looks and casual jokes seriously. She slid into the chair opposite him.

"So," he began after two sips of tea. "I ran into Arv Koch today."

"Arv? You went up to Finster?"

"No, he was here in town. I met up with him coming out of the bank."

He was watching her carefully like he expected her to say something. What was that all about? Was he talking to Arv about her, too?

"So, he's got his own restaurant now, huh?" he asked.

"Yeah," she agreed, stirring two packets of sugar into her tea. "His baby."

Arv had always secretly wanted to do that, open his own restaurant. It was just out of loyalty to Granny that he didn't do it here in Garden Falls. As Marti recalled from what Granny had said, Charleen wasn't too keen on the idea right at first, and their little girl was upset about changing schools, but from everything Marti had heard they were doing great up there.

So East hadn't kept in touch with Arv either? Well, maybe she should find some small comfort in that.

"Is it any good?" East asked.

"What, the restaurant? Yeah, I guess so. Everyone who's been there likes it."

"Have you been there?"

"No, I haven't gotten up there. But they just got invited to that big cook-off Granny's always wanted to get into."

Arv had gotten the invite that should have gone to Granny. Marti had tried to be happy for him, but it was kind of a kick in the pants to think he'd learned everything he knew about restaurants and food from Granny, then he'd gotten invited and she hadn't.

"Hard to believe Arv got in and she didn't," East remarked.

"Yeah, but he's a hard worker. He must have earned that spot."

"So, you two stayed friends after all this time?" he asked.

"I know it's hard to believe people actually can keep in touch after high school, isn't it?"

"Is that all? You kept in touch after high school?"

What was this, an inquisition? What the heck did he care who she stayed friends with over the years?

"We did go to the same college, you know," she said. "You were supposed to be there with us, too, by the way."

"That wasn't for me. You two seemed to do pretty well without me."

"It was college. We had fun. You should have been

there."

"Three would have been a crowd, from what I hear."

Good grief, is *that* what he and Arv talked about? No way. What went on between her and Arv was hardly worth a public mention. Besides, given the details of the situation, it was probably the very last thing Arv would want to discuss with East. Ever.

He must have seen the confusion on her face. "Arv didn't say anything about it. I heard about the two of you from my folks."

She rolled her eyes. Man, and she thought she was living in the past these last couple days! "Oh, so I guess they told you all about how Arv and I were an item until I went off on a field study and he met Charleen."

"You skipped the part about breaking his heart."

"Oh yeah, *that*," Was he serious? Good golly, she had no idea that little rumor was still floating around. She would have laughed, but a the people in the next booth turned to look at her so she settled for a sedate smile.

East, apparently, took this very seriously. "You know he always had a thing for you. He took it pretty hard when you dumped him in favor of some turtles."

"It was the Galapagos Islands, for crying out loud! Look, Arv told me himself I'd be stupid to turn down an opportunity to study there. And they were tortoises, not turtles, by the way."

"See? Even now, you're more keyed up about what to call the damn animals than the fact that you ripped my best friend's heart out."

"So he was your best friend, too? Funny how you didn't keep in touch with him either."

"Like I could have kept up with you, running all over the planet."

"Like you tried," she snapped. More people were staring. Well, let them. Maybe she ought to give them all a good show and just shove East head first into his tea and drown him. No, with that big head and all those lemons there just wouldn't be room.

"Okay, you're right," he said with a sigh. "I should have dropped a post card from time to time."

"Yeah, you should have."

"Well, I'm sorry."

"You should be."

"I am."

The sincerity in his eyes was confusing, to say the least. She never did get used to East being sincere. It did strange things to her, like make her breathe funny again. Maybe having lunch with him was not such a good idea.

"Look, I've got to get back to work."

"You haven't eaten yet," he said softly. "Please stay."

As if she could have left. The way East was looking at her, she didn't seem to have much choice. Her body simply wouldn't respond to her commands right now.

"I shouldn't have said all that," he went on. "I'm sorry. I was gone and you had every right to have a good time at college with Arv and stay friends with him afterward and all that. Okay?"

No, it wasn't okay. But she wasn't about to tell him that.

"You made your choices and I made mine," she said instead.

He nodded. "Right. We did what was best for us, and it all turned out great. I mean, you're Dr. Marti now. You've been out saving the planet."

"And you've got a People's Choice Award for that little cooking show."

"Yep. Things turned out pretty good for us."

Oh, yeah, everything was wonderful. That's why she was back working here and he was living in a furnished unit over by the ballpark. But of course, he had a life to go back to when he was done slumming here in Garden Falls. She still wasn't sure where she could go next.

"Life is good," she said and smiled.

Trisha brought their lunches. She made a special point of advising East to be careful with his soup; it was piping hot, just the way he liked it. Marti half expected her to offer to blow on it for him. She wondered if East would accept. Duh, of course he would. Trisha was female, wasn't she?

They ate in silence for a couple minutes, each taking a turn mentioning how good the soup was, but not saying anything other than that. She was getting used to the quiet when he startled her by talking.

"So let's go check the place out."

"What?" She choked on her soup.

"Arv's place."

"What about it?"

"Let's go up to Finster and check it out. I want to know what he's doing up there that got him into that stupid contest."

Boy, he was full of surprises today.

"You mean, you want go to Finster?"

"Yeah, I figure if he's good enough to beat Granny we ought to check it out."

"We?"

"Yes, 'we'. You said you hadn't been up there either."

"Well, true, I have been meaning to get over there…"

"Then let's go."

"What, you mean *now*?"

"Actually I was thinking more like dinner time."

"You mean, today?" Why wasn't she just telling him a flat

out NO? No way she was driving nearly an hour up to Finster with him. And even if she did decide to go—which of course she wouldn't— she'd need more than just a couple hours to get ready for it!

"It'd be like old times, the three of us getting together."

Oh yeah, that would be a real treat. Arv would be watching them like a hawk, and the two times she'd met her Marti got the idea Charlene wasn't all that fond of her, for some reason. What a real treat indeed. No, she wasn't about to go up there with him. She'd tell him No. She planned to say No. She pictured herself saying No.

What she said was, "Well, I haven't seen Arv and Charleen in ages."

Oh, crap. *Come on, Marti, just say NO!*

"How about if I pick you up at five-thirty?" he offered. "Will you be done working by then?"

Of course the correct answer would be No. Why wasn't that word coming out of her mouth? Jeez, the last thing she wanted was to spend her Friday evening with East under Arv's watchful eye on something almost like a date.

"Sure, that's fine. I'll see if I can get off work a little early." *Oh, damn damn damn damn!*

"Wonderful. We can catch up in the car on the ride over."

And there was that smile again. Ah, hell. As God was her witness, J. Easton Smith would never, ever know what he still did to her with that smile.

"I'll try to stay awake. I'm usually pretty tired when I get off work," she said, adding a little yawn for effect.

There, that sounded like someone who was clearly unaffected by the only man who'd ever seen her naked.

———

It was only 4:37 on Friday afternoon when Milly
Snowden woke from her daily nap. Johnny had picked her up
from her doctor's appointment and brought her back here and
insisted she rest. She didn't argue. He was such a nice boy,
that Johnny.

She'd been enjoying the quiet, but now she heard Marti
coming in the front door. Hmmm. Funny thing. Marti'd been
scheduled to work through dinner, hadn't she? Wonder what
was going on? Hope she wasn't feeling poorly. The girl had
been acting a bit off these last couple days.

Unless of course maybe Johnny had told her about those
papers they signed today. Yeah, that might do to make Marti
so upset she'd come charging home in the middle of the
dinner hour. Well, she'd better get herself up and see what the
damage was.

Such a shame Marti and East never could get things
worked out between them. They'd been the best of friends as
kids, but Marti had been riled against him ever since he took
off just before college. Well, who could blame her? She and
Johnny had been through a lot together. When Johnny's
grandmother was dying of that awful cancer, Marti had gone
next door to spend every day in the woman's sick room with
Johnny.

Heck, all through high school Milly and half the town
expected them to start dating. They never did, though there
were some who just assumed it was a done deal. Course, after
they graduated something changed between them. Milly was
never quite sure what, but she was pretty sure at some point
Marti's feelings toward the boy next door had changed and
gotten a little more womanly. Johnny was an idiot for never
noticing.

They were supposed to go off to the same college; that
big one up in Columbus. Johnny's father planned on the boy

learning accounting and coming back to work with him in the Smith Insurance office, but just a couple days before they were set to go, Johnny up and left. He didn't even say good-bye to Marti. That hurt her something awful. Then he didn't even have the decency to write or make phone calls occasionally. It was six whole months before he even let his folks know where he was. Oh, those had been hard times.

So, probably seeing him again brought back tough memories for Marti. Too bad the girl couldn't just let bygones be bygones. Johnny'd grown into a fine young man and he was just as single as Marti was right now. It would be impossible for an old woman not to get her hopes up. Besides, she'd seen that little spark of something between those two kids when East was in the kitchen this morning. That had to be a good sign.

But now Milly could hear Marti banging around in the house, thumping back and forth from her bedroom to the hall bathroom. And what on earth was that strange clicking sound? Well, clearly she wasn't going to be getting any rest lying here fretting over what Marti was up to.

She got up, silently cursing her frozen joints and that stupid fall she'd taken. It still embarrassed her no end to think about it. She was way too young to be this old, that was for sure.

Slowly she made her way out into the hall and came face to face with clicking, thumping Marti. Good lord, what had happened to the girl?

"What in God's name are you doing?"

Marti just clicked and thumped past her toward the bathroom with a casual flip of her honey colored hair. Was it Milly's imagination or had the girl actually curled it? Never took much curl no matter what a body did to it, but Milly was pretty sure she detected a certain up-turn at the shoulder-length ends.

"I'm getting cleaned up," Marti answered.

"Getting dolled up, more like it."

And it was true. Her own granddaughter, queen of the dungarees, was wearing a skirt and high heels! And she looked darn good in them, too, if she'd just stand still and quit staggering around like somebody drunk. Her ankles kept wobbling in the unfamiliar shoes so every now and then a shoulder would thump into the wall while the shoes clicked an unsteady cadence on the old hardwood floor.

"Well, I'm going to dinner."

Now this was an interesting turn of events! Marti was going to dinner? Going *out* to dinner? That had to mean she was going with someone, and if she was going to the effort of dressing up for it, it must be someone important. Hopefully this meant a *man*.

Milly smiled. Well, well, well. The girl had been pining for that jackass Dr. Hedgeman ever since she came back here. Maybe some lucky somebody finally caught her attention here. But who? She hadn't seen Marti in anyone's company lately except, of course, for Johnny.

Oh dear heavens! But it couldn't be, could it? Had he finally developed a rational thought and recognized what a fine young woman Marti was? And by some miracle had Marti agreed to go out with him? This was almost too much to hope for.

"So who are you going to dinner with that you think you need to dress all up fancy for?"

"It's not fancy, Granny," she said and got a little pink in her cheeks. "It's how people who don't live in little nothing towns like Garden Falls dress every day."

"Well, it's not how *you* dress every day." That much was obvious. "So who's taking you out?"

"We're not going out. It's just dinner."

"Okay, so who will you be eating dinner with?"

The doorbell rang. Trixie came waddling into the hall to bark at them and let them know there was, indeed, someone there. Well, looks like whoever he was he was a gentleman. None of that expecting her to meet him there or just pulling up in the driveway and honking.

Marti checked her watch and gulped. "He's early!"

"Don't worry, I'll get the door. You keep on fixing yourself up. And check your teeth. I think that cheap lipstick you bought is rubbing off."

She left a panicked Marti swiping at her mouth with a Kleenex. Well, well. Now who was she going to find at her front door?

The best way to find out was to open it. She took her time getting out there. Trixie beat her to the door. Well, whoever was here, it wouldn't do to have him thinking the Snowden women were desperate for him, or anything. Even though neither of them were getting any younger and Milly sure as heck would like to see Marti get settled down nice.

She pushed Trixie aside with her foot and pulled the door open. Joy of joys!

"Well, Johnny Smith," she said and didn't bother to hide the smile. "Please tell me you're not just here to borrow a cup of sugar for your mother next door."

"Why, are you out of sugar, too?"

"No, but I'm fixing to send Marti off to dinner with someone and she won't tell me who. I was sincerely hoping it wasn't some old reprobate I'd have to worry about all night."

"Well, as far as I know I'm the only reprobate she's supposed to go to dinner with tonight, but I don't know if that helps you or not."

"It helps," Granny ushered him inside.

He was looking especially well turned-out tonight. That shaggy modern haircut of his kept him looking young, but anyone could see Johnny was all grown up. No way Marti hadn't noticed that even if she still tried to pretend he was nobody special to her.

His shirt looked like silk and was eggplant purple. You didn't see many men in Garden Falls wearing silk purple shirts, but he pulled it off quite nicely. Milly wasn't an expert on young people's dressing habits these days, but it sure looked to her like John Smith had come a'courtin'. Hot damn.

Maybe what she'd thought she'd seen budding between him and her granddaughter ten years ago hadn't been her imagination after all. Maybe Marti wasn't as hopeless as everyone thought. Maybe getting these two together finally wouldn't be as impossible as it seemed.

She was still glad she'd contrived a way to keep Johnny here in town a while by selling him part of the diner, though. That little idea had been a stroke of genius. Knowing Marti, the course to true love was going to need all the help it could get.

"Marti, your date's here," she called.

———

Charleen pushed her hair back. The soot and smoke made it even more mousy than usual. Poor Arv. He'd gotten here just in time to see the roof collapse. She wished at least she'd looked better; anything to give him some kind of hope.

But no. As usual, everything about their life was a pitiful example of unrealized potential. She had been twelve credits short of graduating when she married Arv and went to work to pay for his master's degree. Then Annie came along and Arv got that good job at Pedersund's, so it just didn't seem important for her to finish that last semester. Unrealized potential.

Arv tried to fit in at Pedersund's, but it just never clicked. He had all that talent, those big ideas, but was stuck playing second or third fiddle to the older guys. As far as they were concerned he would always be the new kid. The darn place closed down before Arv ever got to find out if any of his ideas would have worked. Unrealized potential.

And then they started this place. They had two kids to feed, a mortgage to pay, and a marriage that had deteriorated to a series of boring day-to-day routines. The whole idea of dragging the family to a new town and starting up a restaurant hadn't been her first choice, but it was the first time in ages she'd seen Arv excited about anything. Besides, Finster had more opportunities for the kids than Garden Falls. Maybe this was what they needed. So they'd come.

But so far they hadn't had time, energy or cash to make use of any of these opportunities. They'd given it all to the restaurant. And this is what they had to show for it—a pile of stinking, smoking rubble. Talk about your unrealized potential. Even Arv, the King of the Half-Full-Glass, had the look of utter defeat. Yep, the dream was over and this was wake-up time.

"I know you did everything you could, Char," he said.

She wished he'd slip his arm around her, but he didn't even seem to have the energy for that. Still, she figured a lot of husbands would be ranting and raving right now. She should be glad he was at least being calm. It was hard to be glad about anything right now, though.

"I wasn't even here," she said. "I was taking Josh to school."

"Yeah. I'm glad the kids weren't here," he said.

Her chest tightened. "Oh God, me too. What if they'd

been here and…"

"They weren't," he cut her off.

Okay, she could be glad about that. But any minute now she was due for a complete breakdown.

"And no one was hurt," he added. "That's what's really important."

He said it like he meant it, but everything about his posture and expression said it wasn't entirely true. This was an injury they weren't going to get over quickly. If ever.

Well, the best thing to do with loss was to get busy and distracted. Charleen was good at that. She took a deep breath, choked on the thick, charred air, and brushed her hands off on her black polyester slacks. They were kind of gray now.

"So, the kids went home on the bus to the Thomas's," she said. "They can stay there until your Mom gets here to pick them up. She should be on her way already, and I told her we'd meet up at our place and tell the kids what happened."

"Good. I don't want them to be worried."

"They'll be fine." *Probably even dancing in the street*, she thought, but wasn't going to mention that right now.

"I notified our insurance," she went on. "And they're sending someone out, probably tomorrow afternoon. The fire department already got the gas and electric turned off, and the police said they'd be sure to secure the place as soon as the fire people are all done. Is there anything else you can think of we need to do right away?"

"Call the Travel and Tourism Board," he replied.

"Huh?"

"About the cook-off. Tell them we won't be competing."

"Oh."

Wow, that was the last thing on her mind this afternoon! So that silly cook-off had been that important to him? She'd had no idea. What else was she going to be finding out now that it was too late? Yes sir, they were going to be recovering from this a long, long time.

"Look, Arv, there's no reason we can't compete," she said and laid her hand on his wilted shoulder. "So the restaurant's closed for a while. We can get a menu together and whatever we need for that contest. Heck, it's almost a month away, right? I know you were looking forward to it."

His back went rigid but he wouldn't look at her. "I won't compete. We don't have a restaurant, so we don't qualify for this competition."

He pulled out his cell phone and checked the time on it. "They might still be in the office there. I'll call."

He had the number in his speed dial? Wow, this was a *whole* lot more important to him than she'd known. Should she let him go ahead and cancel this thing? Surely if he still wanted to participate they could work something out.

But there apparently was someone in the office and Arv's voice sounded sure. The words came out clearly and there was no doubt about it. Charleen stood by, mute, and listened as Arv cancelled his dream. The worst of it was, all she could think about was how much she was looking forward to getting some time off work.

Yeah, this was a lot bigger than just a fire, wasn't it?

Chapter 6

East had had Marti all to himself alone in his car for the full forty-minute drive to Finster and he still hadn't managed to get around to the two subjects he really needed to bring up. He'd whimped out at lunch today and hadn't told her about the business deal with Granny. He'd tried to, even told her he had a "deep, dark confession", but when it came right down to it he couldn't come through. He ended up just telling her that the whole time he was in California he never quit missing Granny's cooking. How lame.

Subject number two was Arv. East was dying to know exactly how things stood between Marti and their old pal. She seemed awfully nervous about heading out there tonight, and he really wanted to know why. Well, he really didn't want to know if it meant she still had a thing for Arv, but he couldn't quit thinking about it.

She sure hadn't given him much opportunity for asking questions, though. Somehow she'd controlled the conversation and had kept it all on safe topics like religion and politics. No opportunity for him to pry about Arv or remind her about—well, other things. It was pretty impressive, actually, how she kept the conversation going without ever saying anything meaningful. It was like riding with a politician. Where did Marti Snowden learned that?

Probably from politicians. From what he gathered about her work, she had to deal with quite a few of them in her efforts to save the world. Politicians, lobbyists, activist lawyers—fun people like that. No wonder her sense of humor seemed to be a bit lacking these days.

Finally he got her onto a subject related to something personal. Beaverbend Road. Boy, she sure had a lot of opinions about what the Townsend's were up to out there. Just for fun he'd played a bit of devil's advocate and mentioned how the development would be good for the community, providing low-cost housing and giving other avenues for local growth. Boy, she'd jumped all over that! It would have been a real lively debate if he'd actually gotten to put a word in edgewise.

But he was enjoying just listening to her. She was still Marti. All dressed up and world-wise now, she held an even added fascination for him. This wasn't a kid with battered knees and twigs stuck in her hair. This was a woman with a respectable career; a woman with a plan for her life.

A woman who had a thing going with her colleague, that Dr. Hedgeman Granny had mentioned. He kept thinking about that, wondering if it really was over or if the formidable doctor still figured into Marti's life's goals. That was another one of those things he hadn't quite gotten around to asking her.

Well, if he didn't have enough guts to tell her he owned part of the diner, he sure as heck wasn't about to ask about her most recent long-term relationship. She hadn't reacted well to his interest in her thing with Arv, so he'd crossed that Hedgehog person off his list of conversation topics.

But they were going to have to talk about the diner at some point. How was she going to take that news? Well, she dressed up for dinner tonight, so that was a good sign, wasn't it? A woman who usually felt more comfortable in jeans and a sweatshirt didn't suddenly put on pointy shoes with a skirt and don makeup if she wasn't warming up to the guy she was having dinner with. Right?

Then again, what if her reason for the fancy get-up was *where* they were having dinner? This was her first time seeing Arv since she'd come home. Did that have anything to do with her attention to her appearance tonight?

She sure hadn't seemed to care much about what she'd looked like the couple of times he'd seen her at the diner. Why this sudden urge to be beautiful? And she was, he had to admit. She looked great. Not much like his little Marti, but really great. Any guy who didn't know her would still take a second look. Any guy who did know her, well, she'd definitely have his attention.

So, was she after Arv's attention? He didn't like that idea. Arv was a happily married man. He hoped. But was he happy enough to overlook Marti doing justice to hottie clothes tonight? Maybe it was a mistake to suggest they come here.

"So where is this place?" Marti asked as they drove past the Finster main library.

"Fourteen-twenty-eight Park Street," he said, reciting the address he'd read on Arv's van.

He remembered Park Street in Finster from a few years ago when he'd come home for a quick visit. There was a big furniture store there advertising a living room suite his mom really wanted. Country blue upholstery with little beige flecks—she still thought it was gorgeous. He wasn't too keen on it, but she was his Mom and he was just getting used to a regular salary. So in a fit of generosity, he drove her up there and bought it for her. Paid cash, too. It felt good and impressed the hell out of his dad.

He looked in the yellow pages this afternoon for the furniture place and found the address was fourteen-thirty-two, which put it in the same block with Arv's restaurant.

That was convenient. This meant he could get them to The Dutch Pantry and back without having to call ahead for directions. If Marti was getting all fancied up for Arv, he was glad Arv wouldn't have advance warning to return the favor.

"Are you sure it's this way?" Marti asked when he turned east onto Park Street.

"Yeah, pretty sure," he said.

"You didn't call for directions and tell them we were coming, did you?"

Oh, so this was supposed to be a sneak attack? Did she plan to catch Arv unaware and make a big impression on him? Or was she maybe worried about alerting the wife to her presence? Just what did Miss Marti have planned for her tight skirt and perky little hairdo tonight?

"This is the thirteen-hundred block, so it should be right up ahead, on the left," she said.

He glanced over to see her carefully reading street numbers. How did she do it— completely scatterbrained one minute, logical and practical the next? Just one of the million things about her that made her not quite like anybody else.

"Hey, look up there," he pointed, drawing her attention to the road ahead of them. "Lots of police tape. Looks like the road's only open on one lane, too."

"It's smoky," she said, sniffing. "I bet there was a fire around here earlier."

"The furniture store," he said. "It's right over there. Maybe it..."

But right away it was obvious the barricades and yellow tape weren't in front of the furniture store, but the building beside it. A building that looked suspiciously like a restaurant.

"Oh no!" Marti cried. "That's their restaurant!"

And she was right. A policeman was waving them by and

it looked like maybe a fire marshal was still on the scene, too. East had to pay attention to driving so he couldn't really check out the damage, but at first glance it looked bad. Smelled bad, too.

"The roof fell in," Marti said softly. "But the sign's still on the front— it's their place, all right. Oh God, I hope everyone's okay."

"Do you see them around here? Is Arv's van parked somewhere?"

"No, it just looks like official people poking around. Do you think they're okay?"

"Well, I saw Arv at lunchtime today and he was fine then. Oh wait, he got a call from his wife and said she sounded upset. I'll bet this was what it was about. Damn, I had no idea!"

"You don't think the kids were here?"

"They would have been at school, wouldn't they?"

"I don't know. The little boy is pretty young, maybe he's not in school yet. What if he was here and something happened!"

She was looking kind of panicky so he reached out and put his hand on hers where she clenched and unclenched them in her lap.

"I'm sure everyone's okay. It was probably just a kitchen fire and everyone had plenty of time to get out."

"But we don't know that," she said and craned her head around to look out the back window. "Wow, that's a pretty bad kitchen fire."

He thought about making a joke about her being the expert on kitchen fires, but something told him she wouldn't find that amusing right now. Instead he just squeezed her hands.

"I'll tell you what. We'll find out if they're okay," he said.

She perked up. "We will?"

"Sure," he promised. How hard could it be? "Do you know their phone number?"

"No," she said. Well, at least that meant she wasn't in daily contact with Arv.

"No problem." He took out his cell phone and dialed information. In no time at all they were ringing Arv's home phone for him.

"Is it ringing?" she pestered.

"Yes, it is."

"Is it still ringing?"

"Yes, it is. And they must not have the answering machine turned on. Or maybe they've got the phone turned off because they don't want everyone in town calling them tonight to see if they're okay."

"Or maybe they're at the hospital with the little boy!"

"No, calm down. Why don't we just go back by the building and ask the cop?" he suggested.

"Do you think he'd be allowed to tell us anything?"

"Can't hurt to ask, right?"

He turned his rental car around and headed back toward the disaster scene. This time they had to stop for traffic from the opposite direction. Marti put her window down and called out to the policeman who was motioning for them to wait.

"Excuse me," she said. Always polite. "Can you tell me if anyone was hurt in the fire here?"

"I'm sorry, ma'am," he said. "I can't give out any details. Move along, please."

Well, that didn't help to take the stricken look off Marti's face. East drove on by and wondered what to say next.

"No news is probably good news," he tried.

"No, it probably means somebody died and he's not allowed to tell us until all the family has been notified!"

"No it doesn't. Okay, let's find a place to pull over."

She looked at him suspiciously. "What for?"

"Hey, I'm hungry. I thought maybe we could find another place to eat in this town."

"What!? How can you possibly be hungry after seeing that? Don't you care at all about what happened to them?"

He laughed. She may look a little different, but this was his same old Marti after all, ready to save the universe.

"I'm kidding," he assured her, waving his phone in front of her. "I thought maybe I could get online and find Arv's address. I just thought it might be a good idea not to be weaving all over the road while I do it."

"You think you can find out where they live? Can we run by there?"

"Don't see why not. Heck, they might need some old friends about now."

It turned out that was about the last thing they needed.

It took a full half hour to find Arv's house, and when they finally did they could barely get up the quiet little street for all the cars parked at their address. There was a police car and about six miscellaneous minivans and other family-type vehicles.

At first Marti was convinced this meant something awful must have happened, but as they inched their way closer it turned out the Koch family was having what looked like good a old-fashioned family barbecue. Kids ran and giggled in the yard and the cop was drinking a tall glass of something pink.

"There's Charleen, and Arv's mother," Marti said. "Oh, thank heavens. They seem like they're okay. And I think those are their kids back there on the swing set."

"Well, there you have it. So should I find a place to park? There's somebody pretty impatient behind me."

"I don't know… it looks awfully crowded there," she said.

He knew she really wanted to stop in, but he had to admit it did look kind of chaotic. And Arv wasn't outside, so they'd have that uncomfortable thing of having to explain who they were and why they were here to a bunch of strangers. Well, he figured Arv's Mom would remember them, and Marti knew Charleen a little bit, but it would still be awkward.

He went on by the house and the car behind him turned out to be another for the barbecue. Well, he'd give Arv credit for having plenty of friends. East wasn't so sure he'd want this kind of circus if his business burned down, but each to his own.

"They don't need us, do they?" Marti said as East turned around in someone's driveway.

"Doesn't look like it," he replied.

"Well, that's good. It seems like they'll be okay."

"Yeah, it does. It's not like they lost their home or anything."

"No, it's not that bad. They'll be okay."

Of course she was still trying to convince herself to let it go. Giving up a cause wasn't something she'd ever been very good at. Too bad he'd never made it to her list of worthy causes.

"So, do we go home then?" he asked.

"Yeah, I guess so. Maybe they'll be answering the phone tomorrow."

"Yeah. We'll try that."

He found his way back out to the main road and headed for Garden Falls. She didn't seem much for conversation at this point, so he let her stare out the window in silence. He could still smell smoke and wasn't sure if it had seeped into the rental car's upholstery or if he was just remembering it. The image of the burnt-out shell of The Dutch Pantry was going to linger a while, too.

He watched Marti's profile. She sure was quiet now. Well, of course she'd be pretty upset about this. When she cared about somebody, she cared a lot.

———

Marti was glad East wasn't trying to tell her how stupid she was being. Obviously he knew she was crying. He dug a stack of Arby's napkins out of the glove compartment for her but at least had the good sense not to say anything about it. She didn't cry a lot and it bugged her that she was doing it now.

She cried when she was a child and her mother died. She cried when she was fourteen and East's grandmother died. She cried watching Disney when Simba's dad died. Basically, unless someone died Marti didn't cry.

She didn't cry when they'd lost their bid to save yet another hundred acres of forest reserve from the developer in Indiana. She hadn't cried when they'd lost their funding for an after school program teaching kids about conservation in Ft. Lauderdale. Then she hadn't even cried about the thing with Dr. Hedgeman, when he not only dismissed her from his life, but from her *job*, as well. And that really hurt.

But she cried when East left and now she was sitting here crying again and wasn't entirely sure why. It would be nice if she could tell herself she was just getting emotional because she cared so much about Arv and Charleen. That would be a great excuse. But it wasn't the truth.

She was crying because East came back and they were technically friends again but everything was different. Except that it wasn't. She felt exactly the same for East as she'd felt all those years ago when she was still allowed to call him

Johnny. Really, she ought to be used to feeling this way. So why was she crying?

Maybe it was just all these other changes around her. That was probably it. She'd caught Leland Hedgeman in the act—literally—and then she'd lost her job. Granny got hurt so Marti'd moved back here to help, East showed up, and now she'd seen her friends' restaurant burned to the ground. Yeah, changes like that would mess with anyone's emotional stability.

She blew her nose on the coarse napkin and ordered herself to shape up. East had been through a lot, too. He'd lost his job, he'd gotten divorced, he'd had to come back to the shocking changes in their hometown, just like she had. If he could sit there straight-faced, so could she.

"Sorry," she said. "It was kind of a surprise to see the place gutted like that."

"Yeah, I know," he said.

Then they were quiet for a while again. It was going to be a long, long ride back to Garden Falls.

"So how long were you in Florida?" he asked out of the blue, making her jump.

"What?"

"Where you were working last. Wasn't that Florida?"

"Oh. Yeah. It was. We'd been there four years. A federal grant in the Everglades."

"Sounds interesting."

She knew he didn't really think so. "It was."

"You must have hated to leave before it was done, huh?"

It took her a minute to realize what he'd said. "So folks have been telling you all about it?"

"No, just Granny. And my Mom. And a few others."

Great. So now East thought he knew what went on there, too. Well, he didn't. A promise was a promise and even if

Leland was a jerk, Marti hadn't shared any details with anyone. Granny and East's mom and everyone else were just giving guesses.

"Well, people don't know everything."

His eyebrows went up. "Oh? There's more to know?"

Sure, he'd love to hear the sordid details, wouldn't he? Well, he wasn't getting them from her. She knew those details intimately—waaay too intimately—and no part of her was about to discuss them. Especially with him.

"It's a long story and I don't think you really want to hear it," she said.

He just shrugged. "We're still a good fifteen miles from home," he said. "I like long stories."

"Great, then why don't you tell me about your divorce?"

She kind of expected him to get a little prickly over that, but instead he just laughed. Even from sideways that Easton Smith smile was a killer.

"That's not a long story. Treeva said we should get married and I was stupid enough to agree with her. Two years later, I was finally smart enough to get the hell out of her life. She took the house, the cars, the checking account, and got me fired from the only really successful job I ever had. So I came back here. End of story."

"Wow. That's awful! She really took everything? I thought California made you divide it all up."

"A little thing called a pre-nuptial agreement. I was a moron."

"No, you trusted her. And you probably cared about her."

"Probably?"

"Well, you married her. I mean, obviously you cared about her."

"Yeah, I guess I cared about her. Or I cared about getting famous by being her on-TV toy-boy. I don't know. It never dawned on me to find out how much I cared about her, or vice-versa. Huh. Guess I should have."

Typical East. Even getting married was a joke for him.

"Seems like it might have been a good idea."

He laughed again. "Well, next time I get married I'll make sure I'm crazy nuts for the gal."

"Well, she'd have to be, anyway."

"Oh, good one. So how come you never married your Dr. Hedgeman? You were pretty smitten with him."

"You really do think you know everything, don't you?"

"You weren't smitten? That's all I've heard about for six years; 'Marti's taken up with a big-shot professor and they're traveling the country together fixing up the environment.' Sounds like a match made in heaven."

Her mouth must have dropped because it was already open when she tried to speak. "What? Who on earth was saying that about me?"

"My parents. I did keep in touch with them, you know. They're still pretty tight with Granny, and I've seen the postcards you sent them from all over the place. Of course I've been well-informed."

"You could have written me, then."

"You could have written me."

"I was afraid my letter would have gotten lost in all the fan mail."

"No, yours would have stuck out."

"What, mine would have been the only one with swamp muck all over it, or something?"

"No, I got plenty of those. Your letter would have been the only one from you."

She swallowed. He was looking at her with his perfect eyes and perfect nose and perfect cheekbones and if she wasn't careful she might start thinking he was perfectly serious. No warm and fuzzies from East. She was way too emotional right now to risk anything like that.

"Well, nobody wrote anybody and we both got along just fine, didn't we?" she said.

"Yeah, I guess we did. If you call unemployed, uninvolved, and stuck back in Garden Falls getting along just fine."

"I do."

"Well, there you go. We are both unmitigated successes then."

"Yay rah."

"But can I tell you something, in all seriousness?"

Uh oh. "Do you have to?"

"It's weighing heavily on my mind."

"All right. What?"

"I really am hungry."

Hungry? He still wanted to eat after seeing Arv's place burnt to cinders like that? Food was about the last thing on her mind. But then again, she had to admit she hadn't been exactly hungry before they got to Finster. She hadn't been hungry all day, not since making this almost-date with East at lunchtime.

But the poor guy was hungry and she probably ought to get something, too. Skipping dinner wasn't going to give Arv and Charleen their restaurant back. Well, she'd survived this long without a nervous breakdown, another half hour in his presence wasn't likely to destroy her. In fact, what better way to finally exercise those old demons than to face them? Yes, dinner with East might be just what she needed.

"Dixon's," she said suddenly. "Let's go to Dixon's."

He glanced over to see if she really meant it. She must have had a convincing expression because he looked back out at the road immediately. Was he surprised? Yeah, he looked it. She was, too, actually. But if she was ever going to get over this guy, she was going to have to stand up to her greatest fear: a big, greasy box of fried chicken.

Chapter 7

Dixon's, huh? He sure hadn't expected her to suggest Dixon's. Then again, he guessed it made sense. Dixon's would be the first place they'd drive past on their way back into Garden Falls. Maybe she was just being practical. Maybe Dixon's didn't even mean anything to her. Maybe she'd been eating chicken for ten years and not having one single thought of him. Maybe he was a freak with his own, personal fried chicken phobia.

But, damn, he couldn't even smell fried chicken and not think of her. How on earth was he going to munch nonchalantly on Dixon's with her sitting right there across from him? Boy, talk about an opportunity to stretch his acting skills. Dixon's with Marti would be it.

They'd eaten here scores of times over the years. It had never been any place special for them, not until that one particular night, anyway. Hell, he still remembered it like yesterday. Okay, maybe more like last week, but he remembered it clearly. Did she? Probably not. If she did she'd probably have suggested some other place.

But it became obvious when the perky little teenage hostess offered to seat them in booth number eighteen that Marti did remember. Her face went kind of pale and she mumbled something about needing a booth farther away from the smoking area. The hostess assured her this was a non-smoking establishment, but Marti still had some excuse about needing to sit on the other side of the room.

Oh yeah, she remembered, all right. So did he. Good old booth number eighteen. They'd thought the booth number was some sort of omen back then. Somehow as they sat there chowing on chicken they'd discovered an interesting pattern. A spooky, reoccurring number eighteen.

He never could remember what started it, but something made Marti point out that they were both eighteen years old sitting in booth eighteen on the eighteenth of August. Then they realized it was ten-eighteen at night. And in eighteen days they were both supposed to head up to Columbus for orientation at college. A lot of eighteens seemed to converge right then and to a couple of naïve kids it seemed like they must have meant something.

He really hadn't cared what they meant. He only knew he had eighteen days left to make his move on Marti. Once they got up to college she'd probably get caught up in classes and causes and he'd lose her. Eighteen days didn't seem like enough time. He was scared senseless he'd lose her, probably forever.

So, that night, right there at booth number eighteen he made his move. Well, she'd helped a bit.

Looking back he was sure it had been very juvenile and awkward, but at the time he'd been quite proud of himself. He'd been sitting in the booth beside Marti while Arv and their buddy Tony sat across from them. East had known Arv was jealous of his pole-position seat right next to Marti, but he didn't care. Arv couldn't be mad; they were all buddies. Marti was just one of the guys and she never gave a moment's thought to which of them she sat next to.

They'd been at the movies and now were stopping for some food before heading home. Granny never cared about how late Marti was out; she said if Marti was with East, everything was all right. Well, up until then that had been true enough.

But Tony's folks weren't so understanding. East had to admit they had good reason, too. Tony didn't have a lot of sense at that point in time. He was an attorney in Chicago these days, but back then he didn't much care about things like rules. So, he was under a strict ten-thirty curfew.

That night Tony was Arv's ride. In order to get Arv to his place all the way out off County Road Twelve and still make it home by curfew, Tony figured they'd better get going. So, that left East sitting alone with Marti—right smack dab next to her, as a matter of fact—at ten eighteen at night on August eighteenth just eighteen days before college. In Dixon's booth eighteen.

She finished up her milkshake and was going on and on about what classes she was signed up for and other stuff East really didn't pay attention to because he was formulating his plan of attack. Well, turns out there was no attack necessary.

All of a sudden Marti got real serious and for a minute he was afraid she was onto him and he was going to get a swift rejection before even hitting first base. But she had something on her mind and wondered if he wouldn't mind answering a question. No, of course he wouldn't mind. Well, he listened and she asked. It was a real doozie.

He was still impressed that she'd been able to ask him flat out like that.

"Um, have you ever had sex before?"

Just like that, straightforward and unwavering. But that was how Marti did things, so he shouldn't have been so shocked. Probably if he hadn't at that very moment been thinking about participating—with her—in what would have allowed him to answer in the affirmative he wouldn't have been so surprised.

But she caught him off guard that night, just like she'd done tonight by suggesting they eat at Dixon's. He wasn't fooling himself that there would be anything besides eating involved in tonight's events, but just the thought that Marti remembered everything as clearly as he did gave him sort of a warm feeling. He'd always been kind of afraid she'd just shrugged and went on with her life when he left.

Not that he hadn't expected her to be pissed about the way he left, but he knew the whole thing about *them* wasn't much more than a scientific experiment for her. Just biological research in the area of human physiology. Getting ready for college, she called it.

He knew she never expected it to turn into anything else, and it didn't. She must have been waiting all along for someone like her brilliant Dr. Heathcliff, or whatever his freaking name was. Well, he couldn't be that brilliant if he didn't have brains enough to hold onto Marti.

Well, East had at least had enough brains to jump at that opportunity ten years ago. Marti's question had shocked him, but he'd answered her truthfully.

"No, not like really all the way."

She frowned. "Huh. Really? I figured with all the girls you'd been out with probably you had."

"I've messed around some, but never really, you know, done it."

Damn! He wished he could be as calm about this as she was being.

"How about you?" he asked. If she said Yes he was going to be seriously pissed off.

"Me? Oh yeah, like I've been Miss Popularity around here."

"So you never, um, you know?"

She shook her head. "Huh uh. Not even close."

"Huh." He just nodded. He would have occupied himself with his Coke, but his hands were shaking so he didn't dare pick anything up just now.

"So how come you didn't? A lot of the girls you went out with weren't exactly nuns," she asked.

He had waaay too many rampaging hormones to be sitting here having this conversation with her! Where on earth was she going with it? Was this just small talk?

"Well, you know, it just wasn't right." Lame, lame answer.

But it seemed to make sense to her. "Yeah. That's what everyone says."

"You mean you've been going around taking a poll?"

"Well, I asked a couple people."

"Who else did you ask?" he said before he could stop himself.

"A couple people," she replied diplomatically. "Seniors, mostly. Also I talked to Tony's sister and a couple of her friends. They've been up at college and they've all done it now."

"Does Tony know that?"

She shrugged. The emotional ramifications didn't seem to matter. As usual, this was purely scientific for her.

"It seems like everybody has sex in college," she said.

"Well, I'm kind of hoping that's true," he said with a laugh. "Aren't you?"

She just looked at him and he had no idea what she was thinking. Probably remembering some statistics she read or some other perfectly logical way to analyze this. He was busy trying to ignore his own scientific reaction to the conversation. Lots of human biology going on right now.

"I mean," he went on, babbling. "Isn't that something you

sort of hope to do at some point? You know, someday with the right person, and all that."

"Well, that's just the trouble," she said. "Everyone always talks about it being the right person or the right time and all that. But how on earth can you tell? I mean, what if I get it wrong?"

He laughed again. "Yeah, it's not like it's something you get a second chance at."

"No, and if you mess it up you're just left all alone and what are the chances you won't mess it up next time? I mean, how on earth does anybody know it's the right time or the right person or even if they're doing it right in the first place?"

"Doing it right?"

"Well, you know," she said. "I assume there's a technique."

"A technique?"

"Well, yeah. Like everything, some people probably have more of a natural aptitude for it than others. How does someone even know they're any good at it? I mean, what if it's the right time and the right person and you do it and your right person finds out you really suck at it!"

"Actually, I've heard that sucking at it is kind of a good thing."

She jabbed him with her elbow. "You know what I mean."

Boy, this was going way out into space. What on earth was she expecting him to say? "Well, I guess that's why you mess around for a while before you actually do it," he suggested. "Practice."

She bit her bottom lip and pondered this. It made her lip red and puffy when she released it. He wanted to kiss that lip and start a little practicing right here and now.

"I guess that makes sense," she said. "So that's what I

need."

"You need?"

"Yeah. I don't know if you've noticed it or not, but I haven't exactly been busy on Friday nights all through high school. Heck, I didn't even have a prom date until you stepped in and took me out of pity."

It hadn't been pity. He'd sort of put off asking anyone to go with him while he tried to figure out how to convince Marti to be his date. When he finally got around to it she figured he was just being nice and he hadn't had the guts to tell her otherwise. He'd been ready to give her all the practice she'd ever need that Saturday night in May when he walked next door to find her done up like a movie star, thanks to Granny.

But Marti just treated him like the same old Johnny Smith he'd always been to her and they'd had a fun night, but not one to remember for a lifetime.

Tonight, however, he was going to remember, one way or another.

"I'm sure you'll be real good at it, Marti," he said. "When it's the right guy and everything."

"We're going off to school in eighteen days," she said.

She was looking him square in the eye and he wondered how on earth she couldn't see through him to every steamy thought in his head right now.

"I've read the student handbook," she went on. "I've organized my class schedule, memorized the map of the campus and done everything I could possibly think of to get ready for being in college. But how am I going to be ready for the most important thing in my life if I haven't even kissed a guy?"

Oh man. Here was his chance. He'd never get this chance again. He couldn't blow it. He was going to go for it. Okay, make your move, man.

And he did. He slid his arm behind her and leaned in and kissed those gorgeous, puffy red lips. And she let him.

Thank God and hot damn, she didn't haul off and slug him for it! She let him pull her closer and she made it as easy as possible for him. She kissed him back and holy crap the girl did have natural aptitude.

It wasn't the world's longest kiss, but it was amazing. Maybe that was just because he'd wanted it for so long, or maybe it was because Marti worked hard to excel at everything she did. But when he finally came up for air and looked at her he could see she'd been pretty amazed, too.

He saw everything he needed to see right there in her eyes. Marti wanted more.

"How was I?" she asked in a hot, breathy voice that sure didn't sound like her usual scientific tone.

"With practice you might get to be a real pro at this," he said. "Need a tutor?"

"Really? You'd do that for me?"

Oh, hell yeah! "Sure. It might be good for both of us. I mean, practicing. You know."

"Yeah. You're going to college, too, right? Maybe this is the perfect solution."

It sure felt like the solution to his troubles that night.

"We already know everything else about each other," she said practically. "It's not like we're expecting it to last forever, right? What have we got to lose?"

Turned out he'd had everything to lose.

Now here they sat at age twenty-eight, table number thirty-four and East knew beyond a shadow of a doubt what she'd do if he tried to kiss her this time. It wouldn't be pretty.

Also, it would be pretty tough to do considering she was

as far away from him as possible, scooted way back in her seat on the other side of the table.

The waitress came by to take their order. Marti was still upset by the whole Koch thing, so she just ordered iced tea and a salad. She didn't seem to notice anything odd when he skipped the fried chicken—Dixon's was famous for it—and ordered a burger. It was all a lot easier than he'd expected. Good. Now, if they could just get through dinner without any more annoying flashbacks he'd be fine.

Somehow they managed. They talked about old times— the ones before that fateful night—and she wanted to hear all about how he'd made his way from struggling Midwestern wannabe in Tinsel Town to thriving, sought-after cooking show host. Well, co-host, at least.

He'd gone out to California with dreams of being an actor. As with most starry-eyed kids in LA he ended up working as a waiter or a car washer or a dog walker. Marti listened as he told her all about it, even that stint in telemarketing. She laughed, and he remembered again how much he missed her.

Then he got her talking about a rare species of snail she was able to locate in an isolated area that meant a proposed wastewater treatment facility would have to look elsewhere for a building site. And she'd gotten to meet an apparently world famous naturalist who wrote essays about trees, or something. And she'd been given special clearance to conduct a study on something she called a floating bog. Was there such a thing? Whatever, she was pretty excited about it all.

He just wished he could quit wondering how many of those things Dr. Hedgeclipper was involved in with her. And if she'd ever, during those years, thought fondly about those last eighteen days before college.

———

It was still before ten o'clock when East dropped her off at home. Good. Marti was afraid they'd end up staying out late and she'd be tired on her only day off tomorrow.

Not that she'd expected them to actually be doing anything that would keep them out late. No, absolutely not. She just thought the trip to Finster, dinner and then catching up with Arv and Charleen would take longer, so it was a nice relief when they'd only ended up having a casual bite to eat at Dixon's.

And that was perfect. Sitting down with East, right there in their old stomping grounds, was just what she needed. It was like old times again. The really old times, before she messed it all up by throwing herself at him and making him feel sorry for her. Boy, what had she been thinking back then?

But the good news was he didn't seem to hold it against her. She noticed he was a little nervous at first, when she suggested they go to Dixon's, but that was probably because he was afraid she was going to get all stupid again. Well, this time Dr. Marti was cool, calm and collected and didn't act like an idiot. Ha! And she'd even managed not to throw up at the smell of all that fried chicken.

"So, did you have a good time?" Granny asked from her crocheting. Trixie lay at her feet and gave one obligatory yap before going back to sleep.

Marti waved good-bye to East from the doorway. He smiled like an old friend and drove away without looking back. As it should be.

"Yeah," Marti answered, shutting the door to keep the early June bugs out. "It was nice to catch up."

"You're a little earlier than I expected."

Marti just shrugged. "Well, it's nearly ten."

"On a Friday night?"

"Granny, East and I are just old friends, okay?"

"Old friends who haven't seen each other in ten years. I'd have thought you'd have more to talk about."

The best tactic would be to change the subject. Marti plopped down beside Granny and smoothed out the fuzzy afghan she was working on.

"So, what are you making?"

Granny held up the blanket. It was all in pastels, green and blue and pink and yellow and done with a yarn that was just barely sparkly, but remarkably soft.

"For Trisha Broward. She's having twins."

Marti was surprised. "Trisha? Our Trisha, at the diner?"

"Yeah. If you'd have had your eyes on someone other than East this week you might have noticed she was wearing a maternity top."

"Wow, I guess I hadn't noticed." Time to change the subject again. "So, are you going to make two of these?"

"The other one's done. Did it in the hospital when they wouldn't let me do nothing else."

"Oh, before I got here, you mean. I guess you were pretty bored for a couple weeks, huh?" Marti still felt kind of bad she'd been so caught up in her own troubles that it took two weeks to get here and help Granny.

"You had plenty going on for both of us, Sweetie." Granny patted her hand and let her off the hook like all good grandmothers are supposed to do. "I'm just glad you're back here with me now. And Johnny's come home, too."

"Yeah, must be a reunion, or something."

"Well, I'm just glad you have a friend here you can spend some time with. I know a lot of your old gang has moved away, or is busy with families now."

Sure Granny, rub it in. Oh well, she hadn't meant anything by it. And who knew—now that Marti felt securely on the road to recovery from her East-addiction maybe the right man was just around the next corner. With East out of her system, there'd be no more Leland Hedgeman's for her, that was for damn sure.

"It was nice spending time with him again," Marti said. "But I'm pretty bushed. My boss is a slave driver and at the end of the week I'm worn out." She kissed Granny's cheek and stood up to yawn.

"I think your boss is a saint for putting up with you," Granny said. "Taking off early to come home and get dolled up for a date with some hottie from California…"

"Hottie, Granny?"

"Isn't that what you'd call him?"

"No, not actually," Marti laughed.

"Stud muffin, then?"

Marti shook her head and started for the hallway. "I'm going to bed, Granny."

"How about 'Cutie Patootie'?" Granny called after her.

"Oh God."

Granny cackled behind her.

"Don't stay up too late!" Marti called back. "You need your beauty rest."

"Heck, I'm not the one going out on dates with hunky TV stars."

Grrr. Marti stuck her head around the archway and glared at Granny. The old gal just grinned back at her.

"Granny, he's just Johnny from next door, okay?"

"Yeah, and he's all grown-up, just like you are. That's something you might want to take note of."

Well, she could see chatting with Granny wasn't going to

help. "Good night, Granny."

"Sweet dreams, honey. I'll be along in a minute myself."

Marti headed for her old daisy-wallpapered bedroom. Granny's silliness wouldn't be so bad if it wasn't so true. East was a Cutie Patootie, and Marti was going to have to be around him a whole lot more before she was able to entirely overlook that. Well, she was willing to give it a shot.

Funny, but Marti was already tooth-brushed and in bed before she realized she hadn't mentioned the tragedy with Arv's restaurant. Well, she'd tell Granny about it tomorrow. She'd no doubt want to send a card or offer to help out somehow. Granny was one of *those* kinds of people.

Susan Gee Heino

Chapter 8

Milly Snowden put the phone down and made herself take deep breaths and count to ten. Then she took more breaths and counted to twenty. It simply wouldn't do to drop over from heart failure just now.

Well, by golly, she'd finally gone and done it. By the skin of her teeth, apparently, but she'd done it. She'd gotten into that blasted cook-off and, darn it, she was pretty proud of herself. Of course she was too old to giggle, but she went right on and did it anyways.

"What's so funny?" Marti asked. Even just rolling out of bed the girl looked pretty as a picture. That silky mop of honey-brown hair, those hazel eyes like a bobcat—if John Easton Smith didn't notice for himself what a prize Marti was, then he was a halfwit. A hottie, but a halfwit.

"Oh, good-morning, Sunshine. You'll never guess who I just talked to on the phone!"

Marti stretched her arms up over her head. "Judging by the ear to ear smile I'd have to say Elvis Presley. But he's dead."

"Oh, don't be too sure about that. I read magazines, you know."

Marti laughed. It was good to hear her laughing. She'd been so uptight when she first got back to town. Nice to see her loosening up finally. Hmm. Wonder if that might have anything to do with Johnny showing up?

"So who was on the phone?" she asked.

"Well, I'll tell you," Milly cleared her throat. "It was someone from the Travel and Tourism Board."

"Oh yeah? What'd they want?"

"Guess."

"To find out if you'd seen Elvis? I don't know."

But then the bobcat eyes got very large and Marti began to smile. "Wait a minute… they weren't calling about the cook-off, were they?"

"Yes, ma'am, they were. I'm in!"

Marti grabbed her hands and started jumping up and down. "Oh, Granny! You're in! That's amazing!"

Milly was jumping up and down with her. It hurt, but she'd worry about that later. "I know, I can't believe it!"

"So, was it just some mix up with the scores and they finally figured you really were supposed to be in it?"

Thankfully, the jumping stopped. "Well, no, they said one of the other contestants backed out."

"Backed out? Who'd do a dumb thing like that?"

"Well, it's kind of a sad story," Milly said. "And I know I should feel bad for them, and I do, of course. After all, they lost their restaurant."

"What?"

"It was a fire. One of the contestants had a fire. Of course the Board said they could still participate, but the people didn't want to. Guess they figured they had enough stress in their life right now so they backed out. But I was the top alternate and the Board called me to take their place!"

Marti didn't look near as happy as she had a second ago. "Oh no," she said and plunked into one of the high backed chairs at the kitchen table.

"What's so 'oh no'? This is good news for us!"

"Did they tell you who that contestant was?"

"No, I don't think so."

"Well, it must have been Arv," Marti said and she sounded just miserable. "That's why I was home so early last night. When we got over to Finster we found the restaurant smoldering. Burned to the ground, Granny. It was just awful."

"What? You mean that nice little place Arv and Charleen had there is gone?" Her good news was starting not to feel so good anymore. "That's terrible! Those poor kids,"

"Yeah. It looked bad."

Milly sighed. "But was everyone all right?"

"Yeah, I think so. We drove by their house and they had a bunch of friends hanging out. But the restaurant looks like a total loss."

"Lordy lordy." Milly slid into the chair next to her granddaughter. She didn't know what to feel right now. " So, what should I do? Seems kind of cruel to take their spot on that cook-off."

"I know. But, then again, if there's anyone Arv wouldn't mind giving his spot up for it's you. He'd probably be happy to think this was giving you a chance."

"I don't know if 'happy' would be the right word for it. Can I live with myself knowing my gain is at their expense?"

"Well, if you don't do it someone else will," Marti said. "They'll just call the second alternate, or the third. Someone's bound to jump at this chance."

"But still…"

"You didn't have anything to do with what happened to Arv's place," Marti said. "And from what I know about Charleen, she's super organized and prepared for everything. I'm sure they've got all sorts of insurance. They'll be just fine. Arv would want you to take that spot."

"You really think so?"

"Yeah. Go to the contest, Granny. You've been aiming at this for years."

"I have, but…"

"Nobody in the world will think badly of you for finally getting your turn. Arv especially."

The girl seemed so certain. And Milly really, really wanted this. Too much to pass it up just for feeling a little bit guilty.

"All right. I'll do it. And I'll win it, too!"

"That's the spirit!" Marti jumped off her seat and gave an enthusiastic hug. Ooo, it twisted her hip a bit, but Milly didn't mind. Hugs from Marti had been kind of sparse these last few years.

"I'm going to need your help, you know. I've only got a month to get ready!"

Marti let her go and ran to grab a notebook off the telephone desk. "You're right. We'd better make some plans here."

"Well, it's not like I haven't had years to think about this," Milly laughed. "I've planned the perfect menu dozens of times."

"Well, this time it counts. So, what are we going to need?"

Marti scratched at the notebook. She rattled on about supplies they'd need and other people they could get to help out, but Milly quit listening. This was too good to be true. At last she'd get her chance to go to the cook-off, but even better Marti and Johnny would end up having to work together to help her out on this. That's why she'd let Johnny buy into the restaurant in the first place, so he and Marti would be more or less stuck with each other.

Yep, letting Johnny buy into their diner was the best idea she'd ever had. Now he owned it with them and Milly was going to make sure he was an active participant in this cook-off. And that would be a whole month away! Well, that should be enough time to…

And then reality struck. Oh no! She'd just assured the lady on the phone that Granny's Kitchen was still a family owned and operated business! They were sending a representative over this afternoon to verify all her information! Holy cow, she'd made a muddle of this for sure. Oh, this was terrible!

It must have shown on her face. Marti stopped making lists and was looking at her curiously.

"What's the matter?" she asked. "You don't think we'll need to rent a trailer to haul all your cooking stuff up to the contest?"

"No, no… that's not it." Milly sighed. It was obvious East hadn't gotten around to telling Marti. She was just going to have to do it herself and take the consequences.

"Then what's the matter? Are you sick? You don't look so good."

"It's just that I suddenly realized I might have been a little impulsive."

"Impulsive? What, you've been trying to get into this cook-off for twenty years and suddenly you think you've been impulsive?"

"No, it's not that. There's something else, and probably I should have told you about it right away. But they'd already told me I hadn't made it into the contest, and it just seemed like finances were so tight for us, and I really hated to be a burden on you…"

"Granny, what did you do?"

So she told her what she'd done. Marti took it pretty well. Sure, she yelled a bit, but Marti always was prone to drama. At least she didn't break anything.

Milly thought they'd gotten through the initial shock of her revelation pretty well and was about to pat herself on the back for raising such an understanding, even tempered granddaughter, when Marti stormed back to her room and slammed the door. Well, it would take her a little while to get used to the idea of their diner belonging to someone who wasn't family. And since this pretty well ruined their hopes of being in the cook-off, she figured she'd let the girl have some time to herself.

But then Marti came marching out and announced she was going to talk to Johnny—East, she called him. She'd thrown clothes on and was gone before Milly could talk her out of it. Uh oh. She'd wanted to get these kids to spend some time together, but that glint of murder in Marti's eye didn't bode well for the hearts-and-flowers ending Milly had in mind.

She didn't have Johnny's phone number at his new apartment, so she did the next best thing. She called his mother next door. She figured it was only fair someone should warn him to put the knives and lead pipes up somewhere before Marti got there.

——

East managed to get his mother off the phone about ten seconds before Marti started pounding on his door. Well, so much for their budding re-friendship. And things had been going so well when he dropped her off last night. Oh, well. If he didn't want his door broken off the hinges and every neighbor in the complex listening in on what was bound to be a very animated conversation, he'd better let the rabid woman in.

She was fuming.

"Hey, Marti," he said, trying to pretend he had no idea what she was doing here.

"You weasel! Do you have any idea what you've done to my grandmother?"

Last he knew, Marti kind of liked weasels, so maybe she wasn't as ticked off as she looked.

When he took half a nano-second too long answering she pushed past him and marched right into his apartment. Okay, apparently weasels had lost favor. And so had he.

"All right, you've got every reason to be upset. We should have told you what we were doing. It was my job and I meant to tell you last night."

Marti rolled her eyes. "So, I take it she called to warn you I was coming?"

"She called my mom and Mom called me."

"Great, now the whole town knows what's going on."

"Is that a slam against my mother?"

"What? Like this is all about *you*?"

"No, I thought it was about Granny, but you're acting like it's about *you*."

"I'm acting like someone who cares about Granny."

She'd been ranting and advancing on him 'til he was practically in the kitchen. If Marti had been taller, the way she was glaring at him and invading his personal space might have been kind of intimidating. As it was, her attack was backfiring on her. He found he kind of liked getting this much attention from her.

"Look, Marti," he said. "Why don't I get you a cup of coffee—decaf—and we can sit down and talk about this like rational adults."

"Decaf, huh?" she said and frowned.

"Yeah, sorry," he said, and wasn't. The last thing Marti needed right now was any additional stimulant. Him too, but that was a little bit different.

"Well, I'm not planning on staying. I just wanted you to know how your butting-in cost Granny her spot in this cook-off she's been dreaming about for years."

He'd already poured a steaming cup, added the requisite sugar, and handed it to her. She took a tentative sip.

"Now sit," he said and pointed to the little dinette table he'd set for two. "Your waffle's ready."

For the first time she glanced around the kitchen and her eyes got kind of big as she noticed the mountain of food he'd been preparing. "What's all this?"

"It's breakfast. I figured you came barreling over here without eating anything."

"So you just whipped all this up in the ten minutes it took me to drive here?"

The fluffy omelet was still oozing cheese, the sausages sizzled in a pan next to them, and the light on the waffle iron blinked. Yeah, he'd done all right in such a short amount of time. Plus, he'd had to make small talk with Mom on the phone so he'd pretty much done it all one-handed. Not bad, he had to admit.

"Well, I'm hungry," he said. "And I hate eating alone. If you're going to stay long enough to tell me what a bad person I am for ruining an old lady's life you're going to have to do it with food in your mouth."

He flipped her waffle out onto a plate and poured the last of the batter in to make his. He rolled the organic turkey sausages in their pan to get them finished up and halved the sour cream and cilantro omelet. Two glasses of orange juice were already waiting on the counter.

Marti was still standing there silently and he wasn't quite sure if she was planning her exit or just being difficult. If she took off he sure was going to have lots of leftovers. Well, he'd just have to hope she didn't.

He put half the omelet, two sausage links and a couple sliced strawberries on the plate with the waffle.

"Here you go," he said, setting the plate on the table. "Do you like syrup or whipped cream for the waffle?"

She resisted for a moment, then gave in. He hoped his sigh of relief wasn't loud enough for her to notice.

"Can I have both?" she asked, putting her coffee down beside the plate and sitting.

He laughed. Yep, this was Marti, all right.

"Always got to have a third option, don't you?"

"I just know what I like, that's all," she shrugged.

"No kidding."

She scowled at him.

"But, yes, you may have both," he assured her and brought the syrup *and* the whipped cream to the table.

Their glasses of OJ came next, and by the time he'd put sausages, strawberries and omelet on his plate, his own waffle was done. His plate full, he joined her at the table.

"It looks good," she said. There was a distinctly grudging tone to her voice. He grinned.

"You ought to see what I can do with more than ten minutes warning."

"I don't know why Granny thought she needed to 'warn' anybody, anyway. It's not like I was coming over here to do bodily harm to you."

She sure was laying into that sausage, though. Not that he was being Freudian, or anything.

"Oh, she was just worrying for you, as usual. You do have a bit of a temper, you know."

"What? I most certainly do not have…" She stopped as her voice began to rise and she was making a fist around her fork. "Well, yes, I guess I was a little upset when she told me what you'd done."

"I didn't do it on my own, you know. She was in on it, too. You didn't get all bent out of shape at her, did you?"

"Of course not! I'm sure she had no idea what she was doing when you talked her into this."

"Hey, she's not some helpless invalid. She's been managing her own affairs a lot of years all by herself."

"Oh, and is that supposed to make me feel guilty about not coming back home enough?"

"I hadn't meant it to," he said. "But does it?"

"No, not in the least," she replied. He knew a lie when he heard one.

"Good. How are the eggs?"

"Wonderful," she said, grudgingly. "But I'm not letting you off the hook just because you fed me. You had no right to get involved in our business. Granny was doing just fine without you."

"Oh yeah? Is that what you think?"

"So we're not millionaires like you are. We were getting by."

He had to laugh at that one. "Well, I hate to break it to you, but I'm afraid you have some serious misconceptions about finances. I'm about a hundred miles from being a millionaire, and Granny didn't seem to think you two were getting by all that well. Unless you have some resources she doesn't know about."

"I'm not completely broke," she said proudly. "I tucked some away here and there. Granny just never told me she needed anything."

"Don't tell me you didn't know about the refrigerator you burned up." That was a low blow and he regretted it, but too late now.

"I didn't know we were desperate enough to have to take

charity from you!"

"If it was charity you wouldn't be in this predicament, would you?" he reminded her. "I'd have just given the money and you and Granny would still be sole owners."

"Why didn't you do that then?"

"Come on, you think Granny would have stood for it? Hell no, a gift was out of the question."

But Marti wasn't convinced. "You've had her eating out of your hand since kindergarten. If you'd have wanted to help out you'd have found a way."

"I did find a way! I gave her the money in exchange for part ownership."

"That's not giving."

"Oh isn't it? Since you're not exactly a money whiz let me spell it out for you; buying into a homey back-woods diner with faded curtains and two little old ladies in the kitchen isn't exactly a fabulously smart business investment on my part, you know."

"Then why'd you do it?"

"To help her out! I just made sure Granny got to keep a little dignity in the deal. And while we're on the subject, you might want to ask yourself why I was the one who figured out she needed help while *you're* the one who's been living with her for a month."

Marti pushed away from her half eaten breakfast and stood. "I should have known how pointless this would be. You're not the same guy I used to know."

"Well, I'm sure you'll be happy to hear that you are exactly the same self-centered Marti Snowden who used to boss me around and badger me to get her own way."

He stood too, giving him a five or six inch advantage over her.

"I have never badgered anyone in my life," she said, but

he intentionally invaded her personal space and her voice started losing a little bit of its firmness.

"Oh? So why exactly did you come storming over here this morning, anyway? What did you expect me to do for you?"

He was close enough to feel her breath coming out in quick, shallow puffs as she fought to control her anger. She probably wanted to hit him, judging by the golden sparks in her eyes. Her eyes sure hadn't changed over the years.

He wondered if he stood here, looming over her, for another thirty seconds, would she do it? It was a surprisingly interesting thought; Marti hitting him. Would she raise up that right hand and give a good old-fashioned slap, or would she keep it all balled up and pop him in the nose? Either way, he couldn't imagine it hurting very much.

Not that he doubted her strength or determination, but for the life of him he couldn't picture Marti touching him in any way that wasn't, well, pleasant. He tried to focus more on his looming, but the more he loomed the more he wondered if her hair was still as soft as he recalled. Even softer than it looked; that was one thing he distinctly remembered.

And her skin. She'd always had good skin. It didn't look any worse for the wear now, either. Would touching her now send those same thrills of electricity that he'd been so amazed by ten years ago? He kind of thought it might.

But, jeez, this was stupid. Marti was *not* interested in rekindling the old flame that had never really been there for her. If he wanted to see how hard the woman would hit him, putting the moves on her right now would certainly provide the education. Whatever she *was* interested in, it wasn't *that*.

"I came because I thought you might be able to fix it," she said in a much quieter voice than he expected.

He stepped back. The additional air between them helped

clear his mind. But not enough. He couldn't quite remember where the conversation had been.

"Fix what?"

"You know, the contest. We've got to figure out a way to get Granny in that cook-off."

Oh, yeah. "That's easy," he said and was inordinately happy when she almost smiled.

"What? It is?"

"Sure. I'll just sell my part of the diner back to Granny."

Marti frowned. "There isn't time for that. The contest board is sending someone over this afternoon to get Granny to sign some papers—at least one of those papers is an affidavit that the diner is still family owned."

"What?"

"That's the rules," Marti sighed. "You totally ruined this for her!"

"No. We'll just get her lawyer and have him draw up the papers today. I don't want my money back, so we can make it legal for just a dollar or two."

She just shook her head. "Real estate transfers don't go through over the weekend. Besides, that lawyer is out of town. Granny says he's getting his grandkid baptized in Toledo, or something."

"Okay, so we'll have to wait until Monday. But if we're going to do it anyway, how about if we just don't mention it this afternoon and try to sneak on by?"

"Granny won't consider that. She doesn't even lie about her weight on her driver's license."

"Yeah, that's not exactly her style, is it?" he said and sighed. "Okay. This is a problem. Why don't we bury the hatchet, sit back down to our food, and see what we can come up with."

Marti eyed him doubtfully, but finally she slid back into

her chair. He wasn't sure if it was his wonderful powers of persuasion or the spiced currant sauce he drizzled over the waffles, but either way it worked and he was glad for it.

They managed to discuss the issues at hand without coming to blows. They even spent a little time speculating on how Arv was taking it all, but by the time the food was gone and East got up to run another pot of decaf they weren't any closer to a solution.

"So it looks like we're down to two options," he said, handing Marti a fresh cup. "One: we ask the contest people for an extension on that proof of eligibility stuff without telling them why, or Two: we ask them to make an exception on the rule of ownership since it *was* a family-owned business when she was selected as first alternate even though it isn't now."

"Not very strong options," Marti sighed.

"No, but that second one might have a leg to stand on. She can easily show proof the diner was eligible when they selected her; even when she got word she didn't make the cut."

"But I bet the other contestants wouldn't be too happy if they found out Granny got the contest people to bend the rules for her. Someone's bound to make a big deal out of it. That's all we need, poor Granny to be at the heart of some cook-off conspiracy."

They sat in silence, drinking the coffee and wishing a solution would just drop down from the sky. It didn't, and East realized his mind was wandering, again. Marti was chewing her lip as she stared at a waffle crumb on the table. East was wondering how hard she'd hit him if he tried to chew her lip for her.

He figured he'd better not chance it so he cleared his throat and got up to clear the table. He needed something to take his mind off Marti's lips.

Unfortunately, this broke the spell. She put her cup down and helped him carry dishes to the counter. She checked the clock on the wall and exclaimed about the time.

"It's almost ten o'clock," she said. "Granny's probably wondering what's keeping me. I'd better get home and assure her I didn't commit murder, or anything."

"Yeah, and thank you for that."

She laughed. "Right. And thanks for breakfast. I'm a sucker for waffles."

"I know," he said. It sounded way more intimate than he'd meant it to, and Marti's back went kind of rigid again. She edged toward the front door. Yeah, it was a good thing he hadn't offered to help on that lip chewing.

"So give Granny those two options we came up with and see what she thinks," he said casually.

"Yeah, I will," she responded. "I just wish there was a third option."

"Yeah, me too."

Marti was at the front door now and he'd followed her. It was dumb, but he was really trying to come up with an excuse to get her to stay a while longer. She'd already drunk her coffee and eaten his food, and once again he didn't have a third option. Nothing to keep her around.

That's how things always seemed to be for them, one wrong option or another wrong option, never a nice, comfy middle one. That's why he'd left in the first place. It was either follow the course his parents set out for him and end up selling insurance for the rest of his life—without Marti, or set his own course and run away to California—with no Marti. Pretty extreme options, and neither of them really what he wanted to do. What he'd wanted was that third option, the one where Marti wanted him and was willing to work with him to figure out a way for them to live their lives, but live them together.

But that wasn't an option, that was a freaking fantasy. Is that what he wanted? A white-picket-fence fantasy? Hmm. Maybe. Heck, in that fantasy they'd be married by now and talking about what color to paint the nursery. This whole contest thing wouldn't be a problem because he'd already be in the family and…

Holy shit! There it was, that third option. It might not have worked out for them back then, but it sure would help out now!

Okay, maybe it was a little farfetched. All right, it was a lot farfetched. Marti would never agree to it. Then again, she seemed pretty committed to getting Granny into that contest. And that's what they needed: commitment. A legal and binding commitment.

.

Chapter 9

Marti hated herself for wishing she had some reason to stick around at East's place a little while longer. What an idiot—she shouldn't have even come here in the first place. She stood in the doorway of his cute little apartment, the smell of breakfast still lingering in the air.

Granny was right; this mess was no one's fault. Of course Marti knew that. Had she really been so very angry at East, or did she just come running over here because it was an excuse to be with him again? No, she wasn't about to admit to that. She came because she was mad and, for some reason, she thought he'd be able to fix things.

He couldn't. No one could. That's why she was so mad. It was totally, undeniably, out of their hands and those two lame options they'd come up with wouldn't hold water with the contest people. She knew it. They didn't care about a little old lady's dream; they had a contest to run and they had to run it by the rules. The rules said all contestants had to be family-owned and operated businesses. Period. Granny's Kitchen wasn't. Not anymore.

That contest official would be here in a matter of hours and unless Granny was suddenly going to develop a taste for lying or unless East was going to miraculously become part of the family, they were out of luck.

Oh no. A sudden horrifying, mortifying thought streaked through her head. *A third option.*

Well, it couldn't really be called an option because it was completely insane. Totally insane. Absolutely insane. But it would solve the problem. Not that East would think of it as a solution. Hell no.

And she wasn't going to think about it anymore, either. She had to be brain damaged to even think it up in the first place. As if marrying John Easton Smith would fix anything. What a stupid notion. Time to get the hell out of here.

"Bye, East," she said, turning away. "Thanks for the breakfast."

"Marti?" he called her back.

"Yeah?" *Don't look at him, don't look at him...*

"I just… well, I think, uh…" he said and sounded kind of strange.

Marti refused to say anything. She didn't trust herself not to blurt out something stupid right now, something about how she had a really great third option.

"I'm really sorry about all this," he said. "I should have told you what we were going to do. Finding out like this, it's got to be hard. I didn't mean to catch you off-balance."

"Yeah," she agreed.

He had no idea just how off-balance she was. She tried to walk away, but his voice held her in place.

"Marti, wait. I think I've got that third option you wanted," he said quickly.

Just ignore him. There was no third option. They'd already gone over everything possible—everything realistically possible. If she had any brain she'd let him off the hook and just keep walking.

She didn't. She turned and looked at him.

"Now, hear me out," he went on. "At least give it a little thought. I mean, I know it's not everyone's first choice, but it'll solve the problem. It'll get Granny into that contest fair and square, then once that's over we can decide for sure what to do."

"Oh?"

He checked his watch. "It's Saturday. The courthouse is open until noon."

"But we don't have an attorney and it'll take hours to get the papers drawn up for a new business agreement…"

"I'm talking about a different kind of business agreement."

He was silent for a second. Then two seconds. She felt the blood rushing to her face. Oh, God, don't let him say it! He had to be talking about something else.

"No, I…"

"We can fix things in half an hour, Marti."

"No, we can't!"

"Mom works in the probate court. The judge is a friend."

"No, really, you can't be serious!"

Finally he cleared his throat. "I am. Marry me, Marti."

Oh no. He'd said it. He'd honestly gone and said it. At least, she thought he said it. Maybe he didn't say it. Maybe she imagined it. Maybe he said something else and she just heard this because on some awful subconscious level that's what she wanted to hear. Hell, that was even worse! Oh, she was losing it big time.

"I'm sorry. What did you say?"

"I said marry me, Marti," he repeated. She watched his lips carefully so there could be no confusion. Yep, that's what he said.

"I know it's insane," he went on. "And you'd probably rather just kill me, but it's the only way. If you really want to get Granny into that cook-off, you have to marry me."

He *did* say it. Again. Oh crap. Now what? Well, she'd turn him down, of course. No way could she ever marry East, even if it was just a matter of convenience. Or even necessity. It was too ridiculous.

So why wasn't she screaming "No freaking way!" at the top of her lungs?

Probably because he looked so damn wonderful, staring down at her like he was terrified of whatever she might say. And because he was right: this was the perfect solution. They could get a license and a judge to marry them today; right now. They'd be perfectly legal to get that affidavit notarized by lunchtime.

Holy shit. Was she even contemplating this? She wanted to get rid of her pesky Easton Smith hang-up, not end up married to it!

Then again, she knew lots of people who'd been really hung up on each other until they got married. Hell, maybe in some twisted way, agreeing to this wild scheme wouldn't be such a bad idea. Maybe it's just what they needed to fix Granny's problem *and* Marti's, too. And she really did want to help Granny, right?

"Okay," she said finally.

There was dead silence. East blinked at her, his face absolutely blank. Maybe he hadn't expected her to agree. He really didn't want to do this, even for Granny's sake, and he'd been counting on her to refuse. Oops. Well, this was more than a little awkward.

"Okay?" he questioned, his eyes searching hers.

"Well, that's what I said, but if you don't… you know…" She ran out of anything else to say.

More silence.

"All right then," he said at last. "I'll meet you in the car."

"What? No, East, we can't just go out and… East?"

He stalked back into his apartment. What was up with that? Marti leaned in, but he disappeared up the hallway. Was she supposed to follow? Or maybe he'd changed his mind and realized how idiotic his suggestion was. Maybe she should just leave.

But then he came back, carrying a brown envelope.

"Divorce decree," he announced. "I'm pretty sure we'll need this. You haven't been married before have you?"

"Uh, no."

"Good. Come on. I'll drive."

Yeah, he was going to have to. Marti wasn't one hundred percent sure she could remain standing upright much longer. Good God, what had she just agreed to?

Chapter 10

Charleen smiled mechanically as she invited C.J. Smith into her home. Funny, she'd had nearly 24 hours to get used to the idea of the restaurant being gone, but here it was Saturday afternoon and just the sight of their cheerful insurance guy was enough to bring on more tears.

"Hello, Charleen," he said with exactly the right amount of concern to let her know he understood and cared about what they were going through.

Not that he'd ever been through this, of course. Nope, Smith Insurance still stood proudly in the old Henderson Building on Main Street back in good old Garden Falls. But C.J.'s smile was warm and concerned and his handshake felt like he was actually glad to be here to help some old friends. Guess East wasn't the only actor in the family.

"Sure wish we were getting together under better circumstances, though," he went on as Arv ushered them all into the living room.

"Yeah, me too," Arv agreed.

C.J. sank into the couch and Charleen watched nervously. The ugly slipcover bunched up behind him, but he at least pretended not to notice. She cringed.

She'd been to the Smith's home once a couple years ago when they'd been on the same church committee. The Smith's had nice furniture; expensive, and not stained and caked with the kids' Saturday morning grazing. She hoped C.J. couldn't feel under the slipcover where Josh had gotten bored one day and used a hair dryer to melt through the couch fabric and into the foam cushion. God, they'd never find anyone to sell them insurance again.

"I was almost afraid you'd call and say you weren't coming over here at all," Charleen said and added a nervous laugh to make it sound less like an accusation.

On Friday C.J. had said he'd be here first thing in the morning, but now it was well after lunch time. Charleen just knew he'd been going over their paperwork and found things not in order. Like that time a couple months ago when she'd been late on their payment. Things were tight and she'd had to hold off on cutting his check a couple extra days until they could get some funds transferred. Arv hadn't known anything about it—she hated to give him extra stuff to worry about—but now she just knew it was coming back to haunt her.

So probably C.J. was figuring out how to explain that slip-up had somehow gotten their coverage discontinued. He looked remarkably happy about it, too. Well, he ought to. The restaurant was a total loss and what insurance man wouldn't be thrilled to have that disaster off his plate?

"Yeah, sorry about that," he was saying. "I know I told you I'd be here first thing today, but something came up kind of unexpectedly."

Yeah, he checked them over with a fine tooth comb, no doubt.

"Look, about that late payment a while back," Charleen began, not quite sure what to say next.

"What late payment?" Arv said. She could feel the air around him get all prickly with tension.

C.J. looked confused. "What? Oh, yeah, I remember. You called for an extension, right? But you made that payment just a couple days later, didn't you? I don't remember it being late. Jeez, some of my clients leave me hanging on, covering their backsides for weeks."

"We had a late payment? I didn't know about that," Arv said and his eyes burned right into Charleen's. Great, the insurance guy didn't have a problem with it but now Arv did.

"It wasn't late. It just wasn't two weeks early like usual," C.J. laughed. "No, there's no trouble with our covering you guys on this. You're fine. What I meant was something else came up this weekend. Something in my family."

Obviously he was just waiting for them to ask about it. Well, that sure would get the topic of discussion off her failure to mention that late payment to Arv.

"I hope it's nothing bad," she said, giving him the opening he clearly wanted.

Sure enough, C.J. took it and dove in with gusto. "No, nothing bad. But let me tell you, it sure took me by surprise! Could have knocked me over with a feather when Johnny told us about it."

"Oh? Has he got some new show in the works?" Arv asked. Good. The mention of his old friend distracted his attention right away.

"Ha! That'd be nice, but no cigar. Nope, my boy has gone and gotten himself married again."

Now nobody spoke.

"Congratulations," Charleen finally said.

"Yep, they went down to the courthouse just this morning to make it legal. Came and told us after the fact, if you can believe that. Now go ahead, guess who the lucky young lady is."

Charleen slid a quick glance over to Arv. He was staring at C.J. with amazement all over his face. It only took her about a minute to figure out what he was thinking. *Who* he was thinking about.

"Marti Snowden," she said softly.

"You got it!" C.J. said. "So how come I'm the only one surprised by this? Even the missus said she knew all along those two were meant for each other." C.J. shook his head and chuckled. "I didn't even think they'd so much as exchanged postcards over the last ten years."

"Neither did I," Arv said. He looked puzzled.

"Well, he's the famous J. Easton Smith now," Charleen said. "And recently single. Marti's pretty lucky to have been in the right place at the right time."

It didn't sound like a very nice thing to say. Charleen wished she could tell herself she hadn't meant it to sound like it did, but that would have been lying. She'd only ever been marginally successful at pretending she didn't hate Marti Snowden.

Okay, hate was a very strong word. How about "earnestly dislike"? That made her a better person than "hate". Or maybe simple "resent" was more appropriate. Whatever the word, it was all very juvenile and she ought to be over it by now. Or nearly over it. Or at least a little bit over it.

But she wasn't. Arv was frowning at her so she wouldn't look at him. He, of course, still thought the world of Dr. Marti.

The way C.J. was grinning it looked like he did, too. Sure, why not? Everyone loved Marti and her breezy, She's-Like-The-Wind ways.

If C.J. recognized any ill will behind Charleen's words he didn't show it. "Oh, I'm sure there was more to it than that," he said. "I will say, both kids looked a little shell-shocked over brunch today."

"Yeah, marriage is a big step for most people," Charleen said.

"Well, I for one am thrilled for them," Arv said. His faux

cheerfulness was commendable, despite the fact Charleen knew what he must really be feeling about it. "John's had a thing for Marti since junior high, I think."

She rolled her eyes. Everybody had a thing for Marti since junior high, apparently. Well, good for John Easton Smith. He finally got the big Garden Falls prize. Maybe they'd all live happily ever after now.

Or maybe not.

Arv had a brilliant idea. "Hey, Char, we've got to do something nice for them. Why don't you invite them over for a big home-cooked meal to help them celebrate?"

Oh God, doing a couples thing with East and Marti. That sounded pretty much like her worst nightmare. "Sure, Arv," she said. "But maybe we ought to spend a little time with Mr. Smith talking about what's going to happen now that our restaurant burned down?"

"Oh, there's plenty of time for that," C.J. said with his usual flair. "Right now I wouldn't mind hearing a bit more about how my son had a 'thing' for Marti all along and I never knew about it."

"Well," Arv laughed. "It's not like he really wanted it to be common knowledge. But now that they've gone and gotten married, I guess it's fair to say he had it pretty bad way back then. He denied it, of course. Don't know why."

Because Arv was doing enough pining after her like a lost puppy for both of them, that was why. Charleen had heard the stories; been constantly reminded how she'd been Arv's second choice. At first it hadn't bothered her so much, when they were off at college and Marti was way the hell across the globe. No, then Charleen had felt pretty good about being the one to put Arv's pieces back together for him.

Then they'd married and moved to Garden Falls and it seemed like everyone wanted to talk about the "good ol' days". Yeah, those good ol' days for Arv and Marti and John and everyone else but her. None of it had anything to do with Charleen and if it hadn't been for having babies to give them all something new to talk about she would have gone crazy.

Well, here they were back on the Marti kick. Arv was pretending to be happy for his friends and Charleen was going to have to cook them dinner. Well, at least she liked cooking. Or was that something she just picked up because it was important to Arv? She honestly couldn't remember.

"You guys talk. I'll go put some fresh coffee on."

Charleen headed to the kitchen and could tell nobody missed her.

———

Milly opened their unlocked door and waited for Marti and Johnny to follow her inside. They'd been amazingly silent in the car on the way back from lunch, and now she had the distinct feeling Johnny was ready to bolt. What on earth kind of marriage was this?

"You kids want some coffee?" she offered.

"No, thanks, but I need to, uh…" Johnny said uncomfortably.

"Yeah, it's been a pretty hectic morning," Marti said, jumping in with a purely manufactured yawn. "I think I need some down time."

Milly couldn't help but laugh. "Down time? Is that what you kids are calling it these days? Marti, if you two want to get rid of the old lady and spend some time alone doing whatever it is newlyweds are prone to do, that's fine. You don't need to hang around here and entertain me. Go on, get your things and head over to Johnny's place."

Well, now Marti just looked terrified. Johnny looked a

little green around the gills, too. Okay, what the dickens was going on here? Sure, they were going into this rather suddenly, but both of them were way too old to get that nervous about a little hanky-panky that usually went along with getting hitched.

Maybe they hadn't seen each other in a while, but if they were ready to stand in front of a judge and sign the papers, why in heavens wouldn't they be eager to get on with the rest of it? She never had thought of Marti as the shy type, and nobody on the planet would suspect Johnny of being backward in *that* area. So what was going on here?

Well, there was always one sure-fire way of finding something out. Ask a stupid question.

"You two do know what married folks are supposed to do with each other, don't you?"

Marti turned red and Johnny coughed. Lord, the two of them were acting like a couple uninitiated Victorians. Well, will wonders never cease? Maybe Marti *did* pay attention all those years in Sunday School. But still, what was Johnny's excuse? He'd been married for a couple years. That ought to have taught him a thing or two. No, they were up to something, and it wasn't what it should be.

"Jeez, Granny," Marti began with a sheepish grin. "Are you that eager to get me out of your house?"

"Yeah, I figured… I mean, we thought maybe Marti should stay here with you for a while, until you're healed up a little more," Johnny said.

Milly wasn't buying it. "Oh? You got married, but Marti's going to stay living with me?"

"Of course!" Marti smiled, looking awfully relieved. "I came back to Garden Falls to help you. I can't just bail out now."

"So why the big rush to the courthouse, then? Heck,

Johnny, you haven't been in town long enough to have done any *real* damage yet, at least not so anyone would know about it. If Marti does have a little bun in the oven at this point, a smart man wouldn't take it for granted it's his after only a week!"

"Granny!" Marti squeaked.

"Well, I'm bound to think up all sorts of possibilities so you might as well just tell me," Milly said. "Why did you two suddenly have to get married?"

"Because we wanted to," Marti said firmly.

"Why?" Milly persisted.

Marti started to respond, but Johnny interrupted. "Look, maybe you ought to sit down if we're going to have this discussion." he suggested.

Marti glared at him and Milly couldn't help but note East wasn't exactly beaming with husbandly affection. He still looked a little peaked.

"You are not honestly going to tell her, are you?" Marti asked him.

"If he knows what's good for him he will!" Milly said.

"Granny, this is none of your business," Marti shot back.

"Look," Johnny said and his eyes warned Marti. "You might not care what she goes around telling people about us, but I do. And I think she has a right to know."

"You're darn tootin' I do!"

"But she'll get all crazy about it," Marti said.

Johnny just shrugged. "Hell, she's already got you pregnant with some other guy's kid and me not knowing how to, uh, perform. Can't get much crazier than that."

"I don't know," Marti sighed. "That last part sounds believable enough."

"Ha ha," Johnny said dryly. He checked his watch. "We've got go meet that contest person in an hour. So, you going to tell her, or am I?"

"Contest person?" Milly asked.

"For the cook-off, Granny," Marti said. "I, uh, didn't exactly call them and cancel like you asked me."

Now Milly was confused. "But I thought that was already settled. I sold off part of the diner, so we're not eligible anymore. And I'm not going to lie!"

"Of course not," Johnny smiled. "There's no lying about it. Granny's Kitchen is perfectly eligible since it's one hundred percent family-owned and operated."

"But we…" And then Milly figured it out. Good Lord, these kids had gone and gotten married to keep her in the blooming cook-off!

"Oh no," she said. "You did not get married just to keep me legal for a damn cooking contest!"

"Now don't get all upset," Marti said. "It was the only way, and we know how important this is for you."

"There's nothing *that* important, Martha Kay!" Milly said getting downright furious the more she thought about this. "You cannot just go out and get married for a piss poor reason like that! It's… it's sacrilegious, that's what it is. It's wrong, Marti; very, very wrong."

"It's not wrong," Marti said. "What better reason could we have? It helps you out and…"

"And you can't say we don't know what we're getting into," Johnny added. "We grew up together; we're practically like family anyway. What's wrong with just making it legal?"

"Because a marriage is something special, that's what's wrong," Milly sank into the couch and just shook her head. "It's not something a couple young idiots like you two can just jump into and out of. Didn't you learn anything from what happened to your mama?"

"This isn't anything like what happened to Mom," Marti

said.

"No, I don't suppose it is. Johnny would never do you like your daddy did her," Milly had to agree. She shouldn't have compared the two. "Still, this is wrong, Marti. Getting married is supposed to be about love, and commitment, and kids, and taking care of each other for the rest of your lives! It's *not* about helping some old crippled lady get to a cooking contest."

"You're not crippled, Granny," Marti said softly and came to sit beside her.

Johnny followed and sat, too. They were both looking at her with big, concerned eyes. Johnny put his hand against the back of the couch and leaned forward, putting his face near Marti's as he pleaded for Milly to accept what they'd done.

"It's important to us that you do this, Granny," he was saying. "That's why we did it. It *is* about love and commitment and taking care of each other. It's about being a family, and that can't be a bad thing, right?"

Lordy, he was good. No wonder he made such a big name for himself on TV. Damn shame this whole marriage was for all the wrong reasons.

"Come on, Granny," Marti said, leaning back just enough to let her shoulder touch Johnny. "We knew what we were doing when we did this. Let us help you out here."

Yes, it was a damn shame. They looked so good together there, next to each other on the old green couch. Sure, Johnny had sat there watching movies with Marti a hundred times when they were kids, but now things were different. They were grown-up, and just now they were acting like a team.

That was nice, even if she hated what they were doing. Who could deny it felt good to have these two wonderful young people so worried about her that they'd go to these extremes? If she wasn't so darn mad at them she'd probably think it was the sweetest thing anybody'd ever done for her.

Then again, they were sitting awfully close together, weren't they? She knew her granddaughter was as bull-headed as all get out. If she'd gone and gotten herself married to Johnny Smith, it could only be because she wanted to. Johnny couldn't have talked her into it, that was for sure. Heck, Milly had taken longer than a weekend to talk the girl into taking out the trash on more than one occasion.

No, Marti more than anyone had seen Milly recover from the disappointment of missing out on the cook-off year after year. She couldn't really believe it was this important to her, could she? And Johnny just got out of a bad marriage; it didn't seem likely he'd be quick to dive into something he knew was doomed from the start. So maybe down deep he really didn't think it was doomed, after all.

She chewed her bottom lip and watched them watching her. They did seem pretty determined to do this. Well, they'd already done it as far as the law was concerned. And Johnny was right; they knew each other well enough. Hadn't it always been a secret dream to see these two get together? So what if they were doing things a little bit out of order? Heck, if Marti's mother—God rest her soul—had done things exactly in order there would be no Marti.

So maybe this was not such a bad thing. They were at least friendly again, and now they were married. All that was missing was the good stuff; they just hadn't figured it out yet. Surely a little time spent with each other would bring that along, right?

And now it was Milly's turn to help them. They'd done this for her, so she'd just return the favor.

"Well, I think you're both nuts," she said. "But I guess I ought to say 'thank you', at least."

Johnny smiled. "There's no need for that."

"So you're going to go along with it?" Marti said.

"Well, since the state of Ohio already sees fit to call you two married, who am I to argue? I guess we're a family now."

Marti hugged her. "Oh, Granny, I'm so happy for you!"

Well, this was a little backward, but all things come to those who wait. Milly just patted her granddaughter and smiled at Johnny.

"I'm sure we'll do just fine at that cook-off," she said. "You two will be going up to help me, won't you?"

Now Marti pulled away and glanced over at Johnny. He ran his hand through his thick hair and tried to avoid the question. Poor guy, he sure had no idea what he was in for. Well, time to get things rolling for them.

"They're going to expect us all up there if we all own the place, you understand," she said. She had no idea if this was true, but it sounded good. "And they're going to have to believe you two really are married. Can you pull it off, do you think?"

"Hey," Johnny laughed nervously. "How hard can it be?"

"Treeva Kincaid didn't seem to find you all that convincing," Marti noted.

Johnny frowned at her.

Well, this was an unimpressive start. But that was okay. Milly had made a life of turning lemons into lemonade. She'd figure out a way to handle these two misguided young people.

"And by now everyone in town knows what you were doing at the courthouse today," Milly said. "I won't be able to hold my head up if they get wind of what's really going on."

"What do you mean?" Johnny asked innocently.

Marti's eyes narrowed. Yes, she knew her grandmother well enough to begin to suspect. Oh well, so sorry for her. This was her doing so now she'd have to take her lumps.

"I mean if folks know Marti's still living here while you're off in your bachelor pad they're going to talk," Milly explained. "And they won't be saying nice things. At best they'll figure out it's only a ruse to get me into that contest, and at worst there's no telling what they'll be saying. Either way, I'll be a laughingstock. If you kids really want to help me, you'll do what's expected of you."

"Granny, jeez," Marti said. "It's nobody's business what we do… or don't do! We got legally married and that's all they need to know."

"But if you're living in my house they'll need to know a little more, dear," Milly said evenly. "All I'm saying is it would be a lot easier for everyone if you moved out. Into Johnny's place."

"But, you still need me here," Marti whined.

"Not if you're married to him, I don't. Can't you think what a field day that busybody Marge Franklin will have if she finds out about this? Oh, lordy, I don't even want to imagine it."

"But I can't just move in with him," Marti tried again.

"If you can marry him you can live with him, young lady," Milly said. "And as for what you do while you're living with him, that's your business."

Johnny cleared his throat. "Um, well, Granny… we didn't really plan on actually living together."

"Oh?" Milly said. "And your parents are happy about this arrangement?"

"We haven't quite gotten around to explaining it to them yet," Johnny said.

"No, I didn't figure you had. And you're not going to, either."

"Well, they're going to need to know eventually," Marti said.

"No, they don't," Milly announced. "And I'm going to tell you how this will work."

"Uh oh," Johnny sighed.

"Yes, that's right," Milly said. "You two have graciously put us all in a pretty tight spot here. As I see it we can do two things. We can call this off right now and get you an annulment, kiss this contest good-bye and hello to public embarrassment, or Marti can get her things and move in with you, Johnny, and you can pretend to be a happily married couple for the next month."

They were quiet. Marti stared at her knees and Johnny fussed over a loose thread in the back of the couch.

"Damn," Johnny said finally. "No third option."

"This *was* the third option, remember?" Marti sighed.

Milly didn't know exactly what that meant, but she was pleased to see she had them over a barrel. She thought of saying something about making their bed and needing to lie in it, but the analogy seemed a bit strong. She wasn't sure either of these dummies was ready for it yet. *Yet*.

Chapter 11

"That's all of it," Marti said, nudging the door shut with her elbow as she dragged the last bag of stuff into East's apartment. She was painfully aware it was *his* apartment and she hadn't exactly been invited to move in.

He stared at her with a kind of wild-eyed panic. "That's all of it?"

She knew he was desperate for any excuse to head out that door again, but sadly it had only taken two trips each to get all her things out of the car and into his home. Now she—and her things—were here and he was stuck with them.

Really stuck with them. Married kind of stuck.

Married. That was a scary word. Not that she was opposed to the concept of marriage. No, she'd really hoped to end up that way someday, as a matter of fact. There'd even been a time when she'd dreamed of East… but not like this. This felt wrong. Like Granny said, it *was* wrong.

"So, um, you hungry?" he asked. He looked as awkward as she felt.

His parents had insisted on taking them to lunch after that horrible visit to their house to break the good news. She noticed East ate about two bites more of his food than she did of hers. "No, not really."

"Oh."

"But if you are, that's okay," she added quickly. "I mean, go ahead and eat."

"No, I'm not hungry either."

"Oh."

There was a heavy silence while they each tried to look like they weren't as uncomfortable as they really were. She decided he was coming closer to succeeding than she was. It wasn't fair, him being an actor, and all. He ought to seem every bit as jittery and out of place as she did.

"Okay," she said. "I guess I'll just go put this stuff up. Which way to the spare room?"

Now he did look jittery and out of place. "Well, uh, there isn't one," he said.

"What? There's only one bedroom?"

"Hey, it was a hundred and fifty dollars more to rent the two bedroom model. I didn't figure I'd need that much space for the little while I was in town."

"Great," she sighed, dropping her suitcase with a loud thud. "There's no place for me to sleep for the next month!"

"No, I've got a place for you to sleep," he said. "Queen sized, double layer of that high-tech memory foam, and I can personally vouch for the excellent lumbar support."

"Oh, no," she said, hoping she sounded properly indignant. "You are not getting me into your bed, Mr. Easton Smith. I agreed to this for getting Granny into her cook-off, not to provide you with free entertainment!"

He put her stuff down and rolled his eyes at her. "For your information, *Mrs.* Easton Smith, I was referring to my sleeper sofa."

Oh. She hadn't thought about that possibility. "You have a sleeper sofa?"

"Yeah, Mom's idea," he pointed to the large brown suede couch nearby. "She said if Brad Pitt dropped by, I couldn't very well expect him to sack out on the floor. Actually, though, I should probably be a gentleman and let you have the bedroom and I'll camp here on the sofa."

"No, no, you don't have to… You know Brad Pitt?"

"A passing acquaintance, yeah. So, do I carry this stuff back to the bedroom, or leave it out here?"

"Wow. What's he like?"

He shrugged. "He's okay. So, you moving in here, or the bedroom?"

It wasn't easy, but she managed to shove Brad Pitt from her mind. Drat. That left more room for thoughts about East and his bed and their one, solitary bedroom.

"I can't evict you from your own bedroom," she said. "I'll sleep out here."

"Oh?" he said and at last she saw the hint of a smile. "Wouldn't you rather have a little more privacy? I mean, no telling what might happen if I start sleepwalking, or something."

"You'll get a swift kick to the you-know-whats, that's what'll happen," she said and picked up her suitcase again. "But all right then, I'll take the bedroom, since you're being all gentlemanly."

"Fine. I'll sleep out here. That means I get the TV."

"Fine," she said, dragging the heavy case back toward the short hallway. "I prefer reading anyway. Some of us can."

She heard him laughing under his breath as he followed behind her. "This is going to be a very long four weeks."

She ignored him as she pulled the suitcase into the bedroom. Huh. Fluffy pillows on the bed, a floral valance on the windows—not what she expected for East's bedroom. Not that she'd spent any time thinking about East's bedroom. Well, not much, anyway.

With luck these feminine touches would make it easier to forget it was *his* room she'd be staying in.

Then again, one whiff of the air and she knew forgetting

who'd been sleeping here for a week now would be harder to get out of her brain than Brad Pitt. The room smelled like East; probably his deodorant or something. He'd smelled that way in the car Friday night and he'd smelled that way at the courthouse this morning, when she'd signed her name and said "I do". He smelled like that now, standing close enough to touch.

What was she doing, pretending she could go through with this and not end up a hopeless basket case? Was she already nuts, moving in here and planning to live in *his* room where *his* clothes hung in the closet, *his* stuff cluttered the dresser top, and *his* underwear were folded up in the top drawer on the left? (Not that she checked there, or anything.) And now she was planning to start sleeping in his *bed*? Nothing good could come of this.

"Sorry for the mess," he said, dropping his load beside her. "I wasn't exactly expecting company today. At least I made the bed though, huh?"

God, just hearing him say the word "bed" sent shivers down her spine. Not good. How long were they going to have to play house like this? A whole month? She was seriously headed for a major nervous breakdown.

"It's nice," she said and thought she sounded a little bit strangled. Pathetic.

"They put two closets in here. I can cram all my stuff into one so you can have the other."

"Or I can just keep everything in the suitcases over in the corner, maybe."

"What? So my wife'll be going around wearing wrinkled clothes all the time?"

"*Pretend* wife," she corrected.

He proceeded to open one of the closet doors and grab the few items in there to move them to the other closet.

"Well, they wouldn't be pretend wrinkles. You'd better hang your stuff in here, Mrs. Smith."

"*Pretend* Mrs. Smith."

He just laughed at her and shook his head. "Okay, but the state of Ohio thinks otherwise."

"Well I don't. This is just for pretend and only until Granny wins that contest, remember? After that this 'marriage' is history. You've got your life to get back to, and I've got mine."

"Such as it is."

"Whatever. I know you're not planning to stick around here any longer than you have to, so I just think it's really important that we, um, that we don't lose our focus."

"The cook off."

"Right."

"With no distractions, you mean."

"Right."

"Like ten years ago," he added off-handedly. "When we got caught up in having sex all the time. Is that the kind of distraction you mean?"

Well, there it was. He finally said it, didn't he? He brought it up, laid it out on the table and now they couldn't keep on ignoring it. So just how was she supposed to react to this?

Mercifully he didn't wait for her to respond. He just finished moving his clothes and then shrugged his way back toward the hall.

"But *that's* not likely to happen again, is it?" he said with a short laugh.

He was laughing? About what happened between them back then? So that's how he'd felt about it all this time.

"We're both a little older and wiser now," he went on. "We have more important things in our lives. I don't think we're going to be making the same mistakes this time around, do you?"

"No, I don't," she said, glad to hear she agreed with him. She did agree with him, didn't she? "We were ignorant kids then and we just weren't thinking."

"Rampaging hormones and all that."

"Right."

"Too much time on our hands."

"Exactly."

"Nervous about the future."

"Yes."

"Teenage angst."

Was the room getting smaller, or was he moving closer to her?

"Probably," she agreed. It sounded choked. So the room was getting smaller *and* warmer all of a sudden?

"Any warm body would have done."

Yes, he was getting closer.

"It's possible," she mumbled.

"Friendly sheep would have…"

"Okay, already!" She stopped him. Boy, he sure was chipping away at whatever fond memories she'd had of those historic events from her youth.

"All I'm saying is I think it's safe to assume we're beyond that now." He paused. "Aren't we?"

He was next to her and she could hear him breathe. She used to lay there beside him, out under the stars on that old blanket, and just listen to him breathe. He was a really good breather. Oh lord, how on earth was she going to make it through this?

"Yes, we are. Way beyond that," she said, but it didn't come out very loudly.

"Good. Then this arrangement should be no problem."

"None at all."

"We're adults now."

"Yes, that's right."

"We can control ourselves now."

"Of course."

"Something like this doesn't mean anything to us."

"Uh, something like what?"

He moved forward, covering the last few inches that separated them. "Hold still."

She did. There wasn't any way to avoid it. East had one arm wrapped around her and the other was at the back of her neck, subtly angling her head up to face him. She had no clue how it happened.

For one quick moment she got a glimpse into his impossibly blue eyes and knew exactly what he was doing. He was going to kiss her and there wasn't a damn thing she could do about it because for all her tough talk, she really, really wanted him to do it. She would hold still, damn it, for as long as he wanted her to.

He did kiss her. A real kiss, not some wimpy little tentative peck on the lips. He kissed her like a pro.

Her own eyes must have drifted shut because in an instant all she was aware of was East. His body felt bigger, more solid than the wiry youth she had known before. His hands were more confident, his lips more insistent. That little nick in his front tooth was gone now.

His tooth? How on earth would she know what his tooth felt like unless she'd gone ahead and… Yeah, she had. She'd responded to his kiss with all her might. She was tasting him and exploring him and enjoying the hell out of it.

But she missed that little nick.

Of course he would have gotten that taken care of. Famous television personalities had to be perfect, didn't they? That little flaw had been a part of her old Johnny Smith. This was a different guy. Funny how she could feel all these familiar things for a stranger, though.

But it was a different story for East. He broke off way before it had dawned on her that they should. He stepped back to let a little space between them and, surprisingly, he was smiling.

Not the right kind of smile, though. It wasn't the kind of smile that says, "Wow, how have I gone on so long without you?" Nope. It was the kind of smile that says, "Did I really used to get turned on by this chick?"

Jeez, sometimes she was the stupidest woman alive! How on earth did she let herself end up like this, standing here with her tongue in East's mouth? And thinking there was chance this might mean something to him!

Well, she was getting really good at salvaging what she could from her endless blunders. She'd work something out here, as well. She had to.

"So," she said calmly. "At least we got that out of the way."

One of his eyebrows went up. "I guess we did."

"And you're right," she added with a casual toss of her hair. "We really have changed."

"Everything changes."

"Exactly," she said and hoisted a suitcase up onto the bed. Might as well start unpacking. He'd been right about keeping things in the suitcase. Her clothes would get all wrinkled.

"We're not hormonal kids anymore," she said. "Something like a little kiss doesn't faze us anymore."

"Naturally," he agreed. "We're adults."

"The past is the past and this is now."

"Can't argue with that."

"And right now we're trying to help Granny."

"That's the goal."

"So there's no reason we can't live like civilized adults— friends, even—and just share the same space for a while."

"We ought to be able to do that."

"I'll respect your space and you'll respect mine and pretty soon this month will be over," she said. "You've been very hospitable so far."

He laughed, but she was too busy unpacking to look at him.

"Great. I'm hospitable," he said. "That's just what every man wants to hear from his new wife."

"*Pretend* wife," she reminded him.

"I'll try to keep that in mind."

"Good idea. And while you're at it, would you mind bringing the rest of my stuff in here for me?"

"All right, but I ought to warn you," he said.

Warn her? About what? She turned to find him glaring at her from the doorway. He had his actor face on again and she couldn't tell if he was serious or not.

"You're going to find out I'm a very jealous *pretend* husband."

"What does that mean?" *Was there more to that kiss than she thought?*

But he went on. "If Brad Pitt does drop by, he's bunking with *me*."

Oh, right. He was joking. As usual.

She hoped.

It would be just too much to have to compete with The Brad for East's attentions. She'd read Mr. Pitt was a great kisser.

———

East stared at the suitcases in his small living room. Good God, kissing Marti had been a very bad idea. Didn't seem to affect her one way or another, but he was a mess.

Why had he done it? Just to prove they really were older and wiser now, that the past was over and done? Well, it wasn't. Damn, he knew that for sure now. Every inch of his body had reacted when he'd touched her like that.

And she was going to be living in his house now? With him? Oh, this was going to be a very, very long month.

Chapter 12

Charleen plunked the phone on the kitchen counter.

"Will you kids keep it down?" she said in her loudest whisper. "I was on the phone and Daddy's taking a nap."

"He's always taking a nap," Annie said with a dramatic eye-roll.

"Yeah, when's he going to come outside and help us with our fort?" Josh said.

Annie smacked him. "It's not a fort. It's a stable for my pony."

"You don't have a stupid pony," Josh shot back. "It's a fort."

Annie smacked him again and the game was on. Back and forth they bickered and traded slaps and jabs until finally Charleen disregarded her headache and screeched at them.

"Get out of this house!" she yelled. "Get outside and don't even think about coming back in until I say so!"

They argued, of course, but finally she had both of them shoved out into the backyard. Let them pummel each other out there, but at least it was quiet inside. Her head felt like it was splitting open.

So just how much extra-strength migraine medicine could a person take in a four-hour period? She figured she'd better wait another hour before gulping down more pills. It wouldn't do to have her pass out. The kids needed at least one functional parent.

She suppressed another thought of heading upstairs and ordering Arv to get out of bed and take some responsibility around here. It seemed like he'd been sleeping pretty much straight through since the fire. Must be nice.

At first she didn't mind, figuring he probably needed the rest after those first couple of days when they had so many insurance and fire investigator people to talk to. And heaven knew he'd been working long hours all year; of course he'd take advantage of not having to go to work and get caught up on his rest. But three naps a day for a whole week?

No, this was beyond just simple fatigue. This fire had sapped something out of him and it didn't look like he was anywhere close to getting it back. Without that restaurant to give him something to do, he just wasn't bothering to get up. And damned if his wife and kids weren't excuse enough.

But what could she do if he wouldn't even talk to her? He barely looked at her now, as if he knew this whole thing was her fault and he couldn't bear to see her. Of course, it was her fault. Well, Josh's fault, but since he was only six years old and she was his mother that made it her fault.

If she'd have been more in control of him, paid more attention to him, this wouldn't have happened. He'd have taken his jacket to school that day and not left it crumpled there too near the oven. If she'd have been a better mother none of this would have happened. Of course Arv was disappointed and furious and depressed. It was her fault.

Would he ever forgive her? She honestly didn't know. That restaurant was his dream; his whole life. She'd never realized how important it was to him until now, when it was too late. How on earth was she supposed to fix this?

She was pretty sure her Mom's suggestion wouldn't work. Okay, things with Mom were generally a little more than a suggestion. This latest idea was the perfect example of that.

How was Arv going to feel about it?

He'd hate it, of course. Maybe he'd even think the whole thing had been Charleen's idea, pouring salt in his wounds. Well, it wasn't her idea at all. Mom had come up with this one all on her own. Charleen wasn't taking any credit for it.

Only trouble was, she kind of liked the idea.

Arv appeared in the kitchen doorway.

"The kids home from school yet?" he asked. His hair was a mess. Had he even bothered with a shower today? No, of course not. Why should he? No one important around, just her and the kids.

"They're outside murdering each other," she answered.

"Oh. Good," he said absently. At least, she hoped it was absently.

"Maybe when you get dressed you could go out with them. They wanted you to help with something they're building."

Arv just yawned and moseyed over to the fridge. "Okay, I'll try to get out there if I can."

Charleen bit back a smart-alec remark about how maybe he could fit some time with his children into his busy schedule, but of course that wouldn't help anything. Things were strained enough between them. She wondered what he'd say if she ran Mom's idea past him.

"So, I've been thinking," he said before she could formulate how exactly to mention Mom's phone call. "You know what we should do?"

Charleen felt her eyes widen, and not just because Arv—Mr. Follow-the-Proper-Procedure-Arv—was drinking milk directly from the plastic jug. Was he possibly coming out of this funk? Had he been doing more than just sleeping these past couple days? Did he have some kind of plan for the survival of their family?

"No, what should we do?" she asked and tried to sound as casual as he did.

"We ought to do something for East and Marti," he said.

She was stunned. What had he said? East and Marti? Her confusion must have shown because he went on to explain.

"You know, for them getting married. I understand you've had a lot going on and haven't had time to plan anything, but you've met Marti a few times so you know what a great person she is…"

"Yeah, she's a gem," Charleen muttered, but Arv didn't notice.

"And you'll really like East," he went on. "How about if I call Granny and see if maybe we can't put on some kind of to-do for them?"

"A 'to-do'? What, you mean here? At the house?"

He actually had the guts to laugh at her. "Well, we can't very well have it at the restaurant, can we?"

"Look, this has not been my best week, you know? The absolute last thing I want is a houseful of people you went to high school with and I've met twice!"

He seemed to ponder this as he put the milk away. "Yeah, you're probably right."

"You think?"

"You're right, we can't do it here."

"Good."

"I'll call Granny and see if we can do something at the diner. That's a much better idea."

"What?"

"Yeah, that'll be perfect. You can help cater it so Granny doesn't end up working too hard," he said and then wrinkled his nose. "Jeez, I need a shower."

And he was heading for the stairway. Just like that. As if they'd discussed this whole thing and she was in perfect agreement with him! Well, damn it, this time she was going to say something.

"Wait a minute," she called, and he turned back to her.

He was smiling for the first time all week. Great. Their family could go to hell in a hand basket but one little thought of Marti Snowden and Arv was all grins and happy faces.

"We need to talk about this," she said, but she could feel her resolve fading. Arv had found a reason to get out of bed finally. How could she slam him down?

"Yeah, we'll get all the details worked out after I see what Granny says," he replied, as if this was an adequate response.

"No, I mean… about something else."

"Oh? You've got some other idea for them?"

Man, was this guy thick, or what? Sometimes Arv's one-track mind made her want to jump out of her skin and throttle him.

"No, it's about us, Arv," she said. "I need to talk to you about US."

Now he looked really confused.

"My mom just called," she said slowly so he might comprehend. "And she has a suggestion—not about East and Marti—about US."

"You mean, about the restaurant?"

"God, Arv, I said US! Our family—you, me, the kids… US!"

"Oh, okay," he shrugged. "What is it?"

Charleen took a deep breath. "She's booked us a room at the hotel in Cleveland and bought our tickets to be tasters at the Family Favorites cook-off."

"What?"

"Yeah, she did that. She says the kids can stay at their place and she'll take them to the zoo and stuff while we're there so you and I can have some time alone, and it'll be like a little vacation. For all of us. Our family, Arv."

"I'm not going to that cook-off! Especially not as some stupid taster."

"She already bought the tickets. You'd rather they go to waste?"

"She should have asked us first. Why would we want to go there after what happened?"

"I guess she figured it might be a good way to check out the competition for next year, and to have a few nights in a fancy hotel and a little time alone with each other! You know, most husbands and wives are capable of finding interesting ways to enjoy each other's company from time to time."

"We enjoy each other's company," he said, frowning. "We're enjoying each other's company right now, and we don't need to be in some overpriced hotel for it, either. I'm not going."

She dug in her heels. "My mother tries to do something nice for us and you just won't go, huh? Without even asking what the kids and I want, you're just going to say no?"

"You mean you *want* to go? To be humiliated as the couple whose restaurant was so bad it burned to the ground? They'd all laugh at us, or treat us like some kind of charity case, or just be embarrassed for us. No way; I'm not going."

"Well, maybe the kids and I could use a little time off. Maybe we'll go anyway."

"Then I guess your mom will only waste one ticket, huh?"

"You'd rather stay here alone and let us go without you?"

He didn't get to answer her. Annie came storming through the back door, hollering and stomping her feet angrily.

"I hate him! He's the meanest brother in the world and I wish he was never born!"

"What happened now?" Charleen asked, forsaking the argument with Arv.

"Josh is ruining my pony barn!"

"Well, honey, he didn't want to play pony. Maybe you can figure out what to build that you both will want to play."

"No, I don't want to play with him ever again! He ruined it. He ruined everything."

"Annie, Josh is only six. Why don't you find a way to compromise? Play fort with him for fifteen minutes, then he can play stable with you."

"No, he won't. He ruined everything and I can't build my pony barn ever again!"

Charleen kept her voice soft and motherly. She could do this. It was just a little squabble. She'd show Arv who was the expert at winning fights around here.

"Honey," she said and stooped down to be eye level with her tearful daughter. "That's a big pile of sticks you and Josh collected back there. Why don't you two divide them up, and he can build his fort and you can build your stable?"

"No, he ruined it. He took all the sticks and I can't build anything. I'll never have my pony barn."

Now Josh risked his sister's wrath by appearing in the same room with her. He must have known he'd really upset her because the expression on his face said he clearly knew he deserved some sort of scolding. Then again, the poor boy usually did.

"Josh," Charleen began calmly. "Annie said you won't share the sticks with her. Now, I want you to divide up those sticks out there and you each build what you want."

But now Josh's lip was quivering. "No, we can't," he began. "There's kind of a problem."

But Arv was already jogging past them out the back door. Charleen got a whiff of something from the outside air as the door swished open. Oh no, not again!

Annie explained the trouble behind her as Charleen followed Arv out into the backyard and toward the garden hose.

"Josh put all the sticks in a big pile and caught it on fire and now the grass is burning, too!"

Chapter 12

East walked into his apartment. Uh oh, what was that smell? Burnt sugar? Surely Marti couldn't be home so early. For a whole week now she'd been avoiding him by claiming Granny needed her at the diner from sunup to sundown. Needed her? Yeah, right.

He knew for a fact Granny was offering cold hard cash to anyone who could get Marti out of the diner and out of her hair at least a couple hours a day.

"Marti? Are you home?" he called, figuring if it wasn't Marti then someone else was back there in his tiny kitchen scalding something perishable.

"Yeah, I'm in the kitchen," she called back.

She didn't sound panicked, so whatever he was smelling must not be too disastrous.

"Hey, come here!" she said, poking her head around the doorway. Was that flour on her face or had something frightened her?

"Uh, what you got going in there?" he asked carefully, suppressing the urge to run to her aid.

"I'm baking cookies!" she grinned proudly.

Her hair was a mess and looked like maybe it had something sticky in it. Molasses? Well, couple that with the flour on her face and he could believe she was working with the ingredients to make cookies, but based on his sense of smell he wasn't ready to say she was "baking" them.

Incinerating them, maybe.

"Cookies, huh?" he asked, entering his kitchen with much fear and trepidation.

"Yeah, I need to get a little more kitchen practice before this cook-off thing, and Granny sure isn't letting me touch anything in her kitchen anymore. So, I thought I'd try my hand at her sugar cookies. I watched her at the diner today and I'm pretty sure I got everything right. Try one!"

She was practically beaming. God, she was so darn sincere and hopeful and, well, just plain cute. He sure as hell hoped she'd actually baked something resembling cookies today.

She held one out to him. It looked fairly harmless. It was approximately round and for the most part the right color. She'd even gone so far as to stir multi-colored non-pariels into the batter, just like Granny did. So far so good.

He bit into it slowly, afraid at any moment the illusion might be ruined. But, surprisingly, the cookie wasn't half bad. It wasn't exactly like Granny's, but it was easily edible. It was, in all honesty, pretty good. He smiled almost as big as Marti.

"Not bad," he said. "You did all right."

"Yeah," she said proudly. "I did. The first tray came out a little burnt, but I didn't keep this next one in as long and it turned out perfectly!"

"How about the one in the oven now?" he asked, and wished he hadn't. It sounded kind of critical, when really he was trying to explain how impressed he was without sounding like he usually thought of her as totally incompetent.

She jumped. "Oh no! I forgot about it!"

Grabbing up the oven mitts she yanked the oven open. Smoke puffed out. The current tray of cookies was more than a little singed.

"Damn it!" she grumbled, slamming the tray onto the stovetop. "Look at them! I was so proud of the last bunch, then I got so busy scraping off the first batch that I completely forgot about these. Dammit dammit dammit."

"It's okay," he soothed. "These things happen."

"No. No, they don't. Not to most people," she moaned. "It's no wonder Granny sent me home early."

"She sent you home?"

Marti dumped the burned cookies off the tray and into the trash. East had already given his hands a quick wash and was investigating the mixing bowl, still half filled with dough.

"Yeah. She made it sound like she was worried that I'd been working too hard and… uh, neglecting you."

"Yeah, that sounds like her."

"So she told me to come on home. I couldn't very well argue in front of everyone."

No, she couldn't very well argue about it or people might start to wonder if the new East and Marti Smith household was quite as happy as it should be. They might wonder if maybe these two lovebirds spent a little too much time sniping at each other over things like who got to watch what on TV (he ended up hiding the remote) or who left wet towels in the bathroom (well, wet towels belong in the bathroom, don't they?). They might begin to notice that East was a little bit worse for the wear after a whole week of restless sleep, knowing Marti was right there, in the same apartment, and totally off-limits.

Yeah, they might notice a thing or two. East sure had. He noticed how Marti's lips were usually fuller and redder in the morning when she woke up. Her breasts jiggled a lot more without a bra on, too. And she still kept her toenails painted hot pink.

There were other little endearing things he was learning about her. She always sneezed twice. She read romance novels when she thought he wasn't looking. And she used cinnamon toothpaste instead of mint. Now he craved cinnamon. Mostly, he just craved Marti.

It had been a really long week. The good news was Marti seemed to have no clue what her presence in his home was doing to him. She'd gotten more comfortable as the days wore on and if it weren't for a certain perpetual discomfort in his certain perpetual body part he could have said they were getting along just fine.

The truth was, Marti was getting along just fine. East was beginning to wonder how much more of this he could take. It was divine torture, but torture nonetheless.

He was harassing his agent daily just to have something to think about other than those golden eyes and honey colored hair. He even went so far as to stop for lunch one day at the Five Star Grille to let the manager, Carolyn Benton, flirt with him. She'd been most accommodating back in the eleventh grade and it appeared she was just as "friendly" these days.

But he couldn't take her up on her offer. She just wasn't Marti. No one else was. God, he was pathetic.

"I'm just useless," Marti sighed and sagged against the counter.

Uh, oh. With her looking all vulnerable and sad like that he really, really wanted to kiss her again. But that probably wouldn't cheer her up any. She'd made it clear kisses—his kisses, at least—didn't do much for her.

"Why don't we get another tray of cookies in there?" he said, swooping over to help her. "We'll set the timer on the microwave so we don't forget them, okay?"

"There's a timer on the microwave?"

Now if that just wasn't the most adorable thing. He knew this was a woman with several advanced degrees. She wasn't unintelligent. Her gray matter was highly developed—not unlike the rest of her, he couldn't help noting, although he really ought to be concentrating on baking just now—but something about seeing her all helpless like this just drove him nuts.

Yes, he was probably a world class chauvinist for thinking it, but Marti's haplessness in the kitchen when she was so capable in so many other areas was positively irresistible to him. That and the fact that when she leaned over the counter to grab another wooden spoon she got non-pariels stuck to her breasts. Completely, unequivocally irresistible.

Of course he'd get smacked if he offered to remove those tiny candies for her, especially considering how he'd prefer to do it with his teeth, so he kept quiet and just enjoyed the fantasy.

But before he could get totally carried away, the phone rang.

Marti answered it and he could tell right off there was something wrong. She put it down with a frown and started wiping her hands off. Unaware, she managed to get the non-pariels, too. Damn. What a waste of perfectly good boob-candy.

"That was Granny," she said. "There's some kind of problem at the diner and she needs us to get over there."

"What is it?" he asked, forgetting his sweet little daydream.

"I don't know, but she wants us to hurry."

"Well, let's go," he said and shoved the cookie dough into the fridge.

Marti clicked off the oven—he made sure to watch her

carefully—and they abandoned the cookie project. Clean-up and the rest of the baking could wait. There was no telling what Granny had going on at the diner that she needed them for, but it sounded important.

It only took ten minutes to drive across town and when they got to the diner it was surprisingly empty. No cars parked out front, and from what East could see through the front widow there was no one inside. That was unusual, considering it was not even six thirty on a Monday night. Sure, Monday's were never a big night, but there was usually someone here. So what on earth had happened? He was glad Marti was with him and not in Granny's kitchen.

They hurried through the front door and the cowbell clattered loudly. The place looked fine. So where was everyone?

"Granny?" Marti called out. She sounded worried.

Before they could get to the kitchen door, however, it burst open. Out came Granny and a stream of noisy people.

"Surprise!" Granny cackled, grinning like she'd won the lottery.

It took a minute to register, but filing into the dining area from the kitchen was just about everyone they knew. Several people East was pretty sure he didn't know. He wasn't entirely sure what it all meant until Arv appeared in the crowd and made his way over to slap East on the back. Hard.

"Well, old buddy, you got yourself hitched, huh?" he was laughing.

For a minute that didn't make sense, but then of course he realized what was going on. Granny was throwing them some kind of real party in honor of their fake marriage! Oh, fantastic. This was going to be fun.

He glanced at Marti. She was glaring at her grandmother with eyes that implied a threat of dramatic proportions.

Granny just kept on smiling and shrugged. "Hey, it wasn't my idea. Arv called me and suggested it!"

Arv just laughed. Sure, he thought he was doing something nice.

"It's the least I could do," Arv said, putting one arm around East and one around Marti. "It's not every day a guy's best pal from high school gets hooked up with the girl of his dreams."

Yeah, but just whose dreams was he referring to?

———

It was a freaking ambush! Marti gritted her teeth and hoped it looked something like a smile. She was pretty sure it didn't.

What was Granny thinking, to let Arv and Charleen do something like this? True, they didn't know it was just a pretend marriage, but Granny sure as hell did. Why on earth would she allow it?

Because she was an evil, evil little person, obviously. Or maybe she was still harboring a grudge for that certain fire incident a couple weeks ago. Yeah, this was one great way of getting back at her for that, all right!

Jeez, it seemed like half the town was packed into Granny's diner tonight. How long had they been planning this thing? And how were she and East supposed to get out of it?

They weren't, apparently. East's parents were there and were going on and on about how thrilled they were to have Marti in their family. That was good for more guilt.

"Marti has always been like a daughter to us," Mrs. Smith was saying, a weepy catch in her voice. "We're just so happy for both of them."

East and Marti were shuffled through the crowd and

pushed up against the lunch counter where someone was bringing out snacks and a big cake. It wasn't one of Granny's cakes; no, she'd actually gone and gotten one of those fancy decorated cakes from *Lorelei the Cake Lady*. In between the mounds of roses and ruffles and leafy icing designs the cake read, "Together at Last, Marti and East". Marti wondered if a person could die from too much sicky-sweet sentiment.

"Beautiful cake, Milly" Marge Franklin said.

"It's one of Lorelei's," Granny answered.

"Well, we didn't figure Marti made it!" Lloyd Schneider guffawed. Yes, wasn't it just hilarious that Marti Snowden turned out to be such a disaster in the kitchen? Oh, this was putting her in such a bad mood.

"Hey, Marti can bake for me any day," East said next to her, sounding surprisingly positive. She waited for the other shoe to drop. Surely he was setting up another joke.

"She came home tonight and whipped up a batch of sugar cookies," he went on. "They were good—and I know good food."

And then he just smiled at her. That was all he said. Nothing about how he was amazed to find the kitchen still standing, nothing about the two dozen charcoal briquette's she'd made along with the few decent cookies, and nothing about how he would have starved this last week if he hadn't provided his own meals. Huh. And the killing glare he sent Lloyd's way was nothing short of menacing. My God, was East actually defending her?

She was glad she was propped up on a stool at the lunch counter. Her knees were actually going weak and she might have tipped over.

But then again, of course East wasn't going to stand around and let people think he'd married someone with no domestic skills. He probably wasn't defending her as much as his own macho-man reputation. It was silly for her to attach any more meaning to it than that. Silly and dangerous.

All week now she'd been doing her best to keep distance between herself and East. That kiss on their wedding day had nearly done her in, so she was not about to take any more chances and get caught alone with him and her guard down. Good thing Granny liked having her around so much; she'd used the diner as an excuse to avoid going home to East's apartment.

Not that he seemed to mind. His agent had been calling a lot and Marti was getting the feeling there was some hot project in the works. He'd be out of here before too long. All she had to do was get through this.

But it wasn't easy. Living with East was no walk in the park. For starters, he was a much better roommate than she'd expected. All that crap about hoping a few days in close proximity would help purge him from her system was just wishful thinking. He was not out of her system. Not by a long shot.

She'd hoped that watching him chew with his mouth open or scratch himself and belch would get all those girlish notions of him being the perfect male out of her mind. She figured the toothpaste globs on the sink and hairs in the shower would irrevocably gross her out. She expected him to be inconsiderate and bossy.

But it wasn't working out that way. He didn't chew with his mouth open, and there had been no public scratching, belching, toothpaste globs or hair in the shower. He was polite and charming, and now here he was defending her non-existent culinary skills. Damn! His gallantry was making her life a living hell.

"You mean to say my Marti baked you some cookies today?" Granny said over the din of laughter and snacking.

"And you ate them?"

Okay, Granny. No need to go overboard with praise.
Marti scowled at her. That old woman was going to hear
about this afterwards, that much was sure.

But East just winked at Granny. "Marti's got a lot of
hidden talents," he said as everyone laughed.

Boy, the guy sure knew how to play a crowd. He always
had. No wonder so many people turned out here for Granny
and Arv's little soirée. They knew East would make them
laugh and with any luck Marti might catch something on fire
or fall into the cake. A good time was bound to be had by all.

Well, maybe not by all. Charleen sure didn't look overly
glad to be here. But that would only make sense. After what
their family had been through in the last week Marti was
amazed to see them out and about at all. Of course this whole
festive event had to be Arv's idea. It was pretty obvious just
to look at Charleen that it hadn't been hers.

She looked tired. Marti didn't know her well, but the few
times she had met her Charleen always seemed lively and
interested in the society around her. Tonight she appeared
anything but. She sort of blended into the background,
hissing little warnings of "Be careful," and "Don't touch
that!" to her children.

Poor kids. They looked even less thrilled about being
there. That little boy especially. Marti could relate.

But Arv was in high spirits. He and East were laughing
like old times, slapping each other on the back and calling
each other idiotic, juvenile names. God, it was embarrassing.
Arv was seriously going to hate them when he found out he'd
gone to all this trouble for nothing.

"So tell us how the preparations are coming for the big
cook off!" Mavis McAulley asked loudly. She had Chuckie-
the-spoon-thrower with her and Marti wondered how long

before they all should start ducking.

But Chuckie wasn't near the spoons. Instead he was zeroing in on the Koch kids, showing Arv's son how to flick the edge of one of the Formica tabletops so that the plastic veneer pulled up and slapped down with a loud smacking sound. This seemed right up Arv's kid's alley and Marti expected Charleen to swoop down and crush the budding friendship, but she turned out to be distracted.

Oddly enough, she was ignoring her kids and staring at Granny with a puzzled look.

"Well," Granny was saying in answer to Mavis's question. "I think I've got the right recipes picked out. I've still got a couple weeks to decide for sure, and I'm letting Marti and East make the final decision."

Now Marti was looking at Granny with puzzlement. "Marti and East are making the final decision?" she asked, forgetting all about Charleen. This was news to her.

Granny just shrugged. "Well, since you two are the ones who'll be doing the actual cooking up there, I figured I ought to let you do what you feel most comfortable with. But it'll be my recipes, that's for darn sure."

Now Charleen got into the conversation. "Marti and East are cooking in a competition?"

Granny looked a little sheepish and maybe even blushed a bit. "I guess I didn't mention it to Arv when he called to plan this little shindig," she said. "We got invited to the Family Favorites Cook-Off."

"Really?" Charleen said. "I guess I didn't really look at the list of competitors very closely."

"Oh, they only just got put on it," Mavis said, loudly again. "Granny was an alternate, and someone else backed out so now they're in! And just in time for East to be part of the family."

Charleen looked stunned. Well, Marti couldn't blame her. Anyone with half a brain could have put two and two together to realize that Granny probably got in the contest because Charleen and Arv got out of it. But maybe Mavis didn't realize the Koch's had been in it in the first place. Or maybe she was the one person in Garden Falls who hadn't heard about the Dutch Pantry burning. Or maybe Mavis just didn't have half a brain.

But everyone else around them did, and the room got awkwardly quiet. Except for the kids. They were still flicking away at the tabletop. *Smack. Smack.*

Then Arv spoke and it looked like Charleen was ready to do some smacking of her own.

"You guys are going to be in the cook-off?" He grinned brightly. "That's great! Charleen and I were planning to head up there for that—maybe even sit on the tasters' panel."

Okay, based on Charleen's expression of contempt there would be no sitting on any sort of panel. It looked like Charleen had no plans of sitting on anything with Arv. Not that Marti was an expert on the intricacies of marriage, but she was pretty sure hers was not the only nuptial situation represented here tonight that could stand a bit of tweaking. Charleen looked ready to draw blood, and Arv was hopelessly unaware.

Someone should've warned the poor guy, but he bungled on, grinning at East. "Think you newlyweds could stand a bit of company up there in Cleveland at the end of the month?"

"Heck yeah!" East replied, as clueless as Arv. "Sounds like fun. And it wouldn't hurt to have a friend on that tasters' panel."

"Oh, don't go thinking I'm cutting you any slack, Johnny boy," Arv said and punched him in the arm. "You may be related to Granny now, but it doesn't mean you can cook like her!"

"It may surprise you to know, Koch," East bantered. "I wasn't just hired as window dressing for that little TV show I was on. I know what I'm doing."

Arv just laughed. "Is that right, Marti? Does he cook, or just *act* like he's cooking?"

"You should see him in a calico apron," Marti said.

She probably owed it to East to attest to his culinary skill after he'd stuck up for her cookies, but she just couldn't do it. She was already feeling a little too kindhearted toward him. Going on and on about how his kitchen antics made her mouth water would be entirely too much.

"But is it his cooking you like, or what he's got on under that apron?" Lloyd Schneider said with an exaggerated swagger. Everyone hooted at that.

"Hey, who says I've got anything on under that apron, Lloyd?" East teased.

Happily the children in the room were oblivious to the adult humor that circulated at that remark. Ignoring everything, the kids were still working the tabletop, figuring out how to use the loose flap to fling sugar packets at each other. It looked like fun, actually.

Then out of the blue, the fantastic image of East in Granny's frilly calico apron– with nothing else—lodged in Marti's brain and that looked like fun, too. Too much fun. Oh jeez, why did he have to go and brag about her cookies? Now she was feeling all kinds of grateful to him.

"Stop it right now!"

Marti was glad to realize she hadn't said that. She'd been thinking it, trying to get her mind off of the East-apron image, but she hadn't actually said that. Charleen had, finally realizing what the kids were up to.

"Josh, Annie, get away from there," Charleen ordered.

"Look what you're doing to that table!"

Mavis McAulley, not to be out-mommed by Charleen, rushed over and pretended to be upset about what her little Chuckie was doing.

"Oh, no!" Mavis wailed. "Your table, Granny… oh, I'm so sorry."

"Naw, don't fret about it," Granny said. "They can't hurt much around here. Kids gotta play, you know."

"But they don't have to destroy things," Charleen said. She looked about ready to explode. Seemed odd to see someone so stressed-out at a party. Well, actually, Marti wasn't exactly cool as a cucumber. Maybe if she was doing something useful she could help them all out a bit.

"Hey," Marti said brightly. "We've got some coloring books in the back. Why don't you kids follow me and come pick one out?"

Charleen's little boy brightened considerably, although that could simply have been because Marti was offering a chance to get away from his glaring mother.

"Do you have one with dinosaurs?" he asked.

"I don't know," Marti shrugged. "Why don't we go find out?"

She okayed it with the mothers then ushered the kids toward the kitchen and Granny's desk where she knew Peg housed several coloring books and a big coffee can full of crayons. Peg's granddaughter visited occasionally and this kept her pretty busy, so it ought to give these kids something better to do than strip the veneer off the tables. That might help Charleen not to stroke out on them.

"Okay, pick a book and let's go sit down and make some masterpieces," Marti said, hauling out the stack of coloring books.

There were Barbie books, Disney books, truck books,

butterfly books, superhero books and politically correct caring-about-each-other books, but no dinosaur books. Huh, what sort of grandmother was Peg, anyway? No dinosaurs? Unheard of.

"Sorry, kid," she told the little boy. "I don't see any dinosaur books."

"Aw, man!" he griped, rifling the pile.

"He's Josh and I'm Annie," the little girl volunteered.

"Oh?" Marti said with a smile. "Pleased to meet you. This is Chuckie—in case you weren't properly introduced as you tried to peel the furniture out there. And I'm Marti."

"We know who you are," Annie said. "Mommy and Daddy were talking about you. A lot."

"They were?" Marti said.

"Yeah. Daddy says you just got married out of the blue. But I don't know where that is."

Marti tried not to laugh. "Well, it's not really a place. That's just an expression that means people were kind of surprised."

"Oh, like Daddy was really surprised when he heard about it. He got all excited and stuff. Mommy just got mad."

"She got mad?" Marti asked. Okay, so she shouldn't ask about private conversations the Koch's had at home, but this seemed like such an unusual thing for a kid to say.

"Oh, Mommy just gets mad at everything," Annie shrugged and pointed to a coloring book in the stack the boys had been rifling. "Look! There's a Barbie book! Can I have that one?"

"Sure," Marti answered and slid the book out of the stack for her.

"Thank you, ma'am," the little girl said way-too-politely. Probably trying to make the boys look bad.

By the looks of it the Barbie book was Peg's

granddaughter's favorite, too. Marti never had understood the big deal about Barbie, but the blond chick sure was popular. As if in real life a woman with those proportions could even walk, let alone be a ballerina-veterinarian-rock-star with six boyfriends all named Ken.

"I like trucks," Chuckie said, grabbing his choice before Josh had a chance to take it.

Josh didn't seem to mind. "Ooo, cool!" he said, laying claim to another book. "Here's one about lizards!"

From way down at the very bottom of the pile he extracted a thin, glossy-covered coloring book with a fierce-looking iguana on the cover. It looked like no one had ever opened this book before, much less colored in it, but Josh was eyeing it like he'd struck oil. Smart kid.

"Trucks are way better than lizards," Chuckie said.

"No they're not!" Josh defended, flipping through the pages. "Lizards are cool. See? Look, here's a Komodo Dragon."

"Bull," Chuckie sneered. "There's no such thing as dragons."

"Oh, yes there is!" Josh proclaimed. "They live on islands way far away and their spit can kill a buffalo."

"No way," Chuckie shook his head. "That's not true."

"Yes it is! They're real!"

"You're lying!"

"Well, you're stupid!"

"Josh, that's a bad word," Annie inserted.

"I don't care. He is stupid."

"Hey, I'm telling!" Chuckie whined.

Marti figured it was time to be the grown-up. "Okay, okay. Nobody's stupid. It's true there aren't real dragons like in the fairy tales, Chuckie, but Komodo dragons are real animals."

"Yeah," Josh gloated.

"Yeah? So why do they call them dragons if they're not?" Chuckie asked.

"Because they're very big and very aggressive," Marti explained.

"That means they're mean," Annie said proudly.

"Right," Marti confirmed. "With huge sharp teeth."

"And they eat each other, too!" Josh offered.

"Like cannibals?" Chuckie said, happy to show off he knew a big word, too.

"Sometimes they *are* cannibals," Marti confirmed. "And they have such disgusting bacteria in their saliva that even if a victim survives an attack, they almost always die from infection later on."

"Then the dragons eat the stinking rotten bodies with flies all over them!" Josh enthused.

Chuckie was in awe. "Cool! That is *sooo* disgusting."

"Boys are totally gross." Annie cringed, clutching the ultra-girly coloring book to her chest like a boy-proof shield.

"And here's a Gila monster," Josh said, turning the page and ignoring his sister. "It's supposed to be yellow and black, and it's poisonous, too."

"That's pretty good. You really know your lizards, Josh," Marti said.

"He's really into lizards." Annie shuddered. "And snakes and all that slimy stuff."

"Snakes aren't slimy," Marti and Josh said together.

They laughed. Well, how about that? Marti actually had a kindred spirit here at this damn party. Too bad he wasn't quite four feet tall yet.

"My uncle said he saw a copperhead down by the creek," Chuckie asserted loudly. "He said it was coming after him and he barely got away before it bit him. He would have died!"

Brother. The old copperhead-in-the-crik fable. "Oh, probably not, Chuckie," Marti said gently. "Copperheads don't like to chase people, and their venom isn't usually lethal to humans."

"Well, he did see one," Chuckie insisted. "It was by the bridge down at the ballpark."

"Nuh uh, he didn't see a real copperhead," Josh said, the little skeptic.

"Yeah, it's possible," Marti assured three sets of wide eyes. "We have all kinds of wildlife here in Garden Falls, if you know where to look for it."

"Cool! Could you find us a copperhead?" Josh asked.

"Uh, no, I think not," Marti answered quickly, imagining Charleen's expression if she found the kids playing with a venomous snake. "But I could probably get you a toad or maybe a little spotted salamander."

"Oh, wow," Chuckie said worshipfully. "Where?"

"Come on," Marti motioned toward the back door. "There are some old boards piled out back and I can usually dig up something out there."

They practically pushed her through the old screen door. Even Annie dropped the Barbie book on Granny's desk and went eagerly. The sun was still above the horizon, giving off plenty of warm, orange light, and the mosquitoes hadn't come out yet this spring. A perfect night for hunting things that lived under rocks. Then again, what night wasn't?

Chapter 11

Oh, great. Phil and Joetta had just arrived to round out the guest list at this little surprise party. East grimaced. Did Granny invite them, or were they crashers? Either way, it was bound to send Marti over the edge.

Was she still back in the kitchen with the kids? East was pretty sure Marti had used them as an excuse to escape the fawning crowd. Not that East blamed her for that. Heck no. He wished he'd been smart enough with his own excuse to get out of here, too.

Phil swooped down, interrupting the conversation East had been having with Arv.

"So, been giving our little venture some more thought?" he asked loudly.

Their little venture? East assumed Phil must be talking about the destruction they had planned for the Beaverbend Road area. Yeah, he'd been giving it some more thought. Not the kind Phil might have hoped for, though.

But at least East was able to answer honestly. "As a matter of fact, I was just talking to someone about it today."

He didn't bother to mention it had been someone at the county engineer's office he'd been talking to. And neither of them had been saying anything nice.

"Well, I'm glad to hear we've got you in with us," Phil said, giving him a hearty slap on the back. "Won't those nay-sayers around town clam up when I tell them you've gotten involved."

East was glad to hear Phil had been encountering some local resistance. That would make Marti happy. She'd been grumbling about the Townsend's all week. She still hadn't heard anything from her friend at the state capitol and that was making her grumpy.

Phil noticed Arv standing next to East and made a big deal out of introducing himself. From the sound of it, Phil must have had the mistaken impression that Arv was some big-shot friend of East's from out of town. Phil's cheesy grin faded when Arv mentioned that he was just Bob and Margie's son from right here in Garden Falls.

Arv gave East a better-you-than-me grin and excused himself. "Hey, I think I'd better go check on my kids and make sure they're not getting into things."

"Yeah, let me know if you need any help," East called after him. But Arv was already pushing through the big swinging door into the kitchen.

Some old pal Arv was turning out to be, talking Granny into this stupid party and then ditching East here with Phil. Well, at least Joetta was busy elsewhere. She'd found the cake.

East was stuck smiling politely as Phil rambled on about "progress" and made promises East knew for a fact his little project would never be able to keep. Actually, Phil would be lucky if he didn't end up in jail, based on what East had learned when the County Engineer sent him over to the courthouse. Finally East couldn't take anymore and he cut Phil off in mid lie.

"Hey, sorry, but I see someone I need to talk to," he said and pushed his way out of the corner past Phil.

Charleen and Granny were conversing at a booth where Granny had finally retreated to rest her hip. East made a beeline for them.

"Save me from Phil. He's going to drive me nuts!" he said as he sidled up to their booth.

"Well, then quit acting so darn nice to him," Granny chided. "But if you've got a spare minute, maybe you could go in the back and bring out some more ice. I hate to put you to work at your own party, but this old hip isn't wanting to cooperate tonight."

Charleen hopped up, nearly plowing into East. "I'll do that for you, Granny. I need to check on the kids anyway."

But East had kind of liked the idea of heading back into the kitchen. Marti was there. So was Arv. Hmm. Marti and Arv together. That probably didn't mean anything, but he ought to go get that ice for Granny.

"No, that's okay. I'll take care of the ice," East said.

Charleen followed anyway.

But the kitchen was empty. Maybe Marti really had escaped. That didn't explain where the kids and Arv were, though. Charleen folded her arms and looked annoyed. Then voices came drifting in through the screen door.

Charleen glanced at East and he shrugged. "I guess they went outside."

They went to the door and Charleen pushed it open to march out. East trailed along behind her, but stopped when she froze.

The kids were crouched beside a pile of scrap lumber at the back of the building, picking at stuff in the damp grass that grew in stray tufts. Marti and Arv were standing together in the alley, their heads bent close and haloed by the last rays of sunset. They were talking softly.

It would have been a pretty picture if they both hadn't been married to other people at the time. True, Marti's married state didn't exactly count, but judging from

Charleen's reaction, Arv's sure as hell did.

"I guess this is where the real party is tonight, out here in the alley," Charleen said loudly.

If Arv had known what was good for him he probably would have at least acted startled or come up with some lame excuse for being huddled up with his old girlfriend there. But the moron just waved at his wife and stayed right where he was, plastered up against Marti.

"Hey, Char," he called. "Come see what Marti found!"

"No, I think maybe I ought to get the kids in out of the dirt and wash their hands," Charleen said sharply.

The Koch kids must have known this was coming. They were already getting up and wiping their hands on their clothes. That other little boy just frowned.

"But we only found three snails so far," he complained.

"We gotta go," Arv's little girl sighed. "Come on, Josh."

Tension radiated from Charleen. East could feel it, but he honestly had to admit he didn't mind the way her gaze chastised Arv. Plus, he couldn't ignore his actual relief when Arv finally got the hint and stepped away from Marti and toward his silently fuming wife.

"We should probably get back in to our party, don't you think?" East asked Marti as Arv moved away from her to go help Charleen gather the kids.

Marti just looked confused. "What? But we were looking for toads. I've got this cricket and the kids wanted to see if we could feed it to a toad."

East took her arm, carefully avoiding the grime she'd managed to get all over herself. "Sorry, Mrs. Smith, biology class is done for the day."

He called over to the other little boy, still mucking through the rotting lumber in search of treasure for Marti. "Come on, Charlie."

"Chuckie," Marti corrected as the boy ignored him.

"Whatever," East sighed. "Come on, kid, get inside."

Marti huffed. "Great. My new husband hates kids."

She left him standing in the alley to go usher the kid away from the lumber and follow Arv's family inside. East was alone out there. Funny, he never knew the word "husband" could sound like such an insult.

——

Well, Marti and East made it through the party, all right. They made a good team, Milly decided when it was all done and Peg had dropped her off at home. Yep, they pulled off this newlywed thing with flying colors. The whole town was buying it now.

She really hadn't doubted that East would come through, but she half expected Marti to throw a fit or make some kind of scene. A couple times it looked like the girl wanted to, but somehow she held herself back. She even had the good sense to give her old grandmother a big hug when she and East left for the night.

A BIG hug. It hurt, actually, and Milly was pretty sure that hadn't been an accident. She guessed she was lucky Marti hadn't strangled her right there for making them suffer through that surprise party.

But what else could Milly have done? Arv called and was all excited to plan it. Milly already felt so guilty about taking his place in that damned cook-off, how could she tell him he wasn't allowed to do something nice for his two oldest friends? It wasn't as if he could host the event over at his place.

No, she didn't have any choice but to go along with it and hope the kids would forgive her. Or if she was really lucky,

179

maybe they wouldn't have to. Maybe this marriage would end up making itself real after all.

But how was Milly going to make that happen? Those kids might be living together, but they sure didn't spend much time together. From what she'd seen, they avoided each other like the plague. She wanted them to work together on this cook-off, but so far they'd been leaving most of the work to her.

What could she do? She needed a sure-fire way to get those two working side by side on something, putting their heads together, like the good-ol' days. She was sure if they'd just spend a little more time together those kids would fall for each other.

And then she was grinning. Oh, she had an idea, all right. *Fall for each other.* Yeah, that might just do it. Somebody around here ought to take a good fall. She checked the clock.

Just after ten. That was way too early. If this was going to work, the timing would be all important. She needed a time that would produce the optimal effect.

Midnight. That might do it. Get them up and out of their separate beds. Yes sirree. Those kids needed to do a little less sleeping at night.

———

What was that damn noise? It seemed to go on forever before Marti finally woke up enough to realize it was the phone out on the bar in the kitchen. She looked over at the clock radio. Midnight? Who called at midnight? People who called at midnight usually had an emergency.

Her first instinct then was to panic. She sat bolt upright in bed and tried to wake up enough to think. Was something the matter?

Out in the living room she could hear East rustling around. The phone had stopped ringing so obviously he'd gone and answered it. Now she could hear his voice.

Oh. So she didn't need to panic after all. It must be a call for him—probably someone in California who forgot about the time difference. She took a deep breath and told her heart rate to settle down. Nothing to worry about. Probably just his agent.

Or not. It could be a friend. A woman.

Okay, there went that heart rate again. Of course East would still have women friends. Heck, he probably hadn't even bothered to tell anyone out there that he was technically married again. Jeez, he might have some hot actress babe just waiting for him to get his cute little booty back out to the west coast so they could pick up where they left off.

She listened. He was still talking, but she couldn't tell what he was saying. His voice was low, raspy and deep from just waking up. The perfect voice for a long sexy midnight conversation. Cheap, tawdry phone sex, maybe. Just twenty feet away from her.

He wouldn't be doing *that* with one of those actress bimbos, would he? How disgusting! He couldn't, not right here under her nose. She was his… well, she was his wife, damn it!

She swung her legs out of bed and marched to the door. *Let's just see if he can keep it up while I'm out there eavesdropping on him...*

But her grand entrance to the living room was thwarted. She yanked her bedroom door open only to find East standing right there, his hand poised to knock. He jumped a little. So did she.

For a few breathless seconds they just stared at each other. She took in his bare chest and the hastily pulled on flannel pants that hung slightly crooked, showing that marvelous muscular hip indentation on one side. He had more body hair than she remembered; dark, silky hair that gathered in a tempting mass in the center of his chest and trailed down in a tantalizing line toward his... well, to be hidden behind the pants, thankfully.

Then she realized what she had on; a thin pink tank top that was way too short, and white panties. That was it. And the tank top was entirely too tight. Tight enough that he'd have to be blind not to notice that perhaps her room had been just a might chilly tonight.

She wasn't chilly now, however. Nope. She was quite warm as a matter of fact. Without glancing down to draw attention to things, though, she was pretty sure the sudden wave of warmth hadn't done much to solve the too-tight tank top problem. She was frightfully aware of the fabric tugging against certain body parts that she wished to God had stayed asleep for the night.

East took one quick peep then his eyes shot back up to her face. He swallowed.

"Granny called," he said. It sounded ominous. "She fell again."

"She fell?"

Marti said the words but it took a moment for their meaning to sink in.

"Granny fell again?" she repeated herself. "Oh God, is she okay?"

"Yeah, just kind of shaken up, I think," he said.

Marti rubbed her face, trying to wake up enough to figure out what to do next.

"Where's my purse?" she asked, pushing past him into the hallway. "Is she at the hospital? I've got to get over there!"

"Wait, wait," he said, and took her shoulders to slow her

momentum.

She slowed, all right. Everything in her body seized up under his touch except her heart rate. He turned her slowly to face him.

"It's okay," he said carefully, keeping his eyes fastened to hers. "She got up and back into bed. She promises that nothing's broken or anything like that. She didn't even want me to wake you up, but I thought you'd want to know."

Marti shook her head. "She was too tired after that damn party. I shouldn't have left so early. I should have stayed around to help her and Peg clean up. I should have taken her home myself."

"It's not your fault," East said.

His hands on her shoulders took on a soft, caressing motion. She supposed it was meant to calm her, but it was having the opposite effect. She had to pull away from him. She had to go help Granny, not stand here and melt in front of East.

"It was my idea to leave the party early," he said.

His voice was quiet. It still had that raspy, sleepy quality to it. And he was still gently brushing her shoulders with his fingertips.

"I was upset. I wasn't thinking about anyone but myself and it was my idea for us to get out of there," he went on.

Well, it was true that he'd been the first to grumble something about it being time to leave, but Marti certainly hadn't made any argument. They both were in no mood to stick around there with all that goodwill and happiness around them. As soon as Charleen announced it was time to get her kids home to bed, East and Marti had jumped on the chance to duck out, too.

They'd said a few cursory good-byes, thanked everyone for coming, then took off. Arriving back at the apartment, they'd each headed for their respective beds without so much as a word. No, neither of them had given much thought to helping Granny clean the place up.

In fact, Marti had been downright furious with the woman for even throwing the party. Oh God, she felt just awful.

"I was mad at her," Marti admitted. "I hardly even said good night when we left."

Now East's hands left her shoulders and slid right around her back. He wrapped her in his arms. Big, strong arms. Against his chest. Oh no; melting again.

"She's fine. It's okay, Marti. Stop shaking."

She was shaking? Yes, she was. And not because of Granny. Heaven help her, Granny was suffering all alone at home and here Marti was swooning at East's simple attempt to comfort her. But God it felt good to be in his arms again. Way, way too good.

She pushed herself away from him just enough to look up into his face. Was it her imagination or was he just a little bit hesitant to let go of her? Well, it wasn't like she was exactly struggling, or anything. Her body seemed stuck in slow motion when it came to pulling herself away from East's arms.

He touched her face. For a guy who made his living cooking for a TV camera, he had surprisingly rough, manly hands. She liked that. Then she found herself staring at his mouth. It was moving slightly, like he wasn't sure if he should just keep smiling that beautiful little sympathetic grin he'd been wearing for her or if he should say something.

"Don't worry, Marti," he said in barely more than a whisper. "She's just fine."

Good. Then she didn't have to feel guilty about not worrying anymore. She could concentrate all her energy on staring at East's wonderful, perfect mouth. What was he saying now? She wasn't listening. She was breathing him in, feeling him against her.

Thank God his arms were tightening around her. He was pressing her closer to himself. And that mouth? She desperately needed that mouth. If East didn't kiss her soon she was likely to start begging.

Good thing she didn't have to. He was smart enough to take the hint. And he took it well.

East was holding her tightly. His lips were soft, careful with her at first. The way he had been so many years ago when all this was new to them. He tasted her, teased her, touched her. She responded. She would have even if she'd tried not to. Just being close to him again brought everything back.

With her fingers skimming desperately over his naked back, searching for something to grab onto so he couldn't disappear, Marti brought her body as close to his as she could. It wasn't close enough. She wanted more, wanted all of East.

He seemed eager to comply with her demands. His kisses became more possessive, his embrace crushing the breath out of her. Every move she made he followed, his hands roaming over her body the way hers were discovering his. She felt him growing hard against her and the thrill this brought urged her to move against him.

Somebody moaned and their kiss was broken, only to allow East to shift his attentions to her neck and that sensitive spot near her ear. She gasped in as much air as her anticipating body would let her, but it really didn't seem to matter if she breathed or not. East was touching her, moving his lips against her skin, breathing for her. That's all she needed to survive forever.

In the fervor of their encounter Marti was now pressed against the wall of the little hallway. She was glad for the support, because her legs were decidedly too weak to hold her up. There was nothing weak about East, though, and she let him hoist her up so that her tiptoes were barely touching the floor. This put her most sensitive spot right directly where it should be and she arched into East.

He responded with a growl, pressing against her and bringing his mouth back to cover hers. She felt him, right there, held back only by their thin nightclothes. Oh God, if only she were naked.

But she could get naked! Heck, she could get East naked, too. They weren't wearing much, it wouldn't take long.

She slid her hands to the flannel pants. The drawstring waist was not pulled tight. She'd have them out of the way in a jiffy.

But before she'd reached her goal East's hands were off her body and gripping hers, forcibly holding his pants on. The sudden change in atmosphere was earth shattering.

"What?" she breathed.

"Wait," he replied and had the good sense to sound almost pained.

"What?" she repeated, blinking up at him.

His eyes were nearly black, the pupils ringed by violet. The emotion there was unreadable.

"You're only half awake," he said, leaving her to sag against the wall as he stepped back. "And you're upset about Granny."

Granny? What the hell did Granny have to do with making out with East?

But then she remembered. "Oh God, Granny!"

"Yeah." He swallowed. Hard. "We should get dressed."

Dressed. Of course, she had to get dressed and go to

Granny. The old woman needed her and she wasn't there. Damn, how could she have gotten so distracted?

Because East was here, and he was half undressed and even after all these years she still wanted him. Wanted him badly. So she'd gone and made a fool of herself with him, while Granny lay injured across town.

She couldn't meet his gaze anymore and ducked away from him. "I'll go get some clothes on."

"Yeah, me too," he said behind her. "I'll drive you there."

She didn't argue. In two steps she was back in her bedroom—his bedroom—and had the door shut between them. Damn, damn, damn! How could she have let herself get so carried away? How was she ever going to face him again?

Through the wall she heard the shower start up. Cold, she figured. And she smiled.

She may have acted like an idiot tonight, but she hadn't been alone. East was just as guilty as she was.

Chapter 15

East hadn't done anything, not really. So why did he feel like a slug? Like he was guilty, guilty, guilty?

Because he was, that's why. Marti hadn't even been fully awake, plus she wasn't thinking straight from being so upset about Granny. The last thing she needed was some guy pouncing on her like a hot-blooded teenager.

But that's exactly what he'd done. He'd taken one amazed look at her in those nearly-not-there underthings she'd been sleeping in, and he'd lost control. He'd gone after her and he almost hadn't stopped.

She didn't stop him, either. Man, just thinking of it got him heating up all over again. She'd responded to him with a very obvious willingness. For a few minutes there it had been just like ten years ago. He'd almost let himself forget everything that had happened in between.

Almost. But of course he couldn't do it. He'd taken advantage of her trust back then, and he wouldn't do it now. She'd trusted him to usher her into adulthood back when they were lusty teens, but he'd gone and fallen in love.

Today she just needed him to think straight and help Granny. He was damn well going to do that much for her. And nothing else, no matter how fantastic Marti looked just rolling out of bed in the middle of the night.

He pulled up the car in front of Granny's house. The street was dark and quiet, and just the dim hint of a nightlight glowed in Granny's front room window. It didn't look like she'd gotten out of bed to turn the porch light on for them. Too bad. Marti looked too damn good in the patchy light from the street lamps.

"She knows we're coming, right?" she asked quietly.

It was the first time she'd spoken since they hurried out of the apartment ten minutes ago.

"Yeah, I told her we'd be over."

"It's awfully dark."

"Don't worry, she's fine. I told her to stay in bed and wait for us."

He knew she had visions of the poor woman sprawled on the floor somewhere. Hopefully that wouldn't be the case. Granny was just a little shook up, that's why she called. By the time they got inside they'd find her back to her normal, spunky self.

"We should have gotten here quicker," Marti sighed.

East knew what she meant—those extra minutes in the hallway when they should have been on their way here. He put his hand on hers before she could unfasten her seatbelt and bolt inside.

"I'm sorry about that," he said. He was glad she wouldn't meet his eyes. "I was out of line. It won't happen again."

She just nodded and pulled her hand away. By the time he got unstrapped and out of the car she was already running up the sidewalk. Granny's door was unlocked so Marti didn't even have to dig the key out of her purse. He caught up and followed her inside.

"Granny?" Marti called out softly. "We're here, Granny."

Trixie came waddling around the corner, her tail wagging enough to throw her off balance. She didn't bark at them and East hoped that meant everything was fine and she was just glad for the company.

"Granny?" Marti called again.

"I'm in my room," Granny called back.

She didn't sound her old self, after all. Damn it.

Marti walked briskly, not bothering to turn on lights and half tripped over the dog. He guessed she would have run except for not wanting to startle Granny. They made their way back to Granny's bedroom and found her there, in bed with the phone on her chest.

"Oh, good. I'm glad you got here," she said weakly.

Despite what he'd been telling Marti all the way here, East had a really bad feeling about this. The Granny he knew would never just lie around waiting for someone to show up and help her. This was something different. Bad.

Marti sensed it, too. She carefully took the phone from Granny and set it on the nightstand. Granny smiled gratefully and snagged Marti's hand to pat it.

"That's my girl," she sighed. "I'm so sorry I had to bother the two of you, but I just didn't know who else to call."

"That's okay, Granny," Marti assured her. "It's no bother at all! I just wish I'd been here with you."

Granny shook her head.

"No, you've got a husband now, Marti girl. You need to be with him." Then she smiled at East and sighed. "I hated to bother newlyweds in the middle of the night like this."

East waited to catch the little gleam in Granny's eye to say she was just teasing them about the newlywed stuff. But there was no gleam. Just a sort of frightened confusion.

Marti frowned. "But you know we're not… I mean, of course you needed to call us. Now tell me what happened."

"Well, I was getting up for something. I don't know, but I think I was going to get a drink of water," Granny said, crunching up her forehead.

"So you were in the kitchen?" Marti prompted.

"No, no, I was in here. My hairbrush. That's it, I wanted my hairbrush."

"Your hairbrush?"

"Well, of course. I couldn't very well go in to work looking like a rat's nest on my head."

Marti glanced quickly at East. Her eyes said just how concerned she was. He was sorry his own expression couldn't have offered much consolation. Something was very wrong with Granny.

"So you were getting ready for work?" Marti asked slowly.

"Of course, honey. I was trying to call my manager to let him know I won't be in today, but I can't seem to get through."

"Manager?" Marti questioned.

"He needs to know I won't be there. They'll dock me for the whole day if I don't call in."

"You mean your manager at Pedersund? But Granny, that's been years. You haven't…"

"But there must be something wrong with the phone. It won't let the call go through."

Marti was looking more and more alarmed. He could see her chest rising and falling rapidly under the sweatshirt she'd thrown on. It was painfully obvious there was more going on here than they'd expected.

"It's okay, Granny," he said and put a comforting hand on Marti's shoulder. "I'll take care of calling in for you."

"Oh, that's good. I'm so glad my Marti linked up with a competent young man. Always knew you two would be good together."

"Granny, don't you remember why we…"

But East shook his head for Marti to keep quiet on that issue. Granny wasn't fully in touch with reality right now. If they started throwing too much information at her she might start to get scared.

"Right now we're a little worried about you, Granny," he said. "Remember? You called to tell us you fell down."

"Did I? Well, yes, I think I did. That's why my leg hurts."

"Which leg is it?" Marti asked, glancing up and down Granny's nightgowned body. "And did you hurt anything else?"

"No, I'm healthy as a horse," she said. "But maybe my elbow stings a little."

East leaned in to Marti's ear. "Why don't you let her show you where it hurts, and I'll go get some tea started. Come help me in the kitchen when you can."

He hoped she understood that he wanted to talk to her alone. Soon. And only about Granny. She nodded.

He left the room. Marti's voice followed him, light and deceptively calm.

"You must be getting pretty good at these falls, Granny," she said with a warm laugh. "How about if I take a look at your sore leg. Which one is it?"

He wasn't a medical genius, but didn't figure it would take one to recognize Granny was in real trouble. Three hours ago she'd been fine. Now she was laid up in bed thinking she worked at the factory she retired from nearly twenty years ago. And that her daughter was happily married.

There weren't a lot of harmless explanations for that.

———

"It could be a stroke."

"Don't say that!" Marti said.

She couldn't deny East's suggestion was logical, but she didn't even want to consider it. Granny couldn't have a stroke.

She wasn't old enough. She was healthy, aside from that darned arthritis that wouldn't let her hip heal right. She didn't even have high blood pressure. Not that Marti was aware of, anyway. Had Granny been keeping things from her?

No. It couldn't be a stroke.

"I don't like saying it," East went on. "But we have to consider it. She thinks we're really married. A couple hours ago she didn't. So, obviously something happened."

"Maybe she hit her head when she fell."

"Maybe. Either way, we need to get her to the hospital."

"You think it's that serious?"

"Marti, she thinks she still works at Pedersund. Heck, she quit working there when we were kids. The place has been shut down altogether for a couple years now. There's something wrong."

He was right. Something bad had happened to Granny. Denying it didn't make it less true.

"I know. So, what do we do?"

She hated feeling so helpless. Granny was the one who always took care of things. Jeez, even laid up with her hip she hadn't let Marti do much for her. Not that Marti had had a clue what to do anyway. Damn. For all her degrees and formerly successful career, she was totally useless where Granny was concerned.

So here she was turning to East, begging him—once again—to help her do the things that other people just seemed to instinctively know how to do.

"Don't worry," he said. And he sounded like he meant it. "You go in with Granny. Take her some tea. I'll call the squad."

"An ambulance? You think it's an emergency?"

"If she's got a concussion we need to know about it. If it's something worse, we don't want to waste a lot of time."

No, they didn't. All the terrible things that could be wrong with Granny kept running through her head. East was right. They didn't want to waste any time.

"Okay. Call them. You think it's okay if I explain to Granny what's going on?"

"I think that's a good idea."

He was smiling gently at her—fatherly, or something. Great. She was being such a wuss about this that's how he thought of her now, huh? Someone who needed taking care of, special treatment. Extra caution.

Well, he hadn't been being especially careful with her a half hour ago in the hallway. No, he wasn't fatherly then. He was amazing. The full-grown man version of everything she remembered from that summer after high school.

Until he remembered who she was. Or maybe he just realized the education they'd started back then pretty much stalled for her after he left. He'd probably expected her to be more than the naïve eighteen year old who laughed at the notion of heading to Hollywood with him.

Whatever his reason, it was clear he wasn't interested in picking up where they left off.

It won't happen again, he'd said.

And he meant it. The way he was looking at her now, she knew that for certain. He was pitying her, worrying about her, but not wanting her. She'd been stupid to throw herself at him like that.

Especially when she should have been here, with Granny. What was she going to do? Granny was all the family she had left.

Well, all the real family, anyway. Whatever her legal relationship to East, she knew he wasn't going to stick around here forever. And she was pretty sure there'd be no invitation to follow him to California this time.

Not that she'd take him up on it even if he did feel obligated to offer. But she wouldn't be laughing about it this time. That much was certain.

"So, are we going to keep doing this up at college?" she asked, and snuggled closer under the blanket they always kept in his car for just such occasions.

He didn't answer right away. Uh oh. She was afraid of that.

"Um, I don't know. Did you want to?" he finally said.

She'd been holding her breath and let it out slowly. "Well, it's great and all, but I know the whole point of this was to get ready for school. It's going to be awfully hard to meet new people... and stuff... if we're kind of a permanent item. Right?"

"Yeah."

"So, I mean, you weren't considering this kind of permanent, were you?"

She waited forever for him to say something, "Yes!" preferably. She wanted to hear that he really didn't want to meet new people, that she was enough for him. But he didn't. He just shifted his weight off of her and rolled to look up at the sky.

It was a beautiful sky, still streaked with little smears of pink and orange from the sunset. They'd come out here earlier than usual tonight. It had been three days since they'd been able to sneak away together and neither of them wanted to waste any time once they had their opportunity. Loving Johnny out here by the creek was the best thing she'd ever done.

Over two weeks now they'd been at it. Since that first night after Dixon's, when she suggested they give it a whirl. What a whirl it had been! Wow. It took her breath away.

The Bride Can't Cook

But now it was coming to an end, like she'd always known it would. In two days they'd be headed up to college and looking forward to new lives, new relationships. Some other girl was going to start spicing up Johnny's life for him. Heck, probably lots of girls. He'd never had trouble attracting them.

She tried to be glad that she'd always have the distinction of being the first, but lying here on his arm and feeling like he was a thousand miles away, that wasn't much comfort. How on earth were they going to go back to being pals? How was she going to survive seeing him every day in class and knowing all these wonderful things they'd done these last sixteen days had just been basic training for the real stuff? For the girls he'd find up there and make love to out of choice rather than convenience

And some of them would probably be pretty darn good at it. Hell, Johnny was the kind of guy girls flocked to. He'd have his pick of them up there at college; cheerleaders, sorority types, horny feminist professors. How long before he'd forget all about dull Marti Snowden and their simple practice sessions back home?

"You know, I've been thinking," he said and startled her. "What about, well, what if we didn't go to school here in Ohio?"

"What?"

"I know you say they've got a great program, and you've already met with some of the professors in your department and all, but I'm wondering if maybe it might be better somewhere else. For me."

Oh, God! What was he saying?

"I mean, I'm not like you Marti. I'm looking for a different kind of career. Sure, those biology classes you had me sign up for sound great, but am I really going to get the

experience I need... for my career, I mean?"

"There's all kinds of theatre stuff up there, Johnny," she said quickly. "Loads of it. You can take acting classes, directing, even filmmaking. Along with all the real stuff."

Now he was silent again. "So, acting isn't real stuff."

Oops. She hadn't meant to say that. She knew he took his dreams seriously. And he was good! He had the talent to make it, she believed that. Only... it just seemed like something so far away. How could he be an actor in Ohio? What sort of acting career could he really build here? His parents were right. He could do theatre all he wanted, but first he needed something to fall back on.

"I didn't mean that," she said, but it sounded lame. He knew she really did.

"I need to be in California, Marti."

Ouch. That was the last thing she wanted to hear right now. Mostly because she really couldn't argue with it. He wanted to be a movie star. You didn't do that in Ohio.

"Maybe we ought to look into that," he added.

We? She didn't dare let herself get optimistic, but he had said "we".

"It'd be so much cheaper with two of us paying rent and stuff," he went on. "And there are all sorts of opportunities for biologists and environmentalists out there. The place is crawling with them. I bet you'd have no trouble finding a school you liked and meeting the right people. And you'd be there to help me learn lines, and we could sort of help each other along. You know, until the careers really started kicking in, and all."

Oh, so that's what it would be. Roommates. Next door neighbors again. Best pals. "Until the careers started kicking in." Well, there was no way she was going halfway across the continent just so she could watch Johnny Smith become somebody else's sex symbol. Jeez, that would be pretty much the most horrible thing she could think of. By days she'd help him learn his lines and by night he'd be out screwing his leading lady! Actresses, dancers, lifeguards, horny feminist producers... God, it would be her worst nightmare come true.

She laughed at him. "No, Johnny, we're not going to California."

"Yeah, you're probably right," he'd said. Then it was like he forgot the conversation altogether. As the last bits of pink faded to cobalt in the sky, Johnny Smith wrapped her in his arms again and made her forget all about jobs and school and California. For a while.

She'd had no way of knowing that was his good-bye. The next day he was gone. He'd gone after his dream and she'd gone after hers. No, she'd not be laughing this time when he left.

"I'll take Granny the tea," she said and left him in the kitchen.

——

East made good tea. Had he put something extra in it? Some mint, maybe? He was a good kid. Good in the kitchen, too. Milly smiled as she sipped the warm beverage.

"Thanks, honey," she smiled at Marti, but was careful to keep her eyes from meeting the girl's.

Marti was watching her too closely. Had she started to figure things out? It wasn't like her to be suspicious, but she didn't want to take chances. So far this little scheme seemed to be working just fine, but she didn't want to push it.

Marti knew her well. One wrong move and she'd guess what was going on. Dishonesty was something Milly didn't have a lot of experience with, so no sense taking chances on getting found out.

"I'm feeling much better now," she sighed, settling back into her pillows. "You and your hubby took real good care of me."

"I'm just glad you didn't hurt your hip again," Marti said, fluffing and tucking around her.

Milly tried not to smile. Well, it would have been pretty hard to hurt herself in a fall that never happened, wouldn't it?

"I'm fine, sweetie," she assured her granddaughter. "I'll be just fine here. Now, why don't you and that handsome beau of yours head on back to your place. I'm sure you have better things to do that sit up with an old lady all night."

Yeah, lots better things, she thought.

Now that she'd gotten them out of their separate beds, and gotten their protective instincts and emotions all roused up, the best thing to do would be to send them back home where they'd have nobody but each other to think about. Marti would be worried and upset, and East would no doubt try to provide comfort. Yep, that ought to do the trick, or at least get the snowball rolling down the right hillside.

She'd seen glimpses of sparks between the two of them. Oh yes, she hadn't imagined it. All they'd needed was a gentle nudge in the right direction. And now she'd done that. She was actually fairly proud of herself.

"We're not going home, Granny," Marti said, ruining the nice warm feeling that had begun to settle over Milly.

"We're calling the ambulance. We want some of those nice young doctors at the hospital to get a look at you tonight."

Uh, oh! She'd played her part too well.

"What? Now honey, that's not necessary. I'm telling you, I feel much better. You saw for yourself I wasn't even bruising."

"Yes, but some of the things you said," Marti hesitated then broke into a warm, patronizing smile. "Well, we just want to be sure you didn't hit your head or anything."

Dammit, now these young brats thought she was off her rocker. *That* was not part of the plan. Not at all! She just wanted to catch them off guard, get those sentimental feelings flowing again.

"I tell you, Marti, I'm just fine," she insisted.

But Marti wasn't buying it. She just went on fluffing and tucking and patting her arm like she was some damned dementia patient. Well, this was not going to happen. She'd had no plans to visit any damn hospital tonight.

Milly sat up. "Listen here, Martha Kay, I'm just fine. I do not need no silly trip in an ambulance!"

East stepped into the room just as Marti tried to wrestle her back down onto the pillows.

"East," Milly called out to him. "Tell my granddaughter I most certainly do not need to be dragged off to the hospital."

But East just shook his head and came to help Marti.

"Now, Granny," he said like she was a damn two year old. "You've got us a little bit worried about you. We just want to make sure there's nothing wrong."

Milly had no choice but to flop back down onto her bed and let them fuss over her. Hellfire. Now how was she going to get out of this?

Those pimply young hotshots at County Memorial were going to put her through no end of grief when they couldn't find anything obviously wrong with her. No telling what she'd be in for. No. Absolutely she wasn't going.

Then she noticed the doe-eyed expression on Marti's face as she looked helplessly up at East. He gave her arm a light squeeze and smiled a beautiful I'll-take-care-of-things smile at her. Marti wilted a bit and leaned on him. Hell, no living female could resist East when he turned on the charm.

For a couple seconds Milly watched as the two of them just stared at each other. Oh yeah. Heat, sparks, mutual concern… all that stuff. Lordy, lordy. Maybe a trip to the ER was just what these two needed.

Okay, for these clueless lovers Milly could take a little poking and prodding. A *little*.

She could see the lights from the ambulance as it pulled into the driveway. *Well, the game's afoot now, Milly gal.*

"All right," she capitulated. "I'll go peacefully. But I don't want none of those new know-it-all's groping all over me. I want my doctor. You'd better make sure Dr. Traynor's there to look me over tonight."

Marti nodded and sighed in relief. "Okay, Granny. We'll see if the hospital can call him for you."

East went to let the paramedics in. Holy Toledo. What had she gotten herself into now? These gosh darn kids had better appreciate it someday.

——

"They're really worried about you, Milly," Dr. Traynor said.

"Of course they are. That's the idea."

Her old friend just laughed at her. "I've seen you pull some fine stunts to get your own way, Milly Snowden, but are you sure this one is such a good idea?"

"Look. Patient confidentiality means you can't tell them I was faking, and you'd better not, Milton Traynor. Just tell them you couldn't find anything. Keep me here for observation if you have to, but don't you dare breathe a word of this to those kids."

"They'd think I was nuts if I even tried to explain it to them."

Milly pulled the thin green hospital gown closer around her. Stupid contraption, all those snaps and ties that still didn't do a decent job of covering a body. And why in God's name did they see fit to keep this place so dang cold? Heck, if a person wasn't sick when they wheeled them in here they would be after an hour in one of these ice-box rooms.

"I'll tell them eventually what I did, and by then they'll be raising my great-grandkids and we'll all have a big laugh about it," she assured him.

Dr. Traynor just shook his graying head. She wished these blasted florescent lights didn't wash out all her color and highlight the crowsfeet she lotioned up every night. Even after all these years, Milton Traynor was a fine looking man.

"All right, all right. You win, as usual," he shrugged with a resigned sigh. "I'll see about getting you a room."

"Yeah, and make sure it's down in the basement, refrigerated with the morgue. I might be a little warmer there."

He shook his head and smiled at her. "Anything else you need?"

"No, just send the kids in, I guess," she said, then thought of something. "Oh, and one other thing."

"Yes?"

"Tell them… you might mention to them that some of my troubles could be from all the stress I've been feeling over that cooking contest I'm entered in."

"What? Milly, what on earth would that have to do with…"

"Just tell them they need to take it over for me. They've got to spend a couple hours a day working together on menus and recipes and planning a strategy."

"What?!"

"I'm serious, Milt. You tell them that's what I need to help me get better."

"But that's ridiculous."

"You like getting free pie whenever you walk in my door, don't you?"

"Milly, you can't be serious about this."

She glared at him.

"Okay, all right. I'll tell them."

She smiled. He just laughed and opened the door to leave. As an afterthought, he turned back to her and made a big production of marking something on her chart.

"What are you writing there?" she asked.

"As of this minute, you are on a low sodium diet. With high fiber."

He grinned at her just long enough for that to sink in, then he left. The heavy door clicked shut behind him.

Well, of all the… Now how did he think she was going to survive on that kind of crap? And in hospital food, to boot! It was outright cruelty.

She flung the pillow at the door and cursed.

Just because the man was a doctor and still had most of his hair, she was not going to be so liberal with her free pie anymore.

Chapter 16

Charleen scanned the hotel website. The place looked great: pool, sauna, gift shop, workout facility, complimentary breakfast. Not a bad place to spend a long weekend with Arv.

Too bad Marti Snowden would be there, too.

Wait. It was Smith now, wasn't it? Martha Smith. Yeah, that was her name now. Charleen smiled at the frumpy, frustrated housewife that name conjured for her. Sure, it was petty, but the image made her happy.

To go from being Dr. Marti Snowden to Mrs. Martha Smith was more than fitting. Definitely a step in the wrong direction for Saint Marti. Good. Trusty old Charleen could never hold a candle to Arv's fun and free-spirited Marti Snowden. Now maybe she stood a better chance of competing with a dowdy Mrs. Martha Smith.

As if changing names had made Marti any frumpier or dowdier. It hadn't. Last Monday at that damn surprise party Marti had been more glowing and radiant than ever. Especially when Charleen had walked outside and found her entertaining Arv in the sunset with some kind of cricket nymph or whatever the hell he said they'd been studying.

She pushed back in her chair and rubbed her eyes. Was he seeing her again today? Seemed like Arv had invented a reason every day this week to head back to Garden Falls. He had to meet with C.J. about insurance, had to visit the bank, had to borrow something from his dad. Who knew what all else. And every time he managed to find a half hour to stop in at Granny's diner.

She guessed that since he kept telling her all about it she shouldn't worry. It seemed innocent enough. East was there, too, so he said. But how did she know for sure? She didn't know anything anymore.

She thought she knew Arv. Thought she understood his motivations, thought she trusted him. But now that their restaurant was gone, he was a different guy. It scared her, if she was honest about it.

But she didn't want to be honest about it. She wanted to go on pretending things were just fine for Mr. and Mrs. Arv Koch. But they weren't. They hadn't been for a long time. She'd just been too busy to notice before now.

Not busy anymore, that was for sure. These last days since the fire she'd gotten down-right tired of relaxing. Sure, right at first there'd been all sorts of things to do and business to get squared away. But now, two weeks later, even her house was clean. And she hated housework.

It had made sense when Arv was a slovenly, depressed basket case the week after the restaurant burned. *That* she could understand. Hated it, but she understood it.

But this week he was another person. Ever since that stupid party he'd talked Granny into he'd been, well, happy. It was like after that night he'd been recharged, or something. And the only thing she could think of was that night he'd seen Marti again.

He'd been completely against going up to the cook-off once the restaurant burned. If he couldn't compete, no way in hell was he going up just to watch. Only a moron would suggest that, right? Then the minute he found out Granny and her clan were heading up there, he was all for it. So disgusting.

And he just couldn't figure out why she was upset. He barely noticed it, in fact. No, Arv was all caught up in helping his buddies get ready for that damned competition. Since Granny was all of a sudden not feeling well this week, East and Marti had started working overtime to get things ready for the competition. Arv dove right in with them.

Heck, she'd be lucky to get to eat a meal with her own husband up at the hotel in a couple weeks.

Well, that was fine with her. Who needed Arv? It's not like she needed him to enjoy herself. She couldn't remember the last time they'd done anything fun together, so she was pretty sure she'd do just fine without him.

The kids would be visiting at her parents' house nearby, and she'd have the pool and the hot tub to occupy her time. It would give her a chance to think through some stuff. Like whether or not she wanted to come back to Finster with Arv and start rebuilding.

Insurance might be going to cover their burned down business, but C.J. Smith didn't carry anything that covered burned-out marriages.

——

"Thirteen days," East reminded her.

"Shut the hell up," Marti snapped.

He laughed, but didn't let her see it. She wasn't in a laughing mood. Basically this whole week since that party and then Granny's spell, she'd been overly serious.

The doctor hadn't found anything specific, so that was good. Granny stayed at the hospital all through that next day, though by dinnertime she was getting downright militant about the food. It wasn't any surprise when the doctor had her released first thing Wednesday morning.

The only thing he could figure was she'd gotten herself so worked up over the up-coming cook-off that the extra effort of throwing that surprise party Monday night sent her into exhaustion. Didn't make a lot of sense to East, but he wasn't going to argue with a sixty-year-old medical doctor. So, Granny was confined to two weeks of R&R, while Marti and East promised to spend at least two hours a day working on their menus and procedures for the competition.

Supposedly that would help keep Granny's mind off worrying about it, but so far it hadn't seemed to do much of that. Seemed for the last four days that's all she wanted to talk about. How's this going, how's that going? How many hours did you two kids work on the soup recipe today? What sort of bread will you be serving? Do we have the right kind of pans? Need more wooden spoons?

God, it was torture.

And she'd really caught them off guard when she'd drawn up a chart to track the days left before the competition. Tuesday had started the countdown at seventeen days. Didn't seem like a big deal, until that whole thing from Dixon's restaurant ten years ago flashed through his brain.

He wasn't sure why, but somehow it hit him. Monday had been the eighteenth day before this damned cook-off started. Eighteen. There was that number again, out of the blue. And Monday was the night he'd very nearly dragged Marti down onto the hallway floor and made love to her until they were both begging for mercy.

Eighteen was a bad, bad number for them.

But now they were past that. Thankfully, Granny's confusing illness was just what they needed to get their minds out of the gutter and off each other's bodies. Since coming back to their apartment in the early morning hours of Tuesday it had been easy to keep everything focused on

Granny.

Well, it seemed to have been pretty easy for Marti. She hadn't even mentioned what they'd almost done Monday night. He had the distinct impression she might not even remember. That didn't exactly sit well with his manly ego, but at least it made living with her more comfortable.

They discussed their concern for Granny, talked about their game plan for this competition, and basically were getting along better than before. If you didn't count the way East realized he had to avoid looking at Marti if he wanted to avoid having *those* kinds of thoughts about her. And he wasn't sleeping worth a darn, but there wasn't much he could do about that.

The fact of the matter was he really couldn't avoid having *those* kinds of thoughts about Marti. He wanted her, plain and simple. He liked having her around. He even liked when she ignored him because, dammit, it was *him* she was ignoring and not some other guy.

"We have to be up there, turn in our menus, and be ready to cook in thirteen days," he said. "I don't think they're going to let us scrape stuff up off the floor and use it again."

She was ignoring him—again—and kept on scooping up noodles to dump them back into the colander. She ran them under hot water. Yeah, she was planning to use them again, wasn't she?

"Well if the damn strainer here wasn't so hot I wouldn't have dropped them!" she said. "And nobody's really going to eat this."

"*I'm* going to eat this."

"Well, that's what I mean."

"You mean I'm nobody. I'm freaking nobody now!"

Sleep deprivation was definitely taking its toll on his coping skills. That and constantly having to battle those memories of kissing her in the hallway.

"I meant 'nobody' like a paying customer," she said. "Jeez, you're so touchy. It's not like you didn't just bleach down the floor in here anyway."

"You've got to keep any area where food is prepared clean."

"Why? So you still have to throw away a noodle if you drop it on your perfectly hygienic floor?"

"That wasn't just a noodle. It was a whole damn pot of them."

"And it's just for practice! Nobody's going to eat them."

"*I'm* going to eat them!"

God, it was like arguing with a wall. A really sexy wall with breasts that jiggled just right as she shook the water out of the colander, but still a wall.

She turned and glared at him. He tried to ignore the jiggling breasts.

"You are going to *taste* this. You're not going to eat it, you're going to *taste* it. There's a big difference," she said.

He knew what he'd rather get a taste of.

"Okay, okay. You're right. I'm just going to taste it. We've still got leftovers from the last three days in the fridge, so I guess it's safe to say we won't be taking this one home, too."

She smiled. She sure did like winning.

He pulled out the big bowl they were going to use to mix the noodles and white sauce concoction.

"Here's the mixing bowl."

He turned to hand it to her just at the same time that she turned to bring the colander of noodles over to the counter. They collided and—once again—the noodles were on the floor.

The edge of the mixing bowl caught his foot just right as

it fell, pinching a nerve. Sharp stinging pains shot all the way up to his knee. Holy crap! Cooking with Marti was dangerous in just about every way he could think of.

He bent to rub his tingling foot. Marti bent to start scooping noodles again. They crashed heads.

"Ouch!" she yelled, staggering back. Her foot slipped on noodles and she cracked her elbow on the sink. At that point she was yelling a few other things, too.

East grabbed the counter to support himself as he waited for the nerve in his foot to stop spasming. Too late he discovered the vegetable peeler was still sitting out. It left two nice slices in the palm of his hand. When he jerked his hand away, it was his turn to slip on the noodles. He finally stopped gracelessly flailing when he slammed, spread eagle on his back, into the pile of noodles.

Damn it, not again. He stared up at her. She was clinging to the sink with one hand, and covering her mouth with the other. Her golden eyes were huge and damned if he didn't see some honest concern there. Hell, if near-death kitchen mishaps could make Marti worry about him, bring 'em on!

But then she squeaked. It wasn't a worried squeak, either. Nope. She was laughing, and trying to hide it.

So, laughing at his misery, was she? Well, he'd see about that. He grabbed her ankle. When she tried to pull away she lost her footing on the slippery mess and came crashing back down on top of him. He thought it was probably her elbow that dug into his arm.

Yeah, it hurt, but it was a good kind of hurt. He had Marti right where he wanted her. And boy did he want her.

She screeched and squirmed around, trying to get off of him. Arms and legs and pasta went everywhere until finally she gave up and flopped down onto his chest.

"All right, you win," she said when she could finally get

her breath. "We won't be using those noodles again."

He met her eyes, his gaze holding hers as they lay on the floor, breathing in unison. It felt so right, so perfect. Except for the slimy noodles coating them, of course, and the bruises and mild lacerations, but having Marti plastered against him like this was heaven. What would she do if he kissed her again?

Hell, what *could* she do? Beat him up? Too late. Maybe he ought to just give it a shot. He slid his arms around her and felt her body stiffen. Getting ready to slug him, or just to leave? He really shouldn't, but it was just so damn tempting. He held her tighter, pinning her arms down just in case. Maybe a couple soothing words to get her more into the mood.

Yeah, that might work. Maybe he ought to tell her about that little project he'd been working on. It was still in the early stages and he'd wanted to wait until it was more certain, but she sure would be happy to hear about it. In fact, she might even be just a bit grateful. He had some fabulous suggestions for just how she could express her gratitude.

"Marti, I…"

But he was interrupted.

"Jeez, are you two all right in there?"

The kitchen door swung open with a bang. Feet clattered through it as several bodies hurried in to check on what must have sounded like World War Three. Damn. Marti was climbing off him.

Ouch. She wasn't being any too careful about where she put her knees, either. Maybe that was on purpose.

"Holy shit! What happened?"

It was Arv. He came around the counter just in time to see Marti staggering up to her feet. East just glared up at him from the floor. Charleen was right there, too, wide eyed and disgusted.

"Just another day in the kitchen with Marti," East said with a sigh. *Another painful, frustrating day.*

"Oh, so this is all my fault," Marti snapped, picking noodles out of her hair and off her clothes. "It's always my fault to you."

"No, I didn't say that," East said and let Arv help him up.

"You think I'm just worthless for anything but..." Marti began.

She clenched and unclenched her fists a couple times and never finished the sentence. Arv and Charleen took a step back, clearly figuring out they stopped in at the wrong time. Damn. A second ago it had seemed like the very right time.

Finally Marti took a deep breath and continued. "Well, I'm just glad this stupid contest is almost over. Then I won't have to put myself through this anymore and you can just go back to your fake kitchen."

Oh yeah, it was the wrong time for visitors. Arv and Charleen gulped audibly. East felt like clenching his fist and putting it through a wall right now.

Hell, all he'd done was put his arms around her! Was she so pissed off by that she was going to blab the whole thing about their fake marriage and how she really hated him? Had he really been that awful to live with?

And to think he'd been stupid enough to believe they'd been getting along lately. He'd started hoping maybe she would... well, obviously she wouldn't. She'd been working her tail off on this contest for Granny, and that was all there was to it. She was putting up with East just because she had to. Maybe he was still hopelessly stuck on her, but she'd been over him a long, long time. He was an idiot to hope for anything more.

"I'm going to take a shower," Marti announced, throwing

another handful of noodles into the sink. "At Granny's. You can clean this up since you're so much better in the kitchen than I am."

She barely even acknowledged the Koch's as she stormed out. Wow, she was steamed. He hadn't seen her like that for a good long time. It made him want her even more.

"Sorry, we were in town on business and thought it might be nice to stop in," Arv said sheepishly when the door slammed shut behind Marti.

"Yeah, uh, sorry for the mess," East said.

"Mom!" East recognized Arv's kids as they came marching into the kitchen.

"He sucked milk into his straw and then spit it at me!" the girl kid complained.

"It was an accident!" the boy insisted.

"Two times?" the girl added.

"All right, come on," Charleen sighed, kind of like Marti had done a minute ago, then sent Arv a look that said he'd better help with the noodles. Women sure didn't need to use half as many words as they usually did.

Charleen ushered the kids back out to the dining area and Arv dutifully went for the mop.

"Hey, thanks, but that's okay," East said. "This is only the second time today I've cleaned up this pile of noodles. I'm getting really good at it."

Arv snorted and shook his head in a sort of been-there-done-that-didn't-like-it way.

"Man, if you don't want to spend the next two weeks sleeping on the couch," he said. "You'd better get over to Granny's and start groveling."

East just crouched down and started scooping noodles. He couldn't help but laugh. "Buddy, if you only knew."

"Knew what?"

East glanced up at his friend. Arv was a good guy. He'd been through the Marti gauntlet and he'd survived. Come out on top, as a matter of fact. He was crazy about Charleen and loved his kids. All things considered, Arv might actually be able to handle the truth. Okay, why not let him in on their little secret?

"Want to hear something hilarious?" East began. "I've already been on the couch for two weeks."

Chapter 17

"I'm telling you, I don't need to see the stinking doctor," Granny said and sounded like a stubborn little kid.

"Dr. Traynor does not stink," Marti replied. "He usually smells pretty good actually, and he says he wants to see you weekly, so we're going in weekly. Now be a good girl and get your purse."

"I'm not a child, you know," Granny said, but she went and got her purse.

"Could have fooled me," Marti grumbled.

Oh, well. She guessed she could understand Granny's reluctance to get checked out. She'd seemed fine ever since that night they'd taken her to the hospital, just over a week ago. The doctor hadn't found any signs of a stroke or heart attack, so he'd just chalked Granny's fall and subsequent confusion to stress.

That must be it, too. Since then East and Marti had taken over all the contest planning—under Granny's determined supervision, of course—and made sure they kept the bickering and complaining to a minimum. At least around her. Granny seemed to be actually enjoying watching everyone else do all the work. She hadn't had any signs of further difficulty.

Still, Marti was going to be bullheaded about the doctor. If he said he wanted Granny to come in there today, by golly they were going in.

Granny groused about it all the way out to the car.

"Dang doctor knows there's not a thing wrong with me. I told him so myself."

"And I'm sure he appreciated the input. But you're going in, if East has to come over here and carry you," Marti assured her. She knew he'd do it, too. He'd been just as worried about Granny as she had. That seemed to be the only thing they could actually talk about these days.

"I'm going. But I still say there's not a thing wrong with me and I can drive myself."

Marti helped her into the car. "No driving. Not for a couple weeks; until we're sure you won't have another spell."

"I didn't have no spell. I'm fine."

"I know. That's why we're going to the doctor, just to make sure of that."

Granny harrumphed. "It's a waste of everyone's good time."

"Now, I bet Dr. Traynor's been looking forward to your visit all day. You're not going to spoil it for him by being grumpy, are you?"

"I'm going to give him a piece of my mind for dragging me over there when he knows there ain't a darn thing wrong with me."

Marti laughed. Good thing Dr. Traynor had known Granny since high school. He wasn't likely to be put out over her obstinate gruffness. And he probably really *was* looking forward to Granny's appointment today. He seemed to actually get a kick out of dealing with her when she was in the hospital last week.

"So we've got confirmation on our hotel," Marti said, deciding to change the subject and go over some business. "Though I still say I ought to room with you."

"Don't start up with that again, Martha Kay," Granny

said. "It's going to be awful important up there that no one gets the idea things aren't peachy keen between you and your husband."

Here we go again. "Granny, no one's going to care if I'm sleeping with East. I mean, staying in the same room and all. You know what I mean."

"I know what you mean, and it sure will look funny, two healthy young people like you, just married a few weeks, and you rooming with me instead of him. That's all I'm saying."

"Good."

"Besides," Granny added. "I might want to bring someone else up there to room with me."

Marti took her eyes off the road long enough to slide Granny a quick glance. "Oh? Peg?"

"Naw. She's going to be staying with her son who lives up there."

"Oh. So, who?"

"I got friends, don't I?"

"Yeah, I just wondered…"

"Well I thought I might like to invite a friend up there with me. So you just don't worry about it. You stay in your own room with your husband, and I'll take care of myself."

"Okay."

Well, Granny sure hadn't mentioned anyone else coming along on this venture. Huh. Then again, she was just probably trying to make sure Marti didn't talk her way out of rooming with East. Whatever. Let Granny cling to her little fantasy a while longer. This would all be over soon and she'd have to face reality then. In the meantime, Marti knew what she was up to.

Oh, yes, it had been painfully obvious these last couple weeks that Granny was determined to throw Marti and East together as much as possible. She insisted on making a big deal in public about them being "newlyweds" and basically forced them into keeping up the pretense even if she was their only audience. Apparently she liked having East for a grandson-in-law and was hoping to keep him around. Well, sorry for her, but it wasn't going to work.

Ever since that night of Granny's fall, when Marti had been so stupid and practically ambushed East there in the hallway, he'd made it clear this arrangement was very, very non-permanent. Maybe he really hadn't minded her throwing herself at him, but it wasn't anything more than just physical. Yeah, she'd gotten the idea a couple of times that he wouldn't mind if she'd offer just a casual fling to pass the time, but she couldn't bring herself to do that.

So, the only thing they had in common now was Granny and the contest. The only time she really saw him—except in passing—was when they were working on recipes and making plans. The rest of the time he was busy with who knew what else.

Well, she was pretty sure she knew what else. She'd heard him on the phone with his agent. Somebody wanted him for some project that was gearing up. They wanted him now, but she'd heard him putting the agent off, saying he was committed through the end of the month. That meant through the cook-off. But she was pretty sure he sounded interested in this project. That meant he'd be gone soon.

She just wondered when he'd bother to tell her. *If* he'd bother to tell her this time. Maybe she'd just wake up one morning and he'd be gone. Again. Just like ten years ago.

"…So Arv's not sure what they're going to do now," Granny was saying when Marti's mind finally quit wandering.

"What?"

"Charleen's not overly excited about rebuilding there in

Finster so he's not sure where they'll end up."

"Who told you that?" Marti asked.

"East."

"Oh? And how does East know all that?"

"Arv told him. When he was here in town a few days ago."

Oh, yeah, she'd seen Arv, too, hadn't she? Hadn't presented herself very well, harping at East and dripping with noodles. East just hadn't mentioned that he'd actually spent time chatting with Arv that day.

"So, East got a chance to talk to Arv?"

"That's what I was just telling you! Pay attention, dear. Yes, they were in town meeting with C.J. about some insurance issues. I guess Charleen took the kids shopping and Arv hung out with East for a while. Seems like they're best buddies again, getting together and doing stuff. It's nice."

Huh. East told her he'd been working in the kitchen that evening. He hadn't mentioned anything about 'hanging out' with Arv. Wonder how he'd explained that whole noodle incident? Jeez, she sure had made a fool of herself. Arv and Charleen must have wondered what was going on. What did East tell them?

It was as if he couldn't be bothered to have a simple conversation with her anymore. He probably told Arv how there was no way they were going to win this contest since she was so incompetent. Yeah, that's probably why he hadn't mentioned talking to them.

But how insulting! She'd been working her tail end off in that kitchen. She'd come a long way, too. He just hadn't noticed because he was only interested in getting this over with and getting back to his great important job. He was just putting up with her because he had to. And to think she'd practically molested the guy.

Yeah, and that's probably why he was keeping his distance. He knew she still had a thing for him, and he didn't want any part of it. God, how humiliating.

"How nice for them," she muttered.

"Well, I should think Charleen ought to be more supportive of her husband," Granny said. "A man needs to know his woman is behind him."

Yeah, in East's case it was far, far behind him.

"Maybe Charleen just got tired of watching her man spend all his time on everything and everyone else," Marti suggested.

Granny just shrugged. "Maybe. I don't know what goes on behind their closed doors. But I know East is pretty worried for them."

So worried he never even mentioned it to her? "I think East has enough of his own worries right now," Marti said, changing the subject again. "He can't quite decide on the menu for the second day of the competition."

"Oh? The lunch competition? I thought he was going for the beefy and noodles."

"Well, we made a couple attempts at that last night and he just wasn't happy with the results."

"Did he follow my recipe?"

"Yes, but he said it just wasn't right."

"What did you think?"

"Me? Oh, well I thought it was good. But he's probably right."

Granny smiled. "There, now that's the way it ought to be. The woman supports her man and trusts his judgment."

"Stop it, Granny. He's not my man."

"He's your lawful wedded husband."

"Lawful, maybe, but we're not 'wedded'. Not really. You know that."

"So even after living with each other for almost three weeks you haven't…"

"No, we haven't!" Jeez, she did not want to discuss this. Not with Granny or anyone.

"Not ever?"

Ugh. It was her worst nightmare, Granny asking questions like this. What was she supposed to do, start lying to her after all these years?

"Granny, East and I are both adults. I don't think our past experiences are really open for public discussion."

But Granny didn't want to give up. "I wasn't asking whether you two had ever done it with other people. Sheesh, Marti girl, I know East's been married and you were with that Hedgeman fellow…"

"I was not!" Oops, she'd said that a little too fast. Should have thought first before piping up.

"You weren't?" Granny was blinking wide eyes at her now. "Really? But you were living with him!"

"Look, I don't mean to be rude, but it's not really your business what I did or didn't do with Leland Hedgeman."

"Well. All right, then."

Granny sat back, stared primly forward and folded her hands in her lap. Marti could have kicked herself for being short with her like that. Damn. Granny was just being her grandmother, caring about her and all. But she simply didn't know how complicated everything was! And how much Marti really did not want to think about what did not happen with Leland Hedgeman or what did with East Smith.

They pulled into the parking lot at the medical complex. Finally. Marti parked the car and was reaching for her seat belt when Granny laid a hand on hers to stop her.

"What about Arv?"

Marti gulped. "What?"

"You dated him for a while. Did you… with him?"

"Granny!"

"I'm just asking. Nothing wrong with two grown women discussing this stuff. I'd like to know, that's all."

"Okay, fine," Marti sighed. Arv she didn't mind talking about. "No, I did not ever have a physical relationship with Arv. Despite the word that apparently got back to town, he and I were just friends, okay?"

"Well, that's good to hear. I have to say, I was a little concerned about him coming around so much, knowing things might not be happy at home, and all."

"Trust me. I'm not likely to start up a tawdry affair with Arv, okay?"

"Good. What about East?"

"East? No, he's not likely to, either. He might be an actor and all, but I'm pretty sure he prefers girls."

"Oh, stop it!" Granny scolded with a scandalized grin. "I meant *you* and East. Was there ever anything there?"

"Look, you're going to be late for your appointment. We need to get inside."

Granny was just watching her. Darn it, but Marti couldn't seem to get her fingers to work right to unhook the seat belt. Why'd Granny have to go and start asking those kinds of questions, anyway?

Finally Granny just sighed and turned to gathering up her purse and unhooking her own seat belt. Marti managed to get hers done and hurried around to help Granny out of the car. She took a few deep breaths to get her breathing back under control and hoped her face wouldn't tell the whole world just what turmoil her mind was in after being stupid enough to start answering Granny's questions.

"There we go," she said when Granny was up and out of the car. That exercise was still hard on her hip.

Granny held onto her arm and patted it. "What about any of those other boys up at college? Or off on any of those projects you worked on?"

What? She wasn't done with the inquisition yet? Good grief. "Granny!"

"I'm just asking."

"Look, I really did work on those assignments, not just chase after guys, you know," she said.

Granny just smiled and nodded. "All right, I can take a hint. No more questions."

Thank God! She let Granny lean on her as they walked toward the door of Dr. Traynor's office.

"I guess I just didn't realize," Granny said with a sigh. "This must be hard for you. I'm sorry."

"Getting you to the doctor? No, it's no trouble, Granny."

"No, not that."

"Then what are you talking about?"

Granny stopped right there in the parking lot and looked her in the eye. She was perfectly serious. "It's only ever been Johnny for you, hasn't it?"

Marti just blinked back at her, wondering how on earth she came up with that. And wishing it weren't so damn true.

Granny shook her head and started leading them toward the doors. "I guess I shouldn't have made you go off and live with him, then, should I?"

"No, you shouldn't have," Marti agreed. Every second she spent around East was just going to make it that much harder to watch him leave again.

"I'm sorry," Granny repeated.

"Don't be. That damage was done a long time ago."

Granny just shook her head and clucked her tongue. "It's tough being in love with one man for all your life, hon. Especially when that one man ain't around anymore."

Susan Gee Heino

They were at the door and stepping inside so Marti didn't get to ask Granny what she'd meant by that. She didn't really think she needed to, though. Grandpa had been gone nearly twenty years now and Marti sure had never seen Granny look at anyone else. Guess they had a little more in common than she knew. Huh. Go figure.

———

"There's no reason on earth why I shouldn't be allowed to drive my car."

Dr. Traynor stopped thumping her back and leaned around to frown at her.

"Now, Milly," he said. "You're the one who wanted me to play along with your little fainting charade."

"But I'm perfectly fine!"

"But what sort of doctor would let a patient who'd blacked out and had a spell of dementia go out driving a car the day after that?"

"It's been a whole frigging week, Milton."

The overpaid fool had the nerve to actually laugh at her for that.

"You're the one who wanted to fool the kids. You still haven't told me why, by the way. It's not every doctor who will essentially lie for one of his most disagreeable patients."

He was going to start poking around in her ears, so she pushed him away. He knew there was nothing wrong with her, blast him. She shouldn't have to go through these indignities.

"I didn't ask you to lie. Just tell them you weren't really sure what caused my problems that night."

He put his little light scope down on the counter and leaned back, crossing his arms on his chest. Not at all a bad

226

chest for a man his age. Not that Milly Snowden still noticed things like that on a man. Much.

"And just what exactly *did* cause your problems that night?" he asked.

"I told you. It was to help the kids out."

"Yes, that's what you said, but I haven't quite figured out exactly how worrying about you for a week now has been any sort of help for them."

"It's been a lot of help, actually," she was happy to say. "It did exactly what it needed to."

"Which is?"

"Get them thinking about me instead of their own pitiful selves for a change."

Now he shook he head and tsk-tsked her. "Milly. That doesn't sound like you. Are you so jealous of your granddaughter's happiness that you want to come between her and her new husband?"

She went ahead and smacked his arm. Hmm. Still nice and firm. He must do a lot of yard work, or something.

"Don't be ridiculous," she scolded. "I'd never want to do anything to come between Marti and her happiness. In fact, that's what this is all for; to fix things up so she *can* be happy."

"Fix things up? How on earth…"

"Look, I'll tell you because I know you aren't allowed to go around telling anyone else." Milly glanced around to make sure the intercom was turned off and there weren't any pesky nurses just about to step through the exam room door. "Things between Marti and Johnny Smith aren't all that they should be."

His dark, arching brows went up. "Oh?"

"They got married because they *had* to."

His eyebrows went up even more. "Oh? I thought they

hadn't seen each other for years until East got back into town? That was just a few weeks ago."

"Now don't go getting the wrong idea here. It ain't *that* kind of had-to-get-married."

Now the brows came down and he frowned. "I didn't realize there was any other kind."

"There is." And she explained to him how she'd sold off part of the diner and then found out she'd earned her invite to the cook-off after all. He was suitably congratulatory, until she explained that she'd been ineligible until East married Marti. Then he got a bit testy.

"Do you mean to tell me you let those kids get married just so you could get into some dumb cooking contest?"

"It's not just some dumb cooking contest!" she informed him, moving close enough to jab her finger into his chest. "It's a big deal, and of course I didn't know what those kids were up to until it was too late. That's why I said I'm trying to fix things!"

"And just exactly how do you plan to do that?"

"That's where I needed to have that spell for them. See? They get all concerned for me, Marti starts weeping and worrying and East is there with his big strong shoulder to cry on. Bingo! We get fireworks and they end up happily married."

"Bingo, huh?"

"Well, it might be a little bit harder than I thought. I didn't realize they'd already… well, it looks like it's a little more complicated than I planned on."

He chuckled. "You're kidding. Complicated enough to slow you down?"

"Naw. They'll get it worked out," she said and was even surprised herself by the confidence she heard in her voice. "Marti's been crazy about Johnny for years. He's bound to realize eventually how perfect she is for him."

The doctor just sighed and shook his head. She liked the little smile he gave her, even though she had to admit there was something decidedly sad behind it.

"I don't know, Milly," he said. "Sometimes it seems like maybe the other person never quite gets the hint."

She scooted back up onto the table and straightened her skirt. "Then that other person is a flat out idiot. No, these kids are made for each other. One way or another, I'll get East to see the light."

He laughed again and grabbed up his scope. "Fine, Milly. You go right on ahead and do that. And once you've succeeded, be sure and tell me how you did it."

"Tell you? Won't need to. I'm expecting you to help me on this. I might have to get a whole lot sicker before this is all over, you know."

"Oh? You got something planned I ought to know about?"

"Well, actually," Milly paused, then decided to go all the way with it. "How does Friday night in the ER sound for you?"

"Sounds great," he replied and she wasn't quite sure she altogether liked the sly little grin he slid her way. Mostly she liked it. She just wasn't used to liking things like that.

"I mean how about if I pretend to have another spell Friday night," she clarified.

He just chuckled as he got back to checking out her ears. "I know, Milly. It's all for the kids. All right, I'm in. Just tell me what you need."

Well, that was rather open ended. She hoped he meant it. "Actually," she began, wishing she had a little more of that confidence back. "I was hoping I could maybe interest you in going up to a certain cooking contest with me."

Chapter 18

It was the first day of June. A Wednesday. Kind of rainy, but that didn't matter. From the looks of the schedule he'd just been handed, East could see they weren't going to be outside much.

He wasn't going to be alone with Marti in their nice, cozy, king-sized-bed hotel room much, either. She'd nearly thrown a fit when she found out they'd been booked into a king rather than two doubles. He made some excuse to the clerk about how he snored a lot, but they still got some curious looks. Apparently someone had informed the hotel that they were newlyweds and wanted all kinds of romantic extras, like the Jacuzzi tub in their bedroom or the chocolate covered strawberries waiting in the kitchenette beside the chilled champagne.

For a minute Marti had glared at him as if he'd been the guilty party, but that only lasted until Granny made some remark about how Marti should just calm down and make the best of things. Yeah, that pretty much shifted suspicion right away. *Granny.* Yeah, this had her fingerprints all over it. Subtlety had never been her strong point.

But the hotel was full and it would have taken an act of God to switch their room around. Tasters, competitors and spectators from all over the state had arrived and the Family Favorites Cook-Off was set to open tomorrow. East had had no idea this was such a big deal. Or why. But they had celebrity judges from the best of the B list on hand to give the whole thing a glamorous touch. He wondered if they'd turn out to be anyone he knew. Wouldn't that be a hoot?

Marti hadn't been about to waste time sitting in the honeymoon suite with him, so she insisted they get with Granny down in the lobby to go over some last minute plans. It was hard to concentrate in the stuffy little alcove they'd chosen. There was a gently trickling water feature, soft music over the intercom, and Marti sitting right beside him taking copious notes and frowning as if her very life depended on comprehending things. Mostly he just wanted to daydream about what being alone with Marti in a king sized bed might be like. In the past they'd never quite made it past a blanket spread out in the field beside Tylers Branch.

And that had been pretty good. Even after all his wild times out in California, East still had to rank those nights with Marti among the most exciting. He wondered how they still stacked up for her when compared to subsequent experiences? His gut clenched at the thought and he decided he'd better not go there anymore. He'd do well to keep his thoughts fixed firmly in the present.

Granny had them go over their game plan—and over it, and over it, and over it. It couldn't hurt to be too prepared, she kept telling them. Tomorrow morning would come awfully early, and East wasn't likely to get much sleep tonight. And not in the good way, either. His nerves and Marti's proximity were bound to mess him up.

But morning would come and that meant he had to cook get up and cook. Day One of the competition was breakfast, Day Two was lunch, and Day Three was a full course dinner with all the fixin's. That's how this was structured.

Each day the tasters—a panel of regular folks who paid big bucks to sample the entries and be treated like royalty at the hotel—and the three celebrity judges would assign scores. Breakfast and lunch would be worth twenty points while dinner would be worth forty. After dinner on Day Three there'd be a huge black tie awards ceremony. Granny'd bought a new dress and everything. He sure hoped they didn't embarrass her.

"Don't worry," he said, bringing the little pep session to a close before Marti had a nervous breakdown. She was starting to look a pale with all the info Granny was trying to dump on her.

Granny must have noticed it, too, so she patted her hand gently. "Aw, honey, if you're so nervous, I guess maybe I could let you sit out tomorrow and—"

East cringed. They'd been over this already. Repeatedly. Granny was in no condition to take on the pressure of cooking a meal for them. If Marti wasn't up for it, either, he didn't know what they'd do. But she surprised him.

"No, Granny," Marti said, taking a deep breath and sitting up straight. "I've got this. You're a good coach and you've done your bit. I just need to do mine."

Granny didn't seem so sure about that. "I know you're only doing this for my sake, and I appreciate it, but I can see you aren't the least bit happy about it."

"I'm fine," Marti persisted. "I just need to know you're going to relax and not stress out over this, okay? You've been in the ER three times in the last few weeks, Granny. I don't know what's going on, but we are going to follow Dr. Traynor's advice and you'll sit this out. I can't believe you even talked him into letting you come up here with us."

Granny just shrugged her shoulders, but East was positive he saw her try to hide a smile. "He knows what's best for him."

"And we know what's best for you," East assured her.

"Marti and I have been working really hard to get ready for this. We've got everything planned out to the last ingredient, and we've even been within our time limits on every meal for the last three days of practice."

Remarkably, it was true. They were honestly ready. He expected Marti to chime in with agreement, but she didn't. When he glanced over at her, she was staring off into the distance. She looked bug-eyed and a little peaked, actually.

He followed her gaze all the way across the lobby to one of the brightly colored monitors that listed the various events going on in the hotel. The one Marti was studying flashed in bold letters: *Symposium of Environmental Initiatives*.

East's heart didn't stop beating until one specific name popped up: *Keynote Speaker, Dr. Leland Hedgeman*.

Like a moth drawn to a flame, Marti got up and headed for the monitor, scanning the smaller text as details about this event scrolled by. East slumped in his chair feeling as if someone had driven a truck over his chest. Marti's Dr. Hedgeman was here? Giving some kind of keynote speech? Holy shit!

"What's she looking at?" Granny asked.

"That sign. It's about a conference that's going on here along with our big contest."

"Really? Why's Marti so interested in it?"

"Looks like its some kind of environmental symposium."

"Yeah, she would be interested in that."

"The main speaker is Leland Hedgeman," he added.

Granny was silent for a moment. "Well. That's certainly going to make our stay here more interesting, isn't it?"

Interesting wasn't exactly the word East would have used.

———

Arv and Charleen drove the twenty minutes from her parent's house to the hotel in silence. There just didn't seem to be anything to say. Arv was thrilled about going to help his friends, and Charleen was along for the ride. Mostly because she was too embarrassed to tell her mother that she'd rather not go spend a nice weekend at a fancy hotel alone with Arv.

But they wouldn't be alone. Marti Snowden would be there. And Arv was full of plans for her.

"I'm going to recognize everything they cook," he said for no apparent reason as they pulled into the hotel lot. "They wouldn't tell me what menus they'd come up with, but if it's Granny's recipe, I'll know it."

"It's supposed to be blind tasting. Do you think it's fair for you to be on the panel if you're so sure you'll know which entries are theirs?" she asked and hoped it didn't sound snippy. Not that Arv would notice. He'd been in his own little Marti-world for weeks now. Especially since they'd walked in on that spat in the kitchen. Yeah, he'd been really interested in Marti since then. Probably wondered if she'd be single again soon.

"Everyone knows the tasters' scores don't count as much as the celebrity judges," he said matter-of-factly.

"But our scores still count a little," she reminded him. "And I won't recognize their recipes. What if I don't like their food and end up giving them a low score?"

"The panel we're on only counts for 40 percent of the points. Your score won't matter much," he said. Seemed like that was pretty much how he felt about any of her opinions these days. "But don't think I'm going to go easy on them myself!"

"I thought it would be your greatest joy to see Marti win the whole show."

He just laughed. "Yeah, that would be a hoot, wouldn't it?

Although she's got East helping her, and when I talked to him yesterday he said the doctor thought it would be all right for Granny to come up here and be an advisor. Hopefully the two of them can keep Marti from ruining too much."

Charleen fought back the childish urge to grin. No matter how oblivious Arv was, the fact remained that Marti was famously kitchen-challenged. Charleen would always have that over her. The one bright spot of this whole stupid event was that Charleen might get to see Marti embarrass herself. For that thought alone she was happy when Arv parked the car under the sprawling hotel portico and the weekend officially began.

They lugged their suitcases into the lobby. The hotel was huge, and a lot nicer than the usual roadside places they'd stayed at the couple times they'd attempted a family vacation. She was glad Josh wasn't here to break things.

Apparently she didn't need him, though. Charleen's suitcase caught on the welcome mat just inside the door and started rolling it up. She gave it a quick jerk, yanking the case up off the floor and over the curling rug. But she'd packed heavy, and the bag's weight gave her more momentum than she expected. She staggered back into the spacious lobby, right into a person.

A person who was too busy staring up at a large announcement screen to withstand a sudden impact. They both hit the ground, taking down a nearby fern in the process. Dirt and tiny green leaves scattered everywhere.

Arv came running to the rescue and the next thing Charleen knew, he was crouching down beside Marti asking if she was okay.

Marti? Oh, just great! They'd been at this freaking hotel all of twenty-five seconds and already she'd run into Dr. Marti. Literally. And there was Arv, ignoring his wife and worrying over Marti.

Fortunately—for Arv's sake—East was nearby and he stepped in to take over. Arv finally had the good sense to check on his own wife instead of checking out someone else's. He reached for her, but she pushed him away..

"I'm okay," Charleen said. "We're going to need a broom, though."

"What happened?" East was asking. He was dusting Marti's shirt and she was swatting him away. Looked like maybe she'd rather have Arv tending to her.

"I guess I wasn't paying attention," Marti said, gazing down at the mess.

"No, I think it was my fault," Charleen had to admit. "My suitcase got stuck on the rug."

Arv was actively righting that suitcase at the moment and snorted at her. "Yeah, no wonder. It weighs a ton. What on earth did you pack, Char? Giant iron underwear?"

She glared at him, but he was too busy laughing with East to notice. One of the hotel staff hurried over and started helping out with the plant and gushing with apologies. He was probably just hoping for no lawsuit.

But no one seemed in any sort of mood to lay out blame right now. Granny showed up and was laughing over the whole thing, clearly convinced it must have been Marti's fault. Charleen comforted the worried hotel employee and figured the whole fiasco would be forgotten in another five minutes. Then she noticed where Marti had been staring.

Arv was staring, too. The words scrolling across the large monitor on the wall seemed to hold a special message for them. Charleen read along and wondered what the deal was.

She didn't get the chance to ask. Granny ushered Marti out of the way as a couple more hotel workers showed up with a broom and a dustpan. They bustled to work while

Granny took Marti over to a chair. Arv and East, however, let the workers bustle around them while they just stood stiff, staring at the sign.

"Environmental Symposium," Arv enunciated as the announcement flashed before them.

"Yeah," East agreed. He said it as if he'd been confirming an execution.

"Dr. Hedgeman?" Arv said, quietly.

Charleen read the name, Dr. Leland Hedgeman, and noticed he was touted as some kind of keynote speaker. Who the hell was Leland Hedgeman?

"Yeah," East muttered. This time it was clearly his own execution he was referring to.

"Oh, shit," Arv sighed.

"Yeah," East repeated.

The two men just stared at that sign like it was an omen of doom.

"Who's Dr. Hedgeman?" Charleen asked.

Arv shook his head sadly and East cringed.

"Marti's ex," East replied.

"Oh," Charleen nodded. *No wonder.*

Well, how was Marti going to like having her ex around? It was pretty clear East didn't like it one bit. Maybe things hadn't gotten any smoother between him and Marti since that episode with the noodles. Hmm, then this Hedgeman guy might be running Arv a close race. With Marti at odds with East, it was kind of reassuring to think there was some man other than Arv around to offer her a shoulder to cry on.

Could this be a good thing? Hmm, maybe. Suddenly spending the weekend here didn't seem like such a bad idea. Maybe she'd wander the halls a bit, maybe drop in on this symposium and have a look at this Dr. Hedgeman for herself.

And maybe she'd see what she could do to get Marti to

head back out to the swamp with him.

——

"Oh, my God!" the girl at the desk said as East and Marti signed in for orientation a couple hours later. "You're J. Easton Smith!"

Marti was caught off guard. Somehow, over the last month, she'd forgotten East was famous. Now here they were, standing in a room full of people and one of the contest workers was gushing over him. Too bad Granny had stayed up in her room to rest. She'd have loved seeing this.

"Yes, I am," East said with a killer smile.

"You're actually in this contest?" the girl giggled. "I mean, cooking and all?"

The other two women working the registration desk started paying attention, and a few others milling around. Most of them women, of course. Marti inched a bit closer to East.

"Yes, I'll be up there cooking tomorrow, apron and all," he said, obviously loving the attention. He would have said more, but the girl gushed on.

"So you've got your own restaurant? In Ohio? I didn't know that! So cool!"

He didn't seem in any great hurry to inform them all that it was Granny's restaurant and that he'd sort of manipulated his way into *part* ownership.

"You're the guy from *The Passionate Palate*?" a woman standing in line near them said, leaning past Marti.

"That would be me," he agreed. "And you must be *the* Helen Finkle from Cincinnati?"

The woman looked really confused for a second, then put her hand to her chest and remembered the nametag plastered there. She laughed.

The line of people waiting to sign in got very fuzzy as suddenly everyone was more interested in East than in orientation. He was asked to give several autographs, tell a few people where he was living now, and assure everyone that, yes indeed, real men *can* cook and, no, he wasn't going to use any of Treeva Kincaide's recipes. That was when one of the women asked him to marry her.

He laughed and put his arm around Marti. "Sorry, ladies, but that position has recently been filled. This is my wife, Dr. Marti Snowden-Smith."

Since when was that her name? Well, it sounded good, actually. She smiled for everyone. It wasn't as difficult as she expected. Damn it, but she *liked* being introduced to his drooling public as East's wife. Liked his arm around her, too.

East rattled off some crap about her being his high-school sweetheart and how his life was complete now that they were back together. It made all the ladies sigh and Marti want to gag. He sure could act.

But apparently she could, too. Several of his fans wished her well and congratulated them, and she was able to thank them with something remarkably like sincerity. Hell, she was gracious even, saying of course she didn't mind sharing her husband with the public. When some local newspaper guy asked if the Smith's might possibly find time later for a quick interview, Marti easily promised they could do just that.

She fully intended to get Granny's name in the article, along with a plug for the diner. Granny'd get a big kick out of seeing that. Might bring in customers, too.

Somehow East managed to get them signed in and they wandered off to find a seat in the large meeting room. He held their orientation packet in one hand, and wrapped his other around Marti's. Too many people were watching them for her to object, so she didn't.

"Good job back there," he said. "I didn't realize I'd be such a hot commodity."

"Are you kidding? These women have seen you grill seafood kebobs in a tank top and serve passion fruit margaritas in a hot tub. Now they've got you right here in front of them! Of course you're going to be popular around here."

He breathed in her ear. "I thought you never watched my show?"

"I never watched it *much*," she corrected.

He laughed. "At least you caught the hot tub scene."

She blushed. Yeah, she did catch the hot tub scene. Caught it, DVRed it then deleted it because it was just too hard to watch. Or think about. And she was thinking about it now, unfortunately. And the fact that they had a big, sexy Jacuzzi up in their room. Their room with only one bed.

They found some seats and Marti was painfully aware of the whispering around them. It sounded like everyone in the room was finding out just who this J. Easton Smith was. He didn't look the least bit put out by it all. Well, he'd had plenty of practice. Six years he'd been on that show, and he'd caught the public's attention right from the start. Of course he knew how to handle himself amidst the worshipping throng.

But this was all new to Marti. She couldn't help but look around, watching the faces of people as they noticed East and talked quietly amongst themselves about him. Occasionally glances were sent her way, but everyone always went back to staring at East. She couldn't blame them, either. She might have been able to forget his fame, but he was still breathtakingly beautiful every time she looked at him.

She had to hide a smile when word reached the harried and bustling people on the podium. Wallace Beaumont was the head of the Travel and Tourism Board and he was shuffling papers and trying to organize himself for this session. With him were some other important looking people in suits and a couple assistant-type folk, along with Tommy Blue, morning disc jockey from one of the radio stations up here.

A young woman who had the look of someone's administrative person hurried up onto the stage and attempted to get to Mr. Beaumont. Apparently he was too important to be accessible, so one of the other suits intercepted the woman. She started explaining something. Just about the time a pale, startled look came over the suit's face, Tommy Blue stepped up to the mic and began his duties as emcee. Mr. Beaumont took his seat next to the podium. The suit and the secretary tried waving at him, but he was far too busy organizing his notes.

Tommy Blue joked about cooking and made some plugs for his radio station plus a few of the local businesses who were sponsoring this event, then introduced Wallace Beaumont. The man in the suit and the young secretary now waved furiously, but Mr. Beaumont was at the mic and ignored them. They could do nothing but look nervous and sit down. Marti was fascinated.

Beaumont shuffled his notes and proceeded to read the rules. It was immediately obvious he lacked Mr. Blue's charisma. Marti would have quickly fallen asleep if what he was droning on and on about wasn't so terrifying.

The contestants consisted of ten teams, representing the best of the nominated family-owned and operated restaurants in five districts. The districts comprised the four points of the compass, plus one Central district. That's the one they fell into. Each district was then represented by an urban and a rural nominee. Garden Falls was considered rural. No argument there.

Each team would have two official cooks, both of which must be members of the owning family. That much Marti already knew. But Beaumont went on, and that's when things got scary.

Contestants would be marked down for just about everything they did. There would be points lost for slip-ups in hygiene, for not following the recipes as they had been registered with the Board of Trustees, and for exceeding the time limits set for preparations of each meal.

If they did not have exactly the utensils and ingredients they would need before each session began, their team would be penalized and not allowed to procure them. Each serving laid out had to be presented in an aesthetically pleasing manner. Portion sizes and food quantity would be monitored to make certain it agreed with what had been stipulated in the recipes on record. And neatness counted.

The only exception was dinner. Dinner was to be a surprise. They had not been given the opportunity to register recipes for their dinner menu as the meat ingredient for that would not be revealed until the night of that leg of competition. Their meat would be provided for them and they'd have to get instantly creative. Ugh.

So basically, there were about a hundred ways Marti could seriously screw this up. What was she thinking to come here and take Granny's place? They were *soooo* going to lose, even with a famous cooking-show host on their team.

And then there was that other little issue. Leland Hedgeman was here. Aside from the fact that it was more than a little bit insulting that he'd come all the way up here to Ohio and not bothered to contact her, she ached that what used to have been her life was going on and she wasn't a part of it.

How could she not have known about this symposium? How was Leland involved and she wasn't? It was just so damned unfair.

She had pretty well zoned out when something Mr. Beaumont was saying caught her attention again.

"… And as I speak, a well-known celebrity is en route from Hollywood, California, to join us on our panel of judges."

Well, that was good news. One of the first things they'd learned when they got here was that one celebrity judge had just backed out. Peter MacFalton was not going to be here. It was kind of a disappointment.

Not that Marti was a big fan of bowling, but he'd made a surprisingly big name for himself in that sport and the contest coordinators were expecting his presence to draw a good sized crowd. It'd be great publicity for the contest, and for the contestants. But MacFalton had somehow strained his thumb a couple of days ago and needed to stay home and devote himself to extensive physical therapy. Really? Thumb therapy? Who knew that was even possible.

But that left them with only two celebrity judges unless a third could be found at short notice. The good news was that at least these remaining two had names Marti recognized. Laquinta Martinez had been pretty hot stuff a few years ago with a salsa-dance exercise series that went viral in more ways than one, and most people would recognize Greg Vanderbiddle from a reality show about people with strange pets. He was the guy with the albino penguin. ("Snowflake", they were told, would not be attending this event with him. Apparently he was back home in Minnesota sitting on an egg.)

Oh, well. No one came to a cooking contest expecting to rub elbows with the truly rich and famous. Or penguins. But some well-known judges sure would give additional credibility to the winners. Not that Marti really held any hope that they could win. Even with East's charm and string of devoted fans, she was probably going to blow something up.

"You all know we have the charming and spicy-hot Miss Laquinta Martinez joining us on our panel tomorrow," Beaumont announced in his droning fashion. "As well as Greg Vanderbiddle from the TV show *Pimp My Pet*. But sadly, Mr. Peter MacFalton, the Bowl Master, who was also scheduled to be here has had to decline due to an injury."

Everyone waited for him to continue. The secretary and suit-man were shaking their heads and waving at him. He just waved back and went on.

"I'm happy to announce that one of Hollywood's most creative *quiz-ee-neers* has agreed to fly out here on short notice and fill out our panel."

Marti was pretty sure Mr. Beaumont had been trying to say *cuisinière* and she was pretty sure that meant "cook". One of Hollywood's most creative cooks was on the way? Marti glanced at East. He had his actor face on. Still, as Beaumont droned she detected a slight tick at East's left eye.

"I can't tell you how happy we are to have her agree to join us for our event," Beaumont said regally. "She's the queen of the kitchen and a goddess of gastronomy. I'm thrilled to announce that our third judge tomorrow will be Miss Treeva Kincaid, host of *The Passionate Palate*."

Beaumont smiled, waiting for the crowd to erupt in applause. They didn't. It was more like a gasp, or slow leak, as one by one the contestants and others present started whispering amongst themselves. Anyone who didn't already know who Treeva Kincaid was would be soon informed. Hopefully, that would include Wallace Beaumont.

Marti looked up at East. He was remarkably unruffled,

and even smiled at her.

"Well," he said after a pause. "I wonder how on earth she managed this?"

Chapter 19

Mr. Beaumont didn't find out there was a problem until after he'd finally finished up with all the orientation stuff. Apparently situational awareness was a foreign concept to the guy since he never seemed to notice all the whispering and the desperate waving and throat-cutting signals from his on-stage assistants. He'd gone on to praise the many virtues of this grand lady who'd so graciously decided to come on short notice. It wasn't until after he'd dismissed the crowd that finally he'd learned what a fiasco he had on his hands.

"You mean *he's* a famous TV cook, too?" he sputtered when members of the Travel and Tourism Board had finally explained things then invited East and Marti into a special meeting with them.

A small crowd waited in the hallway outside and Marti felt a bit claustrophobic in the boxy little meeting room they'd been hustled into. From the looks of it, this was the biggest thing to happen to the Family Favorites Cook-Off in all twenty years of its existence. Wallace Beaumont didn't look like the kind of guy who dealt with big things very well.

"Yeah, isn't it great?" one of the other board members was saying. "Just think of the publicity! I only wish we'd known who you were months ago, Mr. Smith. We could have put your name into some of our releases."

Marti watched East. What did he think of all this? It was impossible to tell. He was used to being at the center of things. He just kept on smiling and seemed to have an answer or clever remark for everything. He didn't even bother to tell the board guy that a month ago they picked Arv's restaurant instead of Granny's and even if East had been back in the state, his name wouldn't have been in their press release. He just kept being charming.

"But she's his ex-wife," Beaumont said, shaking his head and glancing at his fellow board members. "We can't hype him as a contestant if his ex-wife is one of our judges. What will people say? It's a conflict of interest."

There was a lot of talking about the issue and not a lot of people asking East how he felt. It seemed everyone only cared about what would be the best way to milk this to promote tourism and sell a few more tickets to the tasting sessions and Saturday's big awards ceremony. As far as the PR people were concerned, this was their dream come true.

"The rules clearly state that in instances of conflict of interest, the contestant has the right to ask for a judge's removal," a lawyer-type in a rumpled suit finally announced.

Everyone glared at her. She swallowed. "Well, that's what the rules say."

Now everyone slowly turned expectant eyes on East. Marti felt sorry for him, except that he seemed to thrive under it. And to think she'd begun half believing he was back in Garden Falls to stay. No, he'd obviously missed the limelight.

"But what are people going to say about fairness?" someone piped in. "We've already got a big TV star competing against these little mom and pops. Now we bring in the guy's ex-wife to sit as a judge? That's just asking for complaints."

"There's nothing that says a contestant can't be a nationally known professional," the lawyer defended. She must be a fan, Marti decided. "As long as Mr. Smith is a legitimate family member and actively involved in his restaurant, then I see no reason to entertain unfairness complaints. Unless, of course, they would be complaints raised by Mr. Smith himself regarding the appropriateness of his antagonistic ex-wife being stupidly invited here to sit on our judging panel."

Oh yeah. She was a fan.

"Well?" Wallace Beaumont asked, turning a cold eye toward East. "Are you going to complain? Do you need us to disqualify Ms. Kincaid, after we've gone to all the trouble and expense of flying her out here and promoting her as our third judge?"

Marti was insulted by the obvious guilt trip, but East took it in stride. The guy must be impervious to guilt. She guessed Hollywood could do that to a person.

"Well," he said slowly and turned to Marti. "I think I'd better discuss this with my wife. She might have an opinion in the matter."

The room was dead silent. From the looks everyone was giving her, Marti was pretty sure what they all figured her opinion would be. Clearly if any of them were married to one of *People Magazine's* Most Beautiful People they wouldn't welcome the unexpected arrival of an equally beautiful ex. And they'd be right.

But how did East expect her to react? Surely it really didn't matter one way or the other what her opinions on Treeva were. Unless maybe he was looking for her to be the bad-guy and tell the Travel and Tourism folk to make Treeva hit the road. Or she supposed he might just be keeping up the appearance of a team. Maybe he wanted her to agree with him that Treeva ought to be allowed to stay. Yuck.

She honestly couldn't tell what East wanted her to say.

Man, how could he be so perfectly composed in the face of all this? It just wasn't fair.

Then he smiled at her and gave her hand a little squeeze.

"How about if Marti and I take a little break? It's getting late and I know everyone's hungry. How about if we go up and get settled in our room and grab a bite. Then we'll let you know what we want to do, say, in about an hour. Okay?"

Not hardly. She could see the board members wincing at his suggestion. Clearly they would have rather known right now if East was going to expect them to chuck Treeva back on a plane. They'd have to do some hauling to line up yet another last-minute celebrity. But East apparently didn't mind seeing them sweat. He gave his suggestion with such a dazzling smile no one was up to arguing with him.

He graciously thanked the board for being so sensitive to them and they simply left the room. Just like that, *"Sorry about your panic, but we're going to go get dinner now. We'll tell you the fate of your little contest when we get around to it."* Man, this must be the coolest part of being beautiful and famous.

The loiterers out in the hall tried to get them to talk, but East was just as good at graciously deflecting them as he was answering the board. That newspaper guy still wanted his interview—even more than before—but East flashed the pearly whites and told him he'd have to wait. Mister and Mrs. Smith were going up to their room to discuss things.

He put his arm around her for effect, as if to protect her from raging paparazzi. It was undeniably sweet. If she really was his wife she could have guaranteed he'd be getting really lucky tonight. As it was, she knew that king-sized bed was going to be a much bigger problem than this Treeva Kincaid thing.

What if East was actually looking forward to seeing her

again? Well, *that* would be a problem. Because if Marti hadn't been head over heels in love with John Easton Smith before, she sure as hell was now that his ex-wife was headed for town.

"Sorry about all that," he said as they stepped alone into the elevator, East prominently lacing his fingers in with hers.

"It's not your fault she's going to be here," Marti said, and hoped to heaven it was true.

"It's an awfully big coincidence though, don't you think?" he said. "I just can't understand why she'd do it."

"You mean you think she got herself invited here on purpose?"

They reached their floor and stepped into the hallway. It was empty. East still kept a hold of her hand, though. She couldn't quite bring herself to pull it away. You never knew when the press might be lurking about, after all.

"I think it's too convenient," he said. "She knows I came back here to Ohio. Even if she didn't know I was competing in this she might have accepted the invite just to come on out here and well, you know, check you out."

"Check *me* out?" Marti asked.

East opened the door to their room and ushered her in. "Not to flatter myself, but I think it's pretty safe to say Treeva's not thrilled I got married again."

"But how would she even know about it?"

"I imagine it's big news on the set," he said, tossing the orientation packet down and heading over to adjust the air conditioning.

Marti kicked off her shoes and flopped down on the bed. "On the set? How does everyone there know about it already?"

"I do still have some friends back there. After all, I worked with a lot of those people for six years."

"You mean you *told* them? You told them we got married?"

He frowned up at her. "Well, I didn't know it was supposed to be a secret. They're all real happy for me. I figured someone would probably mention it to Treeva, but…"

"Oh, so that's it," she said. "You wanted to rub her nose in it."

And that made perfect sense. Of course he'd want Treeva to know he'd gone right out and gotten re-married. He made sure he told someone who'd tell her. Heck, Marti would probably have done the same thing if circumstances between her and Leland had been different. She couldn't begrudge East a little well-earned nose-rubbing.

"Hey, that's not it," he said, plunking down on the bed next to her and catching her gaze with those blue, blue eyes. "I would never use you for something like that."

"It's okay. It makes perfect sense. I'd probably do it, too."

"You mean, for your Dr. Hedgeman," he said.

"Yeah. Probably."

He was quiet. So, he *had* recognized the name on that sign. He didn't say anything about it earlier so she wasn't sure. She still wasn't sure what he thought about it. If he thought *anything* about it.

"It's kind of funny, isn't it?" East said.

He dropped down to lie next to her and stare at the ceiling. His shoulder was just barely brushing hers and she felt those horrible, wonderful tingles of desire. No, this bed was not nearly big enough if she had any hopes of getting some sleep in it. Every part of her reacted to East's proximity. She forced herself to continue breathing—slow, regular. Not easy.

"What are the chances of us ending up here like this with

both our exes on the premises?" he continued.

"Yeah, it's hilarious." *Not.*

"Okay, so it's not the biggest laugh riot of the century, but you have to admit it's not something that happens every day."

"Thank God."

"Does Hedgeman know about… us?"

"I didn't exactly send out post cards," she replied.

"No, I guess not," he answered, drifting into silence again.

It turned out lying on a big king sized bed next to East and not talking was even worse than lying here having a conversation. For the life of her, though, she couldn't think of anything to say. Well, nothing that she wouldn't regret ten seconds later. She wished East would crack a joke, or something. Anything to cut the tension.

He didn't though. Instead of a joke he let out a sigh. It sounded a lot like the sigh Marti would have made if she'd made one.

"I can't wait to see how Treeva works this," he said at last. "She'll find some angle to work this in her favor."

"You think she'll do that?"

"It's her super-power. I'll bet anything that's why she's here. She just hates that the press painted her into such a witch after she forced me off the show. My guess is she'll do just about anything for an opportunity to make me look bad right about now. You're lucky you don't circulate with people like that."

"Yeah, right."

"Oh? You mean creatures like that exist outside Hollywood?"

She could hear the bitterness in his voice even though she knew he hadn't meant for it to be so evident. Now she did sigh.

"Yeah. They can occasionally be found in wetlands reclamation projects and university grant programs."

"Hedgeman?"

"Yup. Sounds like he and your Treeva have a lot in common."

"You think?" he said. "Maybe we ought to introduce them."

At that they both laughed, probably for different reasons, though. Oh, she could just picture that, she and East introducing Leland the Asshole to Treeva the Diva. They could all go out for sushi, or something. Then afterwards those two could take turns stabbing everyone in the back with the chopsticks. What a hoot.

"So, do you want her here or not?" East asked after a minute.

"Your ex-wife?"

"Yeah. What do we tell the board?"

Did he really want to know her thoughts on the matter? Let's see, was there a polite way to say she'd prefer seeing Treeva shoved off the plane somewhere over a cannibal-filled island on the other side of the planet?

He was propped on his elbow now, watching her, waiting for her to speak.

"Uh, what do *you* want to tell them?" she managed.

He reached over and touched her hair. Ah, her hair liked that. She wished she kept it longer, like she had in high school. He used to love to slide his fingers through her hair. Maybe that was part of why she chopped it off at shoulder length a few days after he left back then. She couldn't stand to remember the feel of it.

"I guess I don't care whether Treeva's on that panel or not," he said. "But I was sort of hoping you might have an opinion about it."

Why, so he wouldn't have to be the bad guy? Or was it more than that? Gulp. Was he asking if she cared? If she was, maybe, jealous?

He'd said "hoping". Did that mean he'd kind of *like* it if she was? Her heart started thumping so hard in her chest it finally dislodged the lump that had built up in her throat.

"I guess she can stay," she said. "Unless there's the option of caging her with angry baboons and dressing her like a banana. Or, you know, something like that."

He grinned at her. Apparently she'd given the right answer. Wow, the *really* right answer. He leaned in and kissed her.

She'd never been able to think straight when East was touching her. Maybe he knew that and was using it for his advantage, but she didn't care. She slipped her arms around his neck to pull him closer.

If he'd just been going for a friendly peck, he didn't show any disappointment when she responded in force. His lips took control of hers with equal force. He wrapped himself around her and proceeded to let his tongue explore her mouth. She slid as close to him as she could get and concentrated on his sweet, spicy smell and the taste of East that she'd never, ever been able to forget.

The room went a little fuzzy when he whispered into her hair.

"I want you, Marti. Right now."

And she wanted him right back. An annoying little voice murmured inside her head, though. It questioned what he meant by "right now". *Only* for right now, or just *hurry* right now? Shouldn't she get that clarified before she yanked off all his clothes and started screaming out how much she loved him?

Yes, she probably should but she wouldn't. The fact that

the annoying little voice existed meant that she probably already knew the answer and wouldn't really like it. So, she just wouldn't clarify anything. East wanted her right now and she wanted him in return. Who cared if it meant anything or what was going to happen tomorrow? She was back in his arms where she'd wanted to be for ten long, lonely years. Not even if a hundred annoying little voices to keep her from running straight into heartbreak again.

She'd worn a skirt today and was exceedingly glad for it when his hands began to slide it up across her thighs. She squirmed, helping him. It wasn't like ten years ago when making love with East felt desperate and hurried. This time they didn't have a curfew.

Still, she never did like dawdling. She reached for him to speed things up. He just smiled down at her.

"Hey, take it easy," he said. "We're grown-ups now. We can take our time."

"It's been ten years, East. Don't you think we've taken enough time already?"

She latched onto his belt buckle and started working it, but he caught her hands. Surprised, she met his eyes. His lips left hers and he smiled. It was a smile with a lot of promise behind it.

"I've finally got the worldly and educated Dr. Marti in my bed," he said. "I fully intend to let you have your carnal way with me, doctor, but not before I slowly erase every other man from your memory."

Wow. The fire in his eyes was incinerating. Her breath caught inside, suffocated by his heat. This was an East she'd never even imagined. He was miles removed from the energetic, awkward boy she had loved ten years ago. This was a man who knew who he was and what he wanted, and he expected to get it. From her tonight, apparently.

And that thought struck her with terror.

Not that she could ever really be afraid of East, but she cringed to think what he expected. He, no doubt, anticipated a partner who'd have learned a few things about this over the last few years; someone who could maybe bring a few new tricks to the event, even. Someone who, basically, knew what the hell she was doing.

He was not expecting the neurotic, sappy hypocrite that she'd been all this time. J. Easton Smith, heart-throb of America, was just about to be sadly disillusioned here in the bedroom.

Crap. This was going to be embarrassing for both of them. Unless, of course, she stopped this before it went any farther. She could either tell him the truth, or fake a sudden headache. Once again, she only had two options and both of them sucked.

She pushed herself away from him and struggled to sit up. "Wait! We can't do this."

"I'm pretty sure we can. We've got the marriage license and everything."

"But... I've got to go check on Granny." *Yeah, that was way better than faking a headache.*

He didn't seem to agree. "What? Check on Granny n*ow?*"

"I told her I'd check in before dinner."

She furiously fumbled at rebuttoning her blouse and straightening her damned skirt.

"So, call her."

He grabbed up her cell phone where she'd left it lying beside her purse. Rats. She'd turned it off during orientation and forgot to turn it back on.

"I've got three missed calls from her!"

"Then check your messages."

"Granny won't leave messages. She doesn't approve of

talking to machines."

"Figures. So call her, then come back over here."

She was already dialing, but Granny didn't answer. "She's not picking up."

"Maybe she's taking a nap."

"Right through dinner? When she knows we'll be trying to reach her?"

"Maybe she's in the shower."

"Or maybe something happened!"

"Marti, come on," he said, moving to her and resting his big, warn hands on her shoulders. "What could happen?"

God, she couldn't look at him. "What if she needs me?"

"*I* need you!"

Man, she wished that was true! "I'd better go check on her, East. She'll be worried."

She stepped into her shoes and pulled on her purse. She wouldn't meet East's eyes. Why, oh why hadn't she screwed all those guys in college like everyone thought she did? Then this would have been just another interlude, just one more notch on the bedpost and she wouldn't be standing here now with her heart all broken again. She'd be able to keep this in perspective—like East obviously did.

Before he—or that annoying little voice—could get another word in, she was out the door. It was easier to breathe in the hall, but not much. How was she going to face him again? Worse, how was she going to cook with him? Hell, at this point she'd almost rather he met Treeva at the airport and went straight back to California with her.

Okay, that was a lie. She would *not* rather he do that.

It only took a few minutes to get to Granny's room, one floor below them. Originally the rooms had been booked adjoining, but somehow the reservation had mysteriously been changed. The king-size bed and romantic extras strongly implicated Granny's meddling. Boy, wouldn't she be disappointed if she knew what Marti had just walked out on!

At Granny's door, Marti knocked quietly. No response. Where was she? It just seemed odd that Granny would go wandering around right now. She knew they'd been down at orientation—wouldn't she have been eagerly waiting at the phone to find out how it went?

Unless maybe East was right and she was taking a nap. Dr. Traynor told her to be sure and get plenty of rest. Maybe she unplugged the phone or something. Yeah, that was totally possible. But, just to be on the safe side, she'd let herself in and check on her. She'd want to know about Treeva, at least.

The little light showed green when Marti stuck the extra key card in, so she quietly pushed the door open. The radio on the nightstand was playing softly and the curtains were drawn, with only the one, dim nightlight spilling a golden glow over the large bed in the center of the room. Marti could see easily why Granny hadn't opened the door to let her in.

"Oh my God!"

——

Dammit. He'd gone too far and she'd bolted. East shut his eyes and cursed himself for asking more from Marti than she'd wanted to give.

True, she did kiss him and rub her perky little body against him, but if it was really what she wanted why had she dashed out the door just when things were getting promising? She had to check on Granny? *Seriously?*

He tried to remember anything he'd done or said that might have sent her off like that, but it was hard to think straight right now. He was fighting with his body, which was just plain pissed off that one minute he'd felt better than he had in years then suddenly he was hot and alone and tangled in his pants. Why did she leave?

God, she tasted good. He shouldn't have gotten carried away, though. What was that corny bit about making her forget every other man she'd ever known? Obviously it had been stupid enough to chase a willing woman out the door to visit her grandmother.

Hell. At least she hadn't gone off to see that damn Hedgehog person. At least, he prayed to God she really was just going to check on Granny. Was concern for her grandmother really what sent her out of here, or was it the fact that Marti's old flame was in this very building right now? Maybe kissing East had only reminded Marti how much she missed that other guy.

Well, East wasn't about to step aside and let Hedgeman reclaim what he'd already given up. The bastard had been stupid enough to let Marti go and East wasn't handing her back to him without a fight. She was his legal wife now. That had to count for something. And up until about thirty seconds ago he was pretty sure she wasn't opposed to finally consummating this marriage.

She wanted him. He knew it. Just now, in these few hell-yeah moments in this bed, she'd wanted him. It hadn't lasted very long, but she'd wanted him the same way he wanted her. He could work with that. He'd just have to make very sure she had lots of other opportunities to want him again.

And not that damned Dr. Hedgetrimmer.

For starters, he'd be more careful about letting her out of his sight. She had to check on Granny? Well, then he did, too. And he'd damn well better find Marti there.

Chapter 20

He did find Marti. He saw her immediately when the elevator doors opened. She was out in front of Granny's room, leaning limp against the wall. He knew right away something was wrong.

Oh, God. He ran to her and couldn't help but put his arms around her.

"What's wrong?" he asked quickly.

She looked shell-shocked. "I went in… and…"

He pulled the key card out of her listless hand and went to open the door. Suddenly she came to life against him.

"No!" she cried, twisting to pull the card away from him. "Don't open it!"

He watched the color come flooding back into her ashen face. She wouldn't look directly at him and he wished she would. What on earth happened?

"Tell me, Marti. What's wrong? Where's Granny?"

"She's in there," she answered. "But… no! Really, don't go in there. She's not…"

"She's not *what*? What happened?"

Finally he got her to look at him. Her golden cat eyes were huge and dark. Something sure spooked the girl. He didn't like that one bit.

"She's not alone," she said at last.

"Not alone? Well, who's in there, then?"

He was about to slide the key card in and open the door

despite Marti's protests. Before he could, though, the door opened on its own. Standing inside, wearing a fleecy robe with the hotel logo on it, was Dr. Traynor. Cold fear grabbed onto East's heart.

"Doctor! What happened? Is she all right?"

He was still holding Marti fairly close and felt her shudder. Was she afraid? Of Dr. Traynor? Had he done something to Granny?

No, Marti wasn't trembling from fear. She was making a noise now and it wasn't to accuse the good doctor of anything nefarious. It was more like… more like a giggle. Marti was giggling?

East studied her face. Yes, she was trying desperately to hide the giggles. And boy, was she red. Confused, he looked back over at Dr. Traynor. Only then did he realize that the good doctor seemed to have nothing on under that fleecy robe.

Oh. My. God.

"I can assure you, Milly says she's feeling just fine," the doctor said. Then he smiled.

Marti's giggle became more of a snort. Good God. East figured out what was happening.

The doctor had been boffing Marti's grandmother! But was that medically wise? Forget that. Was it even *possible*?

"Hey, I thought she was supposed to be on bed rest? Bed *rest*," East asked, then clarified. What kind of doctor was this, anyway?

"Maybe you two had better come in here," Dr. Traynor invited.

Marti jumped back from the door as if it were the gaping maw of hell. East was inclined to join her. But then Granny came into view, sliding up beside Dr. Traynor. Oh, how cute. Matching fleecy robes. Please, lord, let those belt ties hold fast.

"Now, Marti, everything's okay," Granny said. She seemed to be suppressing giggles, too. "Come on in and I'll explain things."

"No, I think I understand well enough," Marti said.

Granny just kept on smiling. "Yes, I guess maybe you do."

She made a meaningful nod toward Marti's shirt, and it was then East noticed for the first time that Marti had done up the buttons a bit lopsided. Marti must have realized what Granny assumed and her blush got two shades redder. Seemed the Snowden gals had a lot going on this evening.

"Look, there's nothing wrong with Milly," the doctor announced. "Never has been. Well, not lately. I promise you that. Milly is just fine."

East sincerely hoped the doctor was just talking medical things here. Anything else would be entirely too much information.

"But your hip…" Marti began when she finally quit giggling/hyperventilating.

"Is healing well," the doctor said.

"But she was having spells!" Marti said, and glanced from the doctor to Granny. "We took you to the hospital three times in the last couple weeks."

"Faked 'em," Granny said. "Sorry about that. I don't usually go around faking stuff."

Crap. She had to go and give the friendly doctor a little wink with that.

"Faking? But why?" Marti asked. The giggles were way gone now.

"Look, I'll get my stuff and head back to my room," the doctor said. "I think maybe you two ought to sit down and talk."

Susan Gee Heino

Granny looked like she'd rather be tossed to wolves, but she nodded. He seemed understandably relieved. Now that the initial shock and nervous chortling started to fade, Marti was looking a little ticked off.

Dr. Traynor disappeared back into the dim room and shuffled around. East noted that when he left, it was through a connecting door. Oh, so that's who got the room they'd originally reserved for themselves. Didn't look like Dr. Feelgood was going to get much use out of those double beds, though.

"What's going on, Granny?" Marti was asking slowly, calmly. Way too calmly.

East was more than a little curious about the answer to that, too, but a stormy Marti and Granny in a borrowed robe were just a bit more than he could handle right now. He'd have to leave the explanation-gathering up to Marti.

"You go have a chat with Granny," he said. "I need to make a couple phone calls. Why don't we all plan to meet down in the dining room in about half an hour? You can fill me in then. But just the basics for me, please. I don't need the sordid details, okay?"

Granny chuckled and gave a coy little grin. "Chicken."

"You got it," he said, then turned back to Marti. "All right? Dinner?"

"Yeah. Okay," she agreed, back to avoiding his eyes.

Oh, well. He had three days to get her to look at him. Heck, maybe he ought to hit Dr. Traynor up for some pointers. The man seemed to be quite a mover.

———

"All right, you can start explaining now," Marti said, propping herself against the wall in Granny's hotel room and wishing she could totally redo the whole last half hour of her life. She also wished Granny would wipe that smug, satisfied little smile off her face. Talk about unfairness! The sick geriatric one was getting it and Marti wasn't.

Although, from what she'd seen when she walked in on them, Dr. Traynor was not exaggerating when he assured them Granny was pretty darn healthy. That was an image burned on her brain she could do without.

"I've known Milton Traynor since high school," Granny said primly. "He's a good and decent man and we're both adults. I don't think I need to explain myself to my granddaughter."

"I don't mean about that!" Marti said. "God, I don't even want to think about that, let alone have you explain it. Jeez, Granny. If you're healthy enough for that, well, have at it. I just want to know why you lied about the spells? I can guess why you switched our rooms around—you had a couple reasons for that, apparently—but making us think you were really sick?"

"That was wrong. I'm sorry. I just needed a way to ensure that it was you working with Johnny on this contest and not me. I was afraid if you thought I was able-bodied, you might duck out. Go back to your job in some polluted swamp somewhere."

"What? You know I'd never leave in the middle of this. It's your big moment!"

"Yeah, well things were so rocky between you and Johnny. I thought if you had something to worry about—together—it might smooth things over."

"Oh, so that's what this is all about. You decided to take advantage of this contest to get East and me together. And his name is East, Granny. He's not Johnny anymore."

"I'll call him Johnny if I darn well please. He doesn't

seem to mind."

"Don't get upset with me! I'm not the one who's been lying to her family around here."

"A family who doesn't seem to know what's good for her. You've been living with *Johnny*—" she stressed his name so Marti would notice "—a month now, and this is the first hint I've got that you two even recognize you're of the opposite sex!"

She pointed at Marti's still lop-sided shirt. Marti started fixing it.

"You don't know the first thing about me and East."

"I know you're in love with him."

Okay, so maybe she did know the first thing. It was just all the other stuff she didn't know about.

"That doesn't have anything to do with it," Marti sighed. "East has his life and I've got mine. This fake marriage is never going to be anything but that. All right?"

"No, it's not all right," Granny said looking a little forlorn as she stood there in the dim hotel room hugging her robe around herself. "I want my granddaughter to be happy."

"I am happy, Granny," Marti said with the warmest smile she could muster considering how her insides were still fumbling around trying to come to terms with a whole bunch of weird new information. "And I'll be happier when we're finally done with this competition on Saturday. But first we have to get through it, and I can't do that if you're constantly surprising me and going behind my back plotting things. Jeez, I thought I would stroke out when I walked in on you two!"

"He's amazingly virile for a man in his sixties, isn't he?"

"God, Granny, that's not what I want to talk about."

"Stays in shape, too."

"Okay, okay."

"He's a hottie."

Now Marti couldn't help but laugh. She sank down onto the arm of the one chair in the room and shook her head. "Yeah, all right. He's a hottie *and* a cutie-patootie and you have my blessing to boink his brains out."

"Thank you, dear."

"But please, please don't try anymore matchmaking for me, all right?"

"I don't know… I've done so well for myself this week."

"And that's enough. You probably ought to save your energy for, uh, better things. Right?"

"And you'd rather save yours for *cooking*?" Granny said, doubtful.

"Yes. Exactly."

"Youth is wasted on the young."

"You want to win this little contest, don't you?"

"I intend to win this little contest."

"Good. Then let me and East concentrate on that. No more strawberries and champagne delivered to our room, okay?"

"All right. All right," Granny gave in, coming to sit beside Marti. "But can you at least explain why you showed up at my room with your shirt all wonky like that?"

Marti glared at her. "No. I can't."

Granny met her eyes for a moment, then broke into a slow grin. "Okay. I guess it's your business how you muss your clothing. I just hope you weren't busy mussing when you should have been at orientation."

"We weren't," Marti said, double-checking her buttons. She realized too late her quick denial was as good as a confession. Granny's grin got bigger. "Look, we went to orientation, all right?"

"So it's been over for a while, I take it? Glad you kids are making good use of your free time."

"Look, Granny," Marti said with a frustrated sigh. "There's nothing happening between us."

"Hmm. Interesting sort of nothing that can make your shirt crooked like that."

"At least I'm wearing a shirt."

Granny merely chuckled and scooted over to reach for her hands.

"I'm sorry I lied to you and that you had to walk in on us like that."

"Yeah, I bet you are," Marti said.

Granny just chuckled some more. "Although, it was probably encouraging for you."

"Encouraging? Not the word I would have picked."

"I mean it should be encouraging to know that older folks can still... you know."

"No! Stop! It's not encouraging. It's scary. Okay?"

"Oh come on, surely you've wondered what you have to look forward to."

"I would have sooooo much rather found out on my own."

Granny thought that was funny. "Forty years from now you and Johnny will probably…"

"No," Marti cut her off. "In forty years we'll be off on opposite sides of the planet, or something. You've got to quit hoping for something there between us, Granny. It's just not going to happen."

"And you're okay with that?"

Marti didn't even bother to argue. It must be painfully obvious to everyone now that she still pined away after East. But Granny, at least, should know better than to continually wave him in front of her like this. It was way past time for a subject change.

"Look, we learned something at orientation tonight," Marti said.

Granny patiently waited for the explanation.

"They found their third judge to take the place of that bowling guy who can't come."

"Great," Granny said. "So everything is set to go for tomorrow."

"The new judge is on her way here right now. It's, uh, Treeva Kincaid."

For a couple seconds this name didn't seem to ring a bell, then Marti watched realization dawn on Granny.

"You mean, his *ex-wife*?"

"That's the one."

"Lordy lordy! Did Johnny know anything about this?"

"No, he was just as surprised as anyone."

"But they can't keep her on, can they? We can't have prejudiced judges on the panel. That's just wrong!"

"Not really. The judging will be done anonymously, so she won't know which entry is ours."

"They're letting her stay on?"

"I don't know. They said it's up to us."

Granny frowned. "And what does East say?"

It was harder for Marti to answer that than she expected. "He doesn't really care. In fact…"

"In fact what?"

"I think he'd kind of like her around to see him with a new wife."

Granny's frown turned hopeful. "Well, that's promising, isn't it?"

"But I'm not really his wife, Granny," she reminded her. "It's only for pretend. Everything he wants from me is just for show. After Saturday it's all over."

"So what exactly is it he wants from you, Marti girl?"

Susan Gee Heino

Good question. How to answer? "I guess he wants me to make Treeva think he's the happiest man on the planet without her."

"You mean, the happiest man on the planet *with you*, acting like you're blissfully and madly in love. That shouldn't be too hard for you, I would think."

"But I can't do that!"

"You can't do that for East? Your oldest friend?"

"I didn't hear from him for ten years, Granny. That's hardly evidence of long-lasting friendship. And no, I can't do this for East. Not when he's just going to be gone in the end."

This seemed to make sense to Granny. She nodded. Good thing she understood, because Marti sure didn't. What *did* East want from her? Why on earth couldn't she make herself stay with him in their big, inviting bed one floor up? Her reasoning then didn't seem very reasonable now.

"Remember what we were talking about the other day?" Granny asked. "When you were taking me to the doctor?"

"Yeah, I remember." How could she forget? She was getting red just thinking about it. Please, God, don't let Granny be about to launch into another sex-life cross-examination!

"Well, I started thinking about that, about being in love with one man even when he's gone."

"Granny, I don't…"

"Hear me out. It's no secret your grandpa and me got along pretty well. I loved the guy dearly. You were just a kid when he died, but I think you can remember how hard it was for me to go on without him."

Yeah, she had vague memories of seeing Granny grieve. Mostly she'd been more concerned at the time with her own grieving. Grandpa had been a special guy, filling the role as father for her and supporting her young, single mother. Yes, they'd all grieved, that was for sure.

"It nearly killed me to put that man in the ground," Granny said. "But even knowing that, I'd still give just about anything to have him back again just for a little while, even if I knew I'd have to let him go again."

Ah, now she saw where Granny was going. She didn't really want to hear the rest.

"Well, I'm glad you're so strong, Granny. I don't know that I could do that. "

"I guess you're the one to know, but just make sure you're thinking it all the way through. When all this is over and Johnny heads back to California, you're still going to have to go on one way or another. Do you really want to go on knowing you had a chance and didn't take it?"

Marti snorted. "A chance for what?"

"I don't know. You're the one with the rumpled shirt."

Marti gave her a little nudge with her knuckle. Sheesh. Granny had a dirty mind. Granny just laughed and adjusted her robe.

"Did you know Milton asked me to marry him two years ago?" she asked.

Well, someone could have come in and knocked Marti over with a feather at that. Granny'd been doing Dr. Traynor for two years? Wow, this was one spunky old gal. Sort of explained that hip problem, too.

"But I told him no," Granny went on. "I was convinced there'd never be another chance for me, since what I wanted was old age with a man I'd long ago buried. But I got old age anyway, and nothing was going to make Robert Snowden come back to me. After you and I talked the other day, I started wondering if maybe I'd made the wrong decision."

"So you're going to marry Dr. Traynor?"

"Well, that's still to be determined. But at least I've made up my mind that just because I couldn't have everything I wanted, it didn't mean I couldn't have anything."

"So you're still in love with Grandpa and you're just using Doc Traynor for sex?"

Granny sure did laugh at that. "No, I found out I can still love your grandpa *and* find enough room in my heart for Milton."

"So you're telling me to get a boyfriend?"

"No, honey, I'm telling you to figure out that maybe what you think you have to have isn't what you can ever really get. Might be time to let yourself be happy with what you've got."

"Oh, and what exactly is that? A dead career? A pretend marriage? Stuck living with my grandmother for the rest of my life?"

"You're forgetting one thing. You've got the hots for Easton Smith in a big, big way."

Ugh. Like she needed to be reminded of *that*.

"And I've seen the way he looks at you. Don't think I believe you when you say nothing's happened between the two of you this whole time you've been living together."

"Nothing *has* happened."

"Nothing? Or just nothing that meets with your full approval?"

"And what does *that* mean?" She wished Granny would just get to the point.

"You always made a lot of plans for Johnny, didn't you? I remember that poor boy getting roped into helping you with all those Keep the City Clean campaigns you were forever starting up. He never wanted to do that with his summers, but he went along with you because you were friends. Then you decided what college he needed to go to and what classes he should be taking. Heaven only knows what all else you had planned for him; nearly as bad about that as his folks have always been. Actually, I can't say I blame the kid for running off on everyone like he did."

"He could have at least said good-bye."

"If he had, would you have let him go?"

"Like I could have stopped him."

"Maybe you could have. Maybe that's why he left the way he did."

Ouch. She was going to disregard Granny's suggestion right up front but somehow she just couldn't. Was it possible she was right? Could East have possibly cared enough for Marti that she might have persuaded him to give up his dreams? But just think what all he would have missed! God, he'd have been miserable if he'd done what she'd wanted back then, wouldn't he? Yeah, ouch was right.

"Maybe you never could have Johnny on your terms," Granny went on. "But did you ever find out what his terms were?"

"His terms always include him going off to California."

"And you survived that, didn't you? I bet you'd survive it again."

Easy for her to say. She didn't know the full details.

"You know, Marti," Granny said in a voice that meant she was going to say something else Marti didn't want to hear. "If you're going to spend your life being faithful to the guy anyway, you might as well take advantage of the times you are together with him."

Okay, so maybe Granny *did* know the full details.

"I don't plan to spend my life being faithful to him," she said.

"But things don't always go according to our plans, do they? If you're waiting for another East to come along, you'll end up waiting a long, long time."

"I'm not waiting. I've just been busy with my career."

"You're not busy now. And Johnny isn't in California now. What's your next excuse?"

She didn't have one; not a good one anyway. Darn that Granny and her nosey logic.

"Oh, well. You do what you want. It just seems a shame for a beautiful girl like you to waste her life dreaming of something she's never going to get. At least not the way she thinks she wants it, anyway."

Crap. Why did Granny have to be so damn right about this? It was true. She did have her own plans for East, plans that included him declaring an undying passion and eternal love. How corny. Who got that out of life these days? There was no such thing as undying. Any biologist knew that.

But that sure as hell didn't mean Marti was going to go rushing out and throw herself into East's arms. Hell no! It *would* make his leaving harder for her; she knew that for a fact. And if someone ever did come along to sweep her off her feet, she didn't need another group of memories of East to battle every day. Those ones from high school would be more than enough.

Besides, there was still the little matter of her pride. Getting close enough to East for him to guess how she'd spent her nights these last ten years—and why—would be quite a blow to her ego. Sadly, that was about all she had left these days.

"Well," Granny said, putting her hand on Marti's arm to get leverage for standing up. "Maybe that's enough chatter. I'd better get dressed if we're going to meet our men for dinner on time."

Marti frowned at the "our men" bit, then decided to ignore it. Her love life might be crappy, but she was happy for Granny. In fact, she couldn't help another little giggle and broke into song.

"Granny and Milton, sitting in a tree…"

Granny was digging through her suitcase for something to wear. She seemed to like Marti's little ditty and smiled at her with a sly, knowing grin. The singing stopped abruptly when Granny dramatically produced a pair of red lacy underwear.

"Oh, God," Marti breathed, covering her eyes.

"You live your life, Marti Snowden Smith, and I'll live mine. And, personally, I think mine's a little more fun than yours right now."

"I'll let you get dressed."

Granny was still cackling behind her when Marti tugged open the door to escape. But Granny called.

"By the way," she said. Marti turned back slowly, almost afraid of what she'd see now.

"One of the reasons I said no two years ago was because I was afraid," Granny explained, not that Marti had asked. "Milton's a medical doctor, and I know some of his patients; young, attractive women still in the bloom of their youth, if you know what I mean. I had a hard time figuring he'd be thrilled with his choice of an old lady like me."

Uh oh. This was going into Area TMI again.

"But now I know. The plumbing still works—a little slower and slightly rearranged, maybe—but Milton has no complaints. He didn't want one of those young bloomers. He wants me. And that's mighty damn good on the old ego."

"I gotta go," Marti muttered. She didn't want to hear any more about Granny's ego *or* her plumbing. Way, way too much information.

Chapter 21

Charleen wished she had a little more information. Who on earth was this Dr. Hedgeman, and what precisely was his relationship to Marti? Arv hadn't seemed to know much more than that the two had been lovers for several years. He seemed honestly upset that the guy was here at the hotel now, too. Poor baby. Probably figured this was just one more man to stand between him and darling Marti.

Well, Charleen had had just about enough of Arv's lingering juvenile crush. Marti had left him behind years ago, just as she'd left this Hedgeman person and as she'd likely leave East. So far, Charleen couldn't say the two of them had seemed especially lovey-dovey tonight. Maybe Miss Marti was growing bored with her newest conquest already.

Then how handy that there was an old flame nearby!

Charleen sat with her back to the wall in the dim hotel restaurant. She and Arv had been there already when Marti arrived with her entourage. Without even so much as a glance at Charleen, Arv had stood up and waved them over to join them. The server pulled up another table and—just like that—their intimate party of two had become a frustrating group of six. Looked like Granny was getting pretty chummy with that doctor friend of hers she'd brought along. Sheesh.

Arv had at least retained his seat across from Charleen, but he'd been sure to put Marti in the chair right next to him, of course. East didn't seem to like that, which only confirmed

Charleen's suspicions that Arv's attentions toward Mrs. Smith went beyond simple friendship. From what she'd heard, Arv and East had been like brothers at one time. If East felt jealousy toward Arv, Charleen figured he probably had good reason.

She'd really hoped this could be a new start for her and Arv. A fancy hotel, no kids, and no restaurant hovering over their heads. It could be a chance for them to reconnect and dream new dreams. Well, judging by the way Arv fawned over Marti and went on and on about her chances of winning the competition, that was a silly thing to hope for. There were three of them on this vacation whether she liked it or not.

But now a forth had entered the picture. Charleen could see him, but Marti and Arv could not. He was alone, just entering the restaurant and waiting to be seated. He hadn't noticed Marti, either. Wonder what would happen when he did?

Charleen was already grinning inside at the thought of it. Dr. Hedgeman was here and didn't even know what he'd just walked into. All Marti's men gathered together in one spot. Might make for interesting TV.

"Um, I need to run to the little girls' room," Charleen announced, though she doubted anyone cared.

She left the table quietly and headed for the exit. Yes, there stood Dr. Hedgeman all alone. She'd hunted him down earlier and peeped into one of the rooms where he was hosting a break-out session. He'd been eloquent, distinguished, good-looking, and stuffy as hell. Just what Charleen had figured.

Now here he was stopping in the hotel restaurant for dinner, and wonder of wonders, he was wearing the name badge they must have passed out to everyone at that conference. "Environmental Symposium, Dr. Leland

Hedgeman," it read. Perfect.

"Oh, excuse me, sir," she said as she came to halt beside him.

He glanced at her with dark, vaguely interested eyes. However, when those eyes darted down to see she wore no matching name badge, some of the interest quickly faded. Would it return just as fast once she mentioned Marti? One way to find out.

"I couldn't help but notice your badge there," she said. "I see you're with the environmental group. I was just sitting down to dinner with a friend of mine who mentioned she might know some of your colleagues here this week."

"Oh?"

He had a rich, cultured voice. Just what someone would expect from a renowned professor. And the graying temples were a nice touch. One thing was sure; Marti Snowden had good taste in her men. Maybe under other circumstances Charleen could appreciate that.

"Maybe you've met her?" Charleen smiled and watched him carefully. "Dr. Marti Snowden?"

Oh, yeah. He knew her. That waning interest flooded back with a vengeance. Something fairly sizzled there under Dr. Hedgeman's manicured exterior. Apparently, all was not finished between Marti and her professor.

"She's here? Marti Snowden?"

"You know her? Well, what a small world!" Charleen took joy in pointing toward their table. "She's over there, toward the back. Sitting between those two men."

Hedgeman saw her. His dark eyes widened first, then narrowed significantly. He cleared his throat before speaking again.

"So she's here for the symposium then?"

"Oh, no. It's really funny! I mean, what a coincidence.

She's here to compete in a cook-off." Pause, wait for effect. "With her new husband."

Now his eyes got large again. "New husband?"

"Yeah," Charleen gave a wistful sigh. "She married her high school sweetheart. Isn't that adorable?"

"Um, good for her." He didn't quite sound like he meant that.

"She was really surprised to find out so many people she knows from her work are all here at this hotel. Hey, come on over and join us, why don't you? I mean, if you know her, and all."

At first she thought he was going to refuse. Maybe she ought to hope he did—there was no telling how uncomfortable things might get. Maybe she should have just minded her own business. But, darn it, if East couldn't keep Marti distracted from Arv's fawning, something told her this guy could.

"Oh, come on. I'll bet she'd be thrilled to see you again," Charleen prodded.

The restaurant hostess arrived to seat Dr. Hedgeman, and Charleen took advantage of the timing to inform her he'd be dining with their group. A waiter hurried over to procure another chair and, delightfully, it was placed at the end of the table—right between Charleen and Arv and perilously close to Marti. And East.

Oh, yes. Dinner just got remarkably more interesting.

With the arrival of the new chair, and the waiter bustling to get another place setting, conversation understandably ceased. Everyone looked up at Charleen as she and Dr. Hedgeman approached. She didn't care so much what anyone else thought, but Marti's expression was priceless.

"Hey," Charleen announced. "Look who I bumped into in the hall."

———

Oh, God! It was Leland. How on earth did Charleen know him? And what was he doing at their dinner table? Marti realized everyone was silent, and staring at her. She pasted on a smile and hoped there was still some color left in her cheeks.

"Dr. Hedgeman," she said. Everyone would no doubt recognize the name. Granny snorted.

"Hello, Marti," Leland said in his deep, professorial voice. "What a surprise to run into you here."

"Yes, isn't it? I guess my invitation for the symposium got lost in the mail."

More silence.

"I noticed Mr. Hedgeman's badge and mentioned to him that I had a friend who was involved in environmental work," Charleen said to fill in the space. "He said he knows you, so I invited him to join us. Hope that's okay!"

"We're old friends, actually," Marti said. It sounded better than, *"Charleen, you did the dumbest thing possible."*

Oh, well. She was bound to run into him again someday. Better this way than in front of a bunch of their colleagues where she might embarrass herself. At least this would break the ice and maybe establish some way for the two of them to interact on a civilized level in the future. If only Granny and East hadn't already assumed so much!

She chanced a quick look over at East. Yeah, he assumed a lot. He was evaluating every inch of Dr. Hedgeman right now and obviously didn't like what he saw. That's all she needed; for East to get big-brotherly for her and start threatening to rough the guy up.

Granny was sitting across from Marti and one glance at

her said East might not actually be Leland's biggest fear. East had "I-wanna-beat-him-up" written all over his face, but Granny looked positively lethal. Dr. Traynor, sitting next to Granny, just seemed confused. Poor guy. Did he have any idea what he was getting himself into with Granny?

"Your friend says you're here for a cook-off, Marti?" Leland said, sounding more than a little dubious. "Cooking food for human consumption?"

Great, now even he was going to make fun of Marti's legendary kitchen troubles. Sure, he'd cost her her job, why not ridicule her domestic skills in front of her family?

Then again, what the hell did she care what Leland Hedgeman said about her? Everyone at this table already knew she was a menace with a wire whisk. Most of them knew Leland was an asshole, too. Big deal. She could honestly say his words didn't bother her nearly as much as she might have expected them to.

The only thing that mattered right now was keeping professional doors open for the future. She intended to have a career again someday and, fortunately, her cooking skills didn't have anything to do with that. It might, however, have something to do with Leland Hedgeman.

"Oh, Leland, you're so funny!" she laughed, like he'd just said the wittiest thing ever. "Can you believe it? I'll be judged for making *real* food that people will actually have to eat! Isn't that a riot?"

It wasn't, but everyone tittered nervously and pretended to be having a good time. She took a deep breath and dove in with both feet.

"Have a seat and let's introduce everyone."

Charleen nearly shoved Leland down into the chair that had been dragged over for him. She must have some kind of sixth sense to realize this was going to be good. By appearances, she was enjoying herself more now than on any of the occasions Marti had ever seen her. She was really pretty when she smiled. No wonder Arv had gone all ga-ga over her and made a fool of himself back in college.

East brushed against Marti's shoulder. Had he scooted his chair over closer to her? Well, they were all a little more crowded now with yet another body added to their table.

"This is Dr. Leland Hedgeman," she began for everyone's benefit. "We worked together on several projects over the last few years."

There. That was easy. She'd said his name and actually not choked on it. The casual observer would never know she was practically hyperventilating right now. Or that she still harbored a few dirty little secrets for this well-groomed scholar.

She went on and introduced Charleen and Arv, then Granny and Dr. Traynor. None of them seemed to have much to say, which was especially surprising for Granny. Probably even she was waiting to see what would happen next. Marti had left East's introduction for last.

"And finally," she said after a deep, cleansing breath. "This is Easton Smith. My husband."

Leland didn't seem as surprised as she'd expected. And she *had* expected him to be surprised. She may indeed know the truth about Leland, but she was pretty sure he still held onto one of his mistaken beliefs about her. He'd always been convinced she was in love with him.

There was too much table between East and Leland for them to shake hands, and that made for a nice excuse. The firm set of East's jaw and the icy stare on Leland's face made it clear they both had way too many questions for each other to be on hand-shaking terms just yet. Beneath polite nods and how-do-you-do's the air crackled with tension.

Under any other circumstances, Marti might have been flattered. As it was, she knew better than that. If two men ever had less reason to be jealous of one another it was these two! She wished she could give them just a hint of what the truth really was so they could all have a good laugh. Too bad she was sworn to secrecy on both sides.

Leland greeted East with the fake smile he usually reserved for smoke-belching, land-grabbing industry moguls.

"Pleased to meet you. I'm a little surprised, however. Can't remember Marti ever mentioning you before."

"Really?" East responded. His fake smile was much more believable. "She mentioned *you* a couple times."

Leland gave a weak little laugh. "Oh? Nothing bad, I hope?"

He glanced at Marti and she knew he wasn't just making a joke. Most wives *would* tell their husband all the gory details about someone like Leland. Lucky for him the wife thing was just a sham. Sort of like everything about Leland.

But East played it perfectly, giving an uninterested shrug that was just enough to hint that he knew something, but not enough to indicate he cared. Then he slid his arm securely around Marti's shoulders.

"To tell the truth," he went on. "We haven't spent much time talking about Marti's old colleagues. Busy with other things, you might say."

And everyone knew—or thought they knew—exactly what he meant by "other things". Good. That ought to keep Hedgeman guessing for a while. She wasn't altogether comfortable with what East's body heat and protective arm was doing to her blood pressure, but it was well worth it to watch Leland sweat for a change.

Okay, having East practically snarling over her like a jealous dog with a brand new chew toy was worth just about anything.

"So, you're from Marti's little home town there?" Leland asked, understandably changing topics.

"Yep. I grew up right next door to Marti. We went all the way from kindergarten through high school together."

"How sweet."

Obviously, Leland didn't like sweet. Marti was aware of how uncomfortable he must be, sitting with a whole table of folks who would undoubtedly take her side in a fight. It would be driving him crazy, not knowing what she'd told them and what she hadn't. And with so many of their peers here for this conference… yeah, he must really be sweating bullets that no one started sharing info on him. Actually, she ought to be feeling pretty damn good right about now.

Until, of course, Granny broke her silence.

"So you're that Dr. Hedgeman I was always hearing about, huh?"

Leland visibly blanched and East's arm went tense.

"I take it my illustrious reputation has preceded me?" he said with another weak attempt at laughter.

He looked positively miserable. *Thank you, Charleen, for being totally oblivious and trying to be friendly.*

"Have you realized what a damn fool you were for losing my Marti her job down there in that stupid swamp?" Granny went on.

No one said anything. The collective gasp from their table nearly sucked all the air from the room. God, couldn't she have just a little bit of tact? Just this once?

"Well, we've all missed Marti terribly since she left, of course. But our program lost a great deal of funding and some things just had to be restructured."

"My Marti ain't some *thing* to be restructured," Granny snipped. "But, I guess it all turned out for the best. I needed her in Garden Falls with me, and it just so happened East showed up at the same time. He's been out in California for ten years."

"Oh?" Leland asked too quickly. Apparently East was the lesser of two evils and Leland seemed almost happy to turn from Granny back to him. "What do you do out there?"

"I'm self-employed," East said simply.

"He went out there to be an actor," Granny announced.

East grimaced. Leland gave a condescending smile and turned back to East.

"Oh, you started out as an actor. So, what are you now?"

East didn't miss a beat. "I'm Marti's husband."

"He hosted his own TV show," Granny interjected. "You've probably heard of it."

Leland just shrugged. "Probably not. I don't watch TV."

"Well, the rest of the country does," Granny remarked. "And last year they gave him his own Personal Choice Award just because he's so great."

"It's the People's Choice, Gran," Marti corrected, though it obviously didn't matter. Leland was clearly not impressed. Still, it felt good to say it. Her *husband* had a People's Choice Award. Cool. Even if it was just for a couple more days.

"You know, Marti," Leland said turning his focus back to her. "You should have brought him out last year for our Stars for the Glades program."

Ugh. As if she would have wished that pretentious, overly-dramatized fund-raiser/photo-op on East. Even if he hadn't been still happily married to Treeva at the time, he'd have been about the last person she would have dragged into involvement in a circus like that.

Charleen mentioned seeing some of that program on TV, and she seemed starry eyed enough to suit Leland's inflated ego, so he launched into a detailed telling of how he ran the whole show and took credit for pretty much all of it. He sort of skipped the parts about the Audubon Society, the local conservation groups, and hundreds of international volunteers who did most of the work. But, it gave everyone something to talk about and some of the tension at their table faded enough to be bearable.

Leland happily dropped a few names here and there, and when Granny could take it no longer, she blurted out, "East knows Brad Pitt!"

That led to a brief battle of who-knew-whom as Leland kept badgering East with stories of his encounters with the beautiful people of the world. It was pretty funny, really, to see how annoyed East was getting and how desperate Leland was to one-up him. Man, if only East were in on all the details. He'd get a big laugh out of the delicious irony in this.

Then the name-dropping war segued into more personal attacks, such as whose job was more destructive to the environment. Leland really was such an asshole.

"Are you aware how many toxins are released into our environment from the fossil fuels it takes to generate enough electricity to run the millions of televisions American's watch every day?" Leland asked.

"Good thing I haven't been involved in any six-hour telethons lately then," East replied. "I prefer to financially support responsible organizations without all the hoopla and expense of that kind of thing."

"Yeah, a lot of people think giving money is all they need to do. They don't realize the impact their own personal actions have on the planet."

"Which is why we're so lucky to have Marti back in Garden Falls, where she can make a difference on a personal level," East said. "Did you know she's already stopped the rezoning and planned destruction of the last remaining natural watershed in our county? It didn't even take her two months."

"And she's gotten herself married, too," Leland said. "She's really something, I guess."

"Oh, look," Marti interrupted. "Here's our waiter. Are we ready to order yet?"

"I am," Granny said loudly. "But I don't think I have much of an appetite right now." The last part was said glaring at Leland.

He took the hint and stood. "Why don't you folks go ahead and have your dinner? Thanks for the invitation to join you, but I was actually supposed to meet someone down here."

"Oh? Bring a friend with you, Leland?" Marti asked. He would know what she meant.

"No one you would know," he replied.

"Hmm. I guess things have changed since I was last in Florida."

He glared at her. "No, they haven't. My dinner companion is just an old colleague. *She's* currently working for the Department of the Interior."

Marti smiled. So, at least she knew how things still stood. Amazing that he'd been able to keep up with his little games so long. And now he was sucking up to the Department of the Interior? It figured.

"You always did like friends in high places."

Too bad they were so often conflicting high places. One of these days Leland Hedgeman was going to fall, and fall hard. Maybe she ought to think twice before hoping to reintegrate herself into his work. He may be doing some great things for the environment, but his first priority was always himself. Someday that might bite him. Big time.

He made his polite exit, pretending to be so glad to have met everyone. Charleen seemed content to believe him, but from what Marti could tell, everyone else was glad to see him go. How could Marti have been so stupid to practically idolize the man for so long? Sheesh. She was pitiful.

"Well, maybe I will have that braised turkey after all," Granny said, laying down her menu and smiling at the waiter when Leland was gone. "And don't be stingy with the mashed potatoes."

———

East noticed Marti hadn't finished anything on her plate and then passed on desert. She'd been decidedly quiet through dinner, and he knew why. That damn bastard, Leland Hedgeman.

Something was still there between him and Marti; something big. That wounded expression on her face when she looked up to see him standing there next to Charleen… East didn't even want to think about it. That asshole had left his mark on Marti's soul and East wanted to strangle him for it.

He hadn't asked Marti for any details about that relationship and doubted she would have given any if he had, but after five minutes of seeing them together he had a pretty clear idea of what happened. Marti used to worship the guy, and who could blame her? Dr. Leland Hedgeman was just about everything Marti could have ever dreamed of.

He was mature, undeniably good-looking, and had just as big a thing for swamps as Marti did. He probably didn't have to work very hard to sweep her off her feet back when she was a college kid and first met him. But, damn it, why did he have to dump her, and ruin her career in the process?

Their little cryptic mention of Hedgeman's "friend" made it pretty obvious he was a player. Must have been stupid enough to throw her over for someone else. And Marti obviously had no illusions about the "dinner companion" he was supposed to be meeting tonight. The jerk even went so far as to make sure Marti knew he was meeting another woman. Why would he need to rub her nose in it like that? She didn't deserve that. East had never even heard her say anything bad about the guy. When she was loyal to someone, it was to a fault. And it took a lot to destroy that loyalty.

Like screwing her brains out for two weeks then running off to California without so much as a good-bye. Yeah, that would give her reason to feel a little less than warm and fuzzy toward a guy. East frowned at his own realization. As much as he hated to admit it, but he was just as big an asshole as Hedgeman. No wonder Marti walked out on him earlier today.

She glanced up at him and he caught a glimpse of all the pain and longing and unanswered questions in her golden eyes. If only he could wipe all that away and make sure she never, ever had to worry about someone bailing on her again. But he was probably the very last person on earth she'd ever let close enough for that.

"It's getting late," she said, quickly looking away from him and busying herself with folding her napkin. "We've got an early morning. I think I'd better head upstairs."

She probably wanted to be alone, but he didn't. If she was hurting tonight, he wanted to be the one there for her.

"Yeah, prep starts at six-thirty a.m. and we've still got a few things to get ready," he said, crumpling his napkin and pushing away from the table.

Marti didn't complain in front of everyone else and in fact looked almost grateful when he stood and pulled her chair back for her. As far as appearances went, they sure did make a great couple. Too bad it all fell apart the minute their audience left.

Everyone agreed that morning would come early and wished Marti and East well. Charleen had just picked at her food all through the meal, but suddenly she said she wanted to finish her broccoli and fairly ordered Arv to stay put instead of following them to the elevator. Dr. Traynor had already argued about getting to pay the bill, and finally Granny had convinced the others to let the guy take it. He was signing his name when East and Marti headed off alone to the elevators.

Marti seemed really tense and distracted, so it surprised him when she took a big deep breath and spoke as he punched the "up" button.

"Thanks for giving Leland the smack down he needed."

Really? He fully expected her to be mad at him for it.

"He's an asshole and ought to have his balls ripped off for the way he treated you." *Jeez, did he say that out loud?* Marti probably wasn't going to like it.

But instead of getting ticked off she said, "That would be assuming he had any." Then she went so far as to give an evil laugh.

They stepped inside the empty elevator and he couldn't have been happier. It probably wasn't fair to take advantage of Marti's raw emotions after her first meeting with the slug who stomped all over her heart, but he decided not to think about that right now. If she wasn't going to tell him to leave her alone yet, then he was sticking around.

He let the doors shut before pressing number six. No sense rushing things, since Marti was probably going to send him out to sleep in the hall once they got up to their room. For just a few minutes more she was treating him like an ally and he was determined to revel in it.

"He's a little bit in love with himself, isn't he?" he asked cautiously.

"You noticed? Yeah, he's always been number one," she sighed. "But thanks."

"For what?"

"You know," she shrugged, not meeting his eyes. "For being a smart-ass. For acting like we're… well, like everything is great."

The elevator jerked a bit as it started the ascent toward their room. Marti was unsteady on her feet and rocked into East. He put an arm around her out of sheer instinct and it felt really good. When she didn't push him away or back up, he left it there. Instantly everything *was* great.

He was desperately trying to talk himself out of putting the other arm around her when she inched closer to him and made the fatal mistake of looking up at him with big, trusting eyes. Oh, God. How on earth had he not followed her up to college all those years ago? Right now he was pretty sure he'd do anything she asked him.

He hoped she didn't ask him to get the hell away.

Partly to keep her from saying anything like that and partly because he just couldn't help himself, he did slip the other arm around her. And pulled her closer. And said her name softly just before he kissed her.

Chapter 22

It took a hundred years to get from the elevator into their room. Damn, why were these key cards so finicky? Finally on the third try the little light turned green and East clicked open the door. Marti hoped he hadn't come to his senses.

It didn't seem like he had. No sooner were they inside than he grabbed her to him again and the kisses took up where they'd left off when the elevator doors opened. They were wonderful and East tasted like all her best dreams. She was not going to let herself run away this time because of any silly worries about the future.

Granny was right. She might as well take advantage of the time she had with East. Life would catch up with them soon enough and he'd be gone and there was nothing she could do about that. She'd been stupid about Leland and now she'd been stupid about East. It was time to quit being stupid and time to start being happy.

And getting East naked and into that big bed with her tonight would be a very happy thing.

He seemed just as motivated as she was. Hands collided as they reached to fumble with clothing and fasteners. East was apparently more competent in this area than she was and he won by getting her shirt unbuttoned first. She didn't mind since he seemed so pleased with what he found beneath.

"I love the grown-up Marti," he breathed, leaning in to nip her through the thin fabric of her bra.

The grown-up East was pretty darn loveable, too. But she already knew that. She'd seen *The Passionate Palate* a few times over the years and those producers obviously knew they had a gold mine under East's shirt. He seemed to do an inordinate number of episodes without one. Plus, she'd been watching him go in and out of the shower at home for nearly a month. Yeah, the grown-up East was the stuff dreams were made of and she didn't feel much like putting those dreams off any longer.

She got his last button undone and was slipping his shirt over his shoulders while he was sliding her skirt down past her hips. It fell to the floor. God, his hands felt good on her skin. Vice versa, too. She skimmed her fingertips over the solid muscle of his back, then trailed down to his waist and set to work on his belt buckle. He shuddered where she touched him and she knew that was a good thing.

He didn't wait for her to finish with the buckle. Instead, he scooped her up and hauled her easily the last few steps toward the bed. She giggled. Nothing like being stripped down to her underwear and clinging helplessly to a strong, solid body to make her feel eighteen again. The fact that it was East's strong, solid body probably had something to do with it, too.

He tossed her gently down onto the bed and loomed over her, taking in every inch with hungry eyes. She'd seen that look before, years ago, and it melted her then just as it did now. The only difference was that now he wasn't just hungry. There was a promise in those eyes that hadn't been there before. Grown-up East seemed to have a much better idea of just what to do with her than teenage Johnny had back then. Now that made her shudder.

"You're in for it now," he said, confirming her fondest fears.

"Good," she said just before all the breath went out of her.

His buckle was unbuckled and his pants went the way of her skirt. His underwear, too, if he'd had any on, which she wasn't entirely sure he had. Either way, the result was mind-boggling.

He stood at the end of the bed, stark naked and the most beautiful thing she'd ever seen. Literally. Wow, these ten years had been good to the man.

His skin was bronzed from the sun, and only a slight difference was evident around those important areas where he would ordinarily have been covered. Apparently he spent as much time out of his swim trunks as in them. But why waste time contemplating his tanning habits? There were other, more interesting things to consider at the moment.

Like how it was completely obvious why she'd never fallen head-over-heels for some other guy. It would have been a real disappointment to be stuck forever with someone who could never be East. No wonder her love life had always been so messed up. She'd already had the best, and the best had run off to California without her.

But he wasn't in California now. Nope, he was right here with her. It might only be for a little while, but she was sure as hell going to enjoy it while she could.

"You look good," she managed, not bothering to look him in the eye.

"I have to. It was in my contract."

"But you're not under contract anymore, are you?"

He grinned and moved onto the bed, his thigh just barely brushing hers as he stretched out beside her.

"Well, there's this a little legal matter binding me body and soul to a sexy ecologist gal I know."

She reached to trace her fingernails over his perfectly-defined chest. "She sounds like a lucky ecologist."

"She will be as soon as I get these pesky clothes off her."

She didn't argue a bit as he moved over her, taking her mouth in a deep kiss while his hands slid behind her to unhook the bra. It was as agreeable as she was and he had it off her body in no time. When his mouth moved to take in one of the eager nipples, she couldn't help but let out a gasp of surprise at the wave of pleasure his action brought over her.

He smiled. "You like that?"

She nodded, but her voice was lost behind a flood of wonderful sensation. East was manipulating her nipple with his tongue and doing it very well. She'd let him go on for about a week.

Or, maybe not. When he slipped his hand under the silky elastic of her panties, she knew she'd never last out a week. She wanted him so badly her body took over and she found herself pushing up toward him, begging for his full attention on that hot, desperate area of her lower body.

He stroked her with his finger and she made a noise. It was a happy noise, but she hoped he knew the exact translation was something like "you'd better get on with this before I implode right here under you." He appeared to be polylingual—and poly-a-few-other-things, too—because he only waited about ten more seconds before sliding the panties down while never breaking stride with his nipple-seduction.

"I'm going to apologize right now," he said after a while, giving the nipple a little break. His voice sounded about as sturdy as hers.

"Why?"

"Because I'm not going to last very long. Sorry."

"Good," she said, kicking off the underwear and wrapping her legs around him. "Because I'm dam tired of waiting."

——

The first thing East noticed when he slowly returned to consciousness was Marti's scrumptious body tucked up against his. The blanket was bunched around them and her tousled hair brushed against his face, making his nose twitch. He couldn't ever remember being so comfortable in his entire life.

He'd never woken up to morning light with Marti in his arms, either.

He felt tight, his muscles sore. How many times had they made love during the hours of darkness? He'd lost count.

Well, that wasn't quite true. He may have not actually been keeping a mathematical accounting of their activities, but he remembered every precious moment of the hours with Marti. He always would. And looking at her now, the satisfied blush on her cheeks and the happily exhausted smile on her lips, he was pretty sure last night wasn't one she'd forget soon, either.

With luck, maybe neither of them would have to. If he was careful with her and took his time convincing her to take a chance on him, maybe they could have a lot of years ahead of them to grope and pant for each other at night. That would be nice. Years and years of loving Marti.

He just had to convince her to give this a real chance once the whole cook-off thing was over with.

Oh, damn! They had to compete in that blasted cook-off this morning. What time was it?

He jerked awake, shoving himself up to lean across Marti and check the clock on the nightstand. *Damn damn damn.* She would never forgive him if he'd gotten so carried away with lust that he forgot all about the main reason they were here in the first place!

His movement must have disturbed her and she stirred. The little sounds she made were darling, and he couldn't help but watch shamelessly as she stretched and twisted her body like a cat napping in the sun. The blanket conveniently slipped off and for a moment East forgot all about the time or the cook-off or any other important aspect of life not directly associated with getting his hands on Marti's soft girl-parts again.

Her bobcat eyes slitted open and she smiled at him. "Morning."

When she was foolish enough to reach out and touch his face, he gave up all hope of getting to that competition on time. She was wrapped in his arms again and he was as hungry for her as he had been ten years ago. Or five years ago. Or yesterday. He suspected there would never be enough of Marti to end that perpetual longing.

She melted into him and for the first time East decided he could become a morning person. Waking up with Marti in his bed would be more than enough to get him up early every day of his life. And, by golly, he sure was up.

She slithered against him and must have felt that, too. She giggled.

"Again?" she asked with beautifully pretended surprise.

"Hell yes!"

She was amenable until she glanced at the clock.

"Oh, no! Look what time it is!"

He did. It was just after six o'clock. They had about twenty minutes to get dressed and get down to start preparing for the big event. Shit. He was rather enjoying the big event they already had going on up here.

She scrambled out of bed, giving him an enjoyable show

as she tripped over tangled blankets in the dim light filtering through the thick drapes. She grumbled and started shuffling clothes about in her suitcase.

"Quick, you get in the shower while I try to figure out what to wear," she said. "Maybe you can go down first."

"Unless you'd rather go down first," he said, coming up behind her to nuzzle her neck. He wasn't talking about heading to the first floor.

She giggled again, but shrugged him off. "Be serious!"

"I am." *Oh, how serious he was.*

But she shoved him toward the bathroom. "Come on. You can get ready a lot faster than I can, so you have to get going. If we're not ready on time we'll get disqualified! You want to be the one to explain to Granny what we were up to instead of making Eggs Benedict and frying steak filets?"

He met her smoky eyes then glanced down at the raging hard-on that proudly saluted her. "How can I be expected to cook with this going on?"

"Shower," she said firmly and went back to fussing over her clothes.

Well, nothing to do but obey. He hoped she realized he was going to make her pay for this later on. Like the very minute they were done with this stupid breakfast competition. He hoped no one had any afternoon plans for them today.

The water in the shower heated up quickly and he stepped inside with a frustrated sigh. She thought a shower was going to calm him down? Not likely.

There was a tap on the bathroom door and he could see her shadow moving on the other side of the shower curtain as she stepped into the small room. To his surprise, she pushed the curtain back a bit and timidly poked her head inside.

"I'm hurrying," he assured her, grabbing the soap and rubbing up a big pile of lather.

"I know but I thought… well, I thought maybe it would be quicker if I took a shower with you."

Now that sounded like a great idea. He suspected it would actually be a lot *less* quicker that way, but it was a totally great idea. He stepped back and pulled the curtain aside for her. Yeah, he was leering, but he couldn't help that. She was still naked.

"Come on in."

Her gaze traveled up and down him and for a minute he thought she was going to back out. She didn't, though, and he let out a sigh of relief. The warm water sluiced down his back and he held out the handful of suds toward her.

"Can I wash you?" he asked.

She nodded shyly but couldn't hide her greedy eyes. They practically ate him up. "And I thought maybe I could help you a little bit with that… problem… there."

Oh, yeah. She could sure do that, all right. She could do that big time. Hell. What cooking competition?

———

Jeez. What good was having a husband if you couldn't even count on him for sex? Charleen was in a bad, bad mood.

What an idiot she'd been, splurging on a sexy nightgown for their little "vacation" here at this nice hotel. Did Arv even notice? No. He watched something idiotic on TV last night then rolled over and started snoring. She might as well have been sleeping over at her mom's house with the kids.

It was obvious he'd only had Marti on the brain all night. The few words he did say were all about how he hoped Marti and East won that damn breakfast competition in the morning. Oh, and he grumbled about how she was way, way too good for that Hegeman jerk. Yeah, inviting him to their table last night had been a dumb idea.

She'd wanted to stir up a little discomfort, but didn't count on getting Arv's protective streak all riled up. She'd meant for him to see Marti for the flake she was, going after her old boyfriend or something, but instead the woman ended up coming off as the much-abused saint. Not at all the result she'd had in mind.

Oh, well. She should have known this sort of stuff would never work for her. She'd never been big on revenge or game playing. She just wished there was something she could do to get her husband's attention. She'd been competing with Marti Snowden for nine long years now and didn't think she had much more in her. One of these days she'd just have to admit defeat and try to get on with her life.

Man, that would be hard. Arv *was* her life. She only wished there was some way she could tell him that. If he would even care.

She checked her watch again. Still no sign of Marti and East. Ha, wouldn't that be funny? Maybe Marti's infamous bad-luck would kick in and they'd sleep right through this competition. But that would only make Arv feel more sorry and more concerned for Saint Marti the Popular. Charleen didn't think she could deal with that.

A commotion at the judges' table caught Charleen's attention. A couple of the officials were busy setting things up, but a beautiful woman with perfect hair and blindingly white teeth seemed to have a problem with the way the water glasses were arranged on the table.

"But where did it *come* from?" she was asking loudly.

"The kitchen staff brought it out, Ms. Kincaid," a terrified looking contest official replied. He nervously adjusted his tie.

"Well, if this is tap water I can't drink it. Find out, will you? And bring something safer, something that won't give me *e coli*."

The official nodded and scampered off toward the kitchen, or anywhere away from the fuming diva. Ah, now it hit her. The official had called her Ms. Kincaid, hadn't he? Well, this skinny Medusa could be none other than East's ex-wife.

Charleen had heard all about the scandal of the contest people unwittingly bringing her on as a judge. East and Marti had talked about it last night, before Hedgeman arrived. For some reason they'd told the contest people to go ahead and let Ms. Kincaide stay on as a judge, so here she was today.

And, in perfect timing, here came Marti and East, as well. They scurried into the ballroom and found the cooking station that had been set up and assigned to them. Charleen couldn't help but notice Marti looked particularly thrown together this morning. She hadn't even bothered with make-up or jewelry, her hair was pulled into a drab little ponytail and it was still wet from the shower. She looked flushed and a bit off balance. Were those circles under her eyes? It would seem the poor dear had not slept much.

If it were any other couple Charleen would might have attributed it all to newlywed extra-curricular activities. Judging by what she'd seen of Marti and East lately, however, she thought that was unlikely. Probably Marti's ragged appearance had more to do with seeing Hedgeman last night than to snuggling with East.

One quick glance at East showed him to be cheerful and apparently well-rested. He seemed suddenly aware of Treeva, too. He glanced up from his preparations and his eyes locked with her. To Charleen's surprise, the man actually smiled. He gave his ex-wife a quick little wave and proceeded to get right back to work. He didn't even skip a beat. Well, that seemed odd.

What could Charleen make of it all? Marti's ex had turned up last night, and now here was East giving a friendly little wave to his ex. Damn, they were like some big, happy, dysfunctional family. Everyone was getting along too well and Charleen didn't like it one bit.

What were the odds of something like this happening? Not too damn good. Impossible, actually. Maybe Hedgeman's arrival was coincidence, but this whole Treeva Kincaide thing was just too weird to be an accident. Was she hear to get her wayward boy-toy back?

That would mess things up between East and his new wife. Anyone could see that was not sisterly affection simmering in the look Treeva was giving poor, oblivious Marti. She might not have wanted East when she had him, but she sure as hell did now that Marti had him.

This could be bad. East and Marti weren't the tightest pair of newlyweds Charleen had ever seen. In fact, it didn't seem like they were all that thrilled with being newlyweds. Maybe they jumped into things a little too quickly and were regretting it now. So what was keeping East from dumping swamp girl and diving back in with Treeva? That would leave Marti all alone, looking for a sympathetic shoulder to cry on.

And Arv's shoulder would probably be the closest one.

No, this wasn't good. Treeva the Diva was clearly the kind of person who got exactly what she wanted. If she thought there was a chance she could get East back, she would. Then Marti would come crying to Arv and that would be that.

But what could Charleen do? She couldn't very well just go up and tell Treeva to keep her mitts off East. That would probably only make Treeva more determined to have him. But Charleen couldn't let her get him, not until she was sure

Marti wouldn't fall Arv's way. Somehow, she had to know what Treeva was up to.

Lucky for her, Charleen had just bought herself a nice, cold, unopened bottle of Pure Springs sparkling water. Hmm, this could be promising. Yes, a crystal-clear bottled water ought to look pretty good to Ms. Kincaid, as opposed to the pitcher of Lake Erie that sat sweating on the judges' table right now.

True, maybe none of this was any of Charleen's business, and she usually would never stick her nose in like this, but it involved Arv so that made it her business. And hell, this was a pretty extenuating circumstance. The life of her marriage might depend on how far she stuck her nose right now.

There wasn't anything wrong with offering to share a bottle of water, was there? Heck no. It was like being a Good Samaritan. If Ms. Kincaid happened to ask a few questions about their mutual friend East Smith, and if Charleen happened to make up some crap about how happy and perfect for each other East and Marti were, well, wouldn't it all be for a good cause? Hell yes, it would.

Chapter 23

Marti was busy counting out her eggs and pre-measuring her spices when suddenly she was aware of Treeva. She hadn't seen her, but she knew she was there. The feel of her hung over the room like a big dark bird, hovering, scanning for some helpless little mouse to pounce on. Or, it could have just been Marti's own insecurity after about eight hours straight of making wild, passionate love with East and wondering now if he'd done all that same stuff with his ex-wife.

No, it must have just been Treeva's naturally negative aura. There she was, over at the judges' table. Marti would recognize her anywhere, mostly because no other woman in the state of Ohio wore that much make up and looked that perfect at six-thirty-eight in the morning. Plus, she was staring back at her with the look of a bitchy ex-wife. Marti would not give her the satisfaction of looking back.

"I see she didn't disqualify herself when the judges informed her I was in the competition," East said, coming up beside Marti.

Did he have to be so damn friendly? He actually had the nerve to wave at the woman! Marti would have rather pretended she didn't exist.

"I thought she'd look shorter and fatter in person," she said.

"Don't let her hear you say that. Her head will start

spinning around and then green stuff spews out."

It would have been funny if Marti wasn't so sure it could really happen. No, she was not going to look over there again. Ignore her... ignore her. Odd, but was that Charleen going over there to talk to Treeva? Jeez, Marti just couldn't figure that one.

"I think we ought to separate the eggs before we whip them," East was saying. "Do we have enough bowls for that?"

Marti forced herself to forget Treeva and concentrate on their preparations. Let's see, bowls... now, what was a bowl? God, it was hard to think with her insides still all swirling around after last night. Why couldn't she just accept things for what they were? Why did she have to keep torturing herself by wondering what it had meant to East, if he'd been disappointed with her... if Treeva might have been just a little bit more exciting.

Stupid Treeva. If only Marti had thought to pack rat poison in their supplies. Treeva could maybe get a little extra garnish in her breakfast.

But that wasn't nice, nor would it help them win the contest. The other judges would no doubt mark them down. Rat poisoning was not in the official recipes they'd turned in with their registration forms yesterday.

But how on earth was she supposed to get her mind off the fact that East used to be married to her? Awful though she was, Treeva Kincaide was undeniably gorgeous. Man, but she and East must have made quite a scene heading out to all those posh Hollywood parties and whatever other star-studded events they attended.

Shucks, just look at the finery he was surrounded by now that he was with Marti.

She dropped an egg. It landed with an oddly satisfying,

juicy crunch. So much for that twelve-egg omelet she had planned.

"Don't worry," East said, passing her a roll of paper towels he had suspiciously handy. "I had Arv run out and get us another dozen eggs last night. Just in case."

Just in case his klutzy new wife couldn't come even close to being as useful as his glamorous old wife? Very forward thinking of him. Wonder what he had on hand to mop up her heart when it broke into a million pieces after all this was over?

East didn't seem to have a clue how jumbled her brain was right now. He slid up behind her and pulled her into a tight embrace against him. Then he nuzzled her neck. God, how was she ever going to get over him?

"I think you've got a hickey, Mrs. Smith," he whispered.

He was right, of course. She'd noticed it this morning in the five minutes she'd had to get dressed. She didn't even have time to dig out her make-up case and try to conceal it. Mostly she hoped her shirt would cover it, but apparently it didn't. Which was okay, since she sort of wanted Treeva to see it anyway. Petty and childish, yeah, but the thought made her smile.

"I don't know about you," he went on. "But I'm having a pretty damn good morning already."

Good for him, considering that things were just about to change. In exactly eighteen minutes Marti Snowden would have to start cooking in front of East's famously kitchen-savvy ex-wife. She hoped the hotel was paid up on their fire insurance.

———

Sometimes Milly wished she hadn't fallen in love with a

medical doctor this time around. He was entirely too sensible for her. Here it was the perfect time for a fit of nerves and pacing back and forth, but all he could think about was her blood pressure.

"Come on, relax a minute, will you?" he was saying, and looking pretty darn enticing there in his snazzy golf shirt and inviting smile. He pulled out her chair for her.

"I can't relax," she said, and kept right on pacing. There was plenty of space in this ballroom, it wasn't like she was going to be bothering anybody. "There was almond in my pancakes! I never put almond in my pancakes. Don't know what East was thinking."

"It was fine, Milly. Relax. If those almond pancakes were theirs, they were great. The kids did fine."

He was right of, course. The pancakes had been good. Actually, even better than her original recipe. Darn it, but that boy must have picked up a few tricks along the way. Everything East and Marti served up today had been top notch. They had some pretty stiff competition, though.

As one of the owners, Milly wasn't allowed to score anyone, but she and her guest were allowed to taste everything. After a mouthful of one of the other contestant's strawberry crepes, she wished she'd just stuck to East's dishes. That crepe was good, and it was making her pretty darn nervous despite how incredible East's pancakes had been.

But what would the judges think? She knew for a fact one of them wasn't going to be especially fair. That damn floozy from Hollywood kept glaring daggers at Marti and East. It was just plain wrong that Treeva Kincaide had been brought on to judge. Anyone could see she was nothing but trouble.

Oh, sure, those celebrity judges supposedly didn't know who made what, but how anonymous could any of this really be considering the judges had been sitting there, watching the contestants cook everything in their little kitchen units? It wasn't going to be hard at all for the judges to know which recipe came from which contestant.

Milly scanned the faces of the fifty-or-so tasters seated throughout the big room. Marti and East's breakfast offerings had been great, but there sure was a lot of other good food spread out there. The celebrity judges were sitting at a long table on a stage and they'd each been served a small portion of everything from the ten contestants. The rest of the food was then put out for the rest of them, buffet style. The tasters could then pick and chose what they wanted, grading their selections on a score card that listed everything by number. It was supposed to be anonymous and fair, but Milly knew every one of the cooks in this competition had family and friends on the tasters panel.

Only East had a damned ex-wife on the judges panel, though.

"Hey, all they have to do is get enough points to stay in the competition, right?" Milton said, doing his adorable best to soothe her frazzled nerves.

Peg was there, seated with them, and Arv and Charleen, too. They all quickly agreed with Milton that things were going just fine. Considering the fact that Marti hadn't caught the place on fire yet, Milly had to concur. It was going much better than expected, actually.

"I'm just so proud of those kids!" Peg said, wiping her mouth and tucking her scorecard back in its envelope. She wasn't a family member or an owner, so she was allowed to pay the tasters fee and actually participate in judging.

"Yeah. They're bound to take this round, easy," Arv said.

He'd kind of surprised Milly by the enthusiastic way he cheered on his friends. Considering it was his restaurant that was supposed to be here, Milly thought he must be a saint to not harbor any kind of ill-will after that tragedy at his own place. His wife seemed to have some unresolved resentment, but Arv sure was enjoying his time as a taster.

"Just so long as they aren't the two who get eliminated," Peg said, shaking her head. "I think it's a shame to do that, force contestants out of the running after just one meal."

"You won't feel that way once they announce the scores and Marti and East are only up against seven opponents tomorrow for lunch instead of nine," Milly pointed out.

"And two more get weeded out after that," Arv said.

"So there'll only be five left for the dinner contest?" Peg asked.

Milton chuckled. "This is really cut-throat cooking here."

"It's the Patchwork Platter on the line," Milly said, getting jumpy just thinking about it. "The winner really earns the right to take it home and put it up for all the world to see. They've got to be the best of the best."

"And we really don't have a clue what will be on the dinner menu?" Peg questioned.

"No one does," Milly replied. "The kids will be totally on their own for that one. I'll admit, I feel kind of helpless."

"They'll be fine," Milton soothed. "Isn't the point of that final meal to see how creative these cooks can get in a real-life scenario? Just remember who you're dealing with. Your kids will do fine, Milly. Don't worry about them."

"I am worried!" she insisted. "Did you see how nervous Marti was all morning? Poor thing never did like to cook, and now she's got to do it for a hundred spectators… and that *woman*."

The contest official who was walking around gathering up the score cards gave her a funny look. Yeah, he ought to be ashamed of himself, running a contest where one of the main judges hated one of the competitors. Obviously they were more interested in getting their extra publicity than in running a fair contest here. That gorgeous Patchwork Platter, sitting prominently displayed on the official's table, deserved more respect.

"Come on," Milton said, standing and taking Milly's hand. "It'll be a few minutes while they tally the votes. Let's go for a walk."

Milly tried to protest, but she had to agree moving around right now would feel good. Her hip was all tight and bothered from sitting all morning, and she had just about all she could take of Peg's sly little grins every time Milton said anything. Peg had figured out they were carrying on and was getting a big kick out of it. Well, just wait 'til they got home. Milly knew about Peg's thing for the butcher over at Bandy's IGA. Starting next week Peg would be sent out to buy meat. Lots and lots of meat.

Milton led her away from their table and off to the side, where doors opened into the hallway.

"Where are you taking me?"

He just laughed. "Think there's time to run up to our room?"

"You mean *my* room. And no, there isn't."

"Like it or not, Milly, it's *our* room. You're just going to have to get used to sharing your life with me, you know."

"I thought we talked about that?"

"Well, I'm not done talking about that. I still want to marry you."

Oh, crap. This was the third time in two days he'd brought that up and she felt dangerously close to giving in. But how could she? So much was still undecided with Marti and East. They might act like everything was hunky-dory, but Milly knew the truth. East was working on heading back to

California and Marti was still nursing a decade old broken heart.

Just watching the way Marti faded under that evil woman's haughty glare, it was pitiful. And East went on as if nothing was wrong. He seemed overly cheerful today, as a matter of fact. Probably meant nothing, but poor Marti was likely to attribute it to Treeva being here. She must be devastated.

"I told you. I can't make any commitments like that now," she said in her most business-like voice so he wouldn't know how hard it was to say it.

He sighed heavily and she let him lead her into a little alcove beside the big fireplace that sprouted up and through the ceiling in the center of a lounge area. Big comfy chairs had been tucked in there with a couple reading lamps. It was a nice, quiet place and completely private.

"If you're going to turn me down again on account of Marti," he said, pulling her into a tight embrace. "I need to warn you you're about to lose that excuse."

"Let me go. What if someone… what are you talking about?"

Did he know something she didn't? Had Marti said something to him about leaving Garden Falls and going back to work? That horrid Dr. Hedgeman was here, and a whole pack of them botanists, biologists, environmentalists and all sorts of other -ists. Maybe she'd met up with some of them and started making plans to get on another project somewhere. Maybe once this competition was over she and East really would just go their separate ways like they'd been saying all along.

"You keep saying you want to be sure Marti's all settled before you start making plans of your own," he said. "Well, I've been watching them—her and East—and I've got to tell you, if you're hoping to get that girl back under your roof I don't think it's going to happen."

Dang. She *was* leaving. "What do you mean?"

"He's got the look."

"What?"

"And believe me, I know all about it."

"What are you babbling about, Milton?"

"He's a man in love, Milly." He paused for effect and when she couldn't think of anything to say, he went on. "Trust me on this. He's got it bad, and he's not about to let his woman out of his sight."

"Oh? You're so sure about that?"

"Positive. I'm an expert on the subject." He hadn't let go of her yet, and now he bent to kiss her shoulder. Ah that was nice. He even had her shirt pushed aside for full effect. Oh drat, she was crumbling.

"You are talking about East and Marti here, right?"

"And if I was talking about us, too? Would that be so bad?"

"I explained it to you. I can't focus on my own life right now. Marti needs me. You know she and East just got married to keep us from being disqualified for the cook-off. He's still planning to leave her."

"You sure about that?"

It was hard to keep talking while his kisses began migrating around from one shoulder to the other and she felt him undoing the pearl buttons on the front of her blouse. She ought to stop him, but it sure did feel nice.

But no, she wasn't going to get carried away. Not here, practically in public. And they were talking about Marti.

"I am," she went on. "Marti says he's on the phone all the time with his agent, and she's heard him… making plans… and things."

Milton chuckled, but it was muffled by the lingering kiss he was giving to her collarbone. Oh, and what his hands were doing to her pearl buttons! Milly had almost forgotten they'd been in the middle of a conversation when he finally spoke again.

"Well," he began, as if proud of some accomplishment. "From that nice big hickey your granddaughter was sporting on her neck today—right about here—my guess is he's been making plans, all right."

"Hickey?"

Yeah, she had noticed some kind of blemish on Marti's neck this morning, but she didn't think anything of it. Could Milton be right? Someone was giving her girl love bites last night? Well, hallelujah and holy cow! That might explain a little bit about East's strangely chipper mood. Huh. What do you know about that?

"Are you sure it was a…" she started to ask, but then it dawned on her why Milton was grinning like a guilty kid. "You didn't!"

She pushed him away and leaned over to see in the small gilt mirror hanging behind an armchair. Oh, yes he did. She could hardly believe her eyes.

"I've got a blooming hickey!"

Milton rolled with laughter. Good lord, the old man had given her a hickey like some lust-crazed teenager! Heaven almighty, what were people going to think? And they were going to have to walk back into that crowded ballroom in a couple minutes to hear if Marti and East made the cut.

"I swear, I'm going to murder you!"

He just laughed and pulled her back into his arms for another kiss. This one was pretty quick, though, and it was a damn good thing. Somebody came barging into their private little alcove.

"Just give me a minute, Phil," an annoying—and familiar—voice screeched out. "I've got to pull up my damn panty hose!"

Oh, lordy. Here came Joetta Townsend, already hiking her skirt up. She stopped, thankfully, when she saw Milly. For a second the threesome just blinked at each other, then Joetta erupted into greetings.

"Well, Granny and Dr. Traynor! How handy to find you here. We were just going looking for you!"

"You were?" *Good grief. What were these people doing here?* "I didn't realize you and Phil were coming up here for this event."

Joetta tugged subtly at her panty hose. Well, probably she meant for it to be subtle. It wasn't. Milly could feel Milton trying to hold back a chuckle. If the man knew what was good for him, he'd take his eyes and his mind off of Joetta's panty hose right now.

"Yeah, well, we had some, uh, down time at home so we thought we'd come up here and see how East and Marti are doing. They are here, aren't they?"

"Of course they're here. Everyone's over in the ballroom right now waiting for the final scores for the breakfast competition to be announced."

"Great! Then they'll be free for a little while, right?" Joetta beamed. "Phil's got some important business with East, you know."

"No, I didn't know that," Milly frowned.

Now what on earth kind of important business could East possibly have with the land-grabbing and money-grubbing Phil Townsend? It sure as hell wasn't something that would make Marti any bit pleased.

"Hey, what's the holdup…" Phil was bellowing as he came on into the alcove.

"Phil, looky," Joetta said with a smile. "I bumped into Granny, and Dr. Traynor."

Phil's bellowing was replaced by a smarmy grin. "Well, hey there! Fancy running into you folks here."

"Granny says East and Marti are still in the ballroom waiting for their scores."

"Well, then we haven't missed anything yet," Phil said. "Great, great."

"Maybe if we catch him now, East will have a few minutes to talk to you, Phil," Joetta said.

"He's pretty busy cleaning up right now…" Milly began, but neither Townsend seemed very interested in listening.

"Great! I'll only need a couple minutes of his time. Heck, we can get this done before lunch," Phil said.

Lunch? It was only nine-thirty in the morning now. What were these Townsend's up to, anyway? And why on earth did Phil seem to think East would want to be a part of it?

"It's so nice that you could come up here to keep an eye on Granny, Dr. Traynor," Joetta said. "We've all been so very worried about her lately."

Then she had the absolute nerve to pat Milly's hand and take her glass-scratching voice up a notch, as if Milly was some sort of half-deaf half-wit. "So, are we feeling better today, Granny? Is everyone up here being nice to you, and helping you find your way around this big fancy hotel?"

Milton jumped in before Milly had a chance to tell Joetta just exactly what she could do with this big fancy hotel.

"Milly's doing much better, thank you," he answered. "But all this stress of the competition has made her prone to sudden outbursts, so I've been trying to keep her quiet. Too much stimulation, you know. Not good for a delicate constitution."

"Oh, right, right," Joetta said, dropping her voice down to

a whisper and smiling at Milly like she was a naughty three year old. "It looks like someone's already got a nasty bruise."

Damn it, but Joetta was staring right at Milly's brand new hickey. When she finally looked away, it was to smile cluelessly at Milton and start patting *his* hand. The cow.

"The elderly can be so fragile. So wonderful you could be here to take care of her. It's getting harder and harder to find a doctor who really cares about his work, you know."

Milton smiled back at her. "I'm a hands-on kind of guy. I'd take my work home with me every night, if I could." He gave Milly a little wink.

"You're a saint," Joetta said.

"So, which way to the ballroom?" Phil asked.

"It's just up the hall. We're heading back there right now," Milton said, taking Milly's arm. "Why don't you sit at our table? I think there are a couple extra chairs."

Milly glared at him.

"Oh, that would be lovely!" Joetta gushed.

"In fact, you go on ahead of us," Milton said. "Milly prefers to take things slowly."

Now she really glared at him.

"Although my goal is to get her committed to moving forward with the next phase of her treatment by the end of this weekend," he added. "A much more permanent phase."

Boy, if she wasn't such a nice lady, Milly would have thunked him right there for that one. What were Phil and Joetta to think, him talking like this? But, apparently Phil and Joetta didn't bother thinking. They just moseyed on ahead.

Milton laughed when they were alone. Milly slapped him on the arm.

"Hey, watch it," he said. "We elderly bruise easily."

"I can't believe you, talking like that in front of them."

"Oh, they aren't paying any attention to us. They've got

something else on their minds right now."

Milly frowned. "Yeah, and I just wonder what it is. What do you suppose they think they're cooking up with East?"

"Probably more of this development thing they've been hawking all over town. They must figure East for an idiot with plenty of cash."

"Well, he might be an idiot, but from what Marti says, that Treeva person got all his cash."

"Then he should be rid of the Townsends pretty quickly. I know Marti's not exactly in favor of this development deal."

"No, she isn't."

And that was an understatement. If Marti thought for one minute East was getting involved in helping the Townsend's destroy that land out there… well, any budding romance between those two would be pretty efficiently nipped. Of course East knew that. Surely he wouldn't get involved in this thing.

Then again, it wasn't like the Townsend's to go putting themselves out for no reason. For them to drive all the way up here on a Thursday when they could be home making a buck, well, it just seemed a bit out of character. Would they have done it if they hadn't been given some encouragement?

"I just hope for his own sake he doesn't get bamboozled into helping them," Milly said.

"He's a smart man," Milton reassured. "But I wouldn't mind a little bamboozling myself right now. Want to head upstairs for a 'rest'?"

She was planning to say no, but it just didn't come out. Fact was she really wanted to head upstairs with him. Sure, she really ought to be more concerned about Marti and East, but with Milton smiling at her like he was, she sure found it darn hard to think about anyone else.

Until the loud cheer came from the ballroom.

"Oh, lord almighty! They're announcing the winners!"

Milton sighed, and matched her quickened pace. "Okay, bamboozling can wait. We'll go see how they did."

They hurried on into the ballroom. Milly bumped into a man in the doorway, but she was too worked up with worry to notice who he was. Milton mumbled something to him, then quickly ushered Milly on up toward their table. Her ears perked up as the announcer mentioned Marti and Easton Smith, from *Granny's Diner* in Garden Falls. Oh lordy, here it came!

Chapter 23

Marti held her breath. What if they didn't make the cut? What if they were already out of the competition after just one meal? Jeez, wouldn't that be just her luck?

She honestly couldn't say how well their breakfast turned out. With East beside her calling the shots, she just followed along without really paying much attention. Well, she'd been paying close attention, but not necessarily to cooking. It had been impossible to focus on anything besides East. She could only hope their food had been edible.

And even if it was the best meal ever concocted on the planet, there was still that little matter of Treeva. The diva had been scrutinizing them all through the allotted prep time—Marti had felt her evil eye. It didn't matter that the food was served to the judges anonymously; Treeva would have known which meal was theirs long before she took her first bite. She could have slammed them hard. Did she? The anticipation was nauseating.

"Here comes the DJ," East said softly into her ear. It didn't seem to matter what he was saying; her body still reacted as if it was something private, personal, and delightfully dirty.

The contestants had all been clattering away in their areas, cleaning and double-checking their supplies. They'd only be allowed one other opportunity to come in here before tomorrow's lunch competition, so anything they could do to be ahead of the game would help right now. But as Tommy Blue stepped up to the podium, everyone in the ballroom came to a hush and settled in their seats.

Marti propped herself on one of the tall stools provided for them in their cooking area. East sat next to her and placed his hand on her knee. For reassurance, she supposed. It was doing more to set her off balance than it was to support her, though. She was still a little wobbly after last night and getting even more wobbly just thinking about it.

She figured she'd better concentrate on something else. Like why hadn't Granny and Doc Traynor come back in? She'd noticed them walking out a few minutes ago, and they still weren't back. Did they know something she didn't? Had their food been so very bad?

Or had they gone back up to Granny's room for a quickie? Eew. Marti would need years of therapy after walking in on them yesterday.

Thankfully, the announcements began and she had something else to think about. Tommy Blue was making lame jokes about needing to join a gym after sampling all this great food by these great chefs at this great competition. So his vocabulary could use a little variety, it still made Marti smile to think she was included in the bunch. Ha, Marti Snowden was a great chef! What a riot.

No, that's Marti Snowden Smith, she corrected herself and blushed. She was East's wife. Maybe not for long, but for *now*. No matter what scores they got for their food, she knew they'd earned a perfect ten upstairs. Several of them.

"Unfortunately, two of our great teams won't be coming back for tomorrow's competition," Tommy Blue was saying, still clinging to his favorite adjective. "And that's too bad. Everyone did a great job today and there's no doubt that Buckeyes make *Great Food and Great Friends*!"

The room applauded on cue as a big screen overhead displayed the Travel and Tourism Board's slogan for this year. Mr. Blue must have had a hand in crafting it. Oh well, it was for a "great" cause so Marti smiled and clapped along with everyone.

"Beautiful Ohio" played on the loud speakers and Tommy Blue was practically yelling as he introduced the man who would announce the scores.

"Here he is, a man whose love for Ohio is as great as his appetite, Mr. Wallace Beaumont!"

The head of the Travel and Tourism Board stepped up and took a bow. Everyone applauded him, too. It wasn't so easy for Marti to do that, since this was the man who'd been clueless enough to bring Treeva here in the first place, but oh well. East was playing along nicely so she supposed she could, too.

She scanned the audience and saw movement in the doorway. Maybe Granny was coming back. Someone was coming into the ballroom. Granny?

No! Oh, dear lord, it was the Townsend's. Jeez, what on earth were they doing here? And too late to even eat anything. How weird.

Wallace Beaumont was reading off a long list of Thank You's to the many sponsors and appliance providers who had made this *great* competition possible. There was some rustling in the audience and Marti watched as the Townsend's made their way through the crowd, toward the table up front where Peg and the Koch's were sitting. Phil waved at East. He was tapping his watch and mouthing something, but Marti had no idea what that meant.

A quick glance at East told her he did, though. What? He had some kind of private conversation going with Phil Townsend? What was up with that? If this had anything to do with that Beaverbend project Phil had been hounding him about… grr, just the thought of that was enough to make Marti grind her teeth.

But then East was poking her on the shoulder and she took her attention away from Phil and turned to him. He grinned and gave a nice, public squeeze. What? Had she missed something?

"Not bad, Mrs. Smith," he said. "Who'd have ever thought it?"

"What?"

He just laughed. "Daydreaming? Come on, give me a kiss. Mr. Beaumont just announced us in fourth place!"

"What?!"

But he didn't wait for her to give him a kiss. He leaned over and took one for himself. Sigh. She could let East kiss her all day long. And heck, not being eliminated from the contest was pretty great, too.

——

Treeva was staring and East couldn't have cared less. He had good reason to celebrate, so he was damn well going to kiss his wife in public if he wanted to. He was still getting used to being allowed to kiss Marti anywhere at all, so he wasn't going to take this for granted.

He tightened his arm around her. She'd been too busy daydreaming to even hear their score read. He had a good suspicion he knew what she'd been daydreaming about. At least, he hoped he was right. He'd been having a hard time keeping his mind out of the bedroom all morning and it would be really "great" if she'd been having the same trouble. He hoped so. Then she'd be as eager as he was to get their clean-up done, make their excuses to friends—and the

Townsend's who'd shown up a bit ahead of schedule—and go back upstairs.

He finally decided the public had been treated to enough displays of their affection, so he broke off the kiss and had to settle with a lingering embrace. For one second his eyes glanced over the crowd. Ah, there was Granny, finally. Apparently she and her doctor hadn't slunk off for a nooner, after all. But then he noticed someone behind them, a lone figure whose silhouette filled the doorway.

Leland Hedgeman. The damn bastard was standing there, staring this way, an undeniable glare fastened on Marti. He caught East's eye and their mutual dislike for each other was obvious. So, things weren't as finished there as East had hoped. Damn.

Just how long had Hedgeman been standing there watching them? Long enough for Marti to have seen him, and been lost in thought about him? Shit. East was going to be really, really ticked off if *that* was indeed what had distracted her and prompted the daydreams.

Well, Hedgeman or no Hedgeman, East was just going to have to make sure *he* was the one distracting her from now on.

———

Charleen watched it all; Treeva glaring at East, East glaring at Dr. Hedgeman, Granny studying them all, and these silly Townsend folks trying to get a word in edgewise. Wow, she'd never dreamed this little trip would be full of so much intrigue and high adventure.

The high-school-ish love triangle crap she could understand. But what was up with the Townsend's? They were rattling on and on about some secret business they needed to discuss with East "in private". Joetta kept hinting that it was something "super fantabulous" and of course she wanted Charleen to ask all about it and of course Charleen wasn't about to.

It was fun to watch, though, as East did everything in his power to keep Marti from noticing Dr. Hedgeman who was obviously hanging around the place waiting for his opportunity to pounce on her. Treeva the Diva looked a bit like pouncing herself, although Charleen wasn't quite sure who her target was, East or Marti. She seemed equally prepared to tackle either of them and get equal enjoyment.

The whole thing was so darn entertaining Charleen forgot she was pissed off at Arv when he showed up beside her and actually started speaking.

"Hey, East says they've got it all under control here. Why don't we head back upstairs? Just the two of us."

It took a minute for the words to sink in. Arv wanted to head upstairs with her? With *her*, his own *wife*? And not under duress? Wow, that was odd. She almost wouldn't let herself get her hopes up and take him seriously, but darned if curiosity didn't get the best of her.

"Upstairs? With me? Now?"

"Yeah!"

"Uh, sure. Okay."

Now Arv smiled at her like he honestly meant it. "Good."

Well, what do you know about that? Poor guy must be getting desperate. Oh, well. Desperate times called for desperate measures. Charleen was going upstairs with no kids, no restaurant, and no Marti Snowden. East seemed to be doing his part to keep his little wife occupied so maybe things were looking up.

Heck, maybe she hadn't even needed to give that water to Treeva earlier, after all. Too bad. She'd been thirsty all morning.

Susan Gee Heino

Chapter 25

East was pleasantly exhausted as he pulled a charcoal-gray polo shirt over his head. Hungry, too. Ditching the Townsends right after this morning's competition hadn't been easy, but it sure had been worth the effort. He'd been rewarded by a full day alone with Marti—in bed. In fact, he hadn't wanted to risk running into those money-grubbing chiselers later on so he'd convinced Marti to skip lunch.

It hadn't taken much convincing, either. Now that she'd cut loose—for whatever reason, thank God—Marti seemed as one-track-minded as he was. They'd turned off their phones, put up the Do Not Disturb sign and just gone at it. Trouble was, after several hours of making up for lost time, even passion was forced to take a back seat to hunger. East was starving. Good thing they were supposed to meet everyone for dinner in a few minutes.

Man, these last twenty hours had been amazing. Marti was everything he could ever hope for in a lover. She was, well, perfect for him. Sure, it had always been like that in his memories, but over the years he figured he'd probably embellished things in his mind or purposely forgotten some of the less-than-perfect elements from their brief interlude. It wasn't like he'd really known what he was doing back then.

But he hadn't needed to. Things had been so easy between them, even as clumsy, nervous kids. It was no different now. Being with Marti was just plain easy. Like an instinct, he knew where to touch her, what to say, how to get her to relax. And she returned the favor.

But damn, his muscles were getting a bit sore. Six weeks of home-cooking and lazing around was taking its toll. Must be about time he'd get back into some kind of workout routine.

Really, though, the only routine he wanted was to let Marti keep him up all night. Literally. Every night. For always. That would be all the workout he'd ever need.

But he wasn't so sure she felt the same way. That was the one thing that bugged him about all this. At no time had she ever spoken of their future, or about what all this really meant to her. He tried not to notice it, but now that he was fully satiated and able to think clearly for the first time since they'd fallen into bed after sneaking out of the ballroom, he couldn't deny that had been missing.

He tucked his shirt into black Dockers and found his belt hanging from the reading lamp behind the one armchair in the room. Oh yeah, Marti'd been in a hurry to lose the clothes. They'd gone everywhere.

Here were his shoes, and over there his wallet, and his phone… jeez, they'd been wild. Out of habit he checked his phone and discovered a message. From a number in Garden Falls. He dialed it up his voice messages and listened.

Yep, exactly what he wanted to hear. Now he could face the Townsend's. Man, wouldn't Marti be glad to hear about this? But he wasn't ready to tell her yet. No sense getting her hopes up about this business if it wasn't going to work out in the end. Just another couple days, then he could tell her. He had a few details to work out first. One, in fact, that he ought to get started on right away.

He glanced at the clock, then picked up the hotel phone on the nightstand. He'd make one quick call while Marti was still in the shower. He dialed the three-digit extension.

"Hey, I've only got a second," he said when his party answered and they exchanged pleasantries. "I need to talk to you about... well, you know. Is there any chance we can get together?"

He waited for the reply, and hoped there wouldn't be a lot of questions. He really didn't want to get into all that here, while Marti was just a thin wall away.

"That sounds good," he said, relieved. "I still need to keep things pretty quiet around here. Yeah, she'll find out eventually, but let's wait a little while, okay?"

He laughed. It did seem kind of silly, conspiring like this. Still, it never hurt to be careful. He didn't know exactly where he stood with Marti and he wasn't about to take any chances. He had entirely too much to lose now and he really, really hated losing.

"Uh, I've got to go," he said quickly.

The bathroom door opened and Marti stepped out, a fluffy white towel was wrapped around her head but she had nothing else on anywhere. Oh yeah, he would really, really hate losing this.

"Quit staring," she said.

"I can't help it." And he couldn't, either. He hung up the phone, not sure if he actually said good-bye or not.

"Who's on the phone?" Marti asked, ignoring his slack-jawed gaze and digging though her suitcase.

He kept right on gazing. Did they really need to go down to dinner? He suddenly wasn't very hungry, after all. Not for food, anyway.

"Just the hotel, checking to make sure we're happy with the service here," he lied.

"Really? I didn't even hear it ring."

"Are you sure we need to go to dinner?"

"Yes, we do."

"Damn."

She was still digging in the suitcase. "I don't think I packed enough underwear," she said.

"Then don't bother wearing any." It seemed a reasonable enough solution.

"Oh that's a good idea," she said, with unmistakable sarcasm. "And why bother with a skirt at all either, right?"

Sarcasm or not, it *did* sound like a good idea. He moved closer to her and ran his hands over her satin-smooth skin. She smelled clean and fresh and, God, what he wouldn't give to be allowed to get her all dirty again right now.

He kissed her neck.

"Stop it. We've got to get downstairs."

He teased her earlobe between his lips.

"They'll be waiting for us."

"They'll get over it."

"They'll wonder what happened."

"Let 'em wonder," he said.

Heck, if they had half a brain they'd all know what happened and he really didn't give a damn. He wanted Marti back in bed and the rest of the universe could just go on waiting and wondering. He had ten years to catch up on and there was no way he was even close to that yet. He slid his hands around to get a good grip on her breasts. Her breathing sounded irregular. Good sign.

"They'll probably talk about us."

"Good."

"Good?" she asked, but it came out a weak little moan.

"I want everyone talking about how my wife kept me otherwise occupied through two perfectly good meals today."

"Everyone?"

He didn't mind that his lovemaking was potent enough to

send her into repeating his every other word, but he couldn't help but wonder what she meant by it. Was there some part of "everyone" in particular she didn't want finding out how they'd spent their afternoon? That damn Hedgeman guy maybe?

Hell, he'd seen him hanging around the ballroom after this morning's competition. What was that all about? Did the creep think he could get Marti back? *Could* he get Marti back? East hated not knowing where he stood with her.

Well, he knew for a fact where he wanted to stand. Right smack dab between her and every other man on the planet.

"Forget the underwear," he said. "And forget everyone else. You've got better things to think about right now."

But Marti never had been very forgetful. She turned away from him and went back to digging through her suitcase. "Come on, we'll be late. You're already dressed, so why don't you go ahead on down there and tell Granny I'll be just a couple minutes? Okay?"

She sounded firm in her resolve so he knew he'd lost this battle. Worse, she found some underwear.

"Yeah, okay. I'll meet you down there," he said, giving in with a remorseful sigh.

Oh well. He'd had Marti's full attention for half of the day. Once dinner was over, he'd have her for all of the night. *Him*, not Leland Hedgemen. He smiled as he went to the door. She smiled back.

———

It was all happening again, just like before. She gave in to her crazy desire and now there was no way this would end up just being a casual dalliance for her. She was head over heels in love with East and it was going to hurt really, really bad when this whole thing ended.

And it was going to end soon, she knew that for a fact. She'd heard him on the phone. Probably she shouldn't have eavesdropped, but it had been an accident. By the time she realized she'd been listening the damage had been done. She'd heard him.

"Is there any chance we can get together?" he'd been whispering into the receiver. *"She'll find out eventually,"* he'd said. And then he'd lied about it just being the hotel when she asked who he'd been talking to. Damn, but that told her everything she needed to know.

Her heart was already broken and he'd barely just walked out the door to go meet their dinner party.

But who had he been talking with? His agent? So why use the hotel phone and not his cell where he probably had the number programmed? The only logical reason to use the hotel phone would be if he was calling someone right here in the building. And if it was someone like Granny or Arv, why the whispers and lies?

Because it hadn't been someone like Granny or Arv or even his agent or the hotel. That could only mean one thing—he'd been talking to Treeva. She knew there could be no other explanation. Treeva had come all the way out here to Ohio to try to get him back and he had no good reason to stop her. After all, couldn't Treeva offer him everything he'd ever wanted? Who could blame the guy for falling for that?

And if Marti cared at all for him she'd be glad to let him go. He deserved the life Treeva offered; the fame, the fortune, the adoring fans. That's who East was.

The tears started to well up and she was glad she was alone. She'd known her emotions were pretty frayed right now so she'd managed to pry East's tempting hands off of her and send him down to tell everyone she was running a bit late. He didn't seem to notice anything was wrong and he left her with a smile. For his sake she'd pretended to smile back.

And part of her, really, hadn't had to pretend. Despite the heartbreak and the looming grief, a part of her was content. And why shouldn't she be? That hadn't been Treeva East was doing gymnastics with all afternoon, it had been *her*. East liked what she did to him in bed and she knew that for a fact. Heck, she certainly liked what he did to her. Making love with East had been totally, absolutely, mind-blowingly great. Nothing that happened now could ever take that away.

Okay, so she was going to have a broken heart to suffer through. She'd been there before, hadn't she? She'd probably survive. By God, though, for two more days East was her husband and he claimed he wanted everyone to know what they'd been up to. Yeah, let Treeva be jealous! She had good reason to be. Marti and East had a good thing going here— even if it was just temporary—and no way Marti was going to waste the time they had left by wallowing in self-pity and regret.

There'd be loads of time for that later, right?

What she needed to do now was put some clothes on. Hell, she was going to wash her face, put on the sexiest outfit she owned and go down to dinner. Whatever might happen in two days, for right now East was her husband. She was determined to take full advantage of that.

She crammed her underwear back into the suitcase. So Granny thought she was being a wild woman with that red lacy stuff? Well, Marti was just going to head to dinner *au natural* under her skirt tonight, as per East's witty suggestion. She might not be a Barbie doll like Treeva, but Marti could clean up nicely when she had to, and she'd just decided she had to.

Treeva might be able to give East everything *in* the

world, but Marti was determined to give him something *out of* this world.

———

It had to be a fluke. After a full year of one bad thing after another, Charleen actually had a great day. First Arv had suggested they go up to their room after breakfast—just the two of them—and then he'd suggested they call to check on the kids! On his own, without any prompting from her, he'd thought about them and willingly dialed her Mom's phone number.

They'd had a pleasant chat and found out Grandma had been supplying a steady stream of ice cream, Doritos and Cherry Coke. Arv said that was just fine. He didn't even make any snide comments about her parents after the call. And then he'd ignored the TV and turned to her for entertainment!

They'd had great sex. No, it was better than that. He made love to her. Real, good, old-fashioned lovemaking with foreplay and everything. Complete with cuddling and a nap afterward. In the middle of the day!

And then, well then he'd really blown her mind. He brought her down to the hotel gift shop for a little souvenir shopping before dinner. Wow. God was in his heaven and all was right with the world.

She should have known it wouldn't last.

Marti and East showed up late for dinner. They arrived separately, too, which seemed to say something, although Charleen was too busy being happy to care what. By the time the entrees were served, however, it was obvious to one and all Mr. and Mrs. Smith were a wee bit distracted.

East seemed on edge and kept glancing nervously around,

while Marti fidgeted and kept tugging uncomfortably at her clothes. Arv, of course, was all over them with concern. All over Marti, at least.

He told her jokes, he tried to drudge up funny stories of stupid things they'd done as kids, and he even walked her down memory lane with a sappy recollection of their senior prom. Charleen was left just twiddling her thumbs, wondering how she'd lost her husband again. And East didn't help much.

They'd barely ordered their dinners when his cell phone rang. Instead of ignoring it as any decent, jealous husband would, he excused himself to take the call in the hallway. Two more times he took phone calls that were, apparently, too urgent to ignore and too personal to take at the table. Marti wasn't happy about it, either. She didn't even order desert, but excused herself and said she had a headache and needed to get up to bed.

East was going to follow her, but then his phone rang again. So, Marti glared at him and left. He took his phone out to the hall.

No one seemed to know what to do. Except Arv, unfortunately. He suddenly decided their wonderful day of togetherness and marital bliss was over.

"Hey, I just remembered something I've got to check on," he said, handing the check to Charleen and pushing his chair back. "Can you get this for us, hon?"

He didn't even wait for her answer. He left her with the bill and was out of there. He used the same exit Marti had, Charleen noted.

Damn! They'd had such a good day. Arv had seemed so much like his old self, the one who'd been fun and who'd made her believe he'd forgotten all about Marti Snowden and had fallen in love with *her*. Now she wondered if that Arv had ever really existed, or if she'd just imagined him because she wanted to.

Granny tried to smooth everything over, talking loudly about how Marti and Johnny were stressed out over the competition. But Dr. Traynor was the only one left to convince, and he was too darn smart for that. Finally Charleen just signed her check and left Granny and the doctor alone at the table. At least they still seemed to be getting along okay.

Her first impulse was to go find Arv, but she had the nagging suspicion she wouldn't be happy with where she might find him. Like, in Marti's room. So, she strolled past the gift shop again and wondered if a little therapeutic shopping might help. Probably not, but there were some nice handbags and they still had a little credit left on their card.

Then someone called her name. It wasn't Arv, but she turned around anyway.

"Miss Kincaide," she said, finding the diva sauntering up to her.

"Those bags are great," Treeva said, nodding toward Charleen's focus. "I've got last year's and this year's."

And she was carrying an even more expensive designer's bag now. Must be nice to have more handbags than one had hands.

"I'm surprised you remembered my name," Charleen said. "You must be meeting an awful lot of people here."

"Yes, but I always remember a friendly face in a crowd of strangers."

Sheesh, was that from a Tennessee Williams play, or something?

"So, are you shopping with your husband?" Treeva went on as the two of them wandered into the shop.

"No, he had other things to do."

"Really. Well, I thought I just saw East's new little wife out in the hallway a few minutes ago."

"Yeah, we all just finished up dinner."

"All of you? I didn't see East anywhere."

"He said he had something else to do. He and Marti went off in opposite directions."

"Oh, I see," Treeva said, lovingly touching the handbags but her mind was clearly elsewhere. After a pause, she looked back up at Charleen. "So, which direction did your husband go off in?"

"I'm not sure," Charleen replied.

"Oh. Pity," Treeva said with a little shrug. "Maybe Marti saw which way he went and you can ask her next time you see her. I mean, unless you're certain she would have no idea."

"I... really hadn't thought about that."

"Of course you have. And between you and me, you should totally buy the bag," Treeva said. "Especially if *he's* the one who'll have to pay for it."

Charleen had no idea what Treeva was getting at, but the snake-like vibes the woman was giving off were starting to give her the creeps. Still, if this total stranger had seen something between Arv and Marti, then maybe Charleen wasn't being so very paranoid, after all.

"I do like the bag," Charleen confessed.

"You have good taste," Treeva replied.

She loitered about, fingering other merchandise and smiling to herself. Charleen thought maybe the conversation was over, but then Treeva spoke again.

"You know, I've been wracking my brain, trying to remember things East said about Marti over the years. I usually zoned out when he started talking about his boring childhood back in Gardenburg—"

"Garden Falls."

"Whatever. Sometimes he'd babble on about Marti from next door, and your Arv. I take it the three of them did a lot together?"

"From what I've heard."

"Oh, that's right. You weren't there, were you?"

"No, I met Arv in college. I'm actually from Cleveland."

"Ah, big city girl. It must have been hard getting used to Garden Ridge."

"Garden Falls. And it's not such a bad little place," she said and hated that she felt the need to defend herself to this woman. What was Treeva getting at, anyway?

"So, you haven't felt like an outsider? Alone in that hick town, surrounded by your husband's family, his old friends... his old *girl*friends?"

"Arv never had a lot of girlfriends. And Marti's been gone."

"Oh, so she and your husband dated? How nice that you can be on such friendly terms after all these years. It has been several years, hasn't it?"

"Yes. It has."

"Of course. But the Gardenville people must be very glad to have Marti back. She just showed up again, didn't she? Right around the time East did, too. And they got married. Just in time for this cook-off."

Charleen didn't bother to correct her on the name of the town again. Wherever Treeva was going with this, Charleen didn't like it. " Look, Ms. Kincaide, I don't know what you're getting at, but…"

"All I'm saying is that you and I both know there's something a bit odd about the way East went back to Gardenwhatever—"

"Garden Falls."

"Yeah, okay. Doesn't it seem a bit, um, convenient that showed up and married this Marti person after he hadn't seen her for years?"

"Arv said East had a thing for her—ever since high school. God, everyone has a thing for this woman. East came back and saw his chance so he grabbed it."

"Why'd she marry him, though? She picked your husband over him ten years ago, didn't she? So why'd she jump into marrying East now?"

"How do you know she picked Arv over East?"

"All I'm saying is it's quite a coincidence the way everything worked out. What did East offer her?"

"Offer her? What do you mean?"

"Her career's down the toilet, right?"

"You've been doing your homework, I guess."

"Yes, I have," Treeva admitted. "But I can't figure a few things out. What's he up to? Going back home... this contest... getting married... he didn't do all this just for the fun of it, that much I know."

"You do?"

"He's not over me yet. If he came back to Ohio and married someone like her, he must have had a reason. But what kind of deal could he be working? A reality show? Has he said anything about that?"

"Uh, no, not that I'm aware of..."

"Well, he can't do anything that might compete with *my* program. I had a damn good lawyer draw up the papers."

"I bet you did. Look, Miss Kincaide, I don't think—"

"But he's up to something and he's got this Marti cow working with him. She's working all sorts of angles, that one."

"She is?"

"I saw her getting on the elevator just before I came in

here," Treeva said with a spiteful grin. "And she wasn't alone."

Oh, God. Charleen didn't want to hear this. Did Arv go up to her room with her?

"Who was she with?"

Treeva just laughed. It was a harsh, brittle sound with no joy in it at all. "Oh, how quaint. You're worried! No no, it wasn't your darling Harvy."

"Arv."

"Whatever."

Thank heavens. But if Marti hadn't gone upstairs with Arv or East, who had she been with? And why did Treeva care so much?

"So, who was it?" Charleen repeated.

The diva shrugged. "I'm hoping you can tell me. I saw him this morning hanging around after the breakfast. He had some badge on from another conference here, but he was very clearly trying to catch Marti's attention. Nice looking, scholarly type. Little bit older, but classy."

Now Charleen smiled. Yes, she'd seen him, too, at the breakfast. And so had East. "Ah, she went with him, did she?"

"You know who he is! Tell me."

This was good news indeed. Marti and East may be on the outs, but Arv wasn't going to get his chance with her. Sounded like Marti had already found a shoulder to cry on, and this was way better than Charleen could have expected.

"He's Dr. Leland Hedgeman," she announced proudly. "He's Marti's ex and East's arch enemy."

Treeva's collagen pout curved into the first real smile Charleen had ever seen on her.

"Marti's *ex*? You don't say."

𝕮𝖍𝖆𝖕𝖙𝖊𝖗 26

"Leland, do we have to do this now? I've got a really bad headache," Marti said.

Leland didn't seem to care about the headache. "We need to, Marti," he said. "I need to know."

"I told you. I haven't said anything to anyone."

"I know that's what you said, but—"

"But it's the truth," she snapped. Damn him for not trusting her! Did he really think so little of her? "I just need to go to my room and get something for my headache. We can talk tomorrow."

"I'm sorry. I know you're under pressure right now, with this cooking thing, and all." He took the liberty of reaching out and rubbing her neck. Oh well. The guy did have a knack for massage. She didn't brush him off.

"I'll go upstairs with you," he said, and followed her onto the elevator.

Great. She was *so* not in the mood for arguing with Leland right now.

"You're married now," he said after a few seconds of silence.

"Yeah."

"That was fast."

She rolled her eyes. As if Leland had any clue.

"Your high school sweetheart?" he asked, going back to the massage.

Susan Gee Heino

She had to admit it was helping the headache. He'd always been good at that. Especially in public. It took her almost two years to figure out why. Now she just found it sort of humorous. Well, he wasn't hanging on her in public now. No one around but the elevator doors.

"We grew up next door," she answered.

"Well, he's a lucky man."

"Yeah."

"You know, Marti, if things had been different…" he began. "I mean, if it wasn't that…"

"Don't bother, Leland. You can let off my neck now."

"Headache gone?"

"It will be."

The elevator stopped at her floor and she waited for the doors to open. They did, but he followed her out. She sighed and stopped in the hallway.

"I promise you," she said, meeting his eyes. "I haven't said anything to anyone. Okay? I told you I wouldn't, and I didn't."

"Are you sure?"

"You know what, Leland? You've got a guilty conscience. That's why you can't trust me on this."

His eyes darted around the empty hall. "Can we not discuss this here, out in public?"

Oh, so *now* he was worried about what he did in public with her. Funny, she used to have to put up with all sorts of things if people were around. What a stupid little fool she'd been.

But it was nice to finally be getting some of this off her chest. Especially after the icecap that had descended between her and East this evening. All those damned phone calls! She'd been so stupid to hope that maybe he wasn't exactly in a hurry to get back to his life.

She was clearly in a bad mood. She might as well have it out with Leland right now. It would probably do her a world of good.

"All right. Come on in," she said, leading him to her hotel room.

"What about your husband? I don't think he likes me very much."

"And I honestly never had to tell him anything about you. He's a smart man."

"But is he... in there?" he asked as she clicked open the door.

"No, he's still downstairs conducting business. And trust me, he's not really the jealous type." She had to laugh at that. As if East had anything to be jealous of where Leland Hedgeman was concerned.

He followed her inside, looking over his shoulder and then timidly scanning the room. He gave an audible sigh when it was obvious there was no East around.

"See? He's still downstairs."

"You've got a Jacuzzi."

"Oh, yeah, we're living it up."

"Is he really an actor?"

"What, you don't believe that either? After the two of you played dueling name-droppers last night and everything?"

"Well, I just never thought of you as, well..."

"You just never really thought of me as anything, did you?" she said and felt the steam rising in her gut. All the pent up anger and hurt was right there, fresh on the surface and dying to be let out. "You found me and I practically worshiped you, didn't I? And you loved that."

"It's always good to mentor the next generation—"

"Oh, bullshit. You saw me as your chance to hide your dirty little secrets so you reeled me in, hook line and sinker."

"Marti, you know I never—"

"By the time I knew what was really going on, it was too late. I was stuck having to play along. And I did, didn't I? I played your stupid little game to the point that I even forgot it was a game! I thought it was my freaking life, Leland."

"It *was* your life! I took care of you, didn't I?"

"You hung me out to dry! Damn it, don't try to pretend you didn't. It wasn't a funding issue. It wasn't a matter of my incompetence. You screwed up, Leland. And you chose to protect your creepy little rich boy over me."

"Don't talk about him that way."

"Still together, I guess? Isn't he afraid that when push comes to shove you'll do the same thing to him you did to me?"

"No, he knows I'd never do that to anyone I…" he caught himself. So she finished the thought for him.

"Never do that to anyone you really care about? Yeah, well someone needs to tell him that the only person Leland Hedgeman cares about it Leland Hedgeman."

"Marti, you've got to put yourself in my shoes. You have no idea what it's like to go through life stigmatized, ridiculed for what you are, who you love."

She was digging some Advil out of her suitcase, but took time out to glare at him. "Get over it, Leland. You're gay; so what? It's not a disease anymore. No one gives a damn who you're with."

"Oh, and that's easy for you to say, isn't it? You came back to Ohio and married Mr. Testosterone himself. You have no idea what my life has been like."

"Your life is screwed up because *you* screwed up, Leland. People don't care who you love, they care about how you lied, and stole money, and didn't do your frigging job protecting the land you were supposed to be saving! That's what you really didn't want people to know about, isn't it?"

He was speechless.

"And you weren't quite sure if I knew about all that, were you?" she asked after a pause.

"No. I wasn't."

"Well, I did. I knew about all of it, and I was so damned convinced you knew what you were doing that I kept my mouth shut. But you never really trusted me, so you got rid of me just in case. Then when stuff started coming out, you conveniently made it my fault. Do you know three people I used to consider my friends and colleagues have snubbed me in the hallway here? Well, they did and it's because of the lies you told everyone about me. Hell, I'm going to be lucky to get a job for the village parks department after what you pulled. *That's* what I care about, Leland. Not your sexual orientation. I quit caring about that six months after I met you."

He chewed on that for a while. She downed three pills.

"Really? Only six months?"

What? After all that the thing he was going to fixate on was that she hadn't been lusting after him all this time? Wow, the guy wasn't just stuck on himself, he was downright neurotic about it.

"Yeah, six months. I may not be a rocket scientist, but it wasn't too hard to figure out you and I had more than just ecology in common. It took me a while to figure out why you had me move in with you and why you kept up all those pretenses, but I wasn't languishing like you seem to think."

"But you stuck around." He seemed positively floored by this revelation.

"Because it was my job!" Then because he seemed so lost, she added. "And because you were my friend. I really did care about you, Leland."

He sank onto the bed. "So you weren't going to talk about any of it?"

"After I'd been living with you and covering your tracks for almost six years? Hell no!"

"So I didn't need to…?"

"Destroy my career and ruin my life? No, you didn't."

"Damn."

"Yeah."

"So, um, what exactly have you told your husband about me?"

"Nothing. He's heard the rumors, just like everyone else. He thinks we were, you know, involved and that you dumped me. Just like you wanted everyone to think."

"No wonder he hates me."

"I told you. He's a smart man."

He sat for a minute more, digesting it all. She leaned against the counter in the little kitchenette. Funny, she used to have so much respect for this man. At first she even hoped for something romantic with him, that maybe he could fill the hole in her heart that East left. It didn't take long to realize that wasn't possible, but he'd been her friend, nonetheless. Or so she'd thought. God, did it hurt when he stabbed her in the back.

But that hurt was suddenly fading, she realized. The anger, too. Seeing him here with his tired eyes full of fear and regret, she had a hard time keeping up the urge to fight. Leland just wasn't that important to her anymore. All she felt for him now was a dull ache and something like pity. It had been really good to say those things to him but in the end, she just didn't care anymore.

"The EPA's breathing on me," he said after a long time.

"Yeah?"

"They want to tie me to the developers."

"Oh."

And that would be bad. Leland's lover was the son of a big land developer. Aside from any social stigma, they had kept their relationship secret due to the fact that Leland's job positioned him as the one to be responsible for evaluating the developer's plans with respect to any environmental impact they would have on protected lands. For them to be romantically involved was a huge conflict of interest.

But over the years Marti had become suspicious that their secrets had gone much deeper than that. The program that Leland ran was supposed to be a watchdog, to make sure protected lands remained protected and that any nearby development was conducted in a way that caused no negative impact. She had no actual proof, but she had the idea that Leland began looking the other way when reports were turned in with falsified data that favored the developers. She heard rumors of payoffs to government agencies and couldn't help but wonder just who might be involved. Was Leland covering for his lover's criminal acts and becoming part of them himself?

By the time she finally confronted Leland about it, she'd been so much a part of his work for so long that he assured her no one would believe she'd been unaware of what had been going on. She'd known about his lover, after all, and hadn't told anyone despite the potential impropriety. He went just one step further and promised her that if she spoke out, he'd make it appear as if *she* had been the one responsible. Just to keep her in line, he'd whispered so-called suspicions about her in enough ears that if he ever did put those false reports out into the world, no one would doubt him and she'd be completely destroyed.

Despite all this, Leland was the one who appeared completely defeated right now.

"What are you going to do?" she asked, coming to sit beside him.

"I don't know. If I fight it, there's no telling what they might uncover. Brandon might get dragged into it."

"Brandon *is* dragged into it. He's the one making the deals for his father, Leland."

"Well, I'm not giving him up. I'll quit the program first."

"Yeah, that'll solve things."

"It might. If someone who knew what was going on took over and fixed things. Quietly." He was watching her carefully as he said this.

"Wait a minute, if you think I want to get back into all that crap…"

"I could get you on it, Marti. You could be in charge! You know how things work, who to suck up to and who can be ignored. I messed up, I'll admit it. But you can fix it! The EPA loves you, they'll work with you and get everything back on track."

"And you'll get off with Brandon. Figuratively speaking, of course."

"Come on, Marti," he said with a slight smile directed at her. He could be charming when he wanted to. "What do you say?"

"Jeez, Leland. I don't know. What you did was wrong! People already have some questions about my abilities, thank you very much. They're going to believe I wasn't a part of the problem to begin with? I just don't know."

"But you love your work, Marti! And you're damn good at it. You still care, and that's a rare commodity these days."

"Tell me about it," she said and almost laughed.

So she'd suddenly gone from barely-employable waitress to being offered leadership of the whole program? Unbelievable. And no, she didn't believe it. She'd known

Leland too long to trust him. Still, if he really did have to step aside that would leave the position open…

"You're considering it, aren't you?" he asked, grabbing her hand. "Yes you are! I can see the wheels churning there. Already you're wondering how you can convince your husband to let you move to Florida."

Now she did laugh. "Oh, East wouldn't care about that."

"I wouldn't care about what?"

She swiveled quickly to find East standing in the doorway. He didn't look pleased. Leland jumped to his feet, tossing Marti's hand down onto her lap and nervously straightening his collar.

"I thought you said you had a headache?" he asked, glaring back and forth between Marti and Leland.

"I did," she answered. "So I came up here to take something for it."

"I see that. Did it help any?"

"Some," she said.

"Hey, I just stopped in to say hi," Leland said quickly. "But I think I'm done visiting now."

"Yeah, I think you are," East agreed, stepping away from the door so he'd have free access to leave.

Leland didn't waste any time. He was already headed for the door when he paused to glance at Marti. "I think you should tell him. About me."

"We'll see," she answered.

East didn't say anything. He just stood there looking surprisingly threatening and waited for Leland to pass before slamming the door behind him.

"I'm glad you two are working your problems out."

"Yeah," she said, boldly meeting his gaze. "I've missed him more than I thought."

Her heart was hammering in her chest. East really did

look furious. She wanted so much to believe that maybe this meant he was jealous. Was he? The air seemed to get thicker and Marti's chest hurt from forgetting to breathe. East was just standing there, radiating an anger she'd never seen before.

Then he tossed his key card on the cabinet and strode toward her. She couldn't help but stand quickly, not sure his intentions. Just what was going on behind those fiery eyes? For the first time ever, East scared her.

She let out a little cry when he reached for her, grabbing her shoulders so she had no choice but to face him. He held her there and she met his storming eyes.

"I don't care who that man is or how long you lived with him," he began. "Until this damned contest is over, you're my wife. And I don't share my wife."

Gulp. This was a hard, galvanized side of East she didn't even know existed. Never dreamed he even possessed it. She didn't dare look away from him, even if she'd wanted to. And she didn't want to. Strange as it was, she was terrified and, well, kind of hot for him.

"Okay," was all she could muster.

And it was okay. She'd gladly belong body and soul to East, for today, tomorrow or forever. As long as he'd have her.

———

East felt like someone kicked him in the gut. Marti brought her damn Hedgeman up here, thinking East was going to be busy downstairs for a while. God, that twisted a knot inside him so tight he wondered if he'd burst from it.

From the looks of Marti's wide, worried eyes and her strangulated voice, he was taking it out on her. Damn it. He loosened his grip on her arms just a bit and waited for her to pull away and yell at him for acting like a brute.

She didn't, though. She just stayed there, blinking those golden eyes up at him and defying him to tell her what she could or could not do. As if he had that right.

He wanted that right, though. He wanted her; all of her. Not just a few nights of convenience, not just a commitment for Granny's sake or for this stupid competition, but all of her. Forever. Because she wanted it, too.

But she didn't, obviously. Before dinner he'd gotten amorous and tried to lure her into forgetting about everyone else and she'd gone cold on him. She didn't need that much of him, apparently. She enjoyed herself with him because he was there. A few minutes ago, Hedgeman was there. Would she have ended up in bed with him, too? He couldn't even let himself consider that. Just seeing them together in conversation—close, intimate conversation—had been too much.

"You're stuck with me until we get home Sunday, I'm afraid," he said finally.

"Okay," she said again.

It felt too good to be this close to her. If she wasn't going to tell him to leave her the hell alone, he was damn well going to take advantage of their last remaining hours. He pulled her closer and kissed her.

It was a kiss that demanded other things, but she didn't back away. No, in fact she heated right up for him. As long as he could hold onto her, he was going to. Marti was his for a little while longer and it sure as hell was going to be a time she wouldn't easily forget.

He let his hands roam freely over her body. She murmured against him and he took that as adequate encouragement to continue. So he continued, right on until his hands found their way to her skirt and started hiking it upwards. She wriggled against him. More encouragement.

He paused, though, when his hands felt the bare skin of her round little ass.

"Uh, what happened to your underwear?" he asked.

She seemed slightly dazed when he broke off the kiss and her brows knit together as she looked up at him in confusion. He ran his hands around a bit to make sure he wasn't imagining things. No underwear. Not even a thong. Damn, that Hedgeman was a fast worker!

"You're not wearing underwear," he said, choking back the urge to march out into the hallway and murder that damned professor.

"You told me not to," Marti replied simply.

He had to think about that for a moment and then he clearly remembered that she was right. He *had* told her not to.

"But you thought it was a bad idea," he reminded her.

"And then I changed my mind."

"Why?"

He tipped her chin up so he could see into those eyes again.

"I didn't want to waste any more time," she said after a pause that felt like eternity. "I thought maybe I could, um, surprise you at dinner."

"By showing up without underwear?"

"Okay, it was a very dumb idea."

"I didn't say that," he smiled at her. "I'm just glad your pal Hedgeman didn't know about it." Then he paused, and frowned. "He didn't know about it, did he?"

She shook her head. "No, he wasn't interested in my underwear. If you want to know the truth about him…"

"No. I don't," he said. "I want to forget he exists."

He kissed her again. She clung to him and the fire inside her licked at his own soul.

"No more fighting," he said, a promise. "Let's don't talk about the future or people from the past… let's just enjoy now."

"I am," she said.

———

She was sleeping in his arms. He watched her and thought how perfect she was. Every woman he'd ever been with had been compared in his mind to Marti. They'd all come up lacking. Now he had her again. How on earth was he going to hang onto her?

He'd heard from his friend in Garden Falls after dinner, and things were still a go. He'd been afraid that with the appearance of Phil and Joetta this morning something might have happened to mess up his plans, but it sounded like he could be even a little bit encouraged.

The Engineer's Office had found too many discrepancies in the submitted plots, too many places where Phil and Joetta's recorded information didn't match up with flood surveys and old deeds. Basically, the county engineer was going to yank their permits. Now, in fact, the county prosecutor was involved. The Townsend's might be facing charges for fraud.

That land out on Beaverbend Road was not suitable for development. The best Phil and Joetta could hope for was to dump it off on someone else cheap and pay back the few people who had invested in the project. The prosecutor said he might drop the charges then and just consider it all a big mistake.

But who'd be willing to buy worthless, wet land on short

notice?

East smiled as Marti murmured something unintelligible and nuzzled against him. Yeah, who indeed. East knew *exactly* who would do something like that.

What he didn't know, however, was what Marti would say about it. He kissed her head. Would she think he was trying to tie her down? Would she think he was trying to bribe her? He didn't know.

But just now it didn't matter. She was content, sighing in his arms with a satisfied blush on her soft cheeks. Right now, life was good. Marti was in his arms, in his bed, and it had been his name she'd cried out in passion.

His *real* name. She'd called him "Johnny". He smiled. He wasn't sure why, but something about that seemed significant. He wasn't just Easton Smith to her, was he? He was still Johnny. He liked that.

He pulled her closer and kissed her head again. She snuggled close and looked up at him. For one brief second he saw all he ever wanted to see in her eyes.

"My Marti," he said before capturing her lips in a kiss that was gentle, cautious, and more wonderful than the last.

For these moments, at least, she was his friend, his wife, and she loved him. What more could he ask for?

Other than forever.

Chapter 27

It seemed like forever. Where the hell was Arv? Charleen changed the channel on the TV again without paying any attention to it. All she could see was Arv following Marti out of the restaurant tonight.

Well, fine. If he was stupid enough to throw away nine years of marriage and two great kids, that was his problem. She'd be only too happy to move back here to Cleveland and start over. Who knew, maybe she'd meet some guy who hadn't already fallen love with Marti Snowden?

Yeah, like Charleen could ever notice any other guy.

She sank back onto the pillows and stared at the ceiling, absently clicking away on the remote. There was no other guy for her. It had always been Arv and it would always be Arv no matter how stupid he was or how angry he made her. What on earth was she going to do? She'd never be good enough for him because she wasn't Dr. Marti.

The door opened and Arv strolled in.

"Oh, here you are," he said casually.

"Yeah. Where else did you think I'd be?"

"I don't know." He shrugged.

"So, where were *you*?"

He had the nerve to smile. "Oh, just chatting."

"Chatting."

Arv had never been big on conversation. And what kind of "chatting" had he been doing that left him with a smile like that?

"I think I can guess who you've been chatting with, too. I hope she's been enjoying her weekend here."

"Oh, she has. And she has a proposition!" he added.

"Oh, I just bet she does."

Charleen flipped off the TV. So, Arv thought she was going to sit around and discuss Marti's propositions with him? Like she was his best buddy instead of his freaking wife? The man wasn't just clueless, he was demented.

"She says she's been thinking about it for a while," he went on.

"Well, doesn't that make it special."

He didn't even miss a beat. "I know. She thinks I'm perfect!"

"Perfect?"

"Yeah, she says there's nobody better," he gushed. "And you know, I've been thinking about it. She's right."

This was so absurd she had to laugh. "Oh, no doubt."

"It would solve everything."

"I just bet it would."

"I think it'll work out great," he rambled on. "And East is all for it, too."

"He is? You talked to East about it?"

"Oh, yeah! He's the one who brought it up a couple weeks ago. He just wasn't sure how she'd feel."

"*He* brought it up?" Now she was very confused.

"Yeah," Arv gleefully explained. "He called earlier and asked if we could get together again to talk about something. I said maybe we should meet up after dinner. Well, when I saw how he and Marti seemed a little tensed up tonight, I was afraid that's what he wanted to talk about. He's nuts for her and I hate that they just can't seem to get it together for real."

"Um, you do?"

"Yeah, but here's the good part," he insisted.

"Goody. I can't wait."

"Granny had the same idea that East and I did!"

So now Granny was trying to fix Arv up with Marti? Not likely. Charleen tried to rub the tension out of her temples.

"Um, what the hell are we talking about, Arv."

"About our solution. It'll be perfect for all of us. Don't you think?"

"I don't know *what* to think. You aren't making any sense at all right now."

"I know, I know. We've had so much going on, I haven't exactly been myself lately."

"That's an understatement."

"But this will fix it! It's just what we need."

"We?"

"Sure. Granny and East and you and me," he said, his voice getting faster and faster as his enthusiasm apparently sucked away any remaining brain cells. "So all we have to do is get Marti to agree."

"Agree to what? This is getting a little weird, Arv."

He wrinkled his brows. "Yeah, I should probably explain."

"Yeah, that would be nice."

"We've been talking about the diner, Char," he began. "East thought maybe you and I should buy it."

"Granny's diner?"

"Yes! And now that I've talked to her, she wants to sell it to us. We can use the insurance money we'll be getting. Isn't it great?"

Well, she had to admit it was a hell of a lot better than some of the things she'd been imagining. But Granny wanted them to buy the diner? *Her* diner, where Marti worked and was part owner? Uh, that part of the plan didn't seem so great.

"Char?" Arv asked slowly when she didn't say anything. "You do think it's a good idea, don't you? The kids will love being back in Garden Falls, and after being here at this competition Granny's Kitchen gets a year of free publicity and all, whether they win or not."

"And you'll be working with Marti again, won't you?"

"Naw, Granny's pretty sure she'd rather get back to her career. You know, the environment and biological stuff."

"Oh, I know all about Dr. Marti and her wonderful, biological stuff. I've been hearing how great she is for almost ten years now."

She finally seemed to have caught his attention. He frowned at her.

"Why don't you like her?" he asked. "You never got to know her real well, but you just don't like her, do you?"

"I don't like anyone who's more important to you than I am, Arv. Sorry. Maybe it makes me shallow. I can't help it."

"More important to me? What are you talking about?"

"I'm talking about the puppy dog eyes you were making at her all night. About the way you kept reminiscing about all the good times you two had together."

He was starting to look a little less confused. Good. Maybe the last remaining bits of gray matter were still functioning in his Marti-infested brain.

"Wait a minute… I was making puppy dog eyes at Marti?"

"It was embarrassing!'

"And you're jealous!"

"Hell yes I'm jealous! I'm your damn wife."

"And you think I've got some crush on Marti and care about her more than *you*?"

"I've got eyes, Arv."

The bastard had the gall to laugh at her. He freaking laughed right at her, as if she'd said something hilarious. She didn't even let herself think about it, she just jumped to her feet and swung at him.

But Arv was quick. He grabbed her arm and held it firm. She flailed helplessly and he seemed to be having the time of his life.

"You think I've got a thing for Marti! Holy shit, you're really pissed off about this."

"Yes, I'm pissed off!"

They stood there, deadlocked. She couldn't break free and hit him, but he wasn't making any effort to make her feel any better, either. He smiled, in fact.

"You are so sexy when you're jealous," he said finally.

"Don't you dare try sucking up to me now."

"So just how long have you thought I've been burning a torch for Marti?"

"Since you never got over her when she dumped you in college, you asshole. I was stupid enough to think if I caught you on the rebound you'd appreciate it, maybe see I was the better choice. I am, by the way. She never, ever cared about you like I did, Arv."

"I know! Hell, that's why I married you as soon as I could get you to say yes. I knew I'd found the best and didn't want to risk losing you."

"Like you lost her."

Now the tears were starting to well up. Damn it, but she was going to start crying. She really did not want to cry for this man.

"Oh, Char," he said in his softest, most serious voice. "Come here."

He pulled her gently into his arms and she fell against him willingly. She just couldn't lose him to some other woman. She'd die without Arv.

"I never lost Marti," he said softly. "Sure, I guess I kind of had a crush on her in high school, but by the time we hit college and I saw there were other girls out there, well, that went away. Fast."

"But you were dating. She left to go study turtles, or something, and you said you didn't know what to do. If you don't remember all this, I do. You told me she broke your heart and you needed someone you could talk to and get over her."

He was kissing her hair and chuckling. She didn't recall saying anything funny.

"Yeah, that's what I told you," he said. "And I guess you believed it."

Very carefully he pushed her away from him so he could look down into her eyes. He was being awfully sweet and she wasn't quite sure she could trust herself to stay focused. It would be way too easy to get sucked into believing anything he said right now.

"I used to believe everything you told me, Arv."

"Okay," he said ominously. "I will be painfully honest right now."

"Whenever you're ready," she said.

No, she didn't really want to hear the words, but she'd take it like an adult. It seemed like Arv waited forever before saying them, though.

"I lied about dating Marti. We never did."

"What? But I saw you!"

"You saw us?"

"Sure. You were always hanging out with her on campus during our Freshman year. I figured I'd never have a chance, the way you two were like conjoined twins all the time."

"Really? You mean, you knew who I was before I signed

up for that dumb poetry class?"

"It wasn't a dumb poetry class!" she said, then stopped herself. "Wait a minute. You told me you loved poetry—all the symbolism and imagery."

"Sorry. That was a lie, too."

"So why were you there?"

"How else was I going to meet you?"

"You took a whole semester of nineteenth century romantic poetry just to meet me?"

"Hell yes I did! And when I realized you had such a soft spot for hard luck cases, I invented the whole bit about Marti breaking my heart. Sorry, but at the time it worked wonders for me."

"You lied to get me to go out with you?"

"Char, I'm sorry. I was such a geek in college! I didn't know how to get a popular, intelligent, gorgeous girl like you to notice me. I was used to hanging out with Marti, for heaven's sake. What did I know about someone like you?"

"Really? You thought I was intelligent and gorgeous and all that?"

"Yeah. Still do. You're totally all that."

"And the stuff about Marti was just a pack of lies?"

"On my honor."

Well, that was funny. She let herself smile a little. He smiled back, but she wasn't quite ready to let him off so easily.

"So why didn't you ever tell me about this? Why did I have to spend this whole time thinking I was only second best? Do you know all the awful things I've been thinking about you? And Marti? That wasn't very nice of you, Arv."

She turned away from him. It *had* been wrong of him to lie. It *had* been wrong of him to let things go on like this so long. Jeez, it nearly destroyed their marriage! Sure, Arv was always pretty oblivious about stuff like relationships and all, but he should have known his wife needed to hear the truth at some point. He deserved to suffer a bit for what he'd put her through.

Well, at least he was sensible enough to come and put his arms around her again. He was smart enough to kiss her cheek and whisper in her ear, too.

"I'm an idiot, Char. And I'm so, so sorry. Tell me what I can do to make it up to you."

He *had* been kind of a geek in college, hadn't he? But she liked geeks. And she liked him. And she really, really liked knowing she didn't have to worry about the whole Marti thing anymore. Maybe things were going to be all right after all.

"I don't know. I'll think of something," she answered him.

"Well, think fast," he murmured, kissing her neck. "I want to get started right away."

Oh, what the hell. So did she. She turned around and gave in to his embrace.

———

"Second place!"

Marti could hardly contain herself. They had actually gained two places in today's lunch competition. Wow. She'd slightly scalded the gravy when she got caught daydreaming about last night—and this morning—but East managed to salvage it in time. The open-faced pot roast sandwiches were to die for. Or maybe it was Granny's killer custard pie recipe that put them ahead. Either way, Marti was pretty damn pleased with herself.

The last fourteen hours with East had been fabulous. Eyes-rolled-back-in-your-head kind of fabulous. Now they'd come in here and made it all the way up to second place. Heck, tomorrow's meal was the big one. A good showing there and they could walk away with everything. Life was almost perfect.

Almost. Phil and Joetta Townsend had been sitting in the audience today, whispering back and forth. She was pretty sure Phil made some sort of gestures toward East a couple times, too, like he was trying to tell him something. Right in the middle of their competition. Asshole. Fortunately East ignored him.

But he wasn't exactly ignoring him now. The competition was over, the cheers were dying down, and contestants were beginning to mill around in their cooking areas as clean-up and prep for tomorrow could begin. She saw East catch Phil's eye for a second, then he checked his cell phone. Was he waiting for another call? He was always waiting for a call these days. Late last night he'd gotten another one, too.

She'd heard enough of his end of it to know what it was about. He'd agreed to go back to California. She hadn't asked since she knew if she talked about it he might think she wanted him to drag her along. Of course she did want him to drag her along, but she didn't think he'd appreciate knowing that. The very fact that he didn't volunteer any information after the call told her she really wasn't a part of his future, or his life.

Still, she didn't have to worry about saying good-bye to East for another twenty-four hours. And she wouldn't let herself worry about it. Right now East was smiling at her like he thought she was the only female on the planet. At least, the only one who could cook *and* do those things with her tongue.

"Good job, Mrs. Smith," he said, leaning over to give her a quick little peck on the cheek.

"Well, that doesn't seem like a second place kind of kiss," she laughed. "I know you can do better than that."

His smile told her he was well up to the challenge. Without another thought, he grabbed her by the elbow and practically dragged her away from their little kitchenette. There was side door out of the ballroom nearby and he whisked her through it. They were out in a hallway and practically alone. He pulled her into a quiet corner.

"All right, you asked for it," he said and swooped down on her for a hot kiss much more worthy of his great talents.

"Now that's more like it," she said when they came up for air.

His eyes were smoldering. "And there's more where that came from. In fact, what do you say we finish our clean-up and forget that little reception they've got planned for the finalists?"

Oh, jeez that sounded like a good idea. But they'd already promised to meet Granny and the rest of their entourage there. It wouldn't be very considerate to ditch them just for an afternoon of steamy sex.

"What about your parents?" she reminded. "They drove all the way up here today, don't you think they're going to want to spend a little time with you?"

East frowned. He did look pretty disappointed. "Damn. Yeah, I promised Dad I'd get with him about some stuff."

"Stuff?"

He shrugged. "You know, financial things."

"Oh."

Financial things. Things about his life and his future. Things that didn't involve her. She tried not to let him see how disappointed she was now. But he didn't seem to notice. Something else had caught his attention.

"Shit."

"What?"

She glanced up and instantly realized what he meant. Treeva was making a beeline for them.

"So, you're still in the running for the big prize," she said once she and her musky perfume invaded their corner. "You're making quite a name for yourself, Easton. They'll probably start expecting you to do all the catering when you get back to the set!"

Oh God. There could only be one set Treeva Kincaide was talking about. East was going back to *The Passionate Palate*. So that's what she'd offered him; that's what would win him back. Marti should have known. In fact, that must have been what he and his agent had been working out last night on the phone. East was going back to work with *her*.

Now Treeva was watching her and she hoped to God the shock and suffocating hurt she felt weren't evident on her face. They probably were.

Marti swallowed back the pain and figured it was safer just to focus on the anger. Hell yes, she was pissed off that he'd let her find out about this from damn Treeva, of all people! So just when was he planning to mention it? Didn't he think she'd notice when he was gone one morning? And back on the freaking TV?

"No doubt East will be far too busy out there to do any catering," Marti said with venom enough to make even Treeva proud. "I'm sure he's looking forward to being catered *to*, actually."

"And of course that's what you'll be doing, won't you?" Treeva gave Marti a saccharine smile.

"No, actually, I have my own career."

Treeva frowned. Rather, she would have probably been frowning if not for the Botox.

"But does this mean you won't be joining him?" she

asked. "I just assumed that since you're sort of on a break from your career and all, you'd have nothing better to do than tag along with dear hubby."

"Actually, I *was* on a break from my career," Marti replied, sounding a whole lot more confident than she felt. "But right now I'm considering a position as project director."

"Really? How handy that you found something in California."

"It's not in California," Marti informed. "About three thousand miles away, actually."

Ah, so East wasn't the only one with surprises. She could see in his eyes that he wondered why he was just now hearing about this. Well, screw him. If he could have a life, so could she.

"She's just considering it at this point," he put in quickly.

"Well, I'm sure it'll work out," Treeva said with a wave of her hand. "I've known lots of people with long-distance relationships. They were perfectly fine." She paused, then added. "For a while."

"Look, Treeva, we've got a lot to get done here," East began and started to lead Marti back toward the ballroom.

But his action backfired. He ended up running smack into Leland there in the doorway. The two men sort of sneered at one another.

"What the hell are you doing here?" East growled.

Treeva butted in quickly. "Oh, do you two know each other?"

"Yes," East replied. "Do you?"

"Miss Kincaide and I met in the lobby this morning," Leland said. He took a deep breath and tried to pretend East didn't intimidate him. Marti didn't think he was fooling anyone.

Treeva sidled up to Leland and Marti almost fell over

when she slipped her hand under Leland's arm. *Treeva and Leland?* Hell, they looked like a freaking couple, or something.

"It was the funniest thing," Treeva gushed. "I'd gotten myself all twisted around in this big hotel. So, here was this nice looking gentleman coming out of a workshop and I asked him for directions. Well, we got to talking and, oh! He's just so fascinating! I never knew there were so many things in the environment."

Oh, frigging brother.

"Well, then we realized we had some common acquaintances," Treeva went on. "He told me all about how he used to work with you, Marti, down in that big old swamp in Florida. Until that darn funding crunch, and all. I feel just awful for you. So anyway, I invited him to come and sit in on the competition today, since he's an old friend of yours, and all." She smiled. It made her look a lot like that Komodo dragon in the kids' coloring book back at Granny's Kitchen.

But she wasn't done yet. She fondled Leland's arm and glared at Marti. "He *is* an old friend of yours, isn't he?"

"Of course he is," Marti responded and turned a deceptively sweet smile on him. "How's the symposium going, Leland? Anyone asking you any interesting questions about your work down in that big ol' swamp?"

He had the good sense to go a little bit pale at the thought of answering questions about his work. "Sorry, there isn't much interest in the project right now."

"Oh, too bad. Guess maybe I haven't been telling people much about it, huh?"

Apparently East had had enough. He cleared his throat. "Look, Marti and I have a lot of clean up to do. Maybe we can all get together some other time and reminisce. Like maybe in a year or so."

Treeva just smiled. "Oh East, you're a riot. I'm sure you and I, at least, will have plenty of time to catch up once you get back to California. Next week."

God, she was evil incarnate. What was East thinking when he married her?

"I can't wait," he grumbled.

But before Treeva could wander off with her newest arm-candy to gloat about her big scoop, they were all pinned in the corner by the arrival of the Townsends. East's expression said he'd really just like to die right now. Marti was almost ready to help him along in that.

"Congratulations!" Phil was booming. "Who'd have ever thought Marti Snowden could get to second place in a cooking contest!"

Joetta just fidgeted and blushed, staring at Treeva. "I'm a big fan, Miss Kincaide. I can't tell you how upset I am that you've had to start cooking gluten free!"

"Yes, well that's just something we've been experimenting with," Treeva said quickly. "The producers felt audiences are hungry for health-conscious recipes."

Oh. So ratings had been down since East left and they were getting desperate to create a new niche, were they? Hey, why not just have Treeva give up cooking all together and see how long it would take the bitch to slowly starve to death? There'd probably be millions of people who'd tune in to watch that.

"Don't worry, though," Treeva went on, much to Marti's disappointment. "*The Passionate Palate* has all sorts of creative cooking ideas scheduled for this season. We know East has been researching new and exciting things on his little hiatus."

Hiatus? Is that how he and Treeva were going to spin this? Wow, he sure was going back there with bells on, apparently. Maybe if he got paid enough for it he'd even remarry Treeva and pick up where they left off.

"I'm as interested in kitchen tips as the next guy," Phil interrupted. "But I see East looks like he's in a hurry. Maybe if you ladies wouldn't mind, us men folk will just step over here and talk a little business for a few minutes?"

What?! First she finds out East's going back to work with Treeva, now here's Phil Townsend talking business with him? What the hell was going on?

"I don't think now is such a good time, Phil," East declined.

Was he purposely not looking at her? Yeah, he was. The bastard actually had some kind of business going on with Phil Townsend that he clearly didn't want her to know about. That couldn't be good.

"I'm sorry to push you, East," Phil pushed. "But I'm afraid things are getting a little bit urgent here. I sure would hate for you to miss out on a deal like this, just because you had to go help the little woman there tidy up the kitchen, and all."

Marti couldn't believe it when East took a deep breath, and turned to her.

"It is kind of important, Marti," he said. "I'll just be a minute."

No way! East gave her a limp grin and walked away with Phil. She was stuck here, boxed in with three of her least favorite people on the planet. Mind-boggling.

"Don't worry, honey," Joetta said, patting Marti's arm in her annoying way. "I don't think this'll take long. You'll have your kitchen partner back in a minute."

"Oh, but I'm sure East's little woman can handle things just fine while he's off doing important business," Treeva said. "She's quite spectacular in the kitchen, so I hear."

I'm not so bad with a sharp knife, either, you frozen-faced harpy!

Joetta didn't seem to notice the imaginary daggers flying between Marti and Treeva. Her attention had been caught on Leland. She grinned and thrust out her overly bejeweled hand at him.

"Hi, there. I'm Joetta Townsend of Townsend Real Estate and Development."

Treeva grabbed the opportunity. "Oh, I'm sorry. I should have introduced you. This is Dr. Leland Hedgeman."

She said the name very clearly; very precisely. If Joetta had ever heard the guy's name before, she'd have recognized it now. For just a minute Joetta's face was it's usual shiny blank. Then all of a sudden her eyes got real big. Blue eye shadow rose up into her forehead with her eyebrows.

"*The* Dr. Hedgeman?"

"You've heard of my work?" he asked, clueless and smug.

"I heard you were the one that was living in sin with Marti all those years, right?" Joetta chirped.

"I, um, we had we had a professional relationship…" Leland stammered.

Marti rolled her eyes and wondered if this could get any more uncomfortable. Oh lord, yes it could. The doors across the hall opened and suddenly the hallway was being filled with members of Leland's symposium.

Naturally, several of them recognized him. And her.

"My God, it's Marti!" a woman named Kathy squealed. She quickly nudged several of her companions who all came rushing over, exclaiming in happy surprise at finding Marti here with Leland.

Marti didn't bother with introductions, which was a good thing since everyone seemed to be talking all at once. Besides, Marti kind of enjoyed Treeva's snotty little pout when she realized she wasn't the center of attention. But she didn't wallow in Treeva's delightful discomfort for long. Kathy pretty much distracted her.

"So, Marti, I guess Leland told you the project's been put on hold for a while."

Uh, no, he hadn't. He did look distinctly awkward right now, though. Treeva was still hanging on his arm and Kathy was going on and on about all the problems on the project. She clearly didn't believe Leland could ever be guilty of any of the things he was apparently being investigated for, so she seemed to see no reason to shut up about it. On and on she went, nailing Leland's coffin with every word. It sounded pretty much like it was all hitting the fan for the guy.

And yesterday he offered her the job out of the goodness of his heart? Hell, he'd only been trying to screw her over again to save his own smarmy hide! Bastard.

She didn't get the opportunity to share her thoughts with him, though. Kathy had one final tidbit to offer.

"And worst of all, they say he did these crazy things because he was having an affair with some *guy* whose father is a big real estate developer. Can you believe that? Seriously, Marti, if Leland was, uh, *that* way, I think you'd have known about it, wouldn't you?"

She was spared having to answer that. A couple of determined looking women with big cameras noticed their little group in the corner.

"Miss Kincaide!" one of them shouted, pretty much drowning out anything that anyone else might have been saying. "Hey, give us a smile for *Kultured Kitchen Magazine*!"

Treeva was only too happy to finally be getting some attention again. She slipped into star mode and practically blinded everyone with a dazzling smile. Probably more out of habit than anything, she clutched Leland's arm all the tighter as cameras clicked. He turned a bit green around the gills. Marti wasn't sure if that was more from Kathy's blabbering or from Treeva's arm clutching.

"So," one of these reporters called out. "Is this someone new in your life? Care to introduce us to your hunky pal there?"

For a second it looked like Treeva was surprised to be reminded she actually had a hunky pal there. For that same second it looked like Leland was about to be sick. Then all at once everything about him changed. His smile got nearly as bright as Treeva's and he leaned possessively in to her.

"We're just good friends," he said, though his body language and voice said something very different.

Well, the reporters loved that. Their cameras went crazy and one of them whipped out a tiny recorder and held it up to catch whatever words of wisdom Treeva or her hunky pal might utter next.

"We heard Easton Smith is here," the reporter went on. "How does he feel about you finding someone to take his place so soon?"

Treeva practically purred at that one. "Well, he knows I'm not going to sit and pine away. Life does go on, you know."

"Does it?" the reporter questioned. "Have you renewed your contract with *The Passionate Palate* or is this season going to be the last?"

"Well, of course I can't answer that, but let's just say something big is about to happen and I know you're simply going to love it."

They did love it, and they invited Treeva to join them for coffee. Wouldn't she love to give them an exclusive, in her own words, about how things are going for her since the divorce and how she felt about judging her ex-husband in a cooking contest? Treeva very graciously accepted their offer, and Leland was right there by her side as she headed off with them. Kathy and her friends were left slack-jawed and surprised.

"Who on earth is that?"

"That," Marti informed them. "Is a middle-aged bitch who thinks she rules the planet."

"Don't let her hear the part about middle-aged." It was East. He'd come back to her side once Treeva and her paparazzi had left.

Phil was standing there with him and he looked entirely too damn happy. Whatever deal he'd been talking about with East seemed to have gone his way. Marti ground her teeth, wondering what earth-killing things they'd been plotting.

At least East's arrival provided a good opportunity to escape the others.

"Sorry, Kathy," she said, clutching East's arm just a little bit too tightly. "I'd love to stay and chat but we're on a really fixed schedule right now."

It probably wouldn't have mattered what Marti said and her old colleague would have agreed with it. Kathy clearly couldn't take her eyes off East. He smiled politely, but Marti decided he did not need an introduction. She jerked him back toward the doorway into the ballroom. They hadn't bothered to say good-bye to Joetta and Phil but that was all right. They weren't paying any attention to her, either. Joetta was whispering something to Phil and they both had a greedy little grin on their faces.

"Who were all your friends out there?" East asked.

"It doesn't matter."

"Really? They seemed awfully glad to see you."

"Some people are. What were you talking about with Phil?"

"What? Nothing."

"Then why was he smiling?"

"Oh, you know Phil. He's always got some scheme going."

"And you're helping him? Is that it?"

He actually looked hurt. "That Hedgeman really did a number on you, didn't he?"

She was about to assure him that changing the subject was not going to get him off the hook, but an announcement from the podium about how much time was left of their allotted clean-up and prep time interrupted. Damn.

"Come on, we've still got to get everything washed up in there before they kick us out and lock the place up," he said.

The inquisition would have to wait. She swallowed back her anger and followed him toward their kitchenette. She took her spot at their sink and wondered if maybe it was unwise to put someone so obviously angry in charge of washing fragile dishes. Oh well, it gave her something to do beside murder her husband.

Chapter 28

It was getting late. East knew Marti was tired; her eyes were red and she could barely keep them open. But she sat there bravely ignoring him while he got ready for bed. Obviously she was bound and determined to stay mad at him all night.

Well, maybe he shouldn't blame her. It was kind of unfair that she found out about the whole *Passionate Palate* thing from Treeva. Yeah, he should have told her. But he just hadn't been able to bring himself to do that. Something down deep inside knew what she'd have said. It would have been something devastating like, "Oh, that's great. Have a good time out there. Maybe we'll see each other again someday."

No, he'd been in no hurry to hear that. He'd wanted to hang onto his little fantasy about Marti being interested enough in him to maybe even consider going out there with him. But, that was over now. She'd found out and was pissed that he hadn't had the decency to tell her himself. It appeared that she'd sit propped up there on pillows all night reading that damn environmental journal before she'd ever let him come near her in bed again.

Hell, they only had one more night. Then the contest would be over and they could head back to Garden Falls. No doubt she'd come up with some great excuse for immediately moving back in with Granny and he'd be left with just memories of his nights with her. Again.

He'd hoped to keep her interest a while longer, but his little scheme with Phil clearly backfired on him. Marti probably thought he was in cahoots with the Townsend's and was helping to rape and pillage the land. He couldn't tell her what he was really trying to do, though. So far all he had was Phil's handshake, and Phil's hands were notoriously slimy. If the opportunity came up, East knew Phil would screw him over in a heartbeat.

He just couldn't say anything to Marti about what he was planning. Not yet, anyway. It wouldn't be fair. She still had tomorrow's dinner to concentrate on and he doubted she'd be able to do that with Beaverbend Road on her mind. Especially when she was already so ticked off at him about everything else.

He sighed and sat down on his side of the bed. She turned a page in her journal and kept right on ignoring him.

"You know, girls who read make me horny," he said after about five minutes of sitting there watching her.

She still ignored him.

"You're reading," he pointed out.

Nope, that didn't get her yet.

"So I'm horny," he added just in case she hadn't caught the connection.

She slammed the journal down. Success! He had her attention finally. She didn't look thrilled with him, but it was a start.

"You're a jerk, you know that?"

"Because I didn't mention that my agent has been talking with Treeva's producers? You're right. I should have told you. I'm a jerk."

"Yes. You are."

"So we've got that settled. Now, it's getting late and we've got a busy day tomorrow. Don't you think maybe you ought to turn off the light?"

She rolled her eyes. "Fine."

The light clicked off and he heard the magazine hit the nightstand. Okay, that was easier than expected. Too bad it wasn't just the light he wanted to get off right now.

He slid under the covers and felt her shifting around, adjusting her pillows and getting comfortable way, way over on her side of their huge bed. He wondered if he dared reach across her pillows for her or if she had the things booby-trapped. Better not. A man could lose a hand that way; or some other useful body part.

"Damn it, Marti," he said after a long time. "I really, really want you right now. I don't suppose there's any way I could talk you into letting seduce you, is there?"

She was quiet. Hell, maybe he'd waited too long and she was asleep. Maybe he should be thankful for that. Or maybe he should wake her up and ask again.

Finally she answered.

"Okay."

"Okay?"

"Yeah. But I'm still really mad at you."

"You mean, okay I can seduce you?"

"You don't want to?"

"Hell yes I want to!"

"Okay then."

He was kind of frozen in shock. She said *okay*? He honestly hadn't been prepared for that and didn't quite know what to do.

"So are we going to do this by telepathy, or something?" she asked.

"You still sound kind of pissed at me."

"I am. But you offered a seduction and I figured that meant you were going to do more than just lie over there."

He had to laugh. Only Marti could be so damn sexy and so damn bossy all at the same time. He didn't wait for her to change her mind or start making sense. He rolled over and found her right where she should have been. She curled her body around his and let him find her lips. Telepathy would have been interesting, but this was so, so much better.

"You're such a jerk," she whispered when he slipped his hands under her clothing.

"I know," he breathed against her wonderful skin. "And I hope you're not planning to get a lot of sleep tonight, Mrs. Jerk."

She was too busy returning his kisses to insult him again.

———

Charleen felt bad. Sure, she and Arv had connected over the last couple days like they were kids in college again, and she was thrilled to pieces about Granny offering to sell them the diner, but all was not well. Treeva was being a bigger bitch than usual and Charleen knew it was her fault.

Damn, why had she thought it was a good idea to stick her nose in where it didn't belong? She'd been the one to inform Treeva of Marti's past relationship with Dr. Hedgman, and now Treeva had somehow managed to link up with the guy. He was hanging all over her, smiling for the photographers and acting like a smitten teenager for them. Charleen had a sneaking suspicion Treeva herself had arranged for the reporters to be swarming all over the hotel, but her new boyfriend sure seemed happy to pose for them.

Man, she felt just awful. Things had been decidedly tense between Marti and East today, and it was obvious the whole Hedgeman-Treeva thing was a problem. They seemed to be constantly in view, and the glares Marti gave them fluctuated between seething anger and outright disbelief. East seemed to be doing a good job of ignoring them, but clearly Marti was still troubled by the thought of Leland Hedgeman taking up with someone new, especially when that someone was East's gorgeous ex-wife.

How had Charleen let herself get so carried away? It had been undeniably stupid to think Arv would throw away their marriage over some imaginary crush on Marti. How did she let herself get so crazy? Somehow she'd have to make up for it. She wasn't sure exactly how to go about doing that, but she would.

"So, been enjoying your time here?"

Charleen realized Treeva managed to tear herself away from Dr. Hedgeman and had come waltzing over to where she waited for Arv to meet her for an after-lunch coffee. Well, maybe she was going to get her chance sooner than expected.

"Yeah, we've been having a great time," Charleen replied. "How about you? I've seen the cameras following you around. That must get pretty old."

Treeva just tossed her hair. "It's something you get used to. Just part of living a public life."

Not *that* public, despite what Her Highness might think. Treeva Kincaide was a cooking show host, not royalty, or anything.

"It's odd how you really clicked with Marti's ex, isn't it?" Charleen asked, deciding to forgo beating around the bush.

"Isn't it, though?" Treeva grinned. "The poor guy follows me everywhere. But I truly hope this doesn't cause any trouble for you and your hubby."

"Why on earth should it cause us any trouble?" Charleen questioned.

"I'm sure you've got nothing to worry about," Treeva said

sweetly. "I just hope that once Marti sees that she's lost Dr. Hedgeman for good, well... I hope she doesn't go looking for comfort in someone else's backyard, if you know what I mean."

"Marti's not with Dr. Hedgeman. She's married to East," Charleen reminded.

"You and I both know there are some problems there. It doesn't take a rocket scientist to recognize that things are a little bit chilly between them."

"I'm sure this contest has been pretty stressful."

Now Treeva just laughed. It was one of those Wicked Witch kind of laughs, with a little bit of Evil Scientist thrown in just to make it creepier. Charleen shuddered.

"It's going to get a little more stressful for them at the dinner competition tonight," Treeva said, her voice dropping low.

Clearly Charleen was supposed to press for an explanation, so of course she did. This sounded like something she ought to ask about. "Oh? How so?"

"Well," Treeva began, slithering into the seat beside Charleen and glancing around for any eavesdroppers. "Just between you and me, East's final meal isn't going to go over so well."

"Oh? Have you got something planned for them?"

Charleen could hardly believe it. Was the bitch actually planning to sabotage East and Marti's dinner?

But Treeva just giggled maniacally and shook her head. "No, that's what makes it perfect. I don't have to do anything. East can mess this up all on his own. You see, I just found out what the meat will be for tonight's dinner."

"What the meat will be?"

"Oh, you know. For the dinner competition they get assigned a meat. The idea is to see how well they come up with something on the spur of the moment. Well, earlier today Mr. Beaumont had the three celebrity judges vote on what we'd like to see for the meat."

"He did?"

"Yeah. He's such a dear. I told him how nice it would be if the judges got to be a part of that decision, and I guess he wanted to please me."

"Really. So, I'm no genius, but I'm guessing you know something about meat that Mr. Beaumont doesn't, right?"

Treeva was beaming like she'd just been voted most popular on the island. "And you would be right."

"You're amazing."

"I know."

"But how did you make sure the big meat-vote would go your way?"

"The penguin guy is a big fan of mine," she said and it was pretty easy to imagine what she might have done to sway him.

"So, what exactly do you know about meat the rest of these poor saps don't know?"

Now Treeva's voice dropped even lower and she leaned in close. Too close. That cleavage was something Charleen really didn't need stuffed up under her nose.

"East hates chicken," Treeva said. "Fried chicken, to be precise. For as long as I've known him, he can't even stand to be in the same room with it. Hell, it's like a phobia, or something. Can you imagine? A grown man with a fried chicken phobia."

Oh God. "So, of course you made sure the impartial judges voted for fried chicken."

"I had to write it on the ballots myself."

"You really are amazing."

"I know," Treeva said again. "Hey, it looks like Leland's

getting a little lonely for me. I wouldn't want to neglect him and give him any reason to go crawling back to Marti, you know."

"Of course not."

"Well, here comes your hubby with coffee. Maybe I'll just leave you two alone," she said, vacating the chair and eyeing Arv carefully. "Hmm. Looks like he's alone, no Marti in sight. You don't suppose he's finally given up on her, do you?"

Bitch bitch bitch. Charleen managed one last smile. "Don't worry, Treeva. You'll be happy to know his feelings for Marti are just about the same as they used to be."

"Oh, so sorry to hear that for you. Well, you can thank me for the fried chicken. She might still have your husband wrapped around her finger, but at least now you won't have to worry about her winning that stupid Plaid Platter, too."

It's the *Patchwork* Platter, moron. *Patchwork*, just like Granny's curtains. And it was going to look damn good in that little diner, too. Charleen was pretty sure she'd just figured out how to make things up to Marti for the shabby way she'd treated her.

She smiled up at Arv as he sat down and handed her the cinnamon latte she'd requested. He'd been so good to her today, treating her like he used to back before life kind of got in the way. God, she loved him.

"What's so funny?" he said, noticing her catty little grin.

"Honey, do you still have that bottle of your secret sauce you brought to give to my parents?"

"Yeah, it's up in the room. I forgot to give it to them when we dropped off the kids."

"Excellent. Let's make that a gift for Marti and East tonight, okay?"

"Sure, okay. So, are you ready to head out to that antique

mall you wanted to visit before dinner?"

She sipped her latte and shook her head. "I've changed my mind. Let's spend the afternoon up in our room instead."

Arv didn't have to be asked twice.

———

East could tell Marti was nervous. Okay, everyone in the crowded ballroom could probably tell Marti was nervous. She was pale and practically shaking as they got their cooking area ready for the big competition tonight. Well, they'd done all they could to prepare. Another hour and a half and this would all be over, for better or worse. Yeah, she was nervous, all right. So was he.

Tonight's meal would be a bit harder to prepare for since they still didn't know what the main course would be. Well, they'd planned a few side dishes that would go with just about anything and they'd made sure to have a wide variety of spices and seasonings on hand. When Wallace Beaumont finally took the podium to announce it was time to officially start the night's event, East felt as prepared as they could be.

The hall was full to capacity; every seat at every table was taken. Maybe news of the *almost*-scandal involving a celebrity contestant and his ex-wife celebrity judge had drawn extra interest. Or maybe it was like this every year. Either way, tension was high and he could see that Marti was more nervous than ever. He sure had to hand it to her. The girl had guts to come out and face her mortal fear of the kitchen in front of hundreds of hungry critics.

He rolled his shoulders and tried to relax. He didn't dare offer any words of encouragement to Marti; no telling how she'd react. Even after another night of incredible sex, she was not happy with him today. She was still pissed about how he'd handled the Treeva thing and kept dodging her questions about the Townsend's. Just now, as a matter of fact, he had to admit they were standing just a little too close for comfort to some very sharp instruments. He wisely chose to stay quiet.

Mr. Beaumont rambled on about the contest promoters and the many gracious sponsors, yada yada yada. He reminded everyone that after dinner was served and everyone had time to turn in their score sheets they would all be invited to a wine and chocolate reception out in the main lobby. That would give enough time to tabulate the results before everyone returned to the hall one last time for the grand awards ceremony.

The look on Marti's pale face said she didn't really expect that awards ceremony to bring any good news. He glanced around at the four other teams of competitors standing ready in their kitchen units. He had to agree with Marti. These were the best of the best, and in all four cases they were from upscale restaurants in more urban areas. It was kind of silly to think Granny's Kitchen had a chance against any of them. Well, too late for self-doubt now. It was time to find out exactly what gourmet impossibility they would be concocting tonight.

"So, contestants, here is the moment you've been waiting for," Wallace said dramatically. A hush fell over the crowd and he grandly continued. "If the Crawford County Miss Soybean will please bring me the envelope!"

A fresh-faced beauty queen wearing a glittery prom dress strolled out with a large white envelope in her hand and a wide smile on her face. Yes, soybeans had been good to this gal and she knew it. She handed the envelope over with a practiced flourish then stood primly to await the results. Mr. Beaumont was noticeably slow to take his eyes off Miss

Soybean and get to the task of opening the envelope.

He cleared his throat loudly. The microphone squealed feedback through the speakers. He held the contents of the envelope up like a royal edict.

"Tonight's main course, to be prepared by each of our five final teams, will be…" *Pause for dramatic effect.* "Fried chicken!"

The audience murmured amongst themselves, but East was only vaguely aware of it. Had he heard correctly? *Fried chicken?* But he hadn't even eaten fried chicken in ten years! Damn it, he hadn't even *looked* at a fried chicken; he changed the channel for KFC commercials. Even now, the very sound of those words brought memories and regrets flooding over him.

Fried chicken with Marti on a blanket out by the creek. Sitting in that booth at Dixon's, laughing and holding hands. Planning their futures over greasy napkins. Good times they would never capture again no matter how much he might want it.

Hell. Mr. Beaumont might as well have just announced their final assignment to be fried dragon eggs. Fried chicken was impossible.

———

"Did he just say *fried chicken*?" Marti asked. East didn't reply right away and for a minute she thought maybe he hadn't heard her. Finally, though, he nodded.

"Yeah. Fried chicken."

"Oh God."

He looked at her. "What?"

Shit. How on earth could she explain this to him? It was stupid, of course, but she couldn't help it. Just the smell of fried chicken brought on such a wave of memories… well, she hadn't eaten it since then and she was pretty sure she wouldn't be able to start cooking it tonight.

He was watching her, waiting for an explanation.

"I, um, we haven't practiced fried chicken."

She couldn't meet his eyes. He didn't say anything, so she re-organized the spices on the counter in front of her. Maybe he wouldn't think anything of it. Surely with all the cooking he'd done over the years he'd be a whiz with fried chicken and she could just sort of hang back and focus on their side dishes. Maybe the tears welling up in her eyes right now would just go away and she wouldn't end up crying about something so stupid as golden-brown poultry parts.

"No, we didn't think to practice that, did we?" he said next to her.

She shook her head, and made the fatal mistake of glancing over at him. He was still standing there, watching her. Shouldn't he be getting stuff out of the fridge, or something?

The contest workers brought over a huge pan of raw chicken bits and placed it on the counter. Holy cow, when they said fried chicken, they meant it. From the looks of the whole slaughtered flock splayed out there in front of them, they were going to have to fry up enough for an army. How on earth was she going to pull this off?

They just stood there and stared at the pan. She waited for East to say something, or to tell her what to do. He didn't. He just stood there. She could hear him breathing.

"Shit," he said after a long silence.

That didn't sound good. She looked up at him and for the first time realized he looked just about as shell-shocked as she felt. He met her eyes and asked the question she really hadn't expected.

"Don't tell me you haven't eaten fried chicken in ten years, either?"

Oh no! He knew what a sappy nincompoop she'd been. He knew that all this time she'd been pining away, that their casual forays into the world of adult relationships had been more than just experimentation for her. He knew how she'd felt for ten long years, that she'd… wait a minute. What did he say?

"Did you say, *'either'*?"

He nodded. "Sorry. Ever since, well, since back then I haven't been much of a fried chicken fan."

"All those boxes we took with us down to Tyler's Branch..."

"And we hardly ever ate them."

"As I recall, we had other stuff to do."

The memories were flooding over her too fast and too strong to push them back. Lord, but she was drowning in East's eyes and all her aching dreams of what might have been.

"I haven't touched it since then," he said softly, his eyes never leaving hers.

"I can't even smell it," she admitted.

"My car broke down in front of a Popeye's once a few years ago and I left my phone at home. I walked a mile and a half to find Taco Bell where I could call Triple A."

"I told Granny her shipment didn't come in and hid the fryer pieces way in the back of her freezer so she couldn't serve it. Two weeks ago."

She waited for him to start laughing at her, or something. He didn't. Instead, he reached up and touched her face. It was just the gentlest brush of his fingers against her cheek, but heat roared through her body. The responding flames in his eyes were unmistakable. He pulled her to him in a crushing embrace that felt so good she managed to forget all about that hideous pan of raw chicken parts.

And the whole ballroom full of people who were probably watching them have a mutual panic attack in their little kitchen cubicle.

"It's been a long, long ten years, Marti," he said.

His voice was quiet—strained—but she had no trouble hearing him. She knew exactly what he meant, too. It had been a very long chicken-less and East-less ten years.

She replied by kissing him with all her might.

He responded to that, too, and for a moment everything else around them went away. They were silly, idealistic kids again and the only thing that mattered was getting enough of each other. That was something they'd never quite accomplished, either. Maybe now, finally, they'd find a way.

It was the whistles and applause that got her attention. East broke off the kiss and was chuckling in her ear while their forgotten audience cat-called behind them. Oops! What on earth must everyone be thinking, watching them up here like teenagers in heat when they really should be figuring out what to do with all that damn chicken?

"Sorry," she said, pushing away from his tempting warmth.

"Well, I don't forgive you," he said, grinning. "Guess we're not exactly alone here, are we?"

"No. We've got ten pounds of dead poultry staring at us."

He took a deep breath and flexed his shoulders. Hell, and she was supposed to keep her mind on cooking when he had that burning gleam in his eye and his healthy pecs were all dancing around in front of her? Not freaking likely.

"What are we going to do?" she asked.

"I have no idea," he replied, still grinning.

There was no chance of anyone hearing their dismal

discussion. Sparse applause and laughter still circulated through the crowd—at their expense, of course—and D.J. Tommy Blue was making off-color remarks about the newlywed team and their scores tonight reflecting something other than their cooking skills. He and Laquinta Martinez, the salsa-dancing celebrity judge, were holding up signs with big number tens scrawled on them in marker. The audience loved it. Treeva, apparently, did not. She wouldn't even look at them. Good.

"Well, we've got to do something," Marti sighed, turning her focus back to the meat. She glanced at the other teams who were already busy with preparations in their little stations and oblivious to the dire drama in the Smith camp. Great. They were falling behind already.

"Okay. We can do this," East assured her.

"How?" she asked helplessly.

And then she noticed Charleen. She was smiling at them, and doing some kind of nodding eye roll. What? Charleen didn't have any sort of tick, did she? Oh, wait. She was trying to tell her something. What on earth…?

Then Marti remembered. The secret sauce! She grabbed up the bottle she'd left sitting on their counter after Arv gave it to them just before the competition got started. He said it was his Special Chicken Sauce and that he'd meant to give it to them the first day as some kind of good luck offering. She studied the bottle.

"East, what about this?" she asked finally.

"Arv's sauce?"

"He said he swears by it for chicken. Fried chicken especially, Charleen said."

East shrugged. "Huh. Well, okay. What the hell. Let's use that tonight."

Marti glanced back at Charleen. She was grinning ear to

ear. Okay, so maybe she knew something about the chicken. Marti glanced over at Treeva. She was grinning, too. Holy hell.

"East," she asked. "Did your ex-wife know you don't eat fried chicken?"

East shot a glare over at Treeva then frowned. "Yeah. She did."

Marti just nodded. No need to discuss it, they both had a pretty good idea where the chicken thing came from tonight.

"Have I mentioned that she's a huge bitch?" she said under her breath as East started hauling out a pan big enough to fry a respectable portion of that chicken.

"Yeah. But go ahead and mention it again."

God, she was a piece of work. How on earth had Treeva managed to pull this off? Well, that didn't matter. All Marti could let herself worry about right now was how she and East were going to pull *this* off.

"Okay," he said. "Let's get the oil heating up and see if we can't rub some of that sauce into the chicken. We probably should have marinated it, but there's not time for that. You want to peel potatoes and I'll rub?"

Oh, that was sweet. He was going to let her get out of touching the damn chicken. No, they were in this together and she was going to stick by him for every painful moment of it.

"Let's rub together, shall we?" she offered.

"God, I love you Marti."

Aw, hell. She could cook anything he wanted if he was going to go around talking like that.

Chapter 29

Milly darn near bit her fingers down to bloody little nubs. What on earth was taking so long for the judges to count up all those damn score sheets? Anyone with half a taste bud could tell Marti and East's chicken was head and shoulders above the other contestants'.

She downed the rest of the fancy little wine glass Milton had brought her.

"I hate all this waiting," she said.

"Well, I'm sure Marti and East will do just fine," Milton said, patting her hand.

"Yeah, that was some amazing fried chicken," Peg said, pulling threads out of the linen napkin she'd been wringing for about fifteen minutes now.

East's parents were just as enthusiastic in their agreement.

"That boy sure is a whiz in the kitchen," C.J. said and for once he actually sounded like he was proud of that fact.

And he should be. That fried chicken Marti and East cooked up was the best Milly had ever eaten. Funny thing of it was she couldn't recall the kids practicing that one.

"I just wonder where East got that recipe," she said. "I know that wasn't mine."

Charleen was sort of fidgeting across the table from her. Those two sure had a change of attitude today. The last couple days Charleen had been radiating off ice cubes and sending hateful glances at everyone around her. Tonight, however, she and Arv were all lovey-dovey. Hell, even if Marti and East didn't win tonight Milly would have to say this had been a really enjoyable evening here with all these old friends. Not to mention Milton's hovering attentions, and the promise of what additional attention he was planning for later on when they were alone.

"Can I tell them now?" Charleen was whispering to Arv.

"Oh, all right," Arv said.

"That was *Arv's* fried chicken," Charleen announced.

"What?" Milly had to hear that again.

Charleen repeated herself, and went on to explain. "Yeah, he's got a special sauce he's come up with. It makes absolutely the best fried chicken! He gave a bottle to East and Marti as a good luck gift, and I guess they decided to use it. Pretty good coincidence, huh?"

"Yeah, but what if people start associating this with *Granny's Kitchen*?" Peg asked. "I mean, people are going to expect to find these recipes at Granny's. Shouldn't you keep that for yourself, for when you rebuild, and all?"

Charleen and Arv exchanged smiles. Milly figured she'd better go ahead and spill the beans now. The wine and chocolate reception had put everyone in a good mood. Maybe now would be the best time to inform everyone of the big changes.

"I'm selling the diner," she announced. "Arv and Charleen aren't going to rebuild in Finster. They're buying the diner and coming back to Garden Falls."

The table grew quiet for a few minutes. What if nobody else thought this was such a good idea? Hell, she should have at least told Peg about it. This affected the woman's job; she shouldn't have this bomb dropped on her out of the blue like this. Milly realized she should have be a little more sensitive about her oldest friend.

"Well, holy shit," Peg said. Milly wasn't sure she'd ever heard those words come out of Peg's mouth.

"I know I should have told you, but we only just decided all this. I know it'll mean big changes, but they promised me they'd keep you and the rest of the staff on as long as you all want to work there."

"Want to work there? Good lord, Milly, I've been trying for years to come up with a way of getting out of there!" Peg laughed. "I'd have retired a decade ago if I thought you could handle it without me."

What? Well, this was news to her. Insulting news, too. "Handle it without you? Peg MacNamee, are you saying you don't think I can run my own place without help from the girl who made me get a B minus in high school home economics?" Milly said.

"Are you kidding? You were lucky you had me or that would have been a lot lower than a B minus! Remember what you did to those strawberry crepes we tried to make?"

"Oh, don't remind me!" Milly had to laugh. "And if you ever breathe a word of that to Marti, I'll wring your neck."

"What, you don't want her to know exactly where she inherited her kitchen skills?" Peg kidded.

Of course Milton had to hear all the details on that, so for the next five minutes Peg filled him in on just how sorry things used to be in Milly's kitchen. Marti wasn't the only Snowden woman who'd had her share of culinary struggles. But time and trying had been all it took for Milly to overcome her shortcomings and it sure looked like that was true for Marti.

The group at their table laughed as Peg recounted stories from their early days. It was stuff she hadn't thought about in years and Milly laughed so hard her face hurt. God, she sure hoped someday Marti and East could sit around and look back at all this with the same kind of laughter. It was looking like maybe they'd finally figured out just how much they really cared about each other. They made one hell of a good team in the kitchen; it was high time they carried that into other areas.

"Ah, Milly," Peg sighed, catching her breath. "I never could understand why you kept that place going all these years."

"Well," Milly said, thinking about it for a second. "I guess after Marti left I just didn't know what else to do with myself."

"Yeah, it's going to take some getting used to, not working there every day."

"Are you okay with this?" Milly asked her friend. It was kind of unfair to put her on the spot like this, but she guessed they might as well talk about it now as any other time.

"I think it's great," Peg said, then glanced meaningfully over at Arv and Charleen. "Of course, I'll expect the new owners to still give me a discount every time I come in to eat there."

"You got it, Peg," Arv assured her. "But I'm afraid we'll have to make a limit on how many hours a day you and Granny spend there. I know it'll be hard to get used to, but you're going to need to get out and have a life!"

"Shoot," Milly laughed. "You probably won't see hide nor hair of me. I think a woman with a wedding to plan has a lot more to do than sit around in some greasy little diner all day."

It took about half a second for that to sink in before Peg shrieked.

"You're getting married?!"

Well, that was all it took for the floodgates to open. Peg was crying, Arv was congratulating Milton, Charleen was planning a catered meal, East's mom was hugging her, and C.J. was talking annuities and insurance. It was all damn annoying, but she played along with it for their sake. After all, how many more times in her life was she going to get to be the center of attention?

Everyone was babbling on so, they darn near missed when Tommy Blue announced Wallace Beaumont to give tonight's results. It wasn't until the room around them went silent that Milly realized it was time to start being nervous again. Lordy, but she was going to get an ulcer by the time this was all over.

She held her breath as another fresh young beauty queen—Miss Pork Producer this time—brought out an envelope. Mr. Beaumont opened it too damn slowly, then announced the fourth and fifth place winners. Good. Marti and East were not in that group.

Then it was down to the final three. This meant suspense was pretty high. Mr. Beaumont milked it by skipping the third place winners altogether and going right for second. He held up the envelop proudly and announced them. It was the nice folks from Toledo. Still not Marti and East.

Hell, that meant they came in either a respectable third, or holy cow, right up in first place. Damn, why was this taking so long? The anticipation was killing her.

Finally it was time to find out who placed third and who'd be going home with that Patchwork Platter. She reminded herself third was perfectly fine. They could be proud of that. Marti and East had done their very best and they could all be thrilled for them no matter what the outcome. Everyone was a winner tonight, right?

Hell no! She wanted that damn platter and she wanted it bad. She crossed everything on her body that could still be crossed; she clenched her eyes—and her butt cheeks, for good measure—and waited a thousand years for damn Mr. Beaumont to read that last name. Finally he did.

———

It was almost eleven o'clock at night and Marti still hadn't caught her breath. From the minute Granny's Diner had been announced winner of this year's Family Favorites Cook-Off things had been a blur. A nice blur, but a blur nonetheless.

Their scores had been nearly perfect; they'd won by a healthy margin. She hoped they'd deserved it, but she really couldn't say. She hadn't been brave enough to taste her own dinner. *Fried chicken.* Who would have ever guessed?

They'd been presented the coveted Patchwork Platter and had hundreds of photos taken. Marti wasn't quite sure if this was the usual fare, or if East's celebrity was causing more of a stir than usual. She had a sneaky suspicion the latter was true, but he took it in his usual stride. Also, she had to admit she loved the way he made sure to put his arm possessively around her for every shot.

They'd won. Hell, not only had they won, they won with fried chicken! It was still unfathomable, but the grin on Granny's face as she beamed up at them from the ballroom floor was every proof Marti needed to know this was real. She'd done it. She'd worked side by side with East and she'd won a freaking cooking contest. Nothing exploded or burned down, and they'd won. It was a miracle.

But now she was worn out. All the pictures and schmoozing had about done her in. How on earth did East do this? He seemed perfectly fine; rejuvenated, as a matter of fact. The more cameras and note-pad-bearing journalists that accosted them, the more he seemed to thrive. Marti was getting face cramps from smiling so much, and she was pretty sure a definite hump was developing on her back from all the stooping and hugging.

"You look tired," he pointed out needlessly.

"I am."

Her ears were ringing from the constant clatter of tables and chairs being put away, kitchens being cleaned, equipment being hauled, and the drone of a hundred bubbling people still milling around. Tired didn't come close to describing how she felt.

"Then let's get out of here. And up to bed."

He'd said that with promise in his voice. She felt her skin tingle all up and down her spine. East wanted her up in his bed again, and she wasn't about to argue. Somehow over that damned chicken they'd reached an understanding. They hadn't said anything out loud about it, but she knew and so did he. That chicken was their lifeline and they were going to hang on to it.

"That sounds good," she said.

They had to fend off a few more well-wishers and reporters, and even a few catty remarks from Treeva as she muscled her way into their fifteen minutes of fame. East had to promise some morning interviews, as well, before they were finally able to ditch the crowd and say good-night to Granny and East's parents. Arv and Charleen had already gone up to their room to celebrate. She guessed they were really proud of Arv's special sauce.

Finally Marti and East made it up to their room and closed the door on the world. Alone, at last. They just stood there in the doorway and both took a couple deep breaths. The contest was over; they'd done what they set out to do and did it better than anyone ever expected. Tomorrow they'd head back to Garden Falls and life would begin again, right where they left off.

But where was that?

She looked up into East's summer blue eyes. They were still bright, even after all the exhausting interaction with his adoring public. Yeah, that was his calling. That was the life he needed to go back to, wasn't it? And she didn't fit in there at all. Damn.

She was going to tell him what she knew; tomorrow it would all be over and this fantasy would have to end. She wanted him to understand that she was okay with that now. She'd been a shrew this weekend; jealous over his relationship with Treeva and his commitments to his career, as if she had some right to claim him for her own. She didn't, and she knew it for a fact now.

It hadn't just been casual sex for them that summer before college. He really had cared about her. Heck, he'd cared enough that he couldn't eat fried chicken for ten years and for East, that was saying something. For herself, she was only too aware of how much she had cared for him. But none of that had been enough to keep them together, had it? He'd gone off to California and she'd gone up to college. Now, it was happening again and there was nothing either of them could do about it.

He didn't let her explain all that, though. His eyes told her he understood, but he didn't want to waste any more of their precious moments with boring conversation about the future or reality. He liked the fantasy just as much as she did.

"Let's make the best of our last night with a jacuzzi," he said.

Yeah, that sounded like a great idea. She launched herself into his arms. He laughed and wrapped himself around her.

Their kiss started out hot and got hotter. It was a kiss with a lot of lost time to make up for and they both did their best to make it up. Marti was gasping for air when his lips left hers to concentrate on her earlobes and throat. Her skin registered sparks of electricity wherever they made contact. God, he made her feel so good.

"Give me a minute to get the water running," he said after a few more kisses. "I really do want to try this thing out. I want to see if the combination of you in hot, bubbly water causes spontaneous combustion."

She grinned at him and started dropping her clothes. "Who am I to stand in the way of scientific exploration?"

He laughed. The water in the huge tub in the corner of their room was just heating up when his cell phone rang in the pocket of his discarded pants.

"You'd better answer that," she said.

"I don't want to."

"It might be your agent."

"I can call him back."

"It's your career, East. Go ahead, just take a minute. I promise, I'll wait."

He met her eyes for a long moment then kissed her forehead.

"All right," he grumbled. "I'll just check to see who it is."

He dug his phone out of the pile of clothes and answered it. Marti flopped down into the bed. Yes, she'd been right. It was his agent, she could tell. She'd heard their conversations from this end plenty of times and recognized the pattern. East covered the receiver and gave an apologetic grimace.

"I'm sorry," he mouthed toward her.

She just nodded. "I understand."

Yeah, she understood everything. This was reality. Reality was always going to hit their nice little fantasy head on, and reality would probably always win. What a damn shame.

She fluffed a pillow behind her head and settled in. "At

least we'll always have fried chicken."

———

"Wednesday," East said into his cell phone. "Yeah, I promise. I'll know something by then."

His agent wasn't exactly happy with that, but he'd survive. No way was East committing to a yearlong contract when so much was still up in the air. Treeva was still playing her games, making the producers dance to her tune and demanding this crap or that crap. The show might be faltering, but she was still a valuable part of it. They had to humor her.

But East didn't. He could take the show or leave it. True, if he took it he'd also be taking a nice healthy pay increase, but he'd have to put up with Treeva. He wasn't sure it was worth it.

What he really wanted was think up some angle to get Marti involved. That was where his agent came in. Not that he wanted Marti to hear about it yet. Not until something was definite.

A year ago he'd been approached by a soap opera, a really popular one. They wanted to do a storyline about a chef opening a new restaurant and it would have been nice to tap into East's star power and cast him for the recurring role. However, Treeva had been jealous and made such a stink over his contractual agreement with *The Passionate Palate* that he'd had to turn the soap opera down.

Well, it appeared that storyline wasn't quite dead and they were interested in East again. Since if he did decide to return to *The Passionate Palate* he'd have to sign a new contract, his agent said it would be no trouble to make sure this time it left him free to commit to the soap or any other project that didn't directly interfere with his filming schedule. And *he'd* be in control of his schedule, not Treeva. Basically, if he went back to *The Passionate Palate* now it would be as Treeva's equal, not her pet.

He rather liked that. He also liked that the soap opera people were interested in the suggestion he made of including a storyline about a toxic waste dump near the place where his character was building his restaurant. Toxic waste seemed like a perfect explanation for the sudden resurrection and drastically altered appearance of a recently murdered character, they said. They'd canned the actor and wanted to replace him, apparently.

East mostly thought a toxic waste storyline sounded like a really good excuse to hire a prominent environmentalist to consult on the program and give at least a hint of credibility to the wacked out plot. He'd already given his agent the name of a really great environmentalist he happened to be married to. Now he was just waiting to hear if it was all a go or not.

If he was going to work on either of these two shows—even on the short term—he had to make sure things with Marti were settled first. And that meant things back in Garden Falls had to be settled. So much could still go wrong. Well, for better or for worse, he ought to know for sure by Wednesday. Then he'd decide what to do with the next phase of his life.

And he sure hoped Marti would want to be in it.

He'd been on the phone too long and when he finally turned back to her, she'd fallen asleep. He watched her breathing. Poor thing, she really had been exhausted. He didn't have the heart to wake her, either, even though it was physically painful to think about not picking up where they'd left off a few minutes ago. She'd stripped out of her fried chicken scented work clothes and was spread out before him, tempting and amazing. Still, he decided to let her rest.

Taking a deep breath and trying to think happy, plutonic thoughts, he slid the covers out from under her and then pulled them up over her. She sighed a contented little sigh and curled up on her side, her honey-brown hair splayed over her pillow. What he wouldn't give to have this in his bed every night for the rest of their lives. He couldn't even hazard a guess as to what his chances were of getting it.

He let himself sit there and watch her for a couple more minutes, then drained the jacuzzi and climbed under the covers with her. She snuggled against him and he held her there, drinking in the warmth from her body and the scent of her skin. He was content; tonight he would just hold her and let her sleep. There'd be a million more opportunities throughout his lifetime to make love to Marti.

He prayed to God it was true.

Chapter 30

It was Wednesday and Marti was a coward. She'd been back in Garden Falls three full days now and still hadn't gotten up the nerve to have a real heart-to-heart talk with East. She was a big, fat chicken.

But she was also hopelessly in love with him and was willing to do just about anything that would put off the inevitable. Today, for instance, she'd pretended to lose her keys so he'd have to take a couple minutes to pick her up and drive her over to Granny's. They'd planned to look at some stuff for Granny's upcoming wedding and Marti had the brilliant idea that if she somehow got East involved in the festivities he'd stick around a few days longer.

He wasn't complaining about having to chauffeur her around, either. He did, she noticed, miss the turn onto Granny's street.

"Uh, Granny's house is back there," she pointed out.

"Oh, so you can talk," he said.

"You missed the street."

"I missed you talking to me. You've been practically silent ever since we got home Sunday."

True, she had. Unless he was counting the nights, which obviously he wasn't. All her stuff was still at East's place so she'd been staying with him and he hadn't complained about that, either. He did, however, give up sleeping on the couch.

But he'd been busy. He'd been running around town,

meeting with people for heaven only knew what. "Business" is all he'd ever say and she didn't dare ask him any more about it. Clearly it was his business and none of hers.

So, she'd just gone about her daily routine as inconspicuously as she could, keeping her self busy by, oddly enough, cooking. Crazy, but the one good thing to come of all this was, apparently, she'd gained a love of cooking. Go figure! She'd spend her days helping out at the newly bustling and platter-bedecked diner then come home to whip up something that, maybe, would impress East and make him decide to give up his career and stick around. Or at least ask her to go with him.

But of course there really wasn't such a thing as food that could do that. So, he'd thank her for the great meal and help clean up the kitchen. Then she'd snuggle up as close to him as she dared and watch TV while he sent texts or clicked away at his laptop. She made herself not look over his shoulder. If he had wanted to include her in his business, he easily could have. He didn't.

So, she'd spent the last few days holding her breath, knowing at any moment he'd tell her he was leaving. And now here it was Wednesday, the day she'd heard him tell his agent he'd have things all sorted out. And she was trapped in the car with him while he took an obviously intentional wrong turn.

"Where are we going?" she asked and tried to make it sound like she was just mildly annoyed at his unexpected detour and not like her very soul was crashing into a million little pieces.

"Oh, just around," he answered. "There's something I wanted to show you."

Show her something? Well, she supposed showing was better than telling, wasn't it? Unless maybe he was taking her out to show her his lawyer's office where they'd need to sign the divorce papers.

She decided not to think about that. Surely there were plenty of other things he might be planning to show her. Oh yeah, he had things to show her, all right, and she was happy to look at them. True, she'd seen them already, but that never seemed to lessen the effect.

He wasn't driving back to his place, though. Instinct told her this was something else, something that was going to change everything for them. The suspense was killing her.

"So what do you want to show me?" she asked bravely.

"Oh, uh, the sunset."

The sunset? Did he think they needed a romantic setting for their big break-up scene? Great. Leave it to East to be hugely dramatic at a time like this.

He went past the diner then turned up the road that would take them along Tyler's Branch. Oh, just great. A deep pang of dread latched onto her chest and started squeezing tight. She knew where they were headed and she really, really didn't want to go there. Not now, not when this was all over and he was leaving her again.

Sure enough, he turned onto Beaverbend Road.

———

He pulled up the car and put it in park. This area used to be overgrown and pretty rutted, but Phil and Joetta must have had it smoothed out to use for parking. They probably brought prospective clients up here to tell them stories of how they were going to develop the place and make it valuable. Well, it worked in East's favor now. He could park here and not worry about getting stuck. He still wasn't sure how this would go and there was a distinct possibility their visit wouldn't last long.

She was tense. He could feel it radiating off her as she sat there, hands clenched in her lap. She was staring straight ahead, reading and re-reading the big sign that used to show a plot plan of Townsend's proposed development. Now that plan was covered over by a big yellow "Under New Ownership" sign. He'd had that made up special. It wasn't entirely accurate—yet—but close enough for effect.

"I heard Phil was having some trouble," she said.

"Yeah. He had to unload the place quick when the county engineer started double-checking his surveys. He's lucky they didn't prosecute, but since he found a buyer right away he can give his investors their money back and, I guess, no one wants to press charges."

"It's some guy from out of town, I heard," she said. "The new buyer."

"Really? You heard that?" Funny, he thought of himself as a local.

"He'll probably find some way around the flood issues. It's obvious the state isn't interested in helping out."

"You still haven't heard anything from your friends there in Columbus?"

She shrugged. "No. Guess one little near-threatened salamander wasn't enough to get their attention."

"Well, maybe this new owner will care about preserving the land as it is."

Now she snorted. "Yeah, right."

He had to agree. If he didn't already know the whole story, it would be a little hard to believe. In Marti's experience, wetlands-preserving-philanthropists died out with Teddy Roosevelt. Or got bought off by friends of Leland Hedgeman.

Well, it was time to clear things up. He'd procrastinated

as long as he could. Time to bare his soul and reap the consequences.

"Marti, we need to talk," he began.

Her knuckles went white and she shook her head violently. "No, not here. Let's go back home. To your apartment."

Oh no, he was not about to do that. He needed every advantage he could get and he was counting on this place, old memories, and the sunset flaming over the tree-lined sky to help him out. Besides, he'd spent a lot of time out here getting the sign ready.

"No, let's talk here. Come on," he said and jumped out of the car before she could stop him. He trotted around and opened her door for her. She didn't budge. "Come here. Look at this."

He held his hand out and she waited an awfully long time before she finally took it. Thank God. For a minute he thought he'd lost already.

She stepped out of the car and let him lead her to the clump of tall grass where the real estate sign was. They stopped next to it and at last Marti relaxed. The water in Tyler's branch murmured and splashed in the creek bed below them. Birds sang and darted about in the trees and low lying brush. He watched her take a long, deep breath. The magic of the place was finally starting to work.

"It still smells the same," she commented.

She was right. That had been one of the first things he noticed, too, when he'd come back here a few weeks ago. They stood there together, breathing the air and remembering.

"When do you go back to California?" she asked abruptly.

Darn. He shouldn't have let himself get lulled into

silence. Now he'd have to answer her questions before he'd get to ask his.

"Saturday," he said.

"Oh."

He couldn't quite decipher what she meant by that simply syllable. Was she glad to see him go? Wishing he'd stay longer? Did she have no opinion one way or the other? He should have come right out and told her what he'd done.

"They're giving me a bigger presence on the show," he said as if that even came close to a full explanation.

"That's nice."

"Yeah. And I can wear a shirt now, too."

"Won't help your ratings much."

"I told them I'd only sign on for six months. After that they'll have to renegotiate."

She actually raised one eyebrow and took her eyes off the landscape to spare him a weak smile. "Sounds like they must be pretty desperate. Treeva hasn't been doing so well on her own, huh?"

"No, unfortunately it turns out half the audience only watched it for me."

"The female half, of course."

He shrugged. "Oh, you might be surprised."

"Equal opportunity, huh? But what are you going to do after six months? Can you try to get her booted off?"

"Wouldn't that be nice? Actually, though, I'm not sure I still want to do the show in six months. I've got a couple other opportunities. Did you know *Quentin's Fire* wants me?"

"The soap opera? Wow, that'd be great!"

"Yeah, and get this. There's a movie script I'm considering, too."

"A movie? No way!"

"Yeah, way. It looks good, too, but things are still early."

"I guess you're going to be pretty busy for a while."

He shrugged. "I'm not out saving the Everglades, but it's a job."

"Well, I'm not exactly out saving the Everglades, either."

"But you will be, won't you? I heard Hedgeman offering it," he said. "Damn, but I'm going to hate knowing you're all the way on the other side of the country."

"Then you'll be glad to know that sort of fell through." She kicked a dirt clod.

"It did?" He knew he sounded way too hopeful. He should have at least acted disappointed, for her sake, but he just wasn't *that* good an actor.

"Yeah. Leland's being investigated and everything is pretty well shut down, for a while anyway."

"Good. He's an asshole and you can do better than his hand-me-down projects."

She laughed. "I'll put that on my resume: 'Famous actor thinks I can do better.'"

He cleared his throat. "Why not: 'Husband thinks you can do better?'"

He watched her and waited for the response.

"That's going to get outdated pretty fast, isn't it?" she asked.

"Only if you insist," he replied and took her hand. It was now or never. "I'm in no great hurry to get another divorce, Marti. Especially not from you. Can't we wait a while for that? I know you've got things you want to do and I can't expect you to come following me on all my ventures, but can't we find some way to meet in the middle?"

She swallowed hard and blinked up at him. Was he making a mess of this? Yeah, he was. She had no clue what he was trying to say. He'd have to try again.

"Please stay married to me," he said. That was putting it plain enough, wasn't it?

"Stay married?"

"Hell, I know it's a step down for you, but there's a spot for you on *Quentin's Fire*. Believe it or not, they need a consultant on the set. I guess I had wetlands on the brain when I was negotiating my contract and I suggested that we incorporate some environmental issues in this new storyline. Illegal toxic dumping and stuff like that."

"You mean, you want me to come work with you?"

Damn. She sounded more than a little doubtful. He was mucking this up big time.

"I know it's not much, just some little consulting spot, but can't you at least think about it?"

She looked like she was going to be sick or something. Aw, hell. He'd probably insulted her by offering a stupid TV job. She couldn't even come out and say anything about it, just stood there with her eyes glazing over and her hand clamped on her mouth to keep from laughing at him, he guessed.

Well, he might as well play his last card. Get it over with once and for all.

"I did something else, too," he confessed.

"Oh?" No telling what she expected him to say next.

"We're the new owners of this land, Marti. You and me. I bought it for you. At least," he corrected himself. "I will buy it for you once all the paperwork is signed. Right now, I'm still missing a few signatures, Yours."

Now she was clearly convinced he was insane. Her eyes lost that glazed look and got really, really round. She shook her head like she was watching a train wreck in slow motion.

"But you don't have any money, East. Treeva got everything, remember?"

Did he remember! Well, at least he could set her mind partly at ease on his financial score. "Yeah, she did. But I'd given a bunch of money to Mom and Dad back when I first started out. I thought I was doing them a big favor, paying them back for all I put them through when I bailed on college and all that. Turns out, though, Dad was afraid I'd run through my fame and fortune and have nothing to show for it so, instead of spending the money on trips and new cars like I told them to, he put it away for me. He invested it and now he insists on giving it back to us with all the interest he'd earned. It's a pretty nice chunk, as a matter of fact. Something to get us started, he said."

"You didn't tell me about that."

"No, because I knew you'd have a fit and make me give it back or give it to charity or shove it up my… well, you know. So, I found a better use for it. I bought your swamp."

She turned away from him to gaze out over the valley. His eyes followed hers. It really was a beautiful place, with the dark trees outlined against the orange fingers of sunset reaching up across the sky. One lone jet in the distance left a glowing silver trail and the dampness of night was just barely creeping into the air. It was beautiful, and she was beautiful in it.

"Two acres are considered habitable," he said. "The rest is watershed. The county insists it be left untilled and undeveloped. All one hundred and sixty-seven acres."

"One hundred and sixty-seven acres?"

"It's not the Everglades, but it's home. At least, it could be. These two acres that are above flood level, anyway."

She chewed furiously at her bottom lip. "I don't know what to say. Why didn't you tell me you were doing this?"

"Because I was afraid it wouldn't work out. Townsend didn't want to sell, and I wasn't sure we'd actually be able to find enough evidence that he'd done something wrong to be able to force him to sell at my price. We got lucky."

"I guess so."

"It'll take all the money Dad gave me for the down payment. Sorry to say, if you agree to this and sign the papers I really *will* be broke. That's why I figured I'd better go back to *The Passionate Palate* and start earning a steady paycheck again, at least for a little while. *Quentin's Fire* won't need me for two or three months, at least."

She didn't say anything and he had the sinking feeling that wasn't a good sign.

"I don't expect you to be tied down anywhere forever, Marti. I know you've got other goals. But I don't want to go ten more years without you, either. I guess we each can't help what we do for a living, but surely there's got to be some way we can find a middle ground."

Finally she turned to him and smiled. It was like sunset backed up a couple hours to bright midday.

"Middle ground, huh?"

"Yeah. *This* ground. We go do what we've got to do, but we always end up back here. Back home. Together."

"It's your third option, isn't it?"

He shook his head. "No. It's my only option. I can't walk away from you again. Not if I don't know where and when we'll be back together."

They had moved several feet past the big sign. Apparently the orange letters he'd spray-painted on the back of it earlier today caught her eye. *'Future home of Mr. and Mrs. J. Easton Smith'* stood out in the warm glow of sunset.

"What if I'd rather keep my professional name?" she asked, but her smile hadn't faded.

"I'll repaint the sign," he offered.

"Don't bother. We can think up better things to do."

Oh, yeah, he sure as hell could think up some better things to do. He realized he was grinning like a teenager, but he didn't care. She was grinning right back. He figured he could risk touching her then. She melted into him and he wrapped his arms around her. Mrs. Smith, Dr. Snowden— hell, he didn't care what she called herself. He'd been right all along. No way could he leave her again.

"I love you, Marti," he whispered.

She tilted her face up toward his and met his eyes.

"Prove it. Take me to California with you this time."

Not a problem. "First class or coach?"

She honestly seemed to be contemplating that. "Um, which one is more likely to serve fried chicken?"

About the Author

Bestselling author Susan Gee Heino got her start in the theatre where she discovered that writing snappy dialog was much more fun than memorizing it. Today she writes quirky Contemporary Fiction as well as lighthearted Regency Romance full of playful storylines, heartfelt passion, and happy endings. Under her pen name, Serena Gilley, she writes The Forbidden Realm fantasy romance series, with sexy, magical creatures in a world where passion is forbidden and true love plays a dangerous game.

Ms. Heino is an award-winning author, workshop presenter, and preacher's wife who lives in rural Ohio with her heroic husband, two very creative children, and an accidental collection of semi-magical critters. She loves to get to know her readers and invites everyone to connect with her on social media or visit her websites at www.SusanGH.com and www.SerenaGilley.com.